Ghostrider One

Also by Gerry Carroll

North S★A★R

Ghostrider One

Gerry Carroll

POCKET BOOKS

New York   London   Toronto   Sydney   Tokyo   Singapore

POCKET BOOKS, a division of Simon & Schuster Inc.
1230 Avenue of the Americas, New York, NY 10020

Copyright © 1993 by Gerry Carroll

Library of Congress Cataloging-in-Publication Data

Carroll, Gerry.
  Ghostrider One / by Gerry Carroll.
    p.   cm.
  ISBN 0-671-75323-1
  1. Vietnamese Conflict, 1961–1975—Naval operations, American—
Fiction. I. Title. II. Title: Ghostrider One.
PS3553.A7639G48   1993
813'.54—dc20   93-17620
                                                              CIP

First Pocket Books hardcover printing November 1993

10 9 8 7 6 5 4 3 2 1

For my wife, Debbie
And my parents, Gerry and Dee

ACKNOWLEDGMENTS

I've always wanted to find a place to use the word "indefatigable" so I'll use it in gratitude to describe my editor, Paul McCarthy, Blood Enemy of the Dreaded Double Negative.

Thanks also are due in large measure to Tom for his encouragement and support, to Robert for making sense of Byzantium, and to Troll for his "final checking."

Part One

1

Tuesday, January 2, 1968

The two Marine F-4 Phantoms taxied out onto the runway and came to a stop about seventy-five feet from the large rubber-scarred numbers, their pointed noses dipping toward the ground when the pilots applied the brakes. From his vantage point alongside both the runway and a half-case of almost-cold beer, Commander Jim Hogan, USN, watched their canopies come down and the pilots' heads move as they checked their cockpits, ensuring that all the switches and indicators were as they should be. The sound of the engines changed from the nasal metallic whine of idle to a deep roar and then back again as the pilots ran them up and checked the engine controls and the power the huge J-79s could deliver. Trying to fly a combat mission with a sub-par engine was one of the dumber things to do, thought Hogan, even for marines. Probably even dumber than cutting short a stateside shore-duty tour and coming back to the war early.

Hogan absently looked over the ugly green Mk-82 bombs slung under the wings of the Phantoms. It was their size that gave him the perspective on just how big the Phantoms really were. The same load of bombs that the F-4s hid nicely under their wings would make the little A-4 Skyhawk that Hogan flew handle like a wheelbarrow with the load all on one side. Even though the Phantoms were part of a newer, more advanced generation of jets, Hogan wouldn't trade his little "Scooter" for anything.

The lead Phantom issued huge gouts of black smoke from its tailpipes and began rolling as the pilot shoved the throttles forward and released the brakes. After a few feet, the afterburners kicked in with a long flame and the smoke disappeared, leaving

3

only a shimmering blast of superheated air which made the wingman, now beginning to accelerate, seem almost surreal.

Hogan could *feel* the sounds of the takeoff. The thunder vibrated against his chest and blocked out all thought until the jets were 2000 feet down the runway with their nosewheels just beginning to lift off. As the two Phantoms began a shallow climb to the left, he unconsciously took another sip of his beer, imagining himself in the cockpit of the wingman, joining up just underneath and behind the lead and then effortlessly slipping over into a parade position slightly behind and below the upturned tip of the leader's wing.

Hogan picked up the canvas bag that held his beer and what little ice remained in the bottom. Slinging the strap over his shoulder, he began to trudge back toward his room in the Transient BOQ among the tired and sad buildings on the other side of the flightline. He had been stuck here at Danang for three days now, awaiting space on the carrier on-board delivery aircraft (COD) for the last leg of his journey from the States to his new job as the executive officer of an A-4 attack squadron, VA-262, on board the USS *Shiloh*, driving around somewhere off the coast of North Vietnam.

This was the beginning of Hogan's second tour in Vietnam. He had been here as a lieutenant commander when the early "retaliatory" strikes had been flown into North Vietnam in 1964 and later, in early 1965, the end of his tour saw the beginning of the politicization of the air war. Hogan had enjoyed that tour immensely, for he had gotten to do for real what he had been training for since he had gotten his wings in 1954.

Hogan's last three years had been spent in hot and steamy Kingsville, Texas, teaching student naval aviators the various ways they could avoid getting themselves killed and their names in the book in the chapel at Pensacola. Now that he was on his way back to the war, Hogan was very glad to be out of the Training Command routine and free of the deliberately cautious and constricting rules and procedures which governed every minute of every day back there. Here he could once again fly his aircraft to its limits and sometimes, judiciously, a little beyond. Here he felt like a naval aviator.

By the time Hogan arrived at the BOQ, the sun was setting behind the highlands to the west of Danang. As he passed the desk, the clerk called to him and passed the message that his COD flight

4

was scheduled for noon the following day with a "show time" of eleven, one hour prior to takeoff. He had a few hours then to grab a last shower and have a couple of drinks in the "Club" before he had to turn in. No sense wasting a night ashore, he thought. It may be a while before I see one again.

Of all the ways for a naval aviator to come aboard an aircraft carrier, riding backward in a C-1A logistics aircraft is one of the least glamorous. It is also one of the least pleasant. The C-1A COD is loud, leaky, and smelly. Hogan was thinking this as he felt the deceleration caused by the large landing gear being shoved down and forward into the airflow. His stomach took a second uncomfortable leap when the flaps came down and the pilot compensated for the additional lift by lowering the nose.

Part of Hogan's problem was that, like most pilots, he was never comfortable as a passenger in an aircraft. He couldn't see what was going on up front in the cockpit and had to rely on whatever sounds and sensations he could hear and feel for information on how the flight was going. With no reference to the flight instruments and no way of picking up any of the visual cues he was accustomed to having in flight, his imagination always erred toward the bad side. An aircraft as old and noisy as the C-1 just made everything worse.

The other part of Hogan's problem was self-induced. He had fallen in with evil companions in the club the night before. These took the form of a group of pilots from one of the Marine A-4 squadrons stationed at Danang. The evening started with nearly reasonable calm, but as more and more of the pilots began to drift in, things got progressively wilder and louder. The inevitable Klondike and Ship-Captain-Crew games got going over in a corner, and a gang at the bar were playing Horse for rounds of drinks. Hogan had quietly stood at one end of the bar, just watching and sharing the fun from a distance, until the door opened and Hogan saw an old friend from the training command, Major Dick Averitt, walk in.

Hogan found himself very glad to see Averitt. Military men of Hogan's time in service become well used to arriving at a strange new station all alone. The bases are all similar in procedure, if not in layout, and that similarity eases the transition especially if one knows that he will be there for a year or two. But when one arrives as a transient, stopping only long enough to catch a flight to somewhere else, it can be intensely lonely. Even when surrounded by things completely familiar, one always feels as if he is looking at the place and people through a pane of glass, isolated from everything on the other side.

Averitt's arrival in the club and his obvious happiness to see Hogan went a long way to ease Hogan's feeling of isolation. The tall marine walked up and leaned on the bar next to Hogan.

"Well, look what the cat dragged in. As I recall, it's your turn to buy." Averitt signaled the bartender over.

Hogan gestured for another pitcher of beer. "False. Completely false. I bought the drinks when you left Kingsville, figuring, of course, that you were going someplace where you'd be out in the weeds, enduring all sorts of hardships in a noble effort to defend truth, justice, and freedom. But I see you're making the best of the situation with this here club. However, I do happen to have a bunch of travel money left, so I suppose I can waste some on helping out a jarhead in need."

Averitt laughed and stuck out his hand. "How the hell are you, Jim?" He looked at the silver oak leaves on Hogan's shirt collar.

"Congratulations too, Commander, sir, your highness. What are you doing here? I thought you still had a year or so to go as an instructor."

"I did. But I got tired of seeing the same mistakes made when it got up to about a hundred times each. The routine was getting to me, too, and I asked for a transfer early. I was selected for command of an A-4 squadron, so now seemed as good a time as any to get at it."

"Congratulations again. How's the family?"

Hogan sipped his beer. "That was reason number two. Jenny and I split up. It was friendly and all, but she couldn't handle any more transfers or the sea duty. She had a good job and needed to stick with it. And the girls are happy in their schools. It made sense, I suppose."

Averitt nodded and moved to surer ground. "What squadron did you get?"

Hogan grinned. "Two-sixty-two on *Shiloh*. I should take over as X.O. in a month or so once I get my feet on the ground. Then after about fifteen months in purgatory, I'll fleet up to command." He poured beer into both of their glasses.

"How about you? What have they got you doing?"

"You are looking at the Air Liaison Officer of the Twenty-seventh Marines. I finished six months flying in a squadron and took the ground job for the last half of my tour. It's one of those professionally broadening things. But if I do it now, I'll only have to spend six months with the grunts instead of a whole tour. Not that I don't love my brother marines, you understand, but six months is going to be about all I can handle of walking around carrying a rifle.

"At any rate, we operate up in the highlands of I Corps near the DMZ and Laos. I work out of the regimental headquarters so I don't get to go out in the bush much at all. It's really kind of dull compared to flying A-4s."

Averitt turned at a tap on his shoulder. Another marine, a major, invited the two over to their table. Hogan got another full pitcher and followed Averitt across the room.

As the outsider, Hogan was immediately quizzed about his assignment and his experience and then accepted by the group. After the ritual catching up on where mutual friends were and how they were doing, Hogan attempted to get the others to fill him in on how the war was going and what he could expect. He had been a little afraid that war talk might be taboo in the club, but pressed ahead anyway—Hogan felt that all they could say was no, and an apology and a round of drinks would quickly heal any insult. But the others began to answer his questions almost eagerly.

They spoke freely, talking about everything from the restricted zones to maintenance problems with the A-4 aircraft they flew. But there was something they didn't talk about, something lurking just under the surface. Hogan could feel it in their answers, but there were no looks or any other obvious signals being exchanged among them, so their reticence was more of an unspoken agreement than an established policy. They seemed to be typical aviators fighting "the only war we've got."

As the evening wore on, Hogan's desire to find out what lay underneath their words dissipated a little with every round of drinks until he had forgotten what the question had been in the first place. Running on experience alone, Hogan won more games than he lost, so his meager store of money held up until closing time. He managed to get himself back to the BOQ before his brain completely shut down, and had enough left to leave a wake-up call at the desk for 8:30 the next morning.

Now, as the COD was rolling into the groove on final approach to the *Shiloh*, the airplane's engines thrummed slightly out of synchronization and the pilot wiggled the rudder and dipped the wings to maintain the glideslope. Hogan's stomach heaved along with the airplane, and he hoped that the pilot would make it aboard on the first pass, because another trip around the pattern would surely cause his stomach to reject the greasy breakfast that still lay there like his mother-in-law's meat loaf.

The COD leveled out briefly and crossed over the fantail of the carrier. The engine sound dropped off abruptly as the pilot took the cut signal and floated for a few seconds which seemed like hours to Hogan. The aircraft hit the deck and decelerated abruptly as the hook engaged one of the arresting wires. Hogan felt the C-1 pulled backward a little as it reached the end of the cable run-out and the huge hydraulic system below deck released its grip on the tailhook. The pilot immediately added a burst of throttle to the engines, and the COD cleared the landing area, taxiing toward its parking spot just forward of the tall island structure, its long, tapered wings folding over the top of the fuselage. There was a great deal of jerking and twisting as the pilot goosed the throttles and stomped the brakes to make the tiny adjustments required by the increasingly frustrated taxi director outside, who was trying to fit the aircraft in its spot among the other aircraft on the already overcrowded flight deck.

Hogan was on his last reserves of intestinal strength when the passenger door on the left of the C-1 just in front of the tail opened up, allowing some air into the cabin. The only ventilation once the aircraft was on deck had come from the two cockpit escape hatches over the pilots' heads, which were always opened for landings and takeoffs aboard ship. In flight there had been only the totally inadequate vents that scooped in outside air that had been at least cool until the C-1 had entered the low holding pattern on the starboard side of the *Shiloh*.

One of the Air Transport Officer's sailors stuck his head in the door and motioned the passengers to get out. Hogan stood and moved aft to the door, wincing as his back, stiffened by two hours in the worn and no longer comfortable seat, reminded him of each of his thirty-nine years. At six foot two, Hogan could not stand erect in the cabin, so he had to move awkwardly, increasing the stiffness.

Hogan stepped out and squinted into blinding sunlight on the flight deck. The omnipresent haze composed of smoke, jet exhaust, and the red dust of Vietnam that had hung over Danang was missing here at sea, nearly one hundred miles from the coast. From a rain shower that the *Shiloh* had passed through in the past hour or so, the flight deck glistened in spots with small puddles formed in the "padeyes," the small depressions sunk in the deck to anchor the tie-down chains. Hogan looked around at the aircraft being towed about on the deck and at the hundreds of sailors working to prepare them for the next launch. He smiled at the sights and sounds about him. It was good to be back at sea. It felt like home.

Off to one side, Lieutenant Commander Jack Wilson, the Operations Officer of VA-262, stood waiting for the ATO's harried troops to unload and sort out the people, baggage, and cargo from the rear of the C-1. The people were told to stand off to one side until the luggage was pulled out and piled out of the way. Far greater courtesy was given to the sacks of mail, which were last. The white bags of packages and magazines were passed to waiting hands which stacked them on a small cart. The orange bags of first class, containing the letters from home, were carefully placed on top of the pile, and two sailors pushed the cart toward the hatch in the island structure. Once he was sure that the important cargo was safely on its way to the ship's post office, the ATO turned his attention to the people.

The ATO was an officer who really didn't care much for his job. He had dropped out of flight school in Pensacola and was serving his obligatory two years of active service before he left the Navy and got on with his life in just about four months. He cared not at all whether he ever received a promotion and hated every minute he had to spend on the *Shiloh*, watching the other pilots fly the jets he had once dreamed of.

Wilson watched Hogan (it had to be he, the only commander in the group) step from the small crowd and walk over to the pile of baggage, rooting through it until he pulled out an aviator's canvas kit bag and two well-stuffed canvas army duffels. He placed them off to one side and, when the ATO came over and began speaking, Hogan pulled a sheaf of papers from the kit bag, tore one off the bottom, and handed it to the ATO. Hogan's expression was growing darker by the second.

Wilson appraised his new X.O. About six two, broad through the shoulders and muscular. Hogan had light brown hair and intense-looking brown eyes, but Wilson thought that a large part of the intensity came from forcing himself to keep from strangling the

9

ATO whom Wilson had always felt alternated between being a studied asshole and just an idiot. Wilson walked over and introduced himself.

"Commander Hogan? I'm Jack Wilson, Ops Officer of the squadron. Let me help you with your gear."

The ATO began to protest that Hogan had to first go below and check in through his office, but Wilson held up a hand.

"Right, but he gave you a copy of his orders. That ought to do it. Besides, there's no sense carrying his bags down to your office, then back up here and down the other side."

The ATO shrugged and moved away. It wasn't worth the hassle. After all, what could anybody do—give him a shitty job on a carrier?

Wilson helped Hogan sling the duffels on his shoulders and picked up the kit bag and slung that over his own. It weighed a ton.

"C'mon, X.O., this way. We've got Ready Five." Wilson moved diagonally across the flight deck to the port side and stepped down the short ladder into the catwalk. He dropped the bag onto the grating and helped Hogan put his down.

"What have you got in here, X.O.? Bricks?"

"Nope, just some books and my flight gear." He paused a moment. "I'm not the X.O. yet. Quit calling me that."

"You'd better get used to it. Your predecessor, Commander Sands, got himself wounded yesterday. He'll be medevacked to Danang on the COD you just arrived on."

Hogan had expected at least a month to get used to things and to get to know the squadron before he took over as Executive Officer when Sands relieved the incumbent Commanding Officer, or "fleeted-up" in Navy parlance. Now he had no idea what to expect. When the change of command would happen was now up in the air. In normal circumstances Hogan would have been the X.O. for about fifteen months until he relieved Sands as C.O. With Sands now on his way out of the squadron and the war, they might extend the present C.O. for a few months or even send someone out from the States to take over in Sands's place.

"What happened to him?"

Hogan didn't miss the quickly masked expression of disgust that crossed Wilson's face. "He went to the well once too often. Tried to lead his flight over the target for a second time the same way as the first run. He took a hit in the front, near the cockpit. He got a bunch of shrapnel wounds in his leg and a real rough-running engine. He would have punched out, but his ejection seat was damaged, so he brought it back. He'll be okay in a couple of months."

Hogan considered that for a few moments, picked up his duffels again, and nodded. "Okay. Lead on. Where's the ready room?"

Wilson grinned. "Right this way, your lordship."

Wilson pushed open the door to Ready Room #5, or "Ready 5" as the Navy called it, and stepped in. He dropped Hogan's kit bag on one of the seats and walked over to the duty desk. "Where's the Skipper?" he asked the bored lieutenant whose turn it was to man the desk.

"Down in sick bay, seeing off Commander Sands. He's going from there to CAG Office for a meeting and said he'd be back around five."

"Okay, then. How about calling the Admin Chief up here and then one of the paraloft people and a couple of guys from First Lieutenant Division. The new X.O.'s here and we can start getting him checked in." The younger man reached for the telephone and Wilson walked back over to Hogan, who was inspecting the plaques hanging on the walls around the ready room.

"We've got some guys coming up to take care of your gear. The Skipper's running around but should be back in here in an hour or so. Want some coffee?"

The two walked over to the huge coffee urn in the back of the room, and Wilson took down two white china mugs emblazoned with the squadron crest on one side and gold aviator's wings on the other. Wilson's had "Stuka" painted over the crest. The one he handed Hogan had "Hog" over and "X.O." below.

"That's right, isn't it? 'Hog' is your call sign, right?"

"Yep. Hog it is." Hogan was impressed that they already had his mug all made up. It was a small thing, but it always made new guys feel included right away when their mug was hanging on the board when they checked in. It was something that the good squadrons did as a matter of course and something that the bad ones always forgot. It didn't fit what he had expected from VA-262.

Wilson led him to a couple of chairs in the second row just as the Admin Chief came in and looked around. Wilson raised his hand. "Over here, Chief."

He turned to Hogan as the chief approached. "Chief here always gives me crap because I'm the only officer in the squadron shorter than he is. He pretends that he can't find me right away. I play along because he's the guy who takes care of our service records and our pay records. Besides, it gives his ego a boost. You know how yeomen are, all they ever get to do is type and file."

"Don't forget the paper cuts, Mr. Wilson. They're a bitch," the chief said, grinning.

"Yeah, right. Anyway, Chief, this is our new X.O., Commander Hogan. X.O., this is what passes for an Admin Chief, Chief Napier." Wilson paused while they shook hands. "Give him your orders and service record, X.O., and he'll take care of checking you in. You have to go to sick bay yourself and get your medical flight clearance chit. Chief, see if those guys from First Lieutenant can put his gear in his stateroom."

Hogan stood and pulled his paperwork and records out of his kit bag and handed it all to the chief, who then supervised the two young sailors in picking up Hogan's gear before all three left the room.

"The guys from the paraloft will take your flight gear and get it all ready for you. If you want to go down to sick bay and see the flight surgeon, you can be ready to fly day after tomorrow."

"Okay. Where's my room? I'd like to change uniforms before I see the doc."

"Well, Commander, you have the same room that the old X.O. used to have. They haven't moved all his gear out yet, so it's kind of a mess. They ought to be done by the time you get finished with the doc."

Hogan nodded. It was considerate of Wilson to try to help him avoid the encounter with Sands's gear and the resultant reminder of the dangers they all faced and of his own mortality. He looked over at the shorter man, liking what he saw. There was something genuine about him: his solicitousness was not an effort to ingratiate himself. It was simply his natural way.

"You got somebody who can show me the way? I've never been aboard one of these newfangled big deck carriers. I'm used to the old ones like the *Hancock* and *Oriskany*."

Wilson summoned the duty squadron messenger and turned Hogan over to him. After the two had left, he thought of the old X.O. and hoped Hogan would be better. Couldn't be any worse, he thought as he refilled his coffee cup. That would be impossible.

2

Thursday, January 4, 1968

Hogan yawned as he watched as the last of the A-4s was catapulted from the bow of the *Shiloh*. It was just past six in the morning, and he was scheduled for his first flight at 1500. He had come up to Primary Flight Control, or the "Tower," as everybody called it, to watch the launch and to get a feel for how things went on the ship. One of the things he had learned long ago is that the mood and tempo of flight operations on a carrier are controlled and set from Primary. The Air Boss and his deputy, the "Mini-Boss," normally both commanders who have completed a tour as a squadron C.O., are in charge of all flight operations around the ship, and if the Boss is a screamer, as some are, the performance of the pilots and flight-deck personnel suffers in direct proportion to how much yelling and screaming comes down over the radio and the loudspeakers from the Tower. This morning, Hogan was impressed with how calmly things went, even when one of the catapults failed, or "went down," right in the middle of the launch cycle.

The other reason Hogan was there was to make himself known to the Boss and the Mini. Having a familiar face and a good reputation is crucial to how well a pilot and the flights he leads perform. If the pilot has a problem and needs a little extra time to get it fixed, the Boss will usually grant it if he is familiar with the guy and has confidence that the pilot is a good one and will do his best not to screw up the rest of the launch or recovery.

If the Boss doesn't have a warm and fuzzy feeling about the pilot, the exchange in the Tower will go something like this:

"Boss, 105 says he needs a couple of minutes to work on his fuel transfer."

"Who's in 105?"

"Jones, sir."

"Jones? Shut that asshole down and tow him out of the way. 'Two minutes' from him means next week."

After the last jet had launched, Hogan turned to walk back to the hatch leading below. As he did, the Boss, a balding ex-fighter squadron C.O., called to him.

"Hey, Jim. Thanks for stopping by. See if you can get that bunch of yahoos your Skipper calls a squadron squared away, will you?"

The Boss turned his attention back to the flight deck with a smile, but the underlying truth of what he said was impressed upon Hogan. As he made his way to the ladders leading below, Hogan had the uncomfortable feeling that he was going to have to fix not only the squadron's feelings about itself but also everybody else's perception of it. There were more pleasant thoughts he could have had on this fine morning.

After he left the tower and had breakfast, Hogan went aft to the ready room. He grabbed a cup of coffee and began going through the huge pile of paperwork left in Sands's in basket, signed a couple of minor reports "by direction," and sent them back to Admin for mailing. Within twenty minutes the Admin Chief, Napier, came up and almost apologetically explained that there was no 'by direction" signature authority granted by the C.O. to anyone in the squadron, and all Hogan was supposed to do was initial that he had reviewed things and pass them on to the Skipper for signature. Taken aback, Hogan apologized to Napier for the extra work in having the reports retyped, but it was the chief's answer that gave him his first real good clue as to what was wrong with VA-262.

"That's okay, X.O., we're used to this. We retype everything at least twice, usually because the Skipper wants more documentation from somebody. It's always some little thing. Hell, we were three months late in getting the lieutenants' fitness reports out last time."

Hogan got up and looked carefully this time around the ready room. None of the twenty-odd awards hanging on the wall had been earned within the past eighteen months, the length of Blake's tour as C.O., extending back into his X.O. tour. They were all reflective of a formerly great unit that no longer was the best. Even the fourth- and fifth-place squadrons earned something, even if it was only a motivator for them to try harder.

He also realized with some surprise that there were very few pilots present in the room. In other squadrons in which Hogan had served, the ready room was the focal point for everything in the squadron. Guys would spend a lot of time in there, drinking coffee and shooting the bull. Everybody would show up at least five times a day, if only to check and see what the night's movie would be. He began to watch the door, and soon it was obvious that people came in, did what they had to do, and left. There was no hanging around.

The phone rang occasionally, and even though there were fair numbers of officers and sailors coming and going, there was just none of the feeling that should have been there. It was the laughter that was missing.

Hogan sighed and sat back in his seat, picking up the rest of the pile of paperwork. Most of it was routine crap like ammunition expenditure reports. About five folders into the pile was a letter from the admiral who commanded naval forces in San Diego requesting a report on the disposition of a case dealing with the theft of one of the admiral's military vehicles, specifically his duty pickup truck. According to the letter, one of the officers in the squadron had appropriated the truck late one evening and, after "using it for unauthorized purposes," had abandoned it on the pier. It was found shortly after the *Shiloh* sailed, but the culprit had been traced to VA-262 by the patches on his flight jacket. Unfortunately, the driver of the truck had been unable to read the leather name tag on the jacket, so the culprit's identity was still unknown. The admiral wanted him apprehended and punished forthwith and a full report forwarded without delay.

Hogan put that one aside and finished up the rest of the paperwork. He placed the single folder with the truck letter back in his in basket and the rest in the C.O.'s basket. As he did, the duty officer, a bored lieutenant, approached and told him that the C.O. had called and wanted to see him in his stateroom as soon as possible. Hogan thanked the lieutenant and headed aft, thinking over both what he had seen in the squadron so far and his first impressions of Blake.

They had met only briefly in the ready room the evening Hogan arrived, but there had been no real eagerness in Blake's expression.

He had been only civil. Hogan put it down to Blake's still being preoccupied by the loss of Sands.

The day before, his first full day in the squadron, Hogan spent settling in to life on a carrier. He got all the nickel-and-dime things done, like joining the officers' mess and getting the flight surgeon to screen his medical records and give him his flight clearance. He had tried to catch the C.O., Commander Frank Blake, but by the time Hogan had gotten free, the C.O. was briefing for a night mission and would not be back until well after midnight. Hogan gave it up and went to bed. *If the C.O. wants me before tomorrow, he can wake me up,* he thought.

Even in the small world of Light Attack pilots they had never run across each other. Blake was from the East Coast Navy and had come to the Pacific Fleet for his command tour while Hogan was at Kingsville. Hogan knew nothing about the man, not even by reputation.

Blake opened the door to his stateroom almost before Hogan finished knocking. He stepped back, gesturing Hogan to a seat in the straight-backed desk chair and closing the door behind him.

As Blake moved past him to sit on the reddish leather couch that folded out to serve as the room's single bunk, Hogan looked around the room, which was painted with the basic light green that the Navy chose to use in nearly all living quarters aboard ship, but was completely unadorned with any of the normal extra comforts that one would expect a man of Blake's rank and seagoing experience to bring along. A couple of dog-eared paperback books, no small refrigerator, no TV, not even the obligatory WestPac tape deck, which it seemed everybody purchased on their first deployment to the Western Pacific and the Far East. Hogan realized with a mental start that there was not even a picture of a wife and kids. In fact, there was nothing anywhere that would give a clue as to who lived there. It looked like Blake was just a visitor.

Without preamble, Blake launched into a description of the squadron and the personnel in it. Each officer and chief was dissected, his strengths (Blake mentioned only a few for each) and his weaknesses (these seemed to be more plentiful) were dragged out and analyzed, always in relation to the way the squadron "looked." The C.O. led from there into an explanation of proper administrative procedure and how he expected things to be done. Hogan was impressed by the organization of the speech and the detail Blake used to make his case for each point. Whenever a question popped into his mind, Hogan found that it was answered within the next few sentences Blake spoke.

Hogan could feel himself being carried along by the essential *accuracy* of Blake's lecture. It was far from impassioned, but at the same time there was a certainty about it, a conviction which seemed both impregnable and yet fragile, as if one tiny flaw would cause the entire structure to collapse. Hogan tried to focus on one point after another, but each time his attention was torn away and drawn along like a stick in a river. He lost the meaning of Blake's lecture in there somewhere and was simply marveling at the delivery when he realized that he had been asked something. He had no idea what the question had been.

"Sir?"

"I asked whether you had any questions about what I've said."

"Umm. No, sir. Well, the Admin Chief said that there's no 'by direction' signature authority granted. Is that to include the X.O.? I realize there hasn't been much time since Commander Sands left, but . . ."

Blake held up a hand. "As I said, I believe that anything official leaving the squadron reflects the policy of the C.O. If I am to be accountable for that policy, it will be my signature on the paperwork and no one else's. I have found that this both eliminates any question of interpretation and reduces follow-on problems."

Blake's tone was outwardly amiable but left no doubt that he was not about to change his style. Hogan smiled and stood.

"Well, sir. Thanks for the brief. I imagine I should get on with it. I'm getting my first hop this afternoon, so I've got to get some lunch."

Blake held the door for him. As Hogan stepped out, Blake gave him another painted smile. "That's good, Jim. I think we'll get along fine. Good luck on your flight."

The door closed quickly but not insultingly so, leaving Hogan standing in the passageway, staring at scratched aluminum, where a decal of a squadron crest had once been. Hogan turned and went forward to the wardroom, only once looking over his shoulder at the C.O.'s door.

Two and a half hours later, sitting in the cockpit of Ghostrider 407, Hogan absently reran the start checklist through in his mind. He hadn't flown an A-4 in nearly a month, and it had been a little longer since he had flown one from a carrier deck. He had completed the carrier refresher training very near the end of the three months he had spent in the Replacement Squadron, or "RAG," back at NAS Lemoore in California between his last assignment and this one. With well over three thousand hours flying A-4s, Hogan could do it all in his sleep, but no matter how many times one has flown from a ship at sea, the first one after a layoff always demands just a little more attention and an extra shot or two of adrenaline.

He looked around the cockpit at the familiar instrument panel, the long strips on the floorboards, where countless pairs of flight boots had worn away the gray paint, and at the switches, some shiny from a lot of use and some dull silver. He smiled at a memory from long ago, when one of the old hands in his first squadron had explained his own ideas on how to properly fly a jet attack aircraft. It was called "The Shiny Switch Theory."

You were supposed to move only the shiny switches, since they were the ones that everybody who flew the airplane before you had moved. Therefore, the dull, unused ones were not relevant to safe flight. The idea was brilliant in its simplicity—move only the shiny ones, and if something bad happens, put it back the way it was and press on. There was a corollary to this one. Any aircraft with one of the emergency handles shiny is trouble; somebody has had some thrilling moments in it before you, repeatedly.

Hogan reached down and adjusted his kneeboard where he had clipped his chart of the area for this, his first combat mission in several years. He looked to his left at Ghostrider 404. He could see Jack Wilson's helmeted head moving around in the tiny cockpit. Wilson, as the Ops Officer, would be Hogan's flight lead for this and several more missions until Hogan was familiar with the operations around the ship and with the ins and outs of flying combat over North Vietnam.

Hogan heard the Air Boss's drawl over the 5MC, or flight deck loudspeaker system, telling everyone that it was time to start engines for the launch. He pulled on his helmet and clipped the oxygen mask to one of the fittings. On the flight deck, sailors in green, brown, red, yellow, and blue jerseys scurried around the aircraft, plugging in the cables that would supply electric power, and the fat yellow hoses that would shoot high-pressure air into the engine compressors for start. Since there were not enough to these for each aircraft, Hogan had to wait for a couple of minutes

18

until the "huffer," or portable starting cart, finished assisting Wilson.

The sounds of dozens of jet engines winding up filled the air, making all other sound impossible to hear. Everything now would have to be done by hand signals. The two sailors pulled the hose and cable free of Wilson's jet and came over and plugged them into Hogan's.

Hogan received the thumbs-up from his plane captain that everything was connected, raised one finger, and the electrical power came on, bringing his cockpit to life. He quickly checked the few things he needed to and raised the second finger, checking the throttle closed with his left hand. The yellow hose jerked as the pressurized air shot through it and Hogan watched his engine RPM gauge move off the peg. At fifteen percent, he moved the throttle from side to side to engage the igniters and then moved it up to the idle position. Once the engine was running at a stable idle RPM, he raised the third finger to have the start air shut off and the hose disconnected. After the aircraft's generator came on line and took over the job of providing electrical power, he raised the fourth finger and the cable was disconnected and thrown on the top of the huffer, which then drove away to another pair of jets farther down the deck.

Hogan followed the hand signals from his plane captain through the rest of the checklist, cycling the flight controls and then actuating the flaps, tailhook, speedbrakes, finally running through the aileron, rudder, and elevator trim. He raised his hands and placed them on the canopy bow as another sailor ran around and under his aircraft, checking that everything was where it was supposed to be and that there were no leaks or other problems. With the thumbs-up from the plane captain, he closed everything up and set them for takeoff. All he had to do now was close and lock his canopy and wait to taxi to the catapult.

Far up the deck, the first of the F-4 Phantom fighters came up on the power as the ship steadied out into the wind. The huge black plume of exhaust rose high above the jet blast deflector, or JBD, while the pilot did his final engine checks and changed to clear shimmering heat when he selected his afterburners. Then, like a huge arrow, the Phantom was gone, down the catapult track and into the air, zero to one hundred sixty miles an hour in under two seconds and about three hundred feet. The JBD came down as the other bow catapult fired, shooting another twenty-odd tons of aluminum and weapons into the air.

Two sailors ran under Hogan's jet and pulled the landing gear safety pins, rolling them up and stowing them in a small compartment under the belly of the Skyhawk, and then it was Hogan's turn to taxi forward, immediately behind Wilson's A-4. There was a series of brief halts as the line moved forward and stopped, awaiting each launch. To Hogan's left, the waist catapults were adding more aircraft to the formation now joining up overhead the ship.

Wilson went to the right to Cat 1 and Hogan to the left to Cat 2. Following the director's signals, the two jets eased onto the tracks and stopped just over the humps of the turtle-backed "shuttles," the small above-deck parts of the catapults. As the red-shirted ordnancemen pulled the weapons' safety pins from the aircraft's bomb racks, green-shirted crewmen ducked under Wilson's A-4 and attached the steel cable "bridle" from the shuttle to the huge hooks under each wing root, while another crewman attached the holdback to the rear of the plane. Hogan watched the dance as everything came together at once, culminating in a frozen moment, with everyone clear of the aircraft, kneeling against the wind over the deck, holding their arms out and giving the thumbs-up, the Cat Officer standing with his arm raised and fingers giving the wind-up signal. Wilson saluted with his right hand and placed his head back against the headrest. The Cat Officer went down on one knee, touching the deck, and then raised his hand to point forward. For a couple of heartbeats there was no movement until the catapult fired, breaking the holdback fitting and blasting Wilson and Ghostrider 404 into the air.

The Catapult Officer stood and turned his attention to Hogan's aircraft while behind him the JBD came down and the nose of another A-4 poked into Hogan's peripheral vision as it taxied onto Cat 1, which Wilson had vacated less than ten seconds earlier. The redshirts and greenshirts swarmed under Hogan's A-4 and hooked him up. He shoved the throttle forward and released the brakes when the tension sign was given, grasping the throttle and the fixed "cat grip" bar with his left hand to prevent the acceleration of the stroke from pulling his hand and the throttle back.

Hogan ran his controls through full cycle to make sure that nothing was binding, checked his engine gauges carefully, and saluted the Cat Officer. He placed his head against the headrest and took a deep breath from his oxygen mask. Out of the corner of his eye he saw the Cat Officer's arm come down, and then everything blurred as the catapult fired.

When the acceleration of the stroke ended, Hogan slapped up his landing gear handle and eased the jet slightly to the right to get clear of the ship's course, since having an engine quit and crashing into the water directly in front of 87,000 tons of moving steel is not a survivable proposition. When 407 had built enough airspeed, Hogan raised his flaps and continued to seven miles ahead of the *Shiloh* before easing into a climbing left turn. He spotted Wilson's Skyhawk high above, also in a left turn, so he rolled in a greater bank to cut inside his leader's turn and smoothly closed into formation, crossing under to Wilson's right side.

Hogan wiggled his rear end in the seat to get more comfortable and looked over at Wilson, the two jets moving now as one, headed to join the sixteen others forming up high above in their rendezvous circle. The bright sun reflected off his canopy and the sky was as clear and blue for him as it had ever been.

After nearly three years, Jim Hogan was back in the war.

3

Thursday, January 4, 1968

 The radio in the F-4 came alive with the voice of the controller back on the *Shiloh*. "Guntrain Lead, this is Alpha. Launch complete."

"Guntrain 201, roger."

Thanks for small favors, thought the strike leader, Commander Chris Scott, who was not having the best day of his eighteen years in the Navy. Scott was the commanding officer of VF-147, one of the two F-4 Phantom fighter squadrons aboard the *Shiloh*.

21

It seemed as if he had had nothing but problems since he had gotten out of bed that morning. First was the summons to meet with CAG, as the air wing commander was called, for breakfast. What could have been an enjoyable and professionally profitable hour or so had turned unpleasant when CAG had gently mentioned that it seemed that recently a few of the squadron reports had been a day or two late. CAG had even made a small joke of it but, for Scott, that hadn't taken the edge off. When he had returned to the ready room, there hadn't been enough time before this flight to call in the officers responsible and chew their asses, so Scott's anger just lay there and festered.

The second thing that had him going was the briefing the strike had gotten from the resident madman, Lieutenant Nick Taylor, VA-262's AIO, or Air Intelligence Officer. Taylor was without question the best and most professionally competent Intell type in the air wing, and normally his oddball attitude and slightly bizarre style provoked only wan smiles and the odd shake of the head from the more senior officers, but today he had grated on Scott. When Taylor had thrown up a chart and explained that today's target, a major powerplant, was in reality a camouflaged LSD factory and so needed to be destroyed in order to put Timothy Leary out of business, Scott had to bite his tongue in order to keep from exploding at the young man.

Finally, when he had gotten airborne, he'd found that his F-4 was a dog. Laden with Mk-82 bombs and Sidewinder missiles and with engines that had gone too long without major maintenance, it wouldn't economically get up the speed Scott needed. The Phantom was famous for the huge amounts of fuel it gulped in the best of circumstances, but for Scott to maintain the speed he'd briefed back on the ship would put him lower on fuel than he needed to be when he arrived over the target. So he had to throttle back some and accept whatever he could get out of it. The only good news was that his relative pokiness gave the other heavily laden aircraft in the strike a break in keeping up with him.

Scott's backseater, or RIO, Lieutenant Randy Norris, who was a Naval Flight Officer, a nonpilot specialist, watched the last two A-4s slide into formation on the outside of the circle. The "launch complete" call came without any qualifiers, meaning that everybody scheduled had made it and was joined up. None of the manned spares had needed to be launched, so the weight of bombs over

22

the target would be as planned. Norris pressed the foot switch which activated the intercom system, or ICS.

"Okay, Skipper, they're all aboard."

"Roj. Let's go." Scott leveled his wings and began a climb toward 22,000 feet, the altitude at which the strike group would cross the coast. Beside and behind him the seventeen left hands of the pilots of the rest of the strike shoved their throttles forward to keep up. The big Phantom's greater power quickly began to tell as Scott's division of fighters pulled away from the little single-engine A-4s which were lugging nearly their own weight in fuel and bombs. Norris craned his neck around to watch as the A-4s began to fall back. Looking down at his altimeter, he saw that they were passing 20,000 feet and would be easing off the climb soon.

"The Scooters are having trouble back there, Skipper. I don't think they're gonna be able to get much more than three-fifty out of them today."

"All right. We'll let them catch up. Once we head downhill, they'll do better."

One thing that fighter pilots hate is being slow. Speed, which is really stored energy, is their stock-in-trade and is readily convertible into maneuverability, which in turn keeps them from getting hosed by missiles and aimed "Triple-A," or antiaircraft artillery fire. The F-4s which were out to the sides as flak suppressors and as TARCAP, or Target Combat Air Patrol, the defensive fighters that were along in case the Vietnamese MiGs decided to come up and play, at least could weave around and keep their speed up. Being tied to a bunch of sluggish attack bombers was the price Scott was going to have to pay if he was going to be able to lead air strikes.

Scott leveled off and pulled the power back. The rest of the aircraft behind began to spread out across several square miles of sky as a defense against flak and to give themselves room to jink and weave. Once they were over North Vietnam, flying straight and level for any prolonged period, say all of ten seconds or so, could give the Triple-A gunners a chance to shoot them down. Once Norris saw everybody struggle back into their correct positions, he told Scott, who then shoved his throttles forward and got back to the briefed speed.

As the coast of North Vietnam passed under his nose, Scott keyed his radio and called the Navy's radar picket ship, known as Red Crown. These ships, usually destroyers which rotated through the assignment of endless station keeping in the Gulf of Tonkin, took care of several key elements in the air war. Not the least of which were keeping an eye on the enemy's fighters and coordinating rescues of downed fliers. Red Crown grew to have a special place in the hearts of most naval aviators on Yankee Station.

"Red Crown, Guntrain 201 and flight, feet dry." "Feet dry" meant that the aircraft were now over land. When they got back out over the water they would call and announce "feet wet."

"Guntrain, Red Crown. Roger, feet dry. There are no bogies airborne in your vicinity. I have several northwest of Bullseye, but they appear to be no factor."

"Bullseye" was the code word for Hanoi. Today's target was well over ninety miles south of there, but one never knew what the MiGs would do. At full power they could be down here and attacking within ten minutes. Scott looked over and smiled as he watched the TARCAPs ease their way into a position on the side of the formation which would put them between the MiGs and the rest of the aircraft.

"Okay, Skipper. Tipover and on the money too." Norris, as the strike navigator, had them at the point where they were to begin the descent which would bring them over the target at 14,000 feet with plenty of additional speed built up. Scott lowered the nose into a shallow descent and listened for the telltale tones in his helmet which would tell him that the acquisition radars of the Vietnamese surface-to-air missiles, or SAMs, were up and searching for them. So far there had been only little chirps as the radar operators tried to find them without giving the Americans time to locate their own sites in return.

Within three minutes of the start of the descent, the three "Iron Hand," or SAM suppression, A-4s and their escorts accelerated ahead of the main body to try to whittle down some of the SAM sites. The Iron Hands carried Shrike antiradiation missiles which would home in on the radar emissions given off by the sites and fly in and take out the radar vans, which contained the missile guidance systems and their operators. The F-4 escorts carried bombs which would be dropped on the sites to destroy whatever was left when the Shrikes were finished. The plan was, as always, that the Iron Hands would arrive in the target area and engage the SAMs five minutes or so before the rest of the strike arrived. The missileers would have a choice of defending themselves against

24

the Iron Hands or laying low and hoping to survive until the rest of the strike arrived.

Very early in the war, military thinking was that the only real threat to aircraft was the surface-to-air missile. This perception had been given great credibility when Francis Gary Powers had been shot down by one in his U-2 spy plane over Russia. The doctrine that in order to get to the target and back out again, an attacking aircraft had to stay low and be under the minimum altitude for the missiles. What was forgotten was that the enemy was probably going to have a whole bunch of inexpensive, easily deployed, and accurate antiaircraft guns. But, then again, everybody knew that modern jet aircraft were far too fast to be shot down by anything as archaic as a cannon.

So, when the war began, aviators roared in down low, secure in the knowledge that the missiles couldn't touch them, and they were right. But when the Navy and Air Force aircraft got the living hell shot out of them by Triple-A in attacks on North Vietnam, it came as a complete surprise to those "strategists" who had ignored the lessons of past wars in their eagerness for "progressive thinking."

Back up to altitude everybody went. Since Triple-A was statistically by far the greater danger, the aviators learned to take the sites out or dodge the missiles and pull out of their dives above 3500 feet—above most of the gunfire. There was still some of the larger caliber guns to worry about but, by and large, they'd made the best of the situation.

Scott saw the target on the far horizon and waggled his wings. His threat receiver was warbling now almost constantly so, as was his habit, he turned off the mixer switch, cutting off the distracting tones. On his signal the other aircraft in smaller groups eased into turns to the right and left so as to be able to come into the target from different headings, thus foiling the gunners' ability to predict where the next attacker was coming from. Off to Scott's left he caught the flash of a missile's motor igniting as one of the Iron Hand A-4s launched a Shrike, the white smoke trail rushing down ahead of the nearly invisible little Skyhawk. He was tempted to follow the flight of the Shrike, but he had much more important things to do, like keep his head moving and stay alive. From the back over the ICS he could hear the sounds of Norris's breathing into his oxygen mask.

Scott lined his aircraft up on the target and rolled in, his white wings briefly flashing against the blue sky to the other jets in the strike.

On the far side of the target Hogan caught the white of Scott's wings as he rolled in on the powerplant. He was concentrating on following Wilson's jet and scanning the ground every few seconds for the telltale dust cloud that would indicate a SAM launch. If you didn't catch the cloud or the brief five seconds or so of white flame that came from the SAM's booster motor, your chances of spotting a missile coming at you were vastly diminished.

Hogan realized all of a sudden that he really hadn't noticed how much chatter there was on his radio. He was concentrating so intently on getting everything right in his cockpit and remembering all the small things he had learned on his last tour that he unconsciously screened out anything that didn't have his call sign on it. That had not been a particularly good move because everything that happened to anybody else in the strike was at least indirectly important to all. He glanced down, rechecking that his master arm switch was on and he had his weapons selectors set.

Wilson's jet pitched up and rolled over as he began his dive at the target. Hogan waited the proper few seconds and pulled his stick back and left, imitating Wilson exactly. Concentrating on the large reddish building near the center of the complex, Hogan rolled out and banked slightly to put it in the center of his sights. From the corner of his eye he could see Wilson pull up sharply and to the left with little bursts of vapor streaming from his wing tips. Hogan neutralized his controls so that there were no little side motions to throw off his bombs, and, just passing four thousand feet, stabbed the button on the stick, releasing his bombs.

He waited a couple of heartbeats to make sure that the bombs had had time to come off the racks, and hauled back on the stick, climbing away and turning to a different escape heading from Wilson's. He looked down over his shoulder at the powerplant which was wreathed in smoke, steam, and flying debris from the bombs still striking within the complex. Several groups of brown and black explosions went off on the periphery of the target from somebody's near misses. Hogan could not tell exactly where his bombs had landed, but he was sure that they had gone into the maelstrom of smoke and flame that had been the powerplant.

As he passed 10,000 feet he began to relax just a little, but a jolt from his left wing and a bunch of black and gray puffs of smoke from the Triple-A in the sky around and ahead of him stopped that. He had forgotten momentarily that jinking was something you did *always* when you were over enemy territory: you could get just as dead on your flight home as you could on your way in.

Hogan wrapped in a steep bank to the left, and several seconds later another back to the right, all the while heading generally southeast. The flak bursts ceased exploding nearby, but Hogan was under no illusion that it was his brilliant airmanship that threw them off. The gunners simply switched to firing at easier targets among the other aircraft still escaping from their runs over the powerplant.

Scott, as the first to make his run at the target, was the first to get back out over the water. His wingman had joined on him very quickly, and the two had headed for the coast as fast as they could. Norris made the "feet wet" call to Red Crown, and as the others straggled out in loose pairs, they checked in and headed back to the ship.

Scott hadn't heard anybody yelling for help amid the incredible mess of chatter on the radio over the target, and he could remember only one SAM warning call and no maydays, so it appeared that everybody had made it so far.

It was not that the Vietnamese could have been taken by surprise: you could almost set your watch by the timing of the large American air strikes against the North. There was even a joke running around the fleet that they were on a "Dr Pepper" schedule—10-2-4. The Vietnamese even had the help of Soviet "fishing trawlers" which shadowed each carrier. With their impressive suites of radios and radars, these gray and white and rusty little vessels observed and monitored everything that the carriers on Yankee Station did and reported on it to higher headquarters who, in turn, passed it on to the Vietnamese defenders.

Norris's voice on the ICS broke into his thoughts. "Okay, Skipper. Looks like everybody's out."

Scott keyed his radio switch. "Red Crown, Guntrain 201. The strike is feet wet. No stragglers."

"Roger, Guntrain Lead, Red Crown copies that all aircraft are feet wet. Be advised you're clear behind you." This last told Scott that there were no MiGs that decided to try to sneak up behind the strike aircraft as they left and get in a shot or two when the Americans were just beginning to think that they were safe.

"And, Guntrain, your pigeons to mother are 105 at 96, cleared to switch frequencies." Red Crown told Scott that his range and bearing (pigeons) to the *Shiloh* (mother) was a bit south of east (105 degrees) at ninety-six miles and that he could change frequencies to the controllers back aboard the *Shiloh*.

"Guntrain 201, roger, switching and thank you."

Scott heard the radio channelizer tone as Norris switched the radio to the *Shiloh*'s frequency. When it ceased, he called the ship and was told that he could expect the deck to be clear for landing in thirteen minutes and that the weather in the vicinity of the ship was generally pretty good.

Scott looked around at the blue sky and the small scattered white clouds dotting the sea far below. He glanced back at his wingman and smiled at the forbidding beauty of the F-4, its sloping tail and insouciantly upturned wing tips, its huge air intake ducts and the black-tipped nose. There was not another aircraft in the world that looked as mean and tough and solid as did the Phantom. The best thing about it was that it performed just as impressively as it looked. Of all the airplanes he had flown in his career, dating all the way back to the old piston-engine F8F Bearcat in 1951, Scott loved the F-4 Phantom II the best.

For about the thousandth time in the past six months, Scott smiled as he thought of just how lucky he was to be leading a squadron of the world's best fighters. But then, on the other hand, he thought that maybe luck had little to do with it—he had after all carefully planned nearly every professional move he'd made over the past eighteen years just to get where he was, and his success was more a product of work. He was "on the fast track," as they said, marked for higher things. All he had to do was not make a mistake and he'd get there. Someday he'd wear the broad stripes of an admiral.

These thoughts brought him back to his conversation with CAG at breakfast that morning. He remembered his anger at those officers who'd let him down and decided once again that he'd have to do something serious about their mistakes.

Norris's voice from the back telling him that they had a good lock on the ship's TACAN, or tactical air navigational aid, brought him back to the present. His few moments of reverie were over. He was now completely back to flying his aircraft.

* * *

Several miles above and behind Scott's fighters, Hogan was flying comfortably on Wilson's wing. He was playing a small game with himself, trying to see how perfectly he could keep his relative position in the formation. Wilson had joined up on two other aircraft from VA-262 which had been on the strike so that Hogan was now flying in the most difficult spot, number four. The farther one is from the lead, the greater the corrections one has to make to maintain proper position. Since number two flies on the lead and number three flies on number two, the fourth guy has to make corrections that are amplified in response to the corrections being made by the other two wingmen. The effect is like being on the very end of the game Crack the Whip. It is a lot of work but still a lot of fun.

Hogan was generally pleased with his performance today. He had done his job pretty well for a three-year layoff. In a way, he had welcomed the fear he'd felt before the mission like an old friend. He had been worried about how bad it was going to be after those years, but when it had been no worse than he remembered from his last tour, it had come as a relief. Hogan knew that he would never tell anybody about that, but the knowledge that he could still handle it as well as he had before answered the last question for him. He grinned to himself because he knew now with certainty that he would be okay, that he was still a damn good combat pilot and that he would be able to help the others in his squadron become good ones too.

The leader of this flight of four was a lieutenant, Joe Jackson (inevitably nicknamed "Shoeless"). Rather than take the lead, as his seniority entitled him to, Jack Wilson had just joined easily as the number three. Hogan was impressed by that as he had been by everything Wilson had done all day, from the briefing on. At least there's one guy I don't have to train, he thought.

When it was their turn to enter the landing pattern, Jackson led the flight up the starboard side of the ship with their tailhooks down, giving the time-honored signal for intent to land. He gave the hand signal and broke hard left, turning to the downwind leg, followed by the others in order at specific intervals. Hogan watched Wilson break away, waited a few seconds, and shoved his stick hard left, forcing the nose to stay level with the horizon instead of dropping, as it tended to do. He pulled back on the stick a bit, increasing the rate of turn and allowing the G forces to decelerate the A-4 to 150 knots. He rolled out directly behind

Wilson on the downwind leg and dropped his gear and flaps, reflexively compensating for the changes in nose attitude their deployment caused. He was dead on altitude and airspeed and determined to keep it that way.

Ahead, Wilson reached the one-eighty position, directly abeam the landing area on the *Shiloh* but headed in the opposite direction from the ship, and began his approach. Hogan looked inside his cockpit and rechecked that his hook, flaps, and wheels were down and locked, and then looked outside again. He hit the speedbrake switch on the throttle with his left thumb and lowered the nose slightly to get his descent going.

One of the quirks with the A-4 was that the J-52 engine was fairly slow to spool up from a low power setting to full power. This interval didn't matter much normally, but in the landing pattern when the aircraft is slow and very near the ground, if you needed a lot of power to arrest a rate of descent, you didn't want to have to wait long for it. Most pilots have scared themselves nearly white by coming close to hitting the earth inadvertently, and a slow-responding engine was something to be wary of. The solution in the A-4 was to extend the speedbrakes from the sides of the jet into the airstream, which increased the drag and thus required a higher throttle setting to maintain flight. If you needed thrust quickly, all you had to do was close the speedbrakes and the drag went away, leaving you with a whole bunch of extra thrust since the engine was already running at a higher power setting.

Hogan rolled out on final and picked up the "Ball," or visual landing aid system on the port side of the ship. He was dead center on the glideslope and his nose attitude was right. Not too bad for my first pass in a month or so, he thought. He keyed his radio switch. "Ghostrider 407, Skyhawk, Ball, one-point-five." The last was his fuel state, 1500 pounds.

"Roger, Ball, Skyhawk." The LSO, or Landing Signal Officer, answered immediately and then shut up to allow Hogan to continue his near-perfect approach.

Hogan put in just a touch of right bank to correct for the ship's movement and took it out again almost immediately. He crossed the rounddown on the back of the flight deck and slammed down, catching the number-four wire. The number three was the optimum, so he must have floated just a little when he got over the deck, causing him to land long. So much for perfection, he thought as he followed the taxi director's signals to his parking spot on the bow.

4
Friday, January 5, 1968

Hogan filled his cup from the large ready-room urn and with the morning's pile of paperwork under his arm walked up to the duty desk. He asked the young duty officer, Lieutenant Tomlinson, to summon the Operations Officer, Lieutenant Commander Wilson. As Tomlinson reached for the telephone, Hogan moved over to his seat and sat down with the pile of folders on his lap. He had gotten through most of it when Wilson walked in and, after getting his own cup of coffee, sat down in the next chair with a deep sigh.

"Problems, Jack?"

Wilson took a sip and looked over. "Just the usual chickenshit. Strike Ops wants to launch five times as many airplanes as we have aboard and keep them airborne until an hour after their fuel runs out. Nothing new." Strike Ops were the guys who wrote the daily air plan and were known to make a mistake or two. That's why the squadron operations officers all went down and chipped in their two cents before the plan was published. Reasonably often, an Operations Officer would catch an error and fix it, which would necessitate a rewrite of the plan, which would mean that everybody had to do everything all over again. As a normal deployment went along, the Strike Ops/Air Wing team got better at doing things and the problems pretty much went away. For Wilson, today's problems were getting rarer.

"Seriously?" Hogan didn't know Wilson well enough yet to judge his humor.

"Nah. They just had a little glitch we had to sort out. They really do a hell of a job. They're getting tired in there. After four months of this deployment, working eighteen hours a day for this

31

whole line period is getting to them. They'll be okay after we get some liberty."

Wilson took another sip of his coffee. "Anyway, that's all squared away. What did you need to see me about?"

Hogan pulled out the folder about the stolen truck. He handed it to Wilson and waited a few minutes while he read through it. Wilson handed it back, keeping his face deliberately blank. "So what do we do?"

"Well, what do you know about it? I mean, it's not like one of our guys could steal a truck with nobody in the squadron finding out. It had to be one of the j.o.'s and they've never yet been able to keep from telling their buddies about a stunt like this."

Wilson's eyes shifted around the room as if he were looking for an escape route. Hogan firmed up his voice. "I get the feeling that you really don't want to answer. Well?"

Wilson sighed. "It was us who stole the damn truck, X.O. But there were extenuating circumstances."

Oh, shit, thought Hogan. "Us? You mean us as in 'us the squadron' or us as in you were involved?"

"Both. What happened was a bunch of us were in the club and we closed the place. It got to be real hard getting back to the ship with a couple of the guys having trouble walking and then they got too heavy to carry. One of the guys found this truck with the keys in it and borrowed it so we could all get back to the ship. That's about it."

"Why didn't you return it to where you stole it from?"

"Wait a minute, sir, we didn't 'steal' it, we just borrowed it for a little while. We didn't take it back because once we got back to the ship it seemed kinda pointless to leave it where we found it and then have to walk the two and a half miles back again. Besides, by then it was three-thirty in the morning and the ship was about to get under way in a couple of hours. Somebody might have missed movement."

Hogan nodded as if the whole thing were beginning to make sense. "Okay. Where did you leave the truck?"

"Well, we thought this was the clever part. We parked it in the X.O. of the *Constellation*'s parking spot. She was tied up next to us at the pier. We figured that if anybody came looking for us, they'd figure we were aboard *Connie* and waste time looking for us there while we sailed away. It almost worked too. We were sure we'd gotten clean away with it."

"Well, you didn't. Okay, who else was involved? I mean, who actually stole the truck?"

"Come on, X.O., quit using the word 'stole.' We didn't steal it."

"The goddamned admiral says you stole his truck, so you stole his fucking truck. Now, who did it?"

"I did."

"That's bullshit." Wilson was definitely a player, but Hogan was certain that he was not the main culprit. Although he had known Wilson only a couple of days, he was well aware that the little lieutenant commander was far too smart to have gotten caught as easily as this. "Now, who was it?"

A new voice came from behind Hogan. "It was me, X.O."

Hogan looked around to see the squadron AIO, Lieutenant Nick Taylor, standing over him almost, but not quite, keeping the amusement out of his eyes.

"Commander Wilson tried real hard to talk me out of it, quoting scripture and Navy regs and all, but I wouldn't listen. He even said he'd tell my mother."

Hogan took in this figure. Taylor was a big man, six three at least, and broad with laughing blue eyes and blond hair right at the edge of regulation length. He was dressed in the standard khaki uniform and was wearing an aviator's leather jacket with pilot's wings stamped in gold on the name tag. Below the wings was stamped LT PAT MCGROYNE, HIGHLY EXCELLENT ATTACK PILOT. Hogan had already heard stories about Taylor. He'd been wounded in action and restricted from flying, so he'd volunteered to go back to sea in a squadron as an Intelligence Officer. When Taylor briefed the strike the day before, his limp had been barely noticeable.

"Okay. Now that we've solved the crime, do you want to make a full confession?"

"Well, sir, it was like this. You see, my old war wound was acting up in the cold and all, so I tried real hard to get the air station's duty driver to come to the club and give me a ride. The duty officer said that he wasn't authorized or required to provide taxi service for drunks. I told him that I couldn't be drunk because I could still sing and I had gotten his number right on the first try. He said some very nasty things about my family and my squadron and hung up. Anyway, I didn't have another dime, so I was stuck. When we left the club, this truck was just sitting across the street with the keys in it, so I borrowed it. The other guys, especially Commander Wilson, looked so pathetic trying to make it back to the ship that I naturally picked them up, as any Good Samaritan would. That's the story.''

Hogan looked at the papers in his lap and bit his lip. He liked this guy. He let out a sigh. "All right. Then what?"

"Oh. You mean about leaving it? Since we were pulling out in a couple of hours, it didn't seem right to take up a parking space that some sailor's poor pregnant wife would need when she came to see her husband off. So I put it over in the *Connie's* parking lot. I made sure I wiped off my fingerprints just like they do on *Hawaii Five-O*. Pretty tricky, huh?"

"Not quite. It seems that the sailor who was using the truck saw you. He identified the squadron patch, so the admiral knows it was us.''

Hogan frowned in thought and the other two remained silent, Taylor thinking quickly about how he was going to get out of this and Wilson thinking that Hogan had just said "us" in talking about the problem. He could have been like the Skipper and and the old X.O., Sands, and continued with "you," as if the members of the squadron were of a different breed.

Hogan stared absently for a few moments at the back of his own flight jacket hanging on its hook on the wall. Except for the wear and several more squadron patches from his greater time in the Navy, it was identical to everybody else's. That was it—the patches.

He looked up at Taylor. "Did the sailor see your face?"

"I doubt it. It was way too dark. I didn't think he was close enough to see my patches either. Of course, I did hear some yelling behind me, but I put it down to somebody chasing his dog.''

Hogan sighed and closed the folder. "Okay, Nick. That's all. I'll let you know what I decide.''

Taylor opened his mouth as if to speak but shut it again as he caught the level gaze Hogan was giving him. He just nodded and walked out of the room. Hogan looked over at Wilson and saw him trying to hide a smile.

"C'mon, Jack. This is serious shit here. We got caught cold and the admiral is not a happy fellow about this.''

"Wait a minute. I've served with Admiral Becker. He'd never get upset about something as trivial as this. In fact, I remember him doing a few dances on O'Club tables himself. This probably comes from somebody on the staff. Is it signed by the admiral himself or 'by direction'?"

"It's by direction. So what? It still carries the weight of the admiral. We still have to deal with it."

"Yeah, I know, but we don't have to launch the Alert-5 firing squad."

Hogan nodded and broached the idea that had just firmed itself up in his mind. "You know, a squadron patch is not really conclusive evidence. I mean, I've got five of 'em on my jacket. If nobody can positively identify Taylor, a squadron patch isn't enough. I think we can get out of this. What I want you to do is draft an answer to this letter and get it to me tonight. Say that we've investigated the case and can't pin down the guilty party but we'll keep trying. Make it good."

"Okay. But you know the Skipper will never sign it out without a whole lot of fiddling around with it. It'll take so long that we'll get another blast which we won't be able to duck."

"That's my problem. Just get me that answer." Hogan handed the file to Wilson. "Now, tell me about Taylor. I like that name tag he wears."

"Actually, he's got about fifteen of them, but that's his favorite. When CAG Andrews checked in, he thought Nick's name was really Pat. Nobody told him for a couple of weeks, but he found out somehow and went ballistic. Called Nick in and chewed his ass but good for 'embarrassing the Air Wing commander and holding him up to ridicule.' So then he orders Nick to get a proper name tag, one with pilot wings, his name, and his squadron. Taylor went and had one made exactly the way CAG told him to. It said PILOT WINGS on the first line and MY NAME and MY SQUADRON on the other two. He marched into CAG's office and stood at attention in front of his desk. Then he says, 'Here's my new name tag, just like you said, CAG. Did I do good?' "

They were both laughing now. Wilson obviously loved this story.

"So what happened?" Hogan asked.

"Well, a couple of guys who were in the office said CAG didn't say anything at first. He just turned beet-red and sputtered for a while. Then he started to laugh until he couldn't stop. When he finally did, he dragged Nick up to the captain just to show him the name tag. CAG thinks the sun rises and sets on Nick now. Absolutely adores the guy."

"I heard that he was wounded. What happened to him?"

"According to him, it was a mere flesh wound. He took a hit about a year ago. He was flying an A-4 when somebody on the ground got lucky and hit his jet with a 57-millimeter. It tore up the cockpit and put some chunks into Nick's leg. After he got out of the hospital, he couldn't stand sitting around back at Lemoore, so he conned himself a set of orders to us as the AIO. He says he's almost rehabilitated now and is starting to get the paperwork together to get back to flying. I hope he makes it. He really had a great reputation until he got hurt."

Hogan smiled again at the joke on CAG. Anybody with the balls to do something like that was going to be a good man to have around, but the AIO was mostly a position that operated on its own. It was a shame that he was in a job that really had little to do with the running of the squadron. Hogan said so.

"Taylor isn't really normal in anything, X.O.," Wilson said. "Even though he's assigned only as the AIO, he wheedled us into letting him also be the Powerplants Branch Officer down in maintenance. Says it keeps him up to speed on the A-4 and 'infuses a modicum of reality into an existence otherwise fraught with military fantasy.'"

Hogan chuckled again as Wilson stood. "Well, if there's nothing else for me, I'll get going on the reply for the admiral."

"Okay, Jack. Thanks. You know, I'm damn glad we've got you and Taylor in this squadron. That's gonna make my job a hell of a lot easier."

Wilson looked down at Hogan with no trace of the smile he had worn only seconds before. "X.O., let me tell you something. This squadron is loaded with good men. The problem is that they don't know it yet. Nobody's ever given enough of a damn to tell 'em."

The little Ops Officer walked out of the room, leaving Hogan staring unseeingly at the patches on the back of his flight jacket.

Farther forward on the ship, in the Air Wing Office, a conversation was being held that would have great impact upon the men of VA-262. CAG, Commander Sam Andrews, was talking about the future with the squadron C.O., Commander Frank Blake. They were deciding whether Blake should be extended in his present position for several extra months. As was typical with most involving Frank Blake, this discussion had been going on for about forty-five minutes, covering all sorts of minutiae and outright irrelevancies.

What the two men were dancing around was the fact that neither wanted Blake's tenure to last any longer than was absolutely mandatory, but for vastly different reasons.

Andrews was sipping his fourth cup of coffee in the past hour or so and was beginning to feel a sharp pressure in his groin. It's amazing, he thought, how many decisions get made quickly after one or the other parties develops the screaming need to take a piss.

He held up a hand to halt Blake's latest soliloquy. "Okay, Frank, I understand that you have a great job waiting for you in Washington. My concern is that Hogan has been here, what, three days? Do you honestly think he'll be ready to take over as C.O. in four weeks?"

"CAG, it's not without precedent. There have been other men who have taken over in much more trying circumstances. I'll have an entire month to get him up to speed, and that'll give the wing back at Lemoore time to get somebody else out here to take over as X.O."

"Goddammit, Frank, those 'trying circumstances' were mostly taking over when the C.O. got killed or fired, not when there was time to plan for it. I do not want to have one of my squadrons led by a man who is not ready for it. Can't you understand that? Why not have them send out somebody to be the C.O. instead of a new X.O.? How about we extend you for a couple of months?"

"There aren't any qualified guys available. The A-7 transition program is taking most of the command-eligible men into that pipeline. If we take somebody from another squadron, we'll just be dumping the problem into someone else's lap instead of solving it. There just aren't any commanders with more qualifications than Hogan."

Blake sighed. It was time to be completely open. He wasn't sure he knew how, since he had always been careful to caveat everything to meaninglessness.

"As for my staying around, CAG, I don't *want* to be extended. I've done my bit as a C.O. and it's time for me to get on to other things. I hate being in command and I don't think I can handle any more of it. Steal the X.O. from one of the other attack squadrons aboard. I don't care, I want to get on with it."

That was it, Andrews thought, he doesn't want to spend any more time in the high-risk position of C.O. Only in command of the Air Wing for five months now, Andrews had never been able to exert as much influence on the performance of Blake's squadron as he would have wished. Their performance had never been poor enough to warrant firing Blake, but it had never been good enough to stand out. The squadron had taken on the character of a chameleon—blending in and fighting hard to be invisible. One thing which was nagging Andrews was the question of whether he should have done more to help Blake. Was there something he could have done to get VA-262 to rise from the sheer adequacy he had seen so far?

Along with the question came the sudden realization that not only were there things he could have done, but there were also things he *should* have done. He knew down deep inside that he had let it go in the hope that it would cure itself, and he knew that he had been just a little bit cowardly about the whole thing. Perhaps it was the mild distaste he held within for Blake and all the others like him, but whatever the reason, he hadn't done it right.

Blake himself was always ready to go along and avoid making waves just to keep his status from being endangered. He was just getting his ticket punched and only wanted to get back in among the bureaucrats, where he could succeed without succeeding. He could cloak himself in paperwork and instructions and staffing and never be accountable for anything. He didn't care a bit for his responsibilities to his men, only for their responsibilities to *him*.

Early on Andrews had hoped briefly that Sands would be a change for the better, but it became apparent to him that Sands was just going to be more of the same only with a different face. Andrews had given up in frustration until Sands had been wounded.

Now Blake was due to leave and the only replacement available was Hogan. Andrews knew that what he was about to do was not precisely the way the system was supposed to work, but, at this point, anything that had a chance of fixing VA-262 was worth a try to him. Okay, so be it. He'd let Blake get on with his life. And his fucking career, thought Andrews.

"All right, Frank. We'll go ahead with the change of command when we get to Singapore. In the meanwhile I'll get with the wing back in Lemoore and get somebody with experience to help Hogan out. Now, do you want to break the news to him or do you want me to?"

Blake was about to seize on Andrews's offer, when he saw the look in CAG's eyes. "No, sir, I'll tell him, and I'll give him everything he'll need. You can count on it."

Blake stood and almost ran from the room. He couldn't believe his good fortune. He'd soon be out of here and on his way back to Washington via the prestigious War College. And with a successful combat fitness report in his record to boot. This was the last hurdle for him. He'd never have to go back to sea and could spend the rest of his career in Washington. Where I belong, he thought.

With a grimace, Andrews watched him leave. He was thinking of the wording he'd use for Blake's fitness report. It was definitely going to make interesting reading for the people in the assignments and promotions branches in the Bureau of Personnel back in Washington.

He reached for the telephone to call in the C.O.'s of the other two attack squadrons in the Air Wing. He'd need their help in getting Hogan ready to assume command. They all had seemed glad that Hogan was coming when the announcement had been made four months before. Andrews was from the fighter community and had never served with Hogan, but he trusted the judgment of the other attack types.

He placed the phone back in the cradle and stood. I'll save the Navy *after* I go to the head, he thought.

5

Sunday, January 7, 1968

Commander Chris Scott, fighter skipper, yawned mightily as he sat in the ships's Intelligence center and waited for the briefing to begin. It was just after six-thirty and Scott was a bit short on sleep. The coffee he had mooched from the Intell officers was not nearly strong enough for his requirements. He had scheduled himself for the first launch so that he'd have the rest of the day free to catch up on the paperwork accumulating at a prodigious rate in his in-basket.

Scott had called a meeting late the previous evening with his X.O. and the squadron lieutenant commanders who served as the department heads. His first inclination after the conversation with CAG Andrews about the quality of the squadron's paperwork output had been to assume all the responsibility himself and make everything go out through him, but he forced himself to think it all through carefully. Even though it was his own rear end that would take the blistering if the quality continued to decline, he decided to call the meeting to clear the air and lay out, one last time, what he expected from his officers.

He had explained carefully and very firmly that the department heads were in the chain of command also and that he would appreciate it very much if they got off their collective dead ass and helped him run the squadron. He was basically very tired of being embarrassed and did not intend to be so again. He patiently explained once more that the department heads, because of their seniority, no longer had the option of simply doing their own jobs—they also had to train their junior officers. It was just too damn bad that they all had to do this and fight a war too. When he finished with them there was absolutely no doubt where everyone stood.

Scott was fairly proud of himself for using as much restraint as he had the evening before. Instead of screaming and yelling and wanting to strangle somebody, he'd tried reason. He just hoped it would work. If not, he still had the Attila-the-Hun approach in his back pocket.

The door opened in the back of the room and the pilots from VA-262 walked in led by their new X.O., Jim Hogan. Scott had liked Hogan on first meeting him some days before, and the previous evening they'd had dinner together in the wardroom. It had seemed to both that they'd met somewhere before and so they'd played the ancient Navy games of "Do You Know ... ?" and "Where've You Been?" It turned out that they had been near contemporaries in Flight School with Hogan always following about a month or two behind Scott, so they'd at least run into each other before. They also had several mutual acquaintances and spent a lively half hour catching up on where the acquaintances were now and filling in the gaps of their stories for each other.

Hogan nodded to Scott and smiled as he took his place in the row behind, the other three pilots with him sitting in the same row. None of them looked any more awake than Scott felt. They were chatting among themselves and Hogan with them, not because he was trying to ignore Scott, but because a preflight briefing was not the place for socializing. For his part, Scott was arranging his kneeboard cards in the order he'd need them during the brief.

One of the AIOs disengaged himself from the knot over by the coffee urn and moved to the front of the room. He waited until all the aircrew had noticed him and shut up before he spoke. When he did it was in a nasal New England accent which fit his tall and lanky build. He looks just like Ichabod Crane, thought Hogan. Which was exactly what everyone in the air wing called him. His real name, Rance Dunston, just didn't seem to fit. Apparently, his parents had hoped for John Wayne and had gotten a basketball center instead.

Dunston introduced the weather forecaster, who mumbled his way through his part of the briefing and escaped back to his office as soon as he decently could. The next briefer brought anticipatory grins and nudges from the other pilots in Hogan's flight and a resigned shake of the head from Scott.

Nick Taylor was in all his irreverent glory today. He had on several sets of love beads, an amazingly ugly Hopi headband, and some tiny granny glasses. His name tag said, in three lines FREE B. PEACENLOVE, STARSHIP PILOT, HAIGHT-ASHBURY SPACE COMMAND.

Taylor walked to the front of the room and held up both hands in the peace sign. "Good morning, tools of the decaying fascist system. Today you get to fly around, spreading destruction and woe amongst the peace-loving people of North Vietnam. There are no major strikes planned for today, so your mission will be armed reconnaissance, or road recces, as you all so quaintly call them. Your sectors are on the board over there and you are free to take out any target of military significance. This does not include, of course, anything outside the standard Rules of Engagement, which, astoundingly enough, have not changed at all since yesterday. I'm sure heads will roll when that is discovered back in the Five-sided Wind Tunnel on the Potomac." Even Scott had to smile at Taylor's familiar description of the Pentagon.

The AIO limped to a large chart of North Vietnam and Laos and began giving the latest intelligence on what had been accomplished in the past few days over the North, pointing out targets that had been struck and reading off the post-attack bomb damage assessments gathered from various sources which he told the group were "so secret that even the sources don't know who they are."

"We do, however, have a report from Madame Bazoom, the president's palmist, that we're doing good so far. She wasn't specific in exactly what we're doing good at, but there it is.

"Lastly, we have had reports from the *Enterprise* that several MiGs have made feints toward their strikes in the past two days, coming down and then hauling ass away. They're believed to have been MiG-17s and haven't really been a threat so far. We believe that if they do come all the way down and engage, it will be against smaller formations and the 17s will be used as a decoy to draw off the fighters for some of the MiG-21s they have just entering service. Fighter pukes, heads up for that. Red Crown and the EC-121 surveillance aircraft have been able to spot them coming so far, but you never know. We're also listening in on their GCI frequencies, but since nobody in the world can understand their damn language, who knows what the bastards are gonna do."

The North Vietnamese Air Force was set up exactly like their mentors', the Soviets, and relied heavily on Ground Controlled Intercept, or GCI, coordinating their aircraft formations and tactics from various centers on the ground. Eavesdropping on those GCI control frequencies could give some warning of impending attack to the Americans, so this was a key element in the prosecution of the war.

Taylor looked around the room. He had accomplished his goal in loosening everybody up. Like a good showman, he knew when it was time to make an exit.

"Okay, only one more thing. There is some intelligence that there is a *New York Times* columnist or reporter or something running around in North Vietnam, getting the unvarnished truth from their poor but honest public affairs guys so that he can tell everybody back home what barbarians you all are in blowing up orphanages and hospitals. Try not to do that. Any questions?"

There were none, so Taylor gave the peace sign again and moved off, turning the rest of the briefing over to the flight leaders and the men who would have to go in harm's way. He walked back to the coffee urn and poured a cup for himself. He sat off to the side on a stool near a chart table, close enough to listen and be available for questions but far enough away so as not to intrude.

Taylor slipped off the beads and the glasses and the headband.

He put them in his pocket, and pulling out his Pat McGroyne name tag, he replaced the Peacenlove one. He sipped his coffee, being careful not to listen too carefully to the flight leaders' briefings. For what seemed the thousandth time in his five years in the Navy, he listened to the altitudes and frequencies and approach times and emergency procedures and cautions and back-up plans. He watched the pilots' faces grow grimmer, setting into a sort of cocked readiness. They were silent, making little notes on their kneeboard cards, occasionally glancing at the charts on the wall to remind themselves of the geography they knew so well.

Taylor kept his face blank too. He was feeling with them the corrosive knot of fear that had to be forcefully stuffed into its little cage in the chest and kept there only by will and determination. You could walk by the little cage and glance at the creature within, but you could never stop to examine it too carefully. The creature could reach out and grab you by the throat and pull you to it, locking you into an embrace that would leave you outwardly whole but broken and crushed and vulnerable within. Soon that vulnerability would drive you from the sky and into a lifetime of self-doubt wherein, every once in a while, the face in the mirror would stare back coldly, accusingly, contemptuously, leaving you with the knowledge that you once had an opportunity but turned away from it and left it lying there in the dust, along with a large part of your pride.

He sighed, turning away from the briefing and back to the table. He had been there and believed with all his being that he would sit there with them again. He and they were separated by only ten feet but, until he could get back into one of his beloved A-4s, by a vast gulf of purpose.

Through his windscreen an hour and twenty minutes later, Jim Hogan saw the coast of North Vietnam appear on the horizon as a brown smudge on the edge of the sea. The smudge grew wider and thicker as the formation of four attack jets and two fighters eased down toward the landmass. A couple of minutes earlier, Hogan had checked everybody in with Red Crown and had been cleared to proceed on their mission.

This was the first mission Hogan had gone on as a flight leader. He had had a couple of hops as a wingman and all his experience and knowledge of the area had come back quickly, as if it had been only a couple of months since his last combat cruise instead of three years. He felt *comfortable* back in the lead.

Hogan glanced around at the other aircraft in the flight, shaking his head at the waste of assets they were about. Today was a day for flying pin-prick interdiction raids on the supply system throughout the southern panhandle of the North. The fighters were along in case the North Vietnamese decided to get cute and send up a few of their MiGs to protest the American actions. These were the waning days of the Operation Rolling Thunder bombing campaign which Robert S. McNamara's civilian whiz kids in the Pentagon were convinced would bring the enemy to their knees. Rolling Thunder was designed to stop the shipment of war materiel to the south without getting the Communist bloc, especially China, upset. So the whiz kids checked their formulas and numbers, made studied assessments of the entire Southeast Asian situation, diligently ignored the advice of the military, and decided that blowing up dirt footpaths and bicycles loaded with rice would be infinitely more effective than mining the ports or cutting railroad lines. Since these were the same geniuses who brought out the can't-miss car of the future, the Edsel, Hogan and the others flying from the carriers on Yankee Station and the airbases in Thailand were under no illusion about how things were going. They had been ordered to stop the flow of a river with a coffee cup after somebody decided that the floodgates of the dam upstream should be left open.

Since there were no MiGs reported in the immediate vicinity, the fighters almost dejectedly broke away and took up a station off the coast, condemned to an hour of flying around in circles, waiting for something to do and being bored. They were not armed for ground attack and so could not at least get the pleasure of blazing around down low, shooting up targets of opportunity. Sidewinder heat-seeking missiles do not work at all well on bicycles.

Hogan rocked his wings and lowered the nose as he descended toward his sector of North Vietnam, to the north of the city of Vinh. His wingman, Lieutenant Dick Smith, followed at a comfortable tactical spread while the other two A-4s banked away to the left for their sector farther down to the south. This area, very near the coast, offered a greater chance of finding some worthwhile targets than did many of the more mountainous and exposed areas farther to the west, although by now, in early 1968, the North

Vietnamese had wised up enough to keep as much of their supply traffic moving at night and under the cover of the jungle as possible. The main route was the Ho Chi Minh Trail farther to the west which was a system of roads running down through Laos and Cambodia into the South, but there were sometimes choice targets to be found near the coast.

"Red Crown, Ghostrider 400 and 408 are feet dry."

"Roger, Ghostriders. Be advised there are several bandits southwest of Bullseye. They don't appear to be any factor at this time. I'll keep you advised."

Hogan clicked his transmit switch twice in acknowledgment. So there were MiGs airborne southwest of Hanoi. Even though they were fairly far away, about a hundred miles, their presence still made him just a bit nervous. He hoped that Red Crown and the radar aircraft were on their toes. If they weren't, he hoped that he and Smith could dodge and duck long enough for the Phantoms to get there and help out.

Once over land and crossing what passed for a coastal highway, Hogan banked right and began his search of his sector. Out to Hogan's left, or west, side, Smith began to search that way, being careful to jink and weave around to throw off any gunners below who might decide to take a potshot or two. One of the main rules of flying road recces was that you didn't hang around looking for very long. If you couldn't find anything of value, so be it. Get out of there. More than one good man has failed to come back after trying too hard to make something happen and forgetting that rule.

Far out to sea and reasonably safe from any threat from enemy fighters or surface-to-air weapons systems was a unique naval aircraft called the E-2A Hawkeye. This was a relatively new aircraft in the inventory and was replacing the older E-1B Tracer, which was affectionately known as the "Willie Fudd" from its early designation as the WF-2. The E-1's tired-looking airframe and cantankerous and leaky piston engines had for several years supported a large radar system as a means for giving the carrier and the rest of the fleet early warning of enemy attack and for directing fighter aircraft to intercept the bad guys. Among the many problems with the Fudd was that it was an absolute dog in the air. The large radome on the top was billed as "aerodynamically neutral" which meant that in flight it created enough lift to compensate for its ten-thousand-pound weight. However, when one of the engines

45

failed, or shortly after takeoff with all the flaps and landing gear hanging out, the radome was actually a five-ton millstone.

The E-2, known as the "Hummer," was a vast improvement over the Fudd both in mission capability and in flying ability. They had come into service only about three years before and had proven their worth many times already. Given the fact that there really hadn't been any land-based threat to the carriers, the E-2's chief contribution had been in helping other aviators out of trouble and keeping an eye on the movements of North Vietnamese aircraft.

That morning, in the darkened tube which was the back of the airborne Hummer from the *Shiloh*'s squadron, call sign Slug 770, sat three bored naval flight officers who were each responsible for different facets of the E-2's mission. One of them, Lieutenant Doug McCarthy, was keeping track of the several MiG fighters the North Vietnamese had airborne and hoping for the chance to control fighters against them.

One of the interesting rules of this let's-have-a-war-but-not-piss-anybody-off war was that only MiGs which were actually attacking American aircraft could be fired upon. If the enemy fighters were innocently hanging around their own airfield, armed to the teeth and not bothering anyone, the American aircraft were forbidden to do anything except wave as they flew by. Only when the MiGs snuck up and shot somebody in the back was pursuit authorized, but only until they got back to their airfield, because, after all, how could we pick out one MiG from all the other innocents just flying around? To the American pilots this was much like having a madman with a shotgun in the neighborhood picking off the old ladies and all you could do was wait for him to step off his front porch before you could bag him.

Slug 770 had been airborne for nearly two hours and had two to go before they were relieved by another E-2. McCarthy was eating the last cruller he had filched from the wardroom and drinking a cup of coffee from the thermos he always brought along. He watched the little lighted blips on his radar scope move around over North Vietnam. The six-aircraft formation from the *Shiloh* began to separate with two fighters moving to the north toward the CAP station and the four others breaking off and crossing the coast. On the other frequency he could hear Red Crown talking to them and he waited for the two Phantoms to check in on his own fighter control frequency. He glanced up at the small gaggle of lights southwest of Hanoi and saw that they were mostly still there.

He sat up and fiddled with the controls for his scope, counting the dots twice before he was certain that a couple of them were missing. They had been flying in the immediate vicinity of their airfield and most probably had simply made full-stop landings and called it a day. It had been almost a month since McCarthy had seen any threatening moves from the MiGs at all. But one of the good things about men like McCarthy is that they rarely take anything for granted. In an air intercept controller, this trait goes a long way in keeping other people alive. In this case, it would be the four Ghostrider A-4s from VA-262.

McCarthy heard Scott check in his two Guntrain Phantoms and report that they were fully mission capable, that all of their systems were up and ready. Scott's estimate was that they'd be on station in about two minutes. McCarthy rogered the call and adjusted his scope again, looking carefully at the blank space between the airfield and the little blips that represented the northbound A-4s.

He had been looking for about thirty seconds, when he got just a tiny blink of light about one-third of the way between the two. It could have been ground return interference or just one of the many ghosts that this particular scope was noted for. He watched carefully and saw it again, closer to the A-4s. This was enough for McCarthy. If they were MiGs, they were hauling ass to the southeast directly toward Hogan and company. If they were not, all that would be lost was some adrenaline.

McCarthy switched his mike so that he could transmit on both frequencies and keyed it.

"Guntrain Lead, Slug. I have two bandits headed for the Ghostriders, Vector 255 for eighty miles. Break. Red Crown and Ghostriders, the bandits are about 332 for, um, forty from the A-4s."

6
Sunday, January 7, 1968

The land beyond the coast of North Vietnam could be as low and as tangled as any in Louisiana, Hogan thought. Or it could be as beautiful as any on earth.

The sector which he and Smith had been given was mostly lowlands crossed by a small network of roads which, except for the larger coastal highway, seemed to simply wander around from village to smaller village to hamlet. Near the coast, there were a couple of spots where there was some higher ground, but they were relatively few and far between. The terrain gradually rose until, in the far western distance, it became the Annamite mountain range.

Hogan glanced at the chart on his kneeboard which was folded several times, leaving only the immediate area visible. The large blue numbers that gave him the maximum elevation figures for this area said 55, or fifty-five hundred feet. These represented the height of the highest obstacle in the area, so if he stayed higher than that, he was in no danger of running into anything hard, like a mountain.

In the western part of the sector was a wide and desultory river that flowed mostly south and then finally swung back to the north like a huge fishhook until it met the Gulf of Tonkin about ten miles northeast of Vinh. In several places the roads led up to the river's edge and stopped at what had once been a bridge. The metal bridges were now twisted and red with rust, while the wooden ones simply weren't there anymore. All around each former crossing were dozens of circular holes filled with water, the calling cards of American bombers. Hogan had the momentary thought that it took a whole hell of a lot of bombs to guarantee destruction of one lousy bridge.

Hogan had flown almost all the way across the northern border of his sector when he heard Smith's voice in his helmet.

"400, 408. I think I saw one of those underwater bridges back there. I'm going back for another look."

Banking his aircraft around to follow Smith, Hogan looked down at the river. The Vietnamese had quickly figured out that the Americans would wait until a bridge was almost completely repaired from one bombing attack and then come back and destroy it again. Rather than expend all the time and effort of building an entirely new target for the American jets, the Vietnamese would build a bridge a couple of feet below the surface of the river near the old crossing and then use it only at night so that they could escape further harassment. The other trick was to build a floating bridge in sections on the back of several barges and use that, taking it apart and hiding the sections under foliage near the river's edge during the day.

Smith's jet dipped a little as he flew low over the spot and banked up and away to the right.

"Looks like there's one down there. The river kinda churns over a spot about fifty yards downstream from the old bridge. The road takes a little swerve that way under the trees on either side. I'll take the bridge and you can hit the trees on the east side."

"Roger, that. You have the lead."

"I have the lead."

Hogan was rechecking his armament switches when he heard the radio call from the E-2 about the MiGs.

"Slug, Ghostrider 400. Can you give me a range and estimated speed for the bandits?"

"Not yet, Ghostrider. I don't have real good contact, but they looked like they're traveling about five fifty or six hundred. They're down low and headed your way. I can't find them now. The Guntrains are inbound."

"Roger, 400 copies. We're gonna make one run each on this target we found and then haul ass for the water. Copy 408?"

Smith heard all this and clicked his mike switch twice in acknowledgment. He knew that from the last position given for the MiGs and with their speed they would be there real soon. But the sooner he and Hogan could get rid of the excess weight of their bomb load, the sooner they'd be able to get the maximum speed and maneuverability out of their little jets.

He flew halfway around a wide circle to the east of what was now the target and when he was just short of the river hauled back on the stick and pulled it to the right, pitching the Skyhawk up and rolling it nearly onto its back, simultaneously turning and diving toward the target. He rolled out and made small corrections with his wings until he was lined up to approach the bridge from one end with a slight crossing angle.

Pilots had learned long ago that the crossing angle is the best way to attack long, narrow targets like bridges, since it gives the maximum probability of hits. If the run is made along the length of a bridge, the slightest error either in technique or in windage will cause the bombs to fall harmlessly to one side. If the attack is made directly across the bridge, the chances are that the bombs will fall short or long, again with little chance of a hit.

There was no sign of any antiaircraft fire, which didn't necessarily mean much, but it did allow Smith and Hogan to take more care in their runs. Smith's bombs came off and he hauled into a left climbing turn, looking back over his shoulder as his bombs hit and blew huge gouts of mud and water skyward. Hogan took a long enough interval on Smith's aircraft to avoid flying through the massive ball of fragments from his bombs and began his run aiming to the left and short of where the bridge had been. Very often the Vietnamese would hide the trucks and their cargoes under the shelter of the vegetation near a crossing point and wait until darkness fell before moving them across in order to reduce the chance of detection from the air.

Hogan waited until he had the target lined up in his sight, almost automatically made sure that he had induced no drift errors that would throw off his aim, and pressed the release button on the stick. He waited a few heartbeats to make sure that his bombs were gone and hauled back on the stick. He was looking over his shoulder at the explosions of his bombs when he heard Smith yell out a warning.

"X.O., there's a MiG at your left ten o'clock!"

Hogan slammed the stick to the left and looked out to his front. He couldn't pick the MiG out of the mottled background of the earth below, and he saw nothing against the clear blue sky, so the bastard had to be below him. He armed his 20mm cannon by feel as he continued his roll to the inverted, still searching for the enemy, finally following the Skyhawk back upright.

"Can't see him, Smitty!"

"Passing to your left now! There's another one west of him."

Hogan saw several streaks of tracer go past him close by on the left and spotted the MiG as it flashed by below him. It was an old Korean War vintage MiG-17 that had only guns for weapons instead of the deadly Atoll air-to-air heat-seeking missiles that the newer Vietnamese jets carried. He banked around to try to get behind the guy, knowing full well that if the MiG continued on course, he had little chance of getting him with his own nearly worthless cannon. He looked up and spotted Smith's A-4 high and right in a perfect cover position. Good man, thought Hogan. Now, if we can just keep moving for a little bit here, the Guntrains can get these clowns off our ass.

Beyond the first MiG, the wingman saw that his leader had completely blown the attack and began to turn into Hogan, trying to get on his tail. He had completed most of the maneuver when he abruptly broke it off and headed westward to get out of the situation. The leader turned and streaked off to the northwest to follow. Hogan knew he could cut inside the turn and perhaps cut the MiG off, maybe even getting lucky and scoring a couple of hits, but that would draw him farther inland, where other, better prepared fighters could be lurking, waiting for just such a chance at a couple of underarmed attack jets. He broke it off and headed east for the water.

"Ghostrider, Guntrain has you in sight. We're on the bandits."

It was times like this that made a guy almost glad that God had invented fighters, thought Hogan. "Roger, Guntrain. They're all yours. We've had enough fun for today. They were 17s, so watch for an ambush."

"Click-click."

When the original call from the E-2 had come, Scott was level at 20,000 feet and nearly at his CAP station. Since this was the first launch of the day, there had been no one to relieve, so there hadn't even been the distraction of talking on the radio to somebody. His check in with the Hummer had been brief and clipped, and he was prepared to sit back and be bored to tears for an hour or so. In the back of his mind was the vague possibility that he might get lucky and have something to do other than watch clouds go by or observe how slowly the minute hand of the eight-day clock on his instrument panel moved.

When the war began, the North Vietnamese didn't have much of an air force. What they did have were fighters which, in much of the rest of the world, would be sitting on pedestals outside the gate of the airfield, gathering bird shit and corrosion. Their pilots had been trained by other Communist nations, mostly China, and their tactics reflected the mistrust of initiative that pervaded those nations' military forces.

Their tactics were normally to try to sneak up behind the larger strikes and attack, forcing the heavily laden aircraft to jettison their bombs in order to survive. Once the bombs were gone, the MiGs would dash away toward the airfields, which were usually off limits to retaliatory action. They would very rarely go after small groups like Hogan and the other Ghostriders.

So it came as pretty much of a surprise that the MiGs had come up to challenge such a small raid, especially in that the raid could do no real damage to the overall war effort.

Scott had turned around and was just leveling his wings onto the new course, when McCarthy gave him an updated course to intercept.

"Guntrain, Slug. I've got good contact on the bandits now. They're headed 148 at five fifty plus at about angels six. Your steer to intercept will be, um, 230 for about seventy miles. Buster."

"Guntrain, Roger, buster." Scott shoved his throttles forward to full military rated power. He would use afterburner if he needed to, but for now there was little sense in using the horrendous amount of fuel that 'burner required.

"Angels six" meant that the MiGs were flying at six thousand feet and were well below Scott's present altitude. Most of the sneak attacks that came from the Vietnamese jets were from low altitude because their older fighters operated best down low. It was only the few available newer ones that could survive at the higher altitudes against the more sophisticated American jets.

Scott's present huge advantage in altitude could be converted to both speed and maneuverability when he got into the fight.

"Guntrain 212, Slug. Bandits now 245 for fifty, Switch 285.7."

"Roger, two-eighty-five-point-seven."

In the back of Scott's Phantom, Randy Norris, his RIO, or Radar Intercept Officer, rotated the channel selector knob to the new frequency which was the same one that the A-4s and Red Crown were using. Scott told Norris that he had selected one of the Side-winder missiles for the first shot, and Norris acknowledged but still had no targets on his radar.

When the channelizer tone stopped, Norris pressed his foot switch, keying his radio. "Slug, Guntrain's with you."

McCarthy's voice came back instantly. "Roger, Guntrain. Bandits now 240 for forty-five. There are two A-4s in the vicinity. They're finishing up now and should be gone most skosh."

Norris clicked his mike switch twice. The A-4s, if they were still around when the fight started, would be a problem. It would be much easier if the only heat sources for the Sidewinders to lock on to were Vietnamese.

The coast of Vietnam crossed under the nose much more quickly than it usually does when the fighters are tied to a lumbering bunch of attack aircraft. The two fighters were flying nearly at the speed of sound and would be in the area of the MiGs in two minutes. Scott glanced over at his wingman, who was out to the right in a combat spread that gives both aircraft the freedom to maneuver at will while still being able to give support and protection to the other.

"Guntrain, Slug. Bandits are low, on your nose for twenty miles. The contacts are merging with the A-4s."

"Guntrain, roger."

In the "hole" in the back, Norris was looking hard at his radar scope. He picked out the four aircraft which were now almost together in the same block of sky. He switched his scope to a different scale, and the blips spread out a little. Except for the heading the blips were taking, he really couldn't differentiate among them. The MiGs were heading generally south and the A-4s were pretty well stationary over their target. It was useless for him to try to look out the front and help his pilot try to pick anything up visually, because the back of Scott's ejection seat blocked all but two small crescents of the forward view. His job was to get them on radar and guide Scott to the targets and then, once the fight was on, he would be in charge of keeping track of anything to the sides and behind the big Phantom.

Scott switched the intercom to "hot mike" and instantly could hear Norris's breathing over the intercom. From now on there would be no need for either crew member to waste time trying to press the intercom switch when something needed to be said. He was straining to spot the aircraft which were now only a couple of miles away. He glanced in at his instrument panel, checking once again that all was well, and then back out again at the dark green and tan of the land below, trying to find the one small flash of movement that would reveal the enemy to him.

Off to one side in the distance he caught a flash of white as one of the A-4s banked around to the south. Once he had reduced the area to look in, he spotted the other Skyhawk, following in a perfect cover position. The lead Skyhawk turned back to the west and, following his course, Scott picked out one of the mottled green MiGs as it streaked away, heading out for home.

"Ghostrider, Guntrain has you in sight. We're on the bandits."

"Roger, Guntrain. They're all yours. We've had enough fun for today. They were 17s, so watch for an ambush."

Scott clicked his mike switch twice in acknowledgment and headed off after the MiGs which were now flying as low and as fast as they possibly could, headed back to the northwest. In only a few minutes they would be back at their base and safe. Scott was not about to let his first real chance at an enemy fighter slip away, so he shoved the throttles to the left and forward into the afterburner range. He felt the incredible increase in thrust through his back as he was pressed into his seat by the acceleration. He double-checked that he had a Sidewinder selected and looked out forward again at his quarry.

Seventy-five or so miles to the east, in Slug 770, all three controllers were watching the chase. Aside from a couple of battle-damaged aircraft that needed some help in finding an airborne tanker, this was the most exciting thing to happen for them in a week. The other two controllers had flipped up their radio mixer switches to listen in on McCarthy's frequency. It was a pure act of will for them to keep on with their jobs and responsibilities while McCarthy was having all the fun.

McCarthy forced himself to keep looking at his entire radar picture rather than staring at the one little corner where the Phantoms had just taken up the chase. He could see the two A-4s streak for the coast and then slow as they got safely out over the water. The gap between the Phantoms and the MiGs was closing quickly as the greater power of the huge J-79 engines in the F-4s began to tell, but they were still not in missile range. McCarthy could see that it was going to be a real close call whether the Americans would catch the MiGs in time.

He glanced up at the airfield where the MiGs had come from and noted that everything was still as it was but that there were a couple of new contacts to the northeast of the Guntrain flight. These were good, strong contacts, and for an instant McCarthy thought that they might be American aircraft from the other carrier or part of an Air Force strike headed south for the airfields in South Vietnam. But there were no other strikes due in this early from the Air Force and the other carrier hadn't launched anything yet. He hit the switch that would interrogate the contacts' IFF, or Identification Friend or Foe transponders, and received no reply. The new contacts were enemy too.

"Guntrain Lead, this is Slug 770. It's a setup. There are at least two additional fast-moving bandits northeast of you at, um, seventy miles, and headed south fast. They're gonna cut you off from the coast."

Scott had kept the throttles up for only a few seconds and then pulled them back to military power to save fuel. The two Phantoms had been overtaking the MiGs quickly but were still a couple of minutes from being in Sidewinder range when McCarthy's transmission came. This was not good. If he kept up the pursuit, he would be at a huge disadvantage against the other MiGs—he wouldn't have the gas and would be completely defensive. And being on the defensive is near the top of the list of things fighter pilots hate.

He would rather save something for the ambushers if he had to fight his way out. He knew that over in Guntrain 205, his wingman, Lieutenant Bret Croake, had less fuel than he since the wingman *always* uses more fuel than the lead. He had about made up his mind, when he heard Norris from the back.

"Skipper, we have to go *now*. I've got those bandits on my scope and it's gonna be close. Looks like there's four of them—Fishbeds, I think. Our best route out is about 120."

"Okay, let's go." Scott keyed the radio. "205, hard starboard to 120."

Scott hauled the fighter around and glanced back to look for his wingman. He was up and to the left after the turn. He keyed the radio again.

"Slug, Guntrain. We might need some help here. My RIO says that the bandits look like they're Fishbeds." Fishbeds were the advanced MiG-21 fighters that were armed with the latest in Soviet weaponry. They were not as fast as the F-4 but they were maneuverable as hell at the higher altitudes and airspeeds.

"Roger, Guntrain. I concur. They're way too fast for 17s. We've got some F-4s on the way, but it'll be ten minutes or so."

Shit, thought Scott, in ten minutes this'll be all over. He glanced to the left as if he could see the approaching MiGs which were not any bigger than the tiny A-4s that had started this whole thing.

If he continued to run this way, the enemy jets would get missiles off at him before he even knew that the fight was on. Giving something like that to an enemy is not in the nature of a fighter pilot.

With a glance at his fuel gauge, Scott made his decision. He hauled the fighter around to the northeast to put the enemy directly on his nose.

"205, hard port to northeast."

7

Sunday, January 7, 1968

McCarthy watched the gap between the two groups of lighted blips get progressively smaller. It was becoming obvious to him that the F-4s might get to the coast first, but it would be so close that they would be presenting their tails, and therefore their exhausts, to the MiGs and their deadly Atoll missiles. He was just about to say something to the Guntrain lead, when he saw the Phantoms come right and put the MiGs slightly to the right of their nose. Whoever was the lead today was sharp, he thought.

He began to run the whole problem through the filters in his experience store, trying to think of everything he could do to help these guys. They were going to be on their own for a few more minutes until the other fighters could get there, but with some decent timing and a bit of luck they would be able to escape. As long, that is, as nobody tried anything stupid. Or worse, tried to be a hero.

McCarthy looked over at one of his partners. "Did you get that tanker yet?"

The young man looked back and grinned. "Yup. It's a Whale and ought to be on station by the time the fighters get out. He's got pretty near a full bag, so there'll be enough for everybody."

McCarthy nodded. The A-3 Skywarrior, better known as the "Whale" for its comparatively large size, was originally designed as a deep-strike nuclear attack aircraft, and later on a few of them had been converted to airborne refueling aircraft, designated KA-3s. They held an impressive amount of fuel compared to the little "add-on" buddy stores carried by the A-4s, which, in most Phantom pilots' minds, was a good thing, considering that the F-4s were such fuel hogs that it seemed as if they always had a drain valve stuck open somewhere.

He had done all he could for the present. The fighters had the enemy on their own radar scopes, and for the moment no one was in any danger. Each group had the other generally to their front and so could not fire heat-seekers at the other since the missiles had to be fired from fairly close astern. The Phantoms normally would carry a pair of AIM-7 Sparrow radar-guided missiles on CAP, or Combat Air Patrol, missions like this, but all the missiles had been "downed" in another of the incessant attempts to get them to guide properly. In the past it had sometimes been the doctrine to fire *two* Sparrows in the hope that one of them would work. For the past two weeks the Sidewinder heat-seeker had been the only serviceable air-to-air armament available aboard the *Shiloh*.

Scott glanced at his small radar repeater scope which displayed the presentation from Norris's scope in the rear. He was headed directly for the MiGs and the closure rate was approaching 1200 miles an hour, or a mile every three seconds. Things happen very quickly in modern air combat.

He eased the aircraft thirty degrees to the left, putting the enemy's line of approach slightly to the right of the nose. This would give him a better angle for spotting the MiGs and would give him the shortest flight out of North Vietnam after he made his move. He looked out and saw Croake's F-4 matching his every move, all the while performing the jinks and weaves that were so ingrained in pilots flying over the North.

"205, 212. We're gonna break into 'em on my call. Go to 'burner and head due east for the water. If they want to follow, they'll run right into the other CAPs."

"Click-click" was all he heard.

Norris spoke up from the rear. "Skipper, looks like there's two pairs of them. They should be splitting up pretty soon. Want me to call the break?"

"Yeah. I'll be looking outside. Those little fuckers are so damn small, you can't see them head-on. I hope I've got the angles right."

"Looks good to me."

Scott scanned the sky where the MiGs should be. The offset angle he had chosen would give just a little dimension to them, allowing him to judge their relative motion. In the same way that an automobile driver can't accurately judge the motion of another approaching vehicle from head-on unless he is completely stopped or nearly so, a pilot needs to change the angles in order to see the motion of another aircraft. The greater the angle, the quicker, easier, and more accurate the judgment.

Norris watched the blips on his screen move closer to the center, which represented his own aircraft. Timing this move was going to take just the same amount of agonizing patience that dodging SAMs did. The blips began to ease into a turn toward the Americans and to separate slightly so that whichever way the Phantoms moved, one or the other pair would wind up on the Phantoms' tail, as long as the F-4s did what was expected of them. The MiGs and their controllers at the GCI site were well aware that they were going to have only one try at the Americans both because the MiGs had even shorter fuel "legs" than the F-4s but also because their own surveillance and control radars were seeing the other American fighters coming into the area from the east.

Scott was watching his repeater scope and waiting for the right moment. There is no firm step-by-step doctrine for this sort of flying. Nobody, despite the best efforts of modern human thought and science, has been able to quantify or codify or design the human factor out of the cockpit of military aircraft. Despite all the gadgets and computers and displays and studies and reports and programs, it still comes down to somebody with his hands on the controls and his mind and eyes in the middle of the situation who has to make the right move at the right time with no room at all for error.

The pairs of MiGs steadied out on their new courses, and Norris called the break.

Instantly Scott slammed the stick to the right, simultaneously keying his mike.

"Break now, Bret. Due east."

Norris craned his neck and watched Croake, the wingman, match the turn. Both Phantoms were now streaking through the narrow gap between the two sections of enemy fighters. Scott was flying now with no reference to the radar— that was Norris's job— he was looking ahead and to the sides, trying to spot the Fishbeds and trying to will the coastline to approach more quickly. He could hear the sounds of Norris's breathing mixing with his own into the microphones in their oxygen masks. His mind was racing, analyzing the dozens of possibilities that could happen in the next few seconds and planning his responses. He could almost hear snatches of real words jumping from the impressions in his mind, but they were instantly picked up and blown away by the wind from the passage of his thoughts.

It took the GCI controller a few seconds to recognize the Americans' sudden maneuver and, despite his years of experience and training, a few more to figure out what to do. By the time he had transmitted guidance to the MiGs, the two Phantoms had closed the space between themselves and the MiGs to nine miles. In the three seconds that it took for that gap to close, the MiGs were able only to get back to their original course, which meant that the two flights passed nearly 180 degrees out from each other, completely negating the effectiveness of their missiles.

Scott saw the leader of the left pair flash past only two hundred feet away. The MiG was strangely elongated by the combined speed, appearing normal only for the instant before it disappeared beyond his peripheral vision. He glanced to the side and saw the wingman pass farther away, leaving clear, safe blue sky ahead as the coastline passed under the nose. There was no way the enemy could catch them now. By the time they had completed their turn, the Phantoms would be miles away from the effective range of their missiles.

In the back Norris looked to the right and saw the other two MiGs farther away, headed on the same course as the leader. They'd had an extra second to make their turn because of their distance behind their leader but had pissed it away in just a tiny moment of indecision, that second or so that they still had to use to think of their next move. But then, that extra second they needed was why they were wingmen and not the guy out front.

Norris watched them pass and followed them to see how Croake was doing. His heart stopped when he saw that the wingman was not where he should have been. He looked quickly to the other side and saw only empty sky there too.

"Skipper, I can't see Bret. Oh, fuck . . ." Norris spotted him high and to the right, his nose nearly vertical as he pulled up and rolled to get his missiles aimed at one of the MiGs. Croake had obviously decided to try to get a snapshot off at the wingman of the second pair. Unfortunately for Croake and his backseater, he had miscounted.

Norris stomped on the foot switch that keyed his radio. "205, get outa there! That's the lead you're on. The other's at your six!"

Scott heard Norris yell into the radio and whipped his head around to see. He hauled the big fighter to the right and picked up the second MiG just as his nose came up. It seemed as if time stopped in that little corner of the sky. He could see Croake's fighter roll away for a second and then roll back to the pursuit course. He saw a flash from under the wing of the MiG and a white trail of smoke shoot forward toward the Phantom now nearing the apex, and the slowest point, of its maneuver.

Norris screamed over the radio for Croake to break starboard to defeat the missile and watched in horror as the big fighter continued on.

When Scott had called the move that brought the two Phantoms into the gap between the pairs of MiGs, Croake and his backseater, Lieutenant Terry Nalls, had decided to go after the last of the MiGs pretty much on an impulse. If they had stopped to think about things, they would have realized that it was not the smartest move of their relatively brief flying careers. On their second deployment to Vietnam, they were both fairly experienced for junior officers but were in the most dangerous part of those careers.

There is a period after one becomes familiar with his aircraft and its mission during which the average young pilot with his hair on fire honestly becomes convinced that he knows all there is to know about his profession. He knows that nothing bad will ever happen to him and, when others make mistakes and get themselves killed, it happened because the other guys were either stupid or just plain not as good as he is. In naval aviation the majority of fatal or near-fatal accidents happen to pilots in this stage of their careers. No matter how many times they sit through the lectures from the C.O. and Safety Officer, no matter how many times they read about guys just like them dying in pilot-error accidents, no matter how many times they shake their head at the news that another contemporary or friend has turned his very expensive flying machine into a smoking hole in the ground, they know with the unassailable surety of youth that they are better than that. They can hack it.

Croake and Nalls decided that the opportunity to get a shot at the last MiG in the group was too good to pass up. They could line up, fire a Sidewinder, and get out of there and back to the water before the rest of the MiGs could turn around and catch them. They would probably have been right had they gone after number four rather than the MiG they took for the last one. They would have been successful—not right and not smart, just successful.

Out to their left front, Scott led them toward the coast. When they saw the first pair of MiGs pass on the left, they looked back to their side of the formation and waited for the second pair. Croake saw a MiG pass close aboard his right and pulled the stick back into his gut, grunting against the abrupt onset of the G forces caused by the climbing turn. Behind him Nalls tightened his midsection to help his inflated G suit press as much blood back into his head as possible. He looked over his shoulder and spotted the lead MiG below just beginning to turn around to pursue Scott. Nalls called for a "belly check" from Croake and, when the pilot rolled the aircraft momentarily to check for other enemy aircraft coming at them from the blind spot beneath the Phantom, did a fast scan of the horizon and the terrain below. In their excitement the belly check was not particularly thorough.

"Belly's clear. Get the son of a bitch!"

The pilot of the second MiG was a relatively new one. He had completed his training in Red China less than six months before and had been immediately assigned as the number four in this flight. Number four is the most vulnerable in a formation such as this and therefore, sadly, considered the most expendable. Once the guy proves himself, assuming he survives, he will move up to number three, or the leader of the second section of two in the formation. Today the young man would do something that would go a long way in accelerating his advancement. He would shoot down an American fighter.

He had been following his leader carefully and nearly unthinkingly throughout the pursuit of the Americans. His job was to protect the lead and keep the enemy off his tail. He had been afraid when this, his first actual combat mission, started, but had settled down as the voice of the GCI controller had calmly directed them toward the Americans. He had been working as hard as he ever had to maintain his position but had lagged well behind his section leader, just far enough so that Croake didn't see him and mistook the leader for the number two. The young man saw the first Phantom go by to his right, and looked for the second one, expecting it to be somewhere closer. He was stunned when he saw it climbing above him and turning toward his leader.

The young man hauled back on the stick and got his nose pointed directly at the Phantom. Even at this distance he was surprised at the sheer size of the thing that made his little MiG-21 look like a small toy. He began to run through his weapons procedures, reciting them aloud to himself, making sure he had done everything correctly. He heard the tones from his missile's infrared seeker as it found the heat from the Phantom's engines and, unaware that he was holding his breath, fired the missile.

He watched in fascination as the Atoll streaked away toward the tail of the American jet.

Croake pulled the jet harder, forcing the nose to come around and point at the MiG which had leveled out and was heading almost directly away from them. The abrupt pull up and roll had cut inside the MiG's turn and placed them in a nearly perfect firing position. All that was needed was a tone from the Sidewinder that it had found the enemy's heat and he could pull the trigger and fly away. The two young airmen were concentrating so hard on the MiG that they never heard Norris's warning over the radio.

Nalls had not seen the MiG below, for it was almost directly nose-on, and against the background of the earth the telltale black exhaust didn't show up at all. It came as a complete surprise when the Atoll missile detonated just to the right and behind his seat, sending chunks of metal into the right engine, right wing, one of the fuel cells, and Nalls himself. He lived only long enough to see the fire start.

In the front Croake felt the hit too, but by the time he realized that he had no control of the Phantom and that the entire jet was on fire behind the cockpit, the right wing had come off and the aircraft was spinning far too fast for him to reach the ejection seat handle. The forces rapidly drove him into unconsciousness, sparing him the sight of the ground below coming up and hitting him in the face.

Norris had been alternately watching the Phantom and the missile's progress toward it and yelling for 205 to maneuver to avoid the Atoll. Scott banked the Phantom around to follow the MiG, but Norris could see that it was too late. He was just beginning to hope that the missile had missed, when he saw a greasy black-orange ball of flame and smoke erupt against the clear blue sky above. From the initial explosion the stricken Phantom arced toward the ground, its dive increasingly more steep as the forward momentum of the jet ran out and pure gravity took over. In his shock and dismay he only half heard Scott's strident calls to the crew of 205 to eject.

Norris's radar couldn't see the MiGs behind, so he craned his neck around and spotted one of them closing in from his left rear. The others had to be out there too, boring in. There was nothing on earth they could do for Croake and Nalls now. It was time to go.

"Skipper, we gotta get out of here. The bandits are behind us, coming up from our seven o'clock and gaining. Let's go."

Scott watched 205 long enough to see it hit the ground in a surprisingly small explosion and headed the Phantom generally southeast, directly away from the pursuers, who were gradually falling behind. There was no chance of them catching up now.

"Red Crown, this is Guntrain 212. Guntrain 205 is down on, um . . ." Scott realized he had not gotten a range and bearing of the position where 205 had hit the ground. He was about to ask Norris, when he heard the backseater's voice on the radio.

"Red Crown, the position is your 285 degree radial at about 67 miles. There were no chutes visible. 205 got hit by an Atoll. We're approaching feet wet at this time. Request vectors to a tanker."

"Guntrain, this is Red Crown. Your initial steer for the tanker will be 080 for forty, angels fifteen. Do you recommend a SAR effort?"

Scott hesitated. There were two of his men down in enemy territory, two young men for whom he had been responsible. Calling for a search and rescue effort and sending other pilots and aircrewmen in to look for survivors would be putting their lives in jeopardy for what would only be a gesture at best. Scott had been flying long enough to know what the chances were for Croake and Nalls. If they had survived, it would be a miracle on the order of the parting of the Red Sea.

He turned his aircraft and steadied out on a course for the tanker.

"Negative, Red Crown. Not unless they come up on their survival radio. You might have the new CAPs monitor the frequency though."

"Roger, Guntrain. I'm sorry about your boys. You're cleared to switch to Button Two and contact Slug 770."

"Roger, switching. Thank you."

McCarthy turned the mixer switch for Red Crown's frequency off and waited for the fighter to change to his frequency, Button Two. He had watched the whole drama on his radar and was still stunned.

The fighters had been home free. They'd blown right through the enemy formation and had clear sailing all the way home. When he'd seen the sudden turn of the second Phantom and the subsequent disaster, it had been all he could do to keep from shouting warnings and curses over the radio. That might have been somewhat satisfying, but it would have helped not at all. In fact, it would probably have made things worse. As he waited for Guntrain to come up on his frequency, he told the other two controllers in the back to make sure to write down what they had heard and seen. There was sure to be a bunch of questions raised later on, and he wanted to be able to help answer them.

"Slug 770. Guntrain 212 is with you, level at angels twenty."

McCarthy looked at his scope and picked out the Phantom. He looked farther to the east and saw that the tanker was at fifteen thousand feet, still orbiting exactly where it should have been. He keyed his radio.

"Roger, 212. Radar contact. The tanker is on your nose for thirty-six level angels fifteen. You're cleared to switch to the tanker freq."

"Slug, 212. Roger, on the nose for thirty-six. Thanks for your help this morning. Switching."

McCarthy resisted saying anything over his now-empty frequency. He knew that he had helped the fighters, but hearing 212 say so, however sincerely, felt painfully ironic. He leaned back in his seat and reached for his now-cold cup of coffee. All he had left to do was sit there for another hour, keeping an eye on things. The Vietnamese had had their fun for the day and would lay low for a while, so there was small chance of anything else out of the routine happening.

He watched the little blips move around on his scope as he sipped his coffee, feeling like shit.

8

Sunday, January 7, 1968

Hogan left the ready room and headed for the C.O.'s cabin. The summons had come just as he was finishing up his debriefing after the morning's mission. The C.O. did not seem pleased on the phone, so Hogan decided to postpone seeking out Scott to offer both his thanks for getting him out of a serious jam and his condolences on the loss of the two young men in the other fighter.

On the way down I-95 Port, the main fore-and-aft passageway on the O-3 level, or the deck right below the flight deck, Hogan was working hard on stifling his anger. In the few days since he had reported to the squadron, he had come to find out lots of things he didn't like about Blake's style. At first he had thought that the gun-shy attitude of the other officers was caused by the fact that they were in a war and by the recent loss in combat of the old X.O., but everywhere he went in the squadron he had met the same attitude, even down in the powerplants shop in Maintenance. Normally the men who worked down there and in the other shops in that department were pretty much unaffected by the C.O.'s working policies. It was a rare thing when the C.O.

was dumb enough to try to micromanage maintenance policies and procedures, when he had a hundred or so professionals who usually knew more about fixing and maintaining airplanes than he did. When Hogan had been sitting in powerplants, sort of getting to meet everyone, he'd picked up the large binder that contained the minor squadron maintenance instructions. He had been amazed when he found that every single one of them had been signed by Blake himself rather than the maintenance department head, as was the policy everywhere else Hogan had served. He had never seen a man try to insert himself so completely in the day-to-day minutiae of a unit this size. It was fine as long as the unit was small, say, a division of thirty men or so, but when the guy was dealing with a squadron of twenty-odd officers and two hundred men, most of it had to be delegated, or paralysis would set in. And with the paralysis came an attitude that guaranteed substandard performance if not outright failure and, in carrier aviation, failure usually meant that good men died.

As he turned the corner into the small branch passageway that led to Blake's room, Hogan couldn't decide whether he was pissed off because the squadron was in total disarray or because it was he who would have to clean it up.

Blake answered Hogan's knock immediately, as if he had been standing with his hand on the doorknob.

"Come in, Jim. Have a seat."

"Thanks." Hogan sat in the straight-backed gray desk chair. He looked at Blake, who moved to one side of the room but made no effort to sit down himself. Blake picked up a folder and handed it to Hogan. It was the one containing the letter about the truck. It also contained the reply he had asked Wilson to draft.

"I found this in your in basket this morning. The time stamp says that it was received three days ago, but I haven't seen it in my basket. Wilson has drafted a reply. Did you tell him to?"

"Yessir, I did. It seemed that it was a straightforward sort of thing, so I—"

Blake cut him off. "I make the decisions about who does what. Did it occur to you that Wilson might not be the man for the job? That perhaps he was the one who stole the truck?"

"No, sir. All we have there is a request for an investigation. How can we tell who stole the truck until we investigate or, come to think of it, even if it was stolen in the first place?"

"You'll have to learn that when we get something like this from

66

the 'highers' that they have done their homework and know all there is to know. We have to respond in exactly the prescribed manner, or they'll come down on us like a ton of bricks."

"Are you saying, sir, that these things come down as tests?"

Blake smiled. Now he could see that Hogan was getting the picture. All the man needed was a little guidance, just like the other officers in the squadron.

"Yes. Although not everything that comes down is a test. Most of what we deal with is pretty straightforward, but every once in a while they'll slip in a ringer. My last tour was on a staff run by a submariner, and he would send these down and watch the response. If it was what he expected, then that C.O. had passed the test and got rated accordingly. If not, well, somebody has to bring up the rear."

Oh, shit, thought Hogan. He couldn't figure out whether Blake was just blowing smoke or was serious. If he were serious, this was gonna be a witch hunt. He thought of Taylor and Wilson. They were damn good men and this little episode could be disastrous for them. Hogan remembered an old C.O. he once had when he was an ensign. The C.O. told him that he would forgive one of Hogan's more outrageous stunts because if taken out of context, i.e., on liberty in Palma de Mallorca, it could be construed as a serious lack of judgment and maturity. Ever since, for Hogan, there had been transgressions and then, there had been transgressions.

Hogan looked at the C.O. doing his best to keep a subordinate expression glued on his face. "Yes, sir. So what do we do?"

"I want you to investigate this episode. Use the legal officer for advice, but I want this to be a professional piece of work that will reflect positively on the squadron."

And on you, you son of a bitch, thought Hogan. He was silent for a couple of heartbeats and suddenly had an idea. If he stalled on this one, maybe it would just go away.

"Skipper, what the staff wants is a reply soonest. It will probably take me a while to get to the bottom of this, so why don't we send them an acknowledgment now and the investigation report later, after we've done it right?"

Blake stared off at the wall, thinking about all the ins and outs of Hogan's idea. "How long would you say the investigation would take to do properly, X.O.?"

"I don't know. Probably three weeks by the time the report was ready for mailing."

Three weeks, thought Blake. I'll be gone in two and Hogan will be the C.O. so he'll have to sign it out. My name will be on the acknowledgment but not on the report. He realized suddenly that Hogan still didn't know about the conversation between himself and CAG.

"Okay, Jim. That sounds good. I'm glad you understand the system." He handed the folder to Hogan. "Now, to another matter. We've decided, CAG and I, that we're going ahead with the change of command in port in Singapore. We both feel that you will be able to handle it, especially since CAG has diverted someone experienced to be your X.O. Named Terry White. Do you know him?"

Hogan, stunned, just nodded. He had expected that under the circumstances of Sands's departure Blake would be extended for at least a couple of extra months to give him time to get ready. Now he'd be in command almost before he'd gotten unpacked.

White was an old squadronmate and they'd gotten along very well when they'd served together. That would help, but Hogan was very aware suddenly of what he considered the gaps in his knowledge not only about this squadron but also about being its boss. He knew he should be feeling elated at the attainment of a life's goal, but all he could muster was a cold lump in his belly.

Suddenly he began to get angry. He didn't like the feeling of being a puppet on a string. This wasn't how things should be done.

Hogan heard himself speak. "When was this decided? Nobody consulted me about it."

Blake sat back in his chair as if struck. He was surprised at the tone of Hogan's statement, but a refusal was something he hadn't even considered. He'd have to be careful here. He deliberately relaxed and smiled, hoping to put Hogan back at ease.

"We had a meeting, he and I, day before yesterday. We both believe that you are completely prepared for the job, for more than we could have hoped." That's it, Blake thought, pour on the oil. He could see a struggle with the compliment in Hogan's features as he tried to concentrate on his anger.

Hogan shook off the diversion. "Why didn't you ask me?"

"First, I didn't see the need. I was certain that you'd jump at the chance. I would have. Secondly, as I recall, you were either out flying or getting ready to go. Lastly, I wasn't sure when I'd get another chance to talk to CAG about the subject."

"And you waited two days to tell me about it?"

Blake set himself in his best repentant pose. "You're right, Jim, I should have done that earlier, but we seemed to be going in different directions. I suppose I just procrastinated until now. If I'd truly made an effort, I could have gotten together with you and told you, but I didn't. For that, I apologize."

Hogan couldn't think of anything else to argue about since he'd been so neatly disarmed by Blake's surrender. Before he could come up with a new attack, Blake had moved on. Hogan wondered how many other people had been conned by Blake in just this way. He felt slightly soiled at tacitly accepting Blake's little coup. He wasn't sure if it was his own ego or a growing desire to help the squadron which caused him to cease firing. He hoped that it was the latter, but somewhere deep down he was sure that ego, good old aviator's pride, had a lot to do with it.

He saw that Blake knew he had won this little skirmish quite neatly. He was even careful to keep a humble expression for a few seconds before he moved on.

Blake picked up another folder and handed it to Hogan. "Okay, I have no one coming over for the ceremony. Do you?"

"No, sir. I hadn't planned on this at all, so there won't be time for it."

"Good. Then we can have a simple squadron dress inspection and a short reading of the orders. Let's plan on the twentieth. That all right with you?"

"Yes, sir. That's fine."

Blake took another file folder from the top of the pile on his desk and handed it to Hogan.

"All right. This is the change. Give this to one of the lieutenant commanders. He can take care of the arrangements."

Hogan stood and walked to the door. As he pulled it open, he turned to Blake. "I'll draft the acknowledgment for the admiral. I'll have it to you in an hour or so."

"That's great, Jim. I'll see you later," Blake said as he closed the door behind the X.O.

Hogan stood in the passageway, leaning his head back against the wall. He suddenly felt like the loneliest man on earth. He had no one to share his feelings with, certainly not Blake. The chaplain was out too, he thought, I don't even know the guy. Maybe I'll just go and stand in the catwalk for a while. Shit. Shit. Shit!

*   *   *

Ninety minutes later, Scott was sitting alone at a corner of a table in the "dirtyshirt" wardroom. This was the come-as-you-are, cafeteria-style eating area for officers up forward, just beneath the flight deck. Most pilots preferred eating there simply because of the informality. It beat getting dressed for dinner in the formal wardroom five decks below.

He was staring at the wall and wondering what it would be like if the men in dress blue uniforms ever had to walk up onto his front porch to tell his wife that he wasn't coming home. Right about now, two homes were being visited by the men in the dress blue uniforms who would tell the people in the homes that their loved ones were dead, killed in action in the skies of a country on the other side of the world. Neither of Scott's two young men had been married, so it was the parents who were being told.

Scott had two sons of his own and could not think of anything that terrified him more than having something like that happen to them. He hoped every day that those two boys would not follow in his footsteps, that they'd do something smart with their lives instead of risking them flying from a ship for astonishingly low pay. He hoped they'd find a job which not only allowed them to come home every night but also afforded them a better than sixty percent chance of surviving until retirement.

He realized that this was a pretty selfish way of thinking. He didn't want them to fly Navy airplanes to protect himself from the worry he was certain he'd feel if they did. His own father had flown in World War II and probably secretly hoped for the same thing—that Scott the younger would do something less hazardous with his life. But Scott's father had never tried to dissuade him and had known that seeing his son go off to become a naval aviator was a reflection of his own success in imbuing young Chris with the values and ideals that had driven him to do it all those years before. There were always those men who chose to stand between their own people and those of other lands and other ideologies who lurked in the dark forests of the world. Scott and his father were such men. Scott knew almost resignedly that his own sons might be such men too. But another, deeper, part of him hoped that they might escape the need. It would certainly please their mother.

He shook his head to clear these thoughts away. They would do nothing but make him feel worse than he already did. The almost tasteless "slider," or cheeseburger, he was eating was like rubber.

He really didn't feel much like eating, but he had to be at a strike-planning session later and he knew that his stomach would rebel if it was asked to endure one of them empty.

A voice at his side interrupted his reverie. It was Jim Hogan—another reminder of today's events—standing there, holding a tray of food.

"Mind if I sit down?"

Scott smiled wearily. "No. Have a seat."

Hogan sat and placed his plates on the table, handing the empty tray to a steward. He took a sip of milk before he spoke. "I'd like to thank you for getting those MiGs off our ass today. They'd probably have had us if you hadn't showed up." He drew a breath.

"And I'm sorry about your guys. I wish I could say something to make it better, but . . ."

Scott forced a smile. "Thanks. As to the MiGs, that's our job. We're always happy to chase those fuckers. I just wish we could catch them once in a while."

He leaned back in his chair and watched Hogan bite into his slider. "I hear you're going to take over the squadron soon. Congratulations."

Hogan smiled wearily. "Don't you mean 'condolences'? Everybody else around here seems to think that's what's in order."

Scott leaned forward, staring intently at the slightly younger man. "Is that what you think? That 262 is some kind of McHale's Navy? Listen carefully. The squadron is fine—it's only the command that's fucked up. Your predecessor was worthless and your C.O. is so shit-scared of looking bad, he won't make a decision without triple-checking every word on every piece of paper. I'll admit you've got one hell of an uphill battle, but you can handle it. CAG says so, and he's gotten you a super X.O."

"That's what I can't figure out. Don't they usually bring in somebody with more experience in situations like this?"

"Normally, yes. But you have to understand that 262 is flat on its ass. Other than replacing everybody, the fastest way to get a fresh start is to get an entirely new pair of heavies, both a new C.O. and X.O. That way there'll be no carryover from the bad days. You'll also have plenty of help. The other skippers in the air wing will all help you if you need it." He held up a hand. "I know that we're all 'in competition' with each other for fitness reports, but you're the junior guy and really aren't a player yet. The other reason is that one bad squadron can screw things up for the whole

71

bunch of us in combat. You have to be able to trust everybody up there or everybody's in deep shit.

"The other thing you have to remember is that you must, repeat, must, allow the others in the squadron to help you run it. It's not a one-man show."

Hogan nodded and picked up his coffee. "Who in the squadron is considered good? I mean by the rest of the air wing."

Scott smiled. "This'll surprise you. Wilson for sure and a couple of the senior lieutenants, Smith, Tomlinson, and Kane. And as much as he pisses me off, I'll have to admit that Taylor is a damn good man too. You, although that's mostly from CAG's commercial and from your rep from your last tour. But there's really nobody in the squadron who's considered dangerous."

"Okay. That makes me feel a little better. Not much though."

"Well, be careful not to let them get too cocky. Otherwise they wind up like those two I lost this morning—dead. Goddamn J.O.'s."

Hogan was surprised by Scott's vehemence.

"What happened, Chris? I couldn't figure out much from the radio chatter."

"My wingman got cute and figured he could pick off a MiG, but he miscounted. He rolled in on the lead and the wingman shot him in the ass."

"So what do you do about that?"

Scott scratched his chin. He saw the complete openness in Hogan's eyes. It was obvious that Hogan really wanted to know in case something like it happened to him.

"When I got back I went into the ready room and got the Operations Officer and began telling him that I wanted an examination of all crew assignment procedures and squadron training, especially that of the J.O.'s. It was a dumb mistake that cost those two their lives and us a good airplane and I'm not about to have that happen again. I was really getting into a tirade about goddamn J.O.'s and their goddamn attitude. I had gotten to the point where all J.O.'s should be strangled at birth when my RIO, Norris, walks by and moves his gear off the chair next to mine. I looked at him and asked what the hell he was doing. He said, 'It's obvious that you don't want J.O.'s in your airplane. I'm a J.O., so I'm moving my gear.' I said, 'Yeah, but you don't count.' He says, 'You can't have it both ways, Skipper. If you damn all J.O.'s, you damn me,'"

Scott smiled ruefully. "He was right, of course. One of my biggest flaws is that I really can get full of myself, especially now that I'm in command. My X.O. is always warning me that one of these days it's going to get me in trouble. Anyway, Norris left me with a clear choice of continuing to be an asshole or backing down and admitting I was wrong."

"So what did you do?"

"Neither. I told the duty officer to set up an all-officers' meeting after flight ops tonight and stormed out. When we have the AOM, I'll once again reemphasize judgment and the hard-learned lessons of naval aviation. I will not apologize for getting angry or for being an asshole. Both of them are the privileges of rank. I will admit to you, however, that my RIO is the smartest son of a bitch I've ever flown with and I wouldn't trade him for a million dollars."

Hogan chuckled as Scott stood and left the wardroom. It seemed to him that the job of commanding officer was going to require just a bit of creativity. And he had a real good idea of which men in his squadron had creativity to spare.

Wilson answered the knock on his stateroom door and stared sleepily at his X.O.

"Taking a little snooze, Jack?"

"Uh, yessir. I was resting up for the movie tonight. Don't want to miss any of Claudia Cardinale. Not even a little bit."

Naps, jokingly called "ORP" or officer rest periods, were one of the sacred privileges of the pilots in a squadron. Everybody else had to work a more or less regular schedule, but the pilots never could seem to get enough rest between the stress of flying combat often around the clock and holding down at least one and sometimes three ground jobs. There never seemed to be enough time to get a good night's sleep. So whenever the opportunity arose for forty winks, the smart pilots took it.

There was another reason for this attitude. It is an incredibly dumb idea to be tired when the ship pulls into port for some liberty, so the pilots tried to keep their sleep deficit to a minimum.

Wilson indicated a somewhat dilapidated easy chair in the corner and asked Hogan to sit down. Hogan flopped into the chair which was fairly comfortable even with its pronounced list to the right.

"What can I do for you, sir?"

"I suppose you've heard that the change of command will take place in Singapore and that I'll be taking over."

Wilson nodded but kept his expression noncommittal. Everybody in the squadron had been praying that this would happen and that Blake would not be extended. The rumor was that the chiefs and first class petty officers were willing to sacrifice a virgin to make it happen but were having a hell of a time finding one on the ship. There had been a huge debate over whether an extremely effeminate yeoman in the captain's office was in fact a practicing homosexual and, if so, whether that would qualify as loss of virginity or not. Most of the older chiefs were of the opinion that they should sacrifice him anyway just to see what happened.

"Well, I think we're going to have a hell of a time convincing the squadron that they're as good as anyone else, or, at least, that they can be. Do you know Terry White?"

Wilson smiled. "Yup. He's as good as they come. He'll be the perfect guy for this squadron."

Hogan nodded. "Yeah. We've worked together before and I think we can pull this off. What I need from you are two things. First, your discretion." He raised an eyebrow at Wilson, who nodded.

"Okay. I'll keep my mouth shut."

"I thought so. The second thing I'll need is for you to give me some continuing insight into the mood of the squadron." He held up a hand. "Hold it. No. I'm not, repeat not, asking you or even suggesting that you consider thinking about being an informer. What I mean is that this squadron is so afraid of what the response from the Skipper will be that they act like robots around him. It's obvious that that's been going on for a long time even before Blake got here. There is no way that they are going to open up and become Susie Moonbeams just because I'm here. Terry and I are going to have to earn their respect, but we can't do that in a vacuum. Most of what we'll need to know we'll be able to figure out for ourselves, but not everything. I've been watching and we have some of the greatest thought-hiders in the world here. What we'll need is for you, and others, if you choose, to be the sounding board. If what we try fails, tell us. If you have a better idea, tell us that too. There is no way that anyone can fix this outfit alone."

Wilson looked at the floor for a long moment. Then he fixed Hogan with a level gaze. "One question, X.O. Tell me, what are your ultimate goals from this tour and for this squadron."

Without hesitation Hogan said, "To get all of these men home with the same number of fingers and toes as they started with.

And with more pride and self-confidence than they brought with them from California."

Wilson smiled. That was the answer he had hoped for. He'd liked Hogan a lot from their first meeting, but if he'd waved the flag and laid on the party-line bullshit about mission accomplishment and unit reputation, he'd have known he'd misjudged the new X.O. Hogan's answer showed that he knew that if he accomplished his stated purpose, he'd have taken care of the party line. And the squadron would finally be as successful as they were capable of being.

Wilson stood and opened a drawer above his desk. "You play cribbage, X.O.?"

"Yeah, but it's been a while. Since my last cruise over here."

Wilson laid a board and a deck of cards on the desk. "Better get the rust off, then. I've got a feeling that you and I will be playing this quite a bit in the future. Kind of makes conversation easy."

9

Wednesday, January 10, 1968

Taylor stepped into the tiny squadron Admin Office, cursing as his trailing leg struck the sharp edge of the hatchway. There'd soon be another round brown scar on his shin, but only after the scab and the pain went away. The office was about the size of half of a one-car garage and was cluttered with file cabinets, tiny desks on which teetered beat-up typewriters, and file folders in highly unstable-looking stacks on top of every flat surface. The wall toward the stern of the ship, or "after bulkhead," was shared with one of the rooms in which the huge tanks used to store the steam for the catapults were positioned. As a result, the office was stiflingly hot and all three of the yeomen wore white T-shirts instead of their blue uniform shirts. The only pile of anything which was not in imminent danger of collapse was the tall stack of dog-eared *Playboys*.

One of the yeomen looked up and smiled. He yelled over his shoulder. "Hey, Chief. We've got one of those maintenance pukes in here. Hide the supplies."

Taylor grinned, secretly pleased to be called a maintenance puke as opposed to a staff type. He enjoyed his job as the AIO but truly loved his other one, the one he considered his real job, Powerplants Branch Officer.

There was a muffled thump as a pair of black boots hit the deck from the top of a desk carefully positioned out of sight from the door behind a row of file cabinets. The boots and the feet in them belonged to the Admin Supervisor, Chief Napier. It was obvious that the chief had been snoozing back there.

"What brings you all the way down here to our humble fortress, Mr. Taylor?"

Taylor picked up the top copy of *Playboy* and noted the date—January 1963. This was part of the squadron collection that went back at least a dozen years and which several previous Admin department heads had periodically proscribed, with absolutely no success. He flipped through the pages, noting idly that the spectacular centerfold was still in place.

"Well, I came down to see how my request for reinstatement is coming."

The chief reached under a pile of folders and took one out. He opened it and handed a sheet of paper to Taylor.

"Same as last week, Lieutenant. The C.O. hasn't forwarded your request for waiver yet, so until we get that done and returned we can't go any further." Napier hated to see the twinge of pain and disappointment in Taylor's eyes every time he had to tell him about the almost imperceptible progress caused by Blake's dithering and mania for documentation.

Taylor nodded and forced a smile. "So what else is new down here with you titless WAVES?"

Napier smiled at the old jibe which probably went back to WW II when most admin stuff was handled by the WAVES, or Women Accepted for Voluntary Emergency Service for the duration, allowing more men to go to sea and get shot at. He pulled out another folder and handed it to Taylor.

"What you have there is your pardon. It's the reply about the

Great Admiral's Truck Theft Investigation. It seems you're off the hook, or you will be as soon as the change of command is over."

Taylor read the file with great interest which quickly turned to admiration as he ran through the official-sounding and very weighty investigation report. It said essentially nothing but said it so brilliantly, so convincingly, and so lucidly that Taylor realized that he had found a kindred spirit in its author. And a potential ally in his campaign to bring a modicum of fun and humor to the serious business of fighting an air war and, to a greater extent, keeping meddlesome higher headquarters at bay. This report was written in a style that would blow right past the staff weenies. They'd know for certain that they'd been had, but there was no way in the world that they'd be able to prove it, nor were they likely to make an issue of it. The whole thing would be marked complete and soon forgotten.

One paragraph stood out:

A thorough analysis of the ambient lighting conditions, both natural and man-made, similar to those in the area of the incident demonstrates that it would be difficult for a witness to see the perpetrator well enough for a positive identification. Furthermore, since many men, both officer and enlisted, possess flight jackets (the latter through well-documented and serious flaws in the supply system) and nearly all have more than the permitted three patches sewn on them, it is impossible to pinpoint the culprit. Officers assigned aboard, both ship's company and air wing, possess and wear patches that are either actual Attack Squadron 262 patches or ones similar in color, design, and/or size. The investigating officer was unable to accurately gauge the number of enlisted personnel who possess leather flight jackets, given their natural reluctance to admit to unauthorized possession of accountable flight gear.

"This is great! This even puts the whole supply system on report. Who wrote this? There's no way the Skipper will sign this out."

Napier took back the folder. "Mr. Wilson wrote the first rough and then he and the X.O. sorta teamed up on the final product. I think Mr. Wilson wrote the first draft sort of carefully since he didn't know how the C.O. would receive it. Anyway, the two of them came down here and started plagiarizing old investigation reports and laughing their asses off. When they were done, the X.O. said to hold it until after the change of command and he'd sign it out then."

"So you mean there was no 'thorough analysis' and no survey of the enlisted and officers aboard?"

"There sure was. Their analysis consisted of asking me and the other yeomen in here how dark it was the night before we sailed. We said that it was pretty damn dark. X.O. stood up and turned off the lights. Then he asks 'About that dark?' We said that looked like it to us so they asked us if we could tell which squadron patches they had on their jackets. We told them there was no way. Then they turned the lights back on and asked me if I had an unauthorized Navy leather flight jacket with squadron patches on it. I said no even though I was wearing mine at the time. I told them that I had gotten it from an Army-Navy store but I lost the receipt somehow. They said that that meant that my jacket couldn't be unauthorized, since they knew that a chief would never lie to an official investigation. Then they went to dinner and looked at the officers' flight jackets hanging outside the wardroom."

Napier paused and picked up his coffee cup. "See? Nothing in there is untrue."

Taylor felt a great weight lifted from his shoulders. He had been worried about how his little truck episode would end up. If it had gone through in Blake's regular style, he might well have been professionally doomed, but this report not only saved his ass but managed to tweak the system's nose. He wondered how Hogan had managed to get the Skipper to hold off.

Napier handed Taylor another folder and watched as he read it. It was a request from CAG to all the squadrons to provide junior officers to be assigned as assistant shore patrol officers during the next in-port period in Singapore. Napier knew that Taylor always jumped on the chance to take that assignment and this time was no different.

"I already submitted your name, Lieutenant," he said.

The assistant shore patrol job was one of the truly good deals left in the Navy. There is a senior shore patrol officer, usually a full commander who is selected from the X.O.'s in the air wing and who acts as the liaison between the ship and the local authorities. For him, the job is a gigantic pain in the ass because he spends most of his waking hours (about twenty-three of every twenty-four) getting sailors out of custody and apologizing for whatever behavior got them there in the first place. Every morning, bright and early, he gets to go back out to the ship and explain last night's carryings-on to the captain, who usually takes an extremely dim view of it all and wishes that the Navy would bring back floggings and keelhauling. Another thing wrong with this job is that captains often equate the messenger, i.e., the senior shore patrol officer, with the message, i.e., that the crew is a bunch of undisciplined, drunken, and crazy Visigoths who should be kept at sea until their enlistments expire. This sometimes augers poorly for the officer's next fitness report.

But the *assistant* shore patrol officer job is an entirely different kettle of fish. These are junior guys who are only on duty for eight or twelve hours straight and then get sixteen, twenty-four, or thirty-six hours off. The Navy pays for a nice hotel room for them and they are given no other responsibilities. They ride around in cars or hang out in the local headquarters and make decisions for which the senior officer is ultimately responsible. They get to go into all the off-limits places and sections that are forbidden simply because many of the fun things one does in there can be fatal. And since the danger of the off-limits areas is what attracts the sailors in the first place, that's where most of the trouble is. There are even places like Genoa, Italy, where the piers at which the ships' boats discharge passengers are smack in the middle of the off-limits area.

The assistant serves his shift and then turns it over to the next guy. He writes up his report, gives it to the senior officer, and goes either to bed or on liberty himself, leaving the senior officer wondering how the hell he is going to explain it all to the captain and why he ever joined the damn Navy in the first place.

But the absolute best part of the job is that the assistant gets to leave the ship two days early to set things up in port and gets to leave port a day or so after the ship does, in effect getting up to four extra free days of fun on the beach.

"Okay, Chief, thanks. When do we leave?"

"Says there that the ship will be in port on the morning of the twentieth, so *we* should get off on the eighteenth." There were, of course, several chiefs needed to go along to make sure that the paperwork got done, hence the "we."

"All right, then. Thanks, as usual. I've gotta go get a brief ready. Take care."

"Yeah. See you, Mr. Taylor. I don't suppose, by the way, that there's any chance you could send the Skipper off on a scouting mission, say, a hundred thousand miles or so away, is there?"

"'Fraid not. All we can do is keep him out of the ready room so the rest of us can get some work done."

Napier sighed as he closed the door behind Taylor. "Out of the ready room" meant either sitting in his stateroom, creating more paperwork, or down here in admin, bitching about the way it was done after he created it. Soon, thought Napier. Only ten days to go.

Later that evening, as Taylor sat in the wardroom watching the night's movie and admiring the unfettered view of one of Hollywood's spectacular starlets, Hogan sat in the cockpit of his A-4, admiring his view of God's infinitely more spectacular stars. He had the red lights in his cockpit turned down fairly low and was flying with only half his brain, just enough to keep his jet in its assigned orbit, far astern of the *Shiloh* at twenty-three thousand feet. His wingman, Dick Smith, had broken away and was in his own orbit 1000 feet higher and a mile farther out. All Hogan could see of his aircraft was the red anticollision lights when his orbit was pointed that way.

Hogan and his wingman had just completed a relatively uneventful road recce and this was the last recovery of the night. There were still twelve minutes to go before the first aircraft would begin its approach, so there was little chatter on the radio which was tuned to the marshal frequency. Every once in a while the marshal controller would come up and give a time check to the fifteen or so aircraft in holding, making sure that everyone would begin his approach at the right time so that they crossed the rounddown, the rear edge of the flight deck, and landed aboard with exactly the right interval.

One of the most beautiful experiences in life is flying at night when the weather is clear and you are far enough from the creations of man to be free of the perpetual glow caused by his lights. At sea, the air is clear and the stars are undistorted. Their light is simultaneously soft and familiar and harsh and frightening. You can see more stars than you ever imagined existed, more than any planetarium could ever show you, more than enough to give you back the sense of wonder you had when you first looked up and asked your father the impossible question of how many there were.

Your Plexiglas canopy disappears and it seems as if there is nothing at all to keep you from tumbling away from earth, free to join the infinite community of light.

When your body makes the motions to turn your aircraft to follow the patterns and routes and procedures dictated by those far below, it sometimes seems an annoyance, intruding on a moment when you feel you could almost touch the hem of the Divinity's robe, when you could almost peek over the wall to see the spiritual garden beyond. And then, when you realize that the light you are seeing left some of the stars before the first organism on earth gave its first twitch of life, it gives you a chance to gain some perspective on your place in the tapestry.

Some very fortunate men, like Jim Hogan, can take just a touch of that perspective and hold it in their lives, albeit unconsciously. Others, less fortunate and much sadder men, see infinity and, awed or frightened, shy away and force their eyes to the ground beneath their feet, condemned forever to forgo much of the beauty and joy that surrounds them every day. Those men are infinitely sadder than those who never find that it is out there at all.

Hogan forced his eyes back to the cockpit and saw that it was nearly time for him to begin his approach. He turned up his instrument lights a little so that he would be better able to see the gauges as he got closer to the ship and adjusted his pattern so that he would hit his commencement point exactly on time. Several aircraft below him were well into their approaches judging by their flashing red anticollision lights which were now stringing out in a long line, ending at the ship, where they winked out when they caught the arresting wire and their pilots cut off their external lights' master switches.

He was about fifteen seconds from his commencement point when he saw a large flash in the darkness below where the deck of the *Shiloh* ought to have been. It was not the huge fireball one normally saw from a disastrous crash, but, on the other hand, large yellow flashes were not part of the routine of night carrier landing patterns. Hogan's eyes went instantly to his fuel gauge to double-check that he had enough for a prolonged delay. He had enough to stay in holding for a while before he reached "bingo fuel," the state where he would have to divert to a landing ashore. As he was flipping through his small plastic book and making sure he had the sheets that gave the arrival and landing procedures for his primary divert field, Danang, he heard the marshal controller come up on the frequency.

"Ninety-nine, Liberty. The deck is now foul. Remain in marshal at max conserve. Request fuel states in order." "Ninety-nine" was a brevity code word that meant everybody attached to the group being addressed. "Liberty" was the call sign for the air wing as opposed to a specific squadron, so the radio transmission was being addressed to all *Shiloh* aircraft.

The answers began with the low numbers, the 100- and 200-series, the fighters, which, being F-4s, would be the most fuel-critical, and progressed through the rest of the stack. When it came to the 400s, Hogan, in 403, was first.

"Marshal, Ghostrider 403 has two-point-oh."

"Roger, two-point-oh for 403."

Just below the flight deck, Hogan knew that things were going crazy down in CATCC, or Carrier Air Traffic Control Center, pronounced "cat-see." This was a very much smaller version of the centers that the FAA used back in the States to control air traffic flowing around major airports, except that with this one the airport was always moving.

There would be a sailor with a set of headphones writing everybody's fuel state down backward on a large glass status board, so the officers sitting across the room on the other side of the glass could instantly tell how long each aircraft had left in the air and could prioritize the fuel in the tankers which were always orbiting when the rest of the ship's tactical jet aircraft were airborne. Hogan's 2000 pounds of fuel were more than enough to either keep him in his holding orbit for a while or to get him to Danang with more than the level of reserve fuel which would call for sweaty palms.

Once the brain trust, sitting in CATCC, got a good handle on how long it would take to clear the deck and how long the jets holding above could stay there, they'd be able to make the decision whether to "bingo" the jets to Danang or not. One of the dangers in this process occurred when people on the ship screwed around and waited until the last possible moment to decide, usually forgetting that the divert field ashore just might have some problems accepting a sudden influx of strange aircraft. This sometimes caused a whole gaggle of aircraft to arrive simultaneously at the field with their low fuel warning lights flickering. Then, depending on the experience of the controllers ashore, the weather, and the coolness of the pilots, the problem could become somewhat like a cavalry charge in a broom closet.

"Ninety-nine, Liberty. Estimated clear deck in four–five minutes. All Phantoms and Skyhawks to bingo. Primary divert is 232 at one eight seven nautical miles. Contact departure control now."

Hogan thumbed his channel selector to the ship's departure control frequency and waited a few seconds for the controller to finish giving instructions to a couple of F-4s before he spoke. The recovery would resume in forty-five minutes, but there obviously wasn't enough fuel in the tankers to keep everybody around that long. As it was, even with the decent amount he had left he would be approaching a dangerous level by the time the deck was clear. The decision had been made to send the fighters and the attack aircraft to the beach and to keep some of the others, which had more fuel, around for a while. Even if the others were sent in to Danang later, it would still work because there would be less delay in the approach pattern.

"Departure, Ghostrider 403 is with you. Twenty-three thousand."

Hogan waited while the controller gave some instructions to the fighters to help them find a tanker that would give them some fuel for the trip to the beach. When the F-4s had rogered and switched off the frequency, he called Hogan.

"Roger, 403. Your Pigeons to Danang are 232 at 187. Climb to and maintain 250. Squawk 4235 and contact Danang Approach on 314 point 2."

"403 copies. 232 for 187. Squawking 4235 and switching. Good night."

Hogan switched his radio to the new frequency and set 4235 in the windows of his IFF transponder, which would electronically tell the controllers at Danang exactly which of the little lighted blips on their radar scopes he was. He kept his turn in until he was heading 232 degrees, or generally southwest, and shoved his throttle forward into the climb to flight level 250, roughly 25,000 feet.

Hogan looked out to the side as he passed by Smith's holding pattern but couldn't pick out the lights of his wingman hanging out there in the void. He knew that Smith would be hoping like hell that they'd be told to wait until morning to return to the ship. That way they'd be able to get a beer or two in the club.

* * *

Hogan rolled all the way down the runway at Danang and turned off at the end. Ahead of him were several other *Shiloh* aircraft taxiing into spots on the transient ramp. He followed the line and watched his wingman roll out and swing off the runway onto the taxiway. Hogan lowered the "headknocker," the small ejection seat safing lever behind his helmet, unlocked and raised his canopy, and then released his mask, shutting off the flow of oxygen. Immediately, the hot, humid air of Vietnam rushed in and blew away the cool, dry air in the cockpit. In the few days he had been away from the land, he had forgotten how oppressive and smelly the air could be there.

Up ahead, the aircraft were beginning to turn off the taxiway onto the ramp. Hogan approached the turnoff and saw the yellow wands of the taxi director waving him to a parking spot. When he had stopped in the spot, the director ran down to the next spot as two others inserted the safety pins in his landing gear and external fuel tank. One of them ran forward and gave him the shut-down signal and Hogan pulled his throttle back to the cutoff, watching the RPM, engine temperature, and fuel flow gauges decrease normally. When the generator dropped off the line, the gauges quit and the cockpit light died, so he pulled out his flashlight to help him clean up the cockpit. There was no sign of anyone bringing out a boarding ladder, so he pulled off his helmet, released his straps, and pulled himself up, throwing his leg over the side of the cockpit and feeling for the refueling probe beneath the right side of the nose. He found it and climbed the rest of the way out, shinnying along the probe until he could step onto the wing. He walked aft, sat on the trailing edge of the wing, and slid off onto the ground.

As he walked around his jet, looking for any leaks or missing parts, a jeep pulled up in front of the Skyhawk. A young marine officer in camouflage utilities and a black felt brassard on his arm which had "ODO" embroidered on it, walked up, saluted, and introduced himself.

"Lieutenant Schultheis, sir. I'm the Ops Duty Officer tonight. Are you Commander Hogan?"

Hogan returned the salute. "That's me."

"We just got a message for you. The ship says you're the senior man. Your overhead time will be 0930 tomorrow. I've got some transportation coming for you guys and some rooms set up in the transient barracks. You might want to stow your flight gear in my office since we've got some folks around here who love souvenirs."

"Thanks. I think there'll be some more aircraft dribbling in here for a while. We really appreciate the service, by the way. Your controllers did a nice job getting us all sorted out. Best radar approach I've gotten for a while too."

"Great. I'll pass that on. If you'll excuse me, Commander, I'll go see about getting your fuel truck set up. When will you need it?"

Hogan looked at his watch. It was just past seven P.M. "How long does the club stay open?"

Schultheis grinned. "It starts rolling around nine and it closes at 0200. The kitchen stays open until midnight. Tonight ought to be pretty good. They've got a troupe of dancers from the Philippines in for a couple of days."

"Okay. We'll fuel 'em up now so we can sleep in. If they're going to give us a gentleman's overhead time, we'll take advantage of it."

Smith walked over from his A-4, loosening his harness and rubbing his nose where he had red marks from his oxygen mask.

"What's the plan, X.O.? Do I have to come up with a phantom leak so we can spend the night?"

"Nope. We have an overhead time at 0930 tomorrow so, I regret to say, we have to stay here and go to the club. Give me your flight gear so I can stow it in Base Ops. Apparently there are some thieves around here. I've got to send an arrival message to the ship, so get your jets fueled and pass the word on to the other guys to make sure that everything's buttoned up. Ill be back to help out in a little while."

Smith grinned as he handed his torso harness, G suit, and his helmet to Hogan. "This is great. I've never gotten to stay ashore before. They always needed me back right away."

Hogan took the gear and headed for the truck. It's great, all right. I just hope nobody got hurt back on the ship when whatever fouled the deck happened, he thought.

All the A-4s from his squadron which had been on the last airborne cycle were either safely on deck there in Danang or were on the way. There were many things that could have caused the flash he had seen on the deck of the ship, not a one of them good. But that is the nature of a carrier flight deck. It is without question one of the most dangerous places on earth.

10

Thursday, January 11, 1968

Jack Wilson entered the ready room and plopped down in his seat in the front row. He looked up at the PLAT, or pilot's landing aid television, and watched the first of the "bingoed" aircraft, an F-4, from the previous night's mission return from Danang. The Phantom was lined up perfectly in the cross hairs of the camera lens recessed into the flight deck above. There were two of those fixed cameras in the deck, each set for a different-angled glideslope, so that one of them would always have the approaching aircraft centered up as long as the pilot kept the approach within limits. Completely unlike the approach that had caused all the problems last night.

Wilson had been sitting in this same seat watching the last recovery begin. As soon as it was over and the pilots had filled out their postflight paperwork, the evening movie would begin. The first aircraft down, the "sacrificial" A-4, had trapped nicely and the third, sailor-operated, camera on the island followed the jet's rollout. The A-4 taxied out of the landing area and the picture switched back to the deck camera and picked up the lights of the approaching F-4.

Most of the pilots watching in the ready room immediately sat forward in their seats when they saw the lights of the F-4 against the black background, about a mile or so behind the ship. The lights should have all been in a nice, steady row with just little twitches here and there as the pilot made a small correction in either lineup or glidepath.

But these lights were all over the place. The wings rocked as the pilot wandered back and forth, drifting away from the cross hairs on the screen and coming back toward the center, only to

86

pass right through it toward the other extreme. The approach light in the center was shifting in intensity, showing that it was changing colors from red to amber to green and back again. If the pilot had his nose attitude under control and was on speed, the light should have been amber, but the flicking back and forth was a clear indication that he was raising and dipping his nose, going from fast to slow. In concert with his lousy lineup control, it was obvious that the pilot had a bad case of vertigo.

Vertigo, or, more accurately, spatial disorientation, is one of the most dangerous things that can happen to a pilot. When he is flying on instruments, such as in bad weather or at night, he must believe what the gauges tell him about what his jet is doing in relation to the planet. Sometimes, more often than pilots like to admit, their body and mind will tell them that the aircraft, and therefore the pilot, are doing one thing while, in fact, something entirely different will really be happening. That awful feeling of disorientation is called vertigo, and, unless the pilot can force himself to ignore the erroneous signals his body is sending and believe the gauges, he is in very deep trouble indeed.

Somebody turned up the volume on the television so that the radio transmissions between the Landing Signal Officer and the pilot filled the room. The LSO's voice was fairly calm, much more so than Wilson knew he truly was. He finally got the pilot calmed a little and the movements of the lights settled down a bit.

"Easy with it. Bring it back to the right. Hold your attitude."

The pilot, as was the procedure, didn't reply. His job was to fly. The big fighter got closer and closer, the gaps between the lights expanding. The Phantom was centered in the cross hairs and seemed to be holding steady, when it abruptly settled toward the bottom of the screen. The center light rose above the wing lights as the pilot raised his nose to arrest the descent toward the water. The LSO gave him one call for increased power and then, when he saw how bad things were getting, tried to wave him off, sending him around for another try.

"Don't settle! Attitude! Power. Power! POWER!! Wave off!!"

Wilson and the other pilots could see the blinking wave-off cue on the television screen and knew that the LSO had activated the flashing lights on the deck above.

Too late, the pilot shoved his throttles forward. The descent slowed, just enough to get the jet over the rounddown at the back of the flight deck, but the Phantom hit hard, well short of the arresting wires. There was a brief image of black things flying away from the aircraft into the night and then a large flash of light under the wing, where the right main landing gear used to be. The aircraft dropped onto its wingtip and slewed off to the left side of the television picture and the right side of the deck above.

The view shifted to the island camera that followed the F-4 as it veered toward the aircraft parked clear of the landing area next to the island. It stopped just before it would have plowed into the fully fueled row of aircraft.

There was a moment of silence in the ready room broken in a second or so by the muted sounds of the crash alarm going off on the flight deck directly overhead. Wilson was aware suddenly that he had been holding his breath. He let it out as some of the other pilots stared frozen at the image of the Phantom now being surrounded by men, several in silver fireproof suits, shooting fire-suppressant foam on the wreck and working to get the pilot and RIO out of it.

"Holy shit!" The duty officer broke the silence and all the pilots began talking at once. The consensus seemed to be that they couldn't believe that the crew hadn't tried to eject and that if they had, they probably would not have survived.

Wilson didn't stick around for any more but headed out of the room and forward toward CATCC, where decisions were going to have to be made about the aircraft still in the air, including the four from VA-262.

That morning's recovery went well. Everybody got aboard with varying degrees of "perfection" in their approaches. Wilson waited until the X.O. had entered the room and walked up to him. He knew that Hogan would have a bunch of questions and would have heard the story at least twice, mostly incorrectly, on his way down from his aircraft.

"Welcome back. Have a nice time in the club?"

Hogan dropped his helmet into a seat. "Sure did. It wasn't all fun since we had to make sure that we had a couple of beers for you guys. That took most of the evening. I do wish that the Filipino dancers they get for the clubs were a little bigger in the chest department though. I did run into an old marine buddy, an A-4 type, who is over here as an Air Liaison Officer with one of the grunt regiments. He's going on R&R to Singapore at the same time we'll be there, so I invited him to join our Admin. Remind me to add his name to the list." He sat in his seat and picked up the binder with all the maintenance forms he had to fill out.

Wilson nodded and made a note in his "wheel book," the small green notebook most officers carried in their back pocket to remind themselves of the little things easily forgotten in the press of daily living on a carrier at sea. As he did, he knew that Hogan's invitation to the marine was not entirely humanitarian. The pilots from the squadron would have an opportunity to get to know the guy and pick his brain about the war from his point of view.

Hogan looked up at Wilson. "Okay. So what happened last night?"

"We had a deck crash. One of the F-4s screwed the pooch and landed hard and short. He tore up his right mainmount but caught the number-one wire. The stub of his strut went over the number-two and -three wires, so they all had to be replaced. The aircraft almost went into the pack but stopped short of a real mess. The crew stayed with it and got out okay except that when CAG and their C.O. get done with them, they will not be happy fellows.

"The best guess was that it would be a minimum of an hour before they got everything cleaned up, so you all got sent in to the beach."

"Anybody hurt?"

"No, but there were a lot of scared people up there. The guy looked like he saved it after a bad start, but I guess when he got in close he lost the bubble. Probably should have waved him off then, but I think he surprised even the LSO when he screwed it up again. The safety guys are looking at that. Anyway, the nose of the Phantom stopped about five feet from 406 or we'd have lost a jet ourselves. Anyway, everything's up and ready on the flight deck."

Hogan nodded. He'd find out more later, when the rest of the dust settled.

"What's on the schedule for today?"

"We've got a standdown day, so we'll be coming alongside the *Rappahannock* for fueling and replenishment. We can use the time to get some jets back up and catch up on the paperwork. Tomorrow we switch to the midnight-to-noon schedule. We have an all-officers meeting scheduled for 1600. Mostly that'll be a brief on the plan for the next few days and an intelligence review. We also have to reinforce the rules of engagement again. Seems somebody in McNamara's Band back in Washington has his skivvies in a knot about something. CAG also wants everybody to be briefed again on the air wing SOP after that Phantom got shot down a couple days ago."

Wilson noted the expression of distaste on Hogan's face. He hadn't known that the X.O. hated AOMs like everybody else.

"Don't worry, X.O., we can cover all that and be out of here in less than forty minutes." He grinned and walked away to the duty desk.

While Hogan was finishing up his postflight paperwork, Commander Chris Scott was addressing his squadron in their ready room about one hundred and fifty feet forward. They were having their own AOM and had just been visited by CAG Andrews, who had explained to them with a significant degree of vehemence that between them and the other fighter squadron (the one involved in the preceding night's flight-deck crash), they had cost the Navy and the American taxpayer two valuable, multimillion-dollar aircraft and two even more valuable million-dollar naval officers. The point that he was not going to put up with any more of that crap had been crystal-clear.

CAG was going to be a tough act to follow, but as he spoke, Scott caught several glances cast his way from CAG. The meaning of those glances was not lost on Scott. He felt himself becoming increasingly angry as CAG continued his lecture. He knew that his anger was about to get the best of him and fought mightily against himself to suppress it.

After CAG had departed the room in a cloud of silence, Scott stood and faced his men.

"This morning I finished writing a couple of letters to Croake's and Nalls's parents. I had to lie to them and tell them that their sons were killed while honorably defending the freedom of our little allies to the south. I had to spend all morning composing those letters, and it pisses me off that I had to do it in the first place. There was no need at all for those two to get themselves killed like they did.

"You all want to get a MiG. That's why we've trained so hard for so long. That's why our country has provided us with these wonderful airplanes we fly. We all know that if we get a MiG, our reputations are made and we can be pretty sure that a grateful nation will pin a Silver Star upon our manly breasts. It's even a joke among the pilots on the ship that we get Silver Stars for doing what we're trained for while the attack pukes get a smile and a nod for doing *their* job.

"Croake and Nalls died stupidly. They only made one small mistake. They lost count of the enemy. They got so eager to be heroes that they went ahead and acted on impulse. In so doing, they forgot the rules that have cost many lives to learn. Now you will all get to go to the memorial service and listen to the chaplain tell you that there was a divine reason for what happened, while you'll stand there and tell yourselves that that's bullshit and that you could never be that stupid. Well, Croake and Nalls thought that too. They only forgot it for about fifteen seconds."

Scott looked around the room. Most of the faces were intent on what he was saying but a few looked distracted, as if his lecture had to be directed at somebody else. He felt the flames of his anger burst forth, because those very ones who looked so superior were precisely the ones he was trying to get to.

Scott stopped speaking and looked down at his hands which were clenched into fists on the podium. In every squadron he had been in, there had always been a "last row gang" which sat in the back of the ready room, as far from the senior officers as possible. They were always the cocky ones, the ones who knew everything, the ones he was now trying to reach. He looked up and saw again their bored faces; a couple were staring blankly at the walls above his head or at the seats directly in front of them.

That did it. Scott picked up the small green notebook he had laid on the podium and fired it as hard as he could against the back wall of the ready room. The J.O.'s in the back jumped and looked up at Scott, and as they saw him each felt a cold flash drive straight down his chest and into the pit of his stomach. The muscles in Scott's jaw worked quickly, and his white-knuckled hands were gripping the sides of the podium. His eyes, which were carefully taking in each of their faces, had a fire in them that they had never seen before. It dawned suddenly on at least two of them that they were very fortunate to be well out of arm's reach of the Skipper.

When he spoke it was a deep rumble, menacing them with its dangerous evenness.

"Stand up. Yeah, you dumb fuckers in the back row."

They got slowly to their feet, looking guiltily around the room. They had no idea exactly what they were guilty of, but it seemed a good idea to each of them to lose their cockiness right now.

"You assholes, specifically, are the ones who are gonna die. You are going to be buried in little pieces if they can find anything at all after the fire. If not, your mommy and your daddy are going to watch them put a coffin full of bricks in the ground. And all that you'll leave behind will be a picture on the wall and another bunch of assholes sitting in the back row thinking you were a dumb bastard just like the last dumb bastard. Unless you begin to think instead of acting from your balls, you are going to die! Do you understand? Well? Do you?"

Scott stared at each face in turn, forcing them to look him in the eye and say "Yes, sir." When they had all done so, he told them to sit down and stared down at the podium for a long moment. They could see him taking deep breaths, fighting to control himself. When he looked back up at his assembled squadron, he was back in control, but every man in the room knew that it was a tenuous grip at best.

"All right. CAG has just explained to you his feelings on the matter. What he didn't say was that before he gets to you he'll get me first. I'm not going to allow that to happen. I'm not going to allow your stupidity to drive this squadron's dick into the dirt. I'm not going to lose any more airplanes or write any more letters. Now, lately there have been several instances where you have failed to do your ground jobs completely, thoroughly, and accurately. If you can't do your jobs completely, thoroughly, and accurately, and, when you are flying, use good judgment, you can rest assured that I will see to it that your careers are over. Clear?"

Scott didn't wait for an answer but walked out of the room through a silence thicker than the one that followed CAG.

Andrews sat in his office, staring absently at the wall. He hated to have to come down on people as he had had to do that morning. In all his years of flying from ships, in all the squadrons he had served in and, finally, commanded, he had seen this particular wheel reinvented time and time again. It was always hardest on the commanding officers who invariably seemed to forget that they themselves had seen things like this happen before and probably would again. Combat losses were one thing; that was why everybody got the extra pay. But losses such as this, caused by youthful aggressiveness overwhelming good sense, were quite another. They were not as painful as those caused by "flathatting," or showing off, but they were nearly so.

There really was nothing unique at all in what had happened to Scott's young tigers, but when one is in command of the unit, he feels an almost parental pain when somebody screws up. The others in the squadron can and will feel regret and sadness and genuine loss that a couple of their mates have bought the farm. There will, for a couple of those closest to the departed, be a void that will never be completely filled.

But for the C.O. there is the agony of doubt. Did I teach them everything I could have? Could I have seen something in their actions or demeanor that would have given me a clue? Did I pay too little attention to the small things and too much to the big external stuff? Did I not set the proper example and attitude for the rest of the squadron? Did I make them think that they needed to best me in order to succeed?

Andrews thought over the implications of the last question. He remembered a young man he'd had in one of his squadrons who came in determined to be the best there ever was in flying the F-8. He probably could have been too, if he'd not tried to do a second aileron roll next to the ship during a high-speed low-altitude pass. Andrews hadn't seen it, but the witnesses all said that the splash and fireball seemed to stretch for a mile along the surface of the water. A little more experience or a little less aggressiveness would probably have kept the young man alive. The C.O. of the squadron had taken a long time to get over that one. It was the first and only loss he'd suffered during his entire command tour.

That was probably the problem for the C.O.'s—they always seemed to feel that it was happening for the first time in Navy history, that they were under the gun when it did. Unfortunately, thought Andrews with a grimace, they were often right and it was a damned big gun and getting bigger. That was the system.

Andrews shook his head to clear away the thoughts. He picked up the pile of paperwork from his in basket and opened the first folder. It contained the temporary duty orders for the group of shore patrol officers for the port visit to Singapore. He smiled when he saw Lieutenant Nick Taylor's name near the top of the list. Maybe they'd be able to get in some golf this time in. Andrews had yet to beat Taylor in a round, but he was determined to do so before the cruise ended.

11

Monday, January 15, 1968

Blake looked back at the formation of aircraft spread out above, below, beside, and behind his own A-4, each of them moving around in the random jinking pattern designed to throw off aimed Triple-A fire from the gunners below. Ahead, the Iron Hands shrank to near-invisibility as they began their attempts to find and destroy the SAM sites near the target, a large rail bridge complex, and on the approaches to it.

Blake saw the clear blue sky and then the lovely green and brown and tan land below. There had been a time in his life and his career when he would have been struck by the beauty of the moment. Perhaps not immediately when he saw it because of his concentration on the dangers ahead, but there would certainly have come a time when he would have had the thought. He had been younger then, bound up only with the wonder of the world and what he was about. That young man had gotten bored and had gone away somewhere in the past few years when Blake had come to believe that dreamers were suckers, constantly failing to see what was right under their feet, that dreams were intangible nothings, all shiny and bright and soon banished when confronted with the paths and choices that led to advancement and success.

Now, looking at the land and sky, all he could see was sheer malevolence. The ridges could only hide the enemy, the low flatlands could offer no protection or concealment if he were forced to eject, and every ten seconds on this course drew him another mile farther from the ship and safety. And further from his freedom from the operational Navy.

He knew that it would be a matter largely of chance whether he survived this, his last mission over North Vietnam. The odds were good for him because the leader usually is gone before the gunners below can get their aim squared away and their weapons going to maximum effect. He grimaced when he remembered that CAG had assigned him the lead for this one as a traditional token of his good and faithful service as the C.O. of VA-262. And good service it had been too.

After all, there had never been a moment when the squadron as a unit had lagged behind in its administrative detail. They had missed no more sorties than had any of the other squadrons and their aircraft were as well maintained. Weren't those testimonials to his leadership? And how about the inspection results from everything from the weekly zone inspections to the crucial maintenance and administrative inspections from the higher levels of command? True, the squadron had not set any records, but Blake had never felt that records were worthy goals anyway. All they did was upset the careful routine and raise expectations among the inspectors for the next time.

The young officers in the squadron had been different from those of his earlier years. There hadn't been the camaraderie between the C.O./X.O. team and the rest of the squadron that he remembered from his earlier days. They all seemed distant to him, never approaching unless it was about some work-related item, never going on liberty with him, never confiding in him. But that was all right too. Blake was tired of listening to the same stories and woes over and over again. Only the faces changed, never the problems. That was supposed to be the X.O.'s job, wiping all the noses. Blake wouldn't see any of these men again, so why should he concern himself with their tiresome little problems? Only five more days until the change of command. Hogan could have it then and be welcome to it.

"Target's at left ten o'clock."

The transmission from one of the other aircraft brought him back abruptly. The voice hadn't identified itself, but it sounded a little like his wingman, Lieutenant Tony Cordella. Blake felt a sinking in his gut when he realized that he had allowed himself to be distracted for a few moments. He had never done that before. He'd always been careful to keep his mind on the matter at hand.

"Roger, I have it." Blake couldn't remember if he'd given the order to arm the weapons on the way in. He looked down at his switches and saw that they were in the armed position, so he probably had. If he hadn't said anything, the others should have been smart enough to do their job themselves.

Blake saw the ugly black, gray, and white puffs of smoke in the sky, marking bursts of antiaircraft fire. They were all over the place, from well above the formation all the way down to the streams of tracer fire chasing the Iron Hands as they flew away, the last of their bombs and missiles now exploding in geysers of red dirt and evil black smoke.

"Lead's in."

Blake took a deep breath and pulled his Skyhawk up, rolling it to the left. When the bridge was generally in his sights he rolled the jet back over and made small corrections to keep it lined up. Now that he was heading down into it, the Triple-A seemed to intensify. Each burst seemed to be closer to him than was the last, as if he were flying down a funnel. It was obvious to him that the gunners had singled out his plane in particular and trained every gun in the area at him and, if he continued his run, he'd be killed for certain. He hit the release button and immediately banked to the right, pulling his nose back toward the sky for all he was worth and felt several jolts on the pullout, one far more severe than the others. He knew that this hadn't been his most accurate bomb run and that he'd probably missed the target, but his last load of bombs was gone and he would soon be back out over the water, safe and finished with the war.

Cordella, as Blake's wingman, was the second aircraft in on the target. He rolled out and saw Blake's A-4 above and to the side of his own, pulling away. Looking back at the bridge, he saw a rapid series of explosions several hundred feet to the east of the target among a cluster of buildings in the midst of the railroad yard next to the bridge. He had the momentary thought that Blake's aim was worse today than it usually was, but there was a huge secondary explosion which sent red, orange, and yellow streaks of flame in all directions. He couldn't believe that the dumb son of a bitch could screw up like that and still get lucky.

Cordella put his mind back on the task at hand and, when he had it all lined up, hit the release and felt the little jolts as the bombs rippled away in pairs. He waited a couple of extra heartbeats to make sure they were all gone and hauled up and away toward the east, heading out to catch up with his leader.

He spotted the tiny A-4 well east of the target area, streaking along for the water. Cordella had his throttle full forward and was getting everything his engine could deliver, but he was not overtaking his leader at all. At this rate, there was no chance of his rejoining in formation before Blake reached the ship. Cordella cut his course a little to the right so that when Blake had to alter his to get to the ship Cordella would be inside the turn and might be able to complete a rendezvous that way. As the young lieutenant crossed behind and slightly below Blake's aircraft, his aircraft rocked as it normally did when crossing the disturbed air left by another aircraft, but his windscreen was abruptly covered with a fine nearly clear mist that made the view out front fuzzy at first, but it rapidly cleared from the force of the air passing over the jet. He hadn't seen a trail behind Blake that would be caused by a major leak, but there was definitely something coming out.

"Skipper, you're leaking something. Back off some so I can take a look."

Blake heard the transmission, but it really didn't register. He could see the coastline just ahead, and beyond, the Gulf of Tonkin. The pointer on his TACAN indicator showed that the *Shiloh* was on a bearing of 116, so he eased his jet slightly to the right and put the needle on the nose, heading straight for the ship.

"401, 407. You have a leak. Request you slow down so I can take a look."

This one got through to Blake. Its correctness told him that it was not the first call his wingman had made. He pulled his throttle back and banked slightly to the right and left, looking in his mirrors, trying to spot a telltale stream of vapor flowing back from his aircraft. There was a very small trail of some sort coming from somewhere on the fuselage. He adjusted his airspeed to maintain 250 knots and waited for Cordella to catch up.

Blake called Red Crown and reported that both Ghostrider 401 and 407 were feet wet back out over the water and told them that he and Cordella were switching to their squadron common frequency while they checked his jet for damage. He was too preoccupied with his own problem to bother waiting for Red Crown's acknowledgment.

Blake saw Cordella's A-4 join loosely on the right side and then slide back and down. It appeared on the left side a few interminable seconds later and slid into a perfect parade position on the wing.

"Skipper, I don't know what's coming out, but it seems to be getting worse. You have a bunch of small holes under your left

97

wing, and it's coming out of one of them. What do your gauges show?''

Blake looked carefully at his instruments. Everything looked okay. His fuel quantity was just a little low, but it didn't seem to be dropping much beyond what he could expect at this power setting.

"Everything seems okay. It flies fine. I'm pretty sure I can make the ship.''

"Roger. I'll keep an eye on it. Let's switch back to Red Crown.''

Blake switched back to Red Crown's frequency in time to hear a few more aircraft give their feet wet reports. He waited for Red Crown's acknowledgment and keyed his mike.

"Red Crown, Ghostrider 401's back with you. Looks like I took a hit, but everything seems okay. Request pigeons back to mother.'' "Mother" was the brevity code word for whatever carrier that pilot was from.

"Roger, Ghostrider. Mother is at your 116 at fifty-seven. Be advised all strike aircraft are feet wet and you're the only one reporting damage. You're cleared to switch. Good day.''

"401's switching. Good day and thank you.''

Blake thumbed the switch to the *Shiloh's* frequency. "Tower, Ghostrider 401's with you at fifty-four.''

"Roger, Ghostrider. Understand you have some damage. Are you declaring an emergency?''

Blake thought that over. He could declare an emergency and be given priority in the landing pattern. He would be the first one down on deck but if, as he suspected, the damage was not really significant, he'd look foolish getting the ship all excited and probably screwing up the landing pattern for everybody else. He looked his gauges over one more time and decided that he'd rather not look foolish.

"Negative, Tower. Just be aware that I'm leaking something, so expect that on deck.''

"Tower copies. Call at twenty miles. Base recovery course is 160. Expect a straight-in approach.''

That was good, thought Blake. He was already pretty much lined up for his recovery, since the ship was headed away from him into the wind. The straight-in was the safest way to bring back a damaged jet. The normal overhead circling pattern could put too much stress on a damaged airframe.

In the tower, the Air Boss rolled his eyes at his assistant, the

Mini. The Mini chuckled, for he recognized the voice as belonging to the squadron C.O., a man the Boss considered the biggest flaming asshole he had ever met, let alone served with. In the Boss's eyes, the squadron took on the character of the C.O., which explained why VA-262 was considered the largest collection of pains-in-the-ass in the whole air wing. The Boss was determined to attend the squadron's upcoming change of command, not as a well-wisher so much as a witness.

Blake glanced at the mileage indicator, or DME, on his TACAN. He was fifty miles out now. The ship was on a base recovery course, or BRC, of 160, so he was headed almost straight up the wake. He was momentarily glad that he wouldn't have to go through the normal circle-to-land pattern. A couple of nice, controlled descents and an easy final approach would get him back aboard and out of this damn airplane. Then it would be over and he would be on the way home.

"How's it look out there, 407?"

Cordella glanced at the stream of vapor. " 'Bout the same. How're the gauges?"

Blake looked at his fuel gauge and noted with some satisfaction that it was staying pretty steady. He still had plenty for this approach and a couple more if he needed it. The controls were responding nicely and there were no yellow caution lights on.

"Lookin' good."

"Okay, then 407's detaching."

"Click-click."

Cordella slipped back a little and crossed under Blake's aircraft and headed away to take his place in the normal recovery pattern.

Modern jet engines are really very simple. There are only four things they have to do: suck, squeeze, burn, and blow. Air is drawn in by the compressor section and compressed (suck and squeeze). It is then mixed with fuel, burned in the combustor section, and then it is exhausted, producing the thrust that shoves the airplane forward (burn and blow). The things that make the engine do all this properly are what complicate the process. There are lots of lines and wires and cables and tubes that move small valves or sense engine performance and either keep the engine within temperature or RPM limits or tell the pilot that something has failed.

The largest and most intricate thing in the system is the fuel control which is somewhat like the carburetor on a car. It meters fuel into the engine, compensating for altitude, air density, and other variables so that the engine will deliver the power the pilot has told it he wants by his movements of the throttle.

The leak from Blake's aircraft was coming from his fuel control. One piece of the shrapnel from the shell that had exploded near his jet had smashed into the part where his throttle was connected to the unit. It was holding together at present, but only just.

Blake leveled off behind the ship and waited a few seconds until his TACAN said five miles. He went through his checklist and slapped his landing gear and tailhook handles and the flap lever down, compensating for the increased drag by increasing power. He glanced at his indicators which all agreed that everything was down and locked.

"Tower, 401's at five miles. Straight-in."

"Roger." The Air Boss picked up the phone to call down to the LSO platform but had to wait a few seconds for another jet to land. One never disturbed the LSO when he had a jet on final unless it was a dire emergency.

"Paddles, Tower. We've got Ghostrider 401, an A-4, at five miles. Straight-in."

"Paddles, roger." The LSO looked far aft of the ship and spotted the trail of exhaust from Blake's Skyhawk. There would be time to have another aircraft land from the normal pattern, so he gave his attention to the A-6 just turning final. There was a gap behind the A-6, so Blake's straight-in would not really affect the recovery that much.

The A-6 came in with its characteristic metallic whine as the pilot played the throttles to keep the approach going. It crossed the rounddown and slammed down onto the deck, catching the number-two wire. The LSO watched the wire run out and the A-6 raise its hook, freeing the wire. He turned his attention back to Blake's approaching A-4 while the arresting gear crew retracted the wire. It would be "back in battery" and ready to catch Blake long before he crossed over the deck.

Blake pulled his throttle back to start his descent and with his thumb hit the switch that extended his speedbrakes. Once he had the descent begun, he moved the throttle forward to maintain the rate, but nothing happened. The engine stayed at the reduced power setting. He pulled the throttle back and shoved it forward again. Again nothing. His rate of descent was now going well beyond what it should have been, and the Skyhawk was heading toward the water at a frightening speed. He moved the switch that should have restored manual control of the engine and tried his throttle again, simultaneously closing his speedbrakes.

Nothing.

He did not have enough power to arrest the descent and was going to hit the water well aft of the ship.

He pulled his nose up in an attempt to level off, but without the necessary thrust from the engine, all he accomplished was to bring the jet alarmingly close to a stall where there was not enough smooth air passing over the wings to produce lift and where the wings would simply quit flying. He lowered the nose again so that his wings would stay level, reached above his head for the black and yellow striped ejection handle, and pulled.

The LSO was watching the tiny jet approach and saw the descent begin. For a second or so everything seemed normal until the A-4 began to fall toward the sea at an alarming rate. He saw the descent slow as Blake brought his nose up and, only about a half-second later, the flash as the ejection seat fired. He brought his handset back to his mouth to call the plane-guard helicopter but heard the Air Boss's voice already doing it.

His hand fell slowly to his side as he watched the A-4 almost regally steepen its dive and smash into the wake a mile behind the ship with a huge splash. Above it, the parachute with Blake swinging wildly below drifted down well to one side of the plume of white water.

12

Monday, January 15, 1968

In the plane-guard helicopter, Salty Dog 804, sat two young pilots, Lieutenants Barry Browne and Sam Tucker, who were almost stupefied by the boredom of their job. Plane guard had once been carried out by a destroyer which steamed along behind the carrier, waiting for a pilot to wind up in the water and need rescuing. Nowadays, a helicopter flies the station off to the right side in a long, mind-destroying orbit. Somebody once figured out that a helicopter pilot flying from one of the units which were assigned to provide this essential service to a carrier's aviators could fly nearly six times around the world at a pokey 100 knots during his career. Most pilots figured they'd rather do that because they would at least have a destination as opposed to four hours of right-hand turns over the endless sea.

In the first half hour of the scheduled four-hour flight, Browne and Tucker had almost been animated, discussing the upcoming port visit to Singapore. After that, they'd tuned in the world service of the BBC on their ARC-94 high frequency radio and swapped off the flying duties in thirty-minute intervals. When Blake ejected, their pattern had them flying along the ship's starboard side headed away from the crash. The Air Boss's transmission had torn them away from the BBC's learned discussion by two scientists (who sounded like their mouths were full of marbles and their nostrils full of mustache hairs) of the migratory habits of some goddamn who-cares-anyway North African butterfly and back to reality. It took a few seconds for them to cage their brains and swing around to head for Blake's descending form.

*   *   *

Blake felt all the tugs and jerks and twists as he was blasted from the cockpit of his A-4 into the 150-mile-an-hour windblast. He was separated from the ejection set and the parachute dragged from its casing. He was headed forward flat on his back when the parachute fully inflated, jerking him into a pendulumlike swing below the canopy.

He opened his eyes and looked up to see that the parachute had worked. He was still marveling that it had when he splashed into the warm sea. There was not much wind, so when he popped to the surface he found that the parachute had come down on top of him. He began to struggle, trying to pull it off, but succeeded only in making the entanglement worse. Several shroudlines had wrapped themselves around his upper body, and the more he thrashed, the more they tightened. He released his oxygen mask and found himself breathing more quickly. Several of his gasps brought in seawater, which made him gag and retch in the middle of his struggle to breathe.

Blake tried desperately to force himself to follow all the training he'd had over the years which dealt with exactly this situation, but his mind failed him. It would not calm down: his body needed air and it needed freedom from the soggy restraints that threatened it with extinction.

The parachute began to sink, and one of the shroudlines that had wrapped itself around his neck pulled his head under. He clawed at it and finally got it off, only then remembering that he hadn't inflated his LPA, or flotation bladders. He did it and felt some buoyancy return, but the pull of the parachute was strengthening by the second. His head was submerged for progressively longer periods, and he realized that he was going to die stupidly, all alone, drowned by a piece of cloth that, dry, weighed less than a tenth of what he did.

Browne hauled the nose back to slow the helo down and stomped the right rudder pedal, skidding the huge H-3 to a hover forty feet over the deflated parachute in the water. No one in the crew called out that they had the "survivor" in sight. Normally, when a crew got to the scene of an ejection, the pilot was clear of the parachute and floating merrily in his one-man raft. At worst, his helmeted head would be visible nearby. But this time their first fast scan of the area produced nothing except the parachute fluttering in places where the helicopter's rotor wash moved it around.

Over the intercom the crewman said, "Mr. Browne, I think he's under the 'chute. It looks like he's really entangled. I'm ready to go in the water after him if you need me to."

Browne, as the HAC, or aircraft commander, did not like this at all. His crewman, Petty Officer Joe Guzman, was going to have to go in if the pilot was going to have any chance at all.

"Okay, Guz. You all set?"

"Yessir. If you go straight down here, it'll be best."

"Roger, comin' down."

Browne lowered the collective control and gently let the helo down to only ten feet from the water. In the other seat, Tucker watched the instruments and kept an eye on the parachute in case it started to blow up out of the water and envelop the rotor system. Brown watched his radar altimeter touch ten feet and called the hoist operator.

"Okay, ten feet. Jump the swimmer."

In his mirror Browne saw Guzman kick out and away from the helo. Browne was moving it up and back, well clear, before the hoist operator, Sackey, told him to. He watched Guzman swim carefully toward the parachute, avoiding the floating shroudlines and moving the parachute ahead of his hands. Browne could see what looked like a pair of hands thrashing at the 'chute from beneath and that Guzman had about twenty feet to go. He hated this part: his crewman was risking his life in the most dangerous type of rescue possible and Browne could only watch from his seat in the helo.

Guzman carefully moved toward the nylon-shrouded pilot, and when he was only about five feet away, he ducked under the edge, holding it above and in front of him. He reappeared, still holding the fabric over his head, but in his other hand he gripped the pilot's wrist. He shoved the parachute away from the pilot and began to turn him around, but the panicking man grabbed Guzman around the neck in the classic drowning man's embrace.

Guzman grabbed the pilot's arms and ducked under the surface, taking him down too. The pilot quickly released his grip and kicked and struggled his way back up to the surface. Guzman carefully surfaced nearby but well out of reach.

Blake struggled to the surface and looked for the man who had just been there. He gagged up some seawater and spotted him a few feet away, saying something Blake couldn't make out until he pulled off his helmet and let it drift away.

"Okay, sir. You're all right. Calm down. You have to stop thrashing around 'cause you're only making it worse. Now I'm gonna turn you around and begin dragging you away from the 'chute. You're all entangled in your shroudlines and I have to get them off you. The helo can't hook you up until you're free of the parachute. I can't cut them because that'll only make more problems. I have to pull them off, but I can't do that until you calm down and quit grabbing me. I can stay right here until you calm down because I'm free and you're not. Clear?"

Now that he could breathe, Blake began to get control of himself. His LPA was keeping him afloat, but he could feel much of his body being tugged gently by the shroudlines, reminding him that the parachute would certainly sink and he would go down with it. Guzman's voice was working too. It was comforting just to have another human being close by. He nodded at the swimmer: no sense wasting breath speaking.

Guzman moved in carefully and took Blake's wrist. He gently turned him around and began pulling him away from the nylon which was now entirely below the surface. The young sailor was aware that they had arrived just in time—another couple of minutes would have been the end of this guy. The fact that the parachute was now beginning to sink was a bad sign, but he was not about to say anything to the pilot and start another round of panic.

For Blake, the next couple of minutes went by both quickly and with agonizing slowness. Guzman would pull him away until he was brought up by one of the shroudlines and then would move down his body until he found the tight one. He would carefully work it free and then pull Blake away a little more until the next line tightened its grip. Finally, there were no more lines and Blake was attached to the parachute only by the risers which were still fastened to his torso harness at his shoulders. Guzman popped each fitting free and let them follow the rest of the parachute to the bottom of the sea. He moved himself and Blake farther away from the nylon to be sure that there would be no further entanglements.

Browne had watched this whole thing carefully, hearing the running commentary from the hoist operator with only a part of his mind. When he saw Guzman's signal calling the helo in for the pickup, he became aware that he was biting his lip and it hurt like hell.

He moved the helo over the two men in the water, allowing his hands and feet to maneuver the helo at the directions from Sackey in the rear of the H-3. It was almost as if Browne's brain were not involved, so well had the crew trained together.

"Easy right. Easy right and easy forward. Swimmer and survivor are at two o'clock and thirty yards. Move easy right."

Browne moved the stick almost imperceptibly and the huge helicopter began to slide steadily forward and to the right. He followed Sackey's direction, trying not to look down at the two men in the water, but he could see them move under him in his peripheral vision.

"Easy right about ten yards. Easy forward . . . stop forward, easy right. Easy right five yards. Stop right. Steady hover."

When Browne had the hover stabilized, he followed Sackey's minute corrections which accounted for the natural tendency of the helo to move to the left and rotate a bit. In the back Sackey lowered the hoist with the yellow rescue sling attached.

"Hoist and sling are going down. Steady. Hoist is halfway down, steady hover. Hoist is in the water. Swimmer and survivor are approaching the sling. Survivor is hooking up. Stand by for weight on the aircraft. Okay, survivor is clear of the water coming up. Steady hover. Survivor is halfway up . . . survivor is at the cargo door . . . steady. Survivor is in the aircraft. Unhooking him now."

Browne wiggled his fingers to relax them some as Sackey unhooked Blake and gestured him to a seat on the deck. The crewman ran the hoist down again, guiding Browne back to a proper hover. Guzman climbed into the sling and was hoisted aboard.

Once Guzman was safely in the aircraft, Browne turned control over to Tucker and tried to relax the rest of his cramped muscles. He keyed the radio.

"Tower, Salty Dog 804 has the pilot aboard. He appears to be okay. It'll take us a few minutes to get there. Is the recovery complete?"

"Roger that, 804. Expect a ready deck."

"Click-click."

Blake lay facedown and trembling on the deck where the young helo crewman had indicated. He retched a few more times and got only a little seawater out. He had left most of whatever else had been in his stomach in the water below. He felt the hands of the crewmen on him as they rolled him onto his back and helped him sit up. They handed him a flight-deck helmet to wear to protect his ears from the noise of the helo. He sat up against the wall of the aircraft and nodded when they asked whether he was all right. He saw the hoist operator speak into his helmet mike and then lean down to shout to Blake that they'd be on deck in two minutes. He let his forehead fall onto his arms, which were crossed over his knees. In all his life he had never been as afraid as he had been under that parachute, nor was he ever as spent as he was then.

The helo crossed over the deck edge and settled down on Spot Four abeam the island structure. The crewmen helped him up and guided him to the cargo door, where several white-shirted medical people helped him out of the aircraft and laid him down in a Stokes litter, the wire stretcher used on ships. Several men picked up the litter and hustled across the deck to the elevator on the starboard side. Blake saw the flight-deck personnel gawking at him as he was carried through the crowd that always gathered when something happened on the deck. He put his arm across his face to shut out their stares.

In the Tower, the Air Boss watched the little drama play itself out on the deck below. He called the helo and asked if they needed any fuel.

"Negative, Boss. We're good for another hour or so. But if you've got a couple of beers handy, we'll take them."

The Boss chuckled at the request. Despite the fact that he was a dyed-in-the-wool jet aviator, he had a great deal of respect and fondness for the helo guys. If any bunch were still carrying on the Terry and the Pirates tradition, it was the helicopter crews. But they had to be crazy to fly in those damn things in the first place, so it kind of figured.

He watched Blake carried across the deck and had the momentary thought that he'd have to be really badly hurt to allow himself to be carried in a stretcher like that. A pilot should have more pride. He shook his head rather than sharing those feelings with the Mini standing next to him.

He really didn't need to though. The Mini was having exactly the same thought himself.

13

Tuesday, January 16, 1968

★ Jack Wilson met Hogan as he stepped down from his A-4. Hogan had launched on a road recce as Blake's mission was returning to the ship, and had been on other frequencies and so did not as yet know what had happened to the C.O.

Wilson waited until his X.O. had stuffed all his charts and his kneeboard into his helmet before he spoke.

"How'd it go, X.O.?"

"Fine. Blew up some trees around a road intersection and we got some good secondaries. Came back and trapped. Looks like I brought back all the parts of my jet too." He looked at Wilson carefully. "So what brings you up here?"

"Skipper punched out on final. He's okay but he's not taking it too well. When I went down to sick bay, he would only tell me the bare facts, and it was like pulling teeth to get that much. I got most of the story from Cordella, his wingman. It ain't too good, X.O. I got Cordella to keep his mouth shut until you talk to him. The Skipper's in his room now and wants you to report to him as soon as you land. I assume you can visit the head first though."

"Well, what did Cordella say?"

"Trust me on this one. I think you'd better see the C.O. without hearing anything more. It'll keep until you're finished. Okay?"

Hogan gave Wilson a long, considering stare. "Okay. Is there anything I *should* know?"

"No, sir. The C.O. punched out on his last mission and has never had to do that before. He's always bragged that his takeoffs were equal to his landings, so that's probably what has him going."

"All right. I'll go down there as soon as I'm finished debriefing." He unzipped his torso harness and headed for the catwalk.

Twenty-five minutes later, Hogan was admitted to Blake's room. He found the C.O. packing some of his things into his footlocker. His eyes were a little wild and glassy, the normal reaction of a man who has just come through an experience like combat followed by an ejection into the sea.

Hogan waited for a few seconds for Blake to begin the conversation, and when nothing happened, started it himself.

"How're you doing, Skipper? Read any good books lately?"

Blake gaped at the question for a second or two and then began to laugh. Too merrily by far, thought Hogan.

"That's good, Jim. That's good." He chuckled again and sat in the desk chair, gesturing Hogan to a seat on the bed.

"I'm fine. Just a little wet and, um, keyed up is all." Hogan suspected he had been about to say "scared" but had stopped himself in time. Hogan dearly wished he'd said "scared," but that sort of admission was not Blake's style.

Hogan leaned back on his elbows. "So what happened? I didn't get much from Wilson when I landed."

"I took a hit coming off the target. Except for a small leak, everything was fine until I dirtied up for landing. When I tried to come up on the power, nothing happened. I switched to manual and still had no response, so I ejected. The helo came and picked me up. That's the first time I've ever failed to bring my aircraft back. I hate to see that record spoiled, but I suppose I've been fortunate."

Hogan thought back on his own flying career. He sure couldn't say that about himself. He'd had to eject twice so far, and only one of those was from combat damage.

"Okay. Well, you're out of it now. We're heading for Singapore after the last recovery tonight. I see you're packing up. Need any help?"

"No, thanks. I'm just getting it started. One of the things I wanted to see you about was to tell you how well I think you're doing. I've been really impressed with how you fit yourself in here and how the squadron has taken to your leadership. You'll do well here. I'll admit that makes me a little envious, but I guess that can't be helped. We just have different styles."

Hogan said nothing, only nodding his thanks for the compliment. Blake's experience today must have put him in this mood.

He waited a second for Blake to continue. When he did speak again he was all business. The thoughtful mood had been nice while it lasted.

"I only have about five days left here, so I'm gonna back off and let you have your head. The only thing left for me before the change of command is to get the officer-fitness reports done. Then it's just a plane ride home. My wife has already set up a house for us in Vienna, Virginia. We'll take a couple of weeks vacation and then I go to work in the Pentagon."

Blake's mood had changed again. Now he was staring unseeingly at the wall over Hogan's head, as if speaking to himself. He caught himself and smiled almost shyly.

"Sorry about that. It's just been a long-standing dream for me to get that job."

Hogan smiled. "That's okay. I dream about getting a job handing out towels on the beach at Cannes."

That went over Blake's head. His mind had already moved on. Hogan waited to see where.

"I've filed my report with CAG on what happened today. It was a combat loss, so there needn't be a safety investigation. Just the standard forms and all."

"Okay, Skipper. If that's all you've got, I'm gonna go get some chow."

Blake smiled and simply nodded his dismissal.

Hogan stood. Blake had said whatever he'd wanted to and had made his point, although, for the life of him, Hogan couldn't see what in this conversation had required his presence with the immediacy that Wilson had conveyed. As he walked to the door, he felt that whatever doubts he might have about taking over were far outweighed by the relief he would feel when Blake was gone. He just hoped he'd be able to get the squadron headed in the right direction.

Hogan walked forward to the ready room and stuck his head in. He spotted Wilson standing by the duty desk and called for him. The banty pilot wagged a finger at Cordella and Taylor, who were in the rear of the room, idly flipping through dog-eared *Stars and Stripes*. Taylor picked a file folder from the chair next to him as the two got up and followed Wilson out of the room.

Hogan was in the passageway when the three came out.

"You guys mind if we talk while I eat?"

Wilson looked uncertain. "This might be a little heavy for the wardroom. Maybe your stateroom would be better."

"Is it going to take long? I mean, from the look on your faces, it's got to be serious, and I don't want you to think that I'm not concerned. It's just that I'm starving. I missed breakfast and the wardroom closes in a half hour."

Wilson smiled for the first time. "Okay. You go eat and we'll meet you in your room in twenty minutes. That'll give Nick here time to get some more pictures."

"Pictures? That doesn't sound good at all. Tell you what, here's the key to my room. You go wait there and I'll grab a peanut butter sandwich. Nick, you get your pictures. Ten minutes. okay?"

The three headed off in different directions, looking relieved and reprieved. Hogan didn't like that look because on the face of a junior officer it usually meant that he was about to dump some responsibility on the senior guy and thus relieve himself of the problem. It also meant that whatever it was, it was something way over his head.

Once everyone had gathered in Hogan's room, the three younger pilots looked at each other, waiting for somebody else to start. Finally Wilson broke the ice.

"X.O., we think that the Skipper took out something this morning which is going to really stir up the shit." He saw Hogan's expression and realized that that hadn't been a particularly good opener, so he started again.

"Okay. What happened is that the Skipper dropped his bombs way early and walked them across some buildings close to the target but well short of where you could call it just plain bad aim. Show him the pictures, Nick."

Taylor looked down at the folder in his hand almost regretfully. "First, let me explain how we got to this point. When Tony got back aboard, he came to me in the debrief and told me about what he thought he saw happen over the target. I sort of hurried up the post-strike bomb damage assessment reconnaissance pictures from the Vigilante that went over the target about eight minutes after the strike departed the area. There's so much normal crap going on down in the photo lab that it will be about another day before anybody gets around to examining the pictures. Then I grabbed the pre-strike pictures from the target planning folder for comparison. I do believe we, as a squadron, ought to figure something out now before it comes down from above."

He opened the folder he was carrying, took out several photographs, and handed the top one to Hogan. It had a label crediting the RA-5C reconnaissance squadron and giving the date and time it had been taken, shortly after noon, two days before. Taylor explained what Hogan was seeing.

"The first one there is a view of the whole target area with the buildings in question circled in white. The actual target is in red. The distance between the foot of the bridge and the closest building is exactly 1.4 nautical miles, or twenty-eight hundred yards. The farthest building from the foot of the bridge is twenty-nine hundred and fifty yards."

Hogan set that picture down on his bunk and took the next one as Taylor continued.

"Okay. This one shows the buildings themselves. Notice the huge loading docks in the rear, where the railroad tracks pass, and the docks in the front, where trucks can pull up." He pointed to small blotches in the picture. "On the roofs, here, here, and here are Triple-A batteries that look to be thirty-seven millimeter. There are several more, bigger, guns out of the frame on the far side, the side away from the bridge."

Hogan stared silently at the buildings. He knew what was coming next, and he wished he were anywhere else in the world just then except there looking at the pictures. Prominently painted in several places on the roofs and sides of the buildings, all three of them, were huge white squares with red crosses in the center.

He looked up at Taylor and Cordella. "Were the strike pilots briefed about this?"

Both men nodded and Taylor said, "Yeah, but it really was only sort of in passing. It seemed to be far enough removed from the main target that a guy would have to try real hard to miss by that much."

"Oooh, fuck." Hogan sighed and reached for the rest of the pictures. They were blow-ups of various scale, but all showed just what Hogan didn't want to see. With absolutely no emotion in his voice, Taylor described them.

"Here's the post-strike BDA pictures from the A-5. You can see that nearly all the bomb craters are well within two hundred yards of the center of the target and that the main span of the bridge is down. The only real misses are right here all over the buildings."

The buildings were now completely gone. Most often after a building had been hit directly by a five-hundred-pound bomb, there was at least one windowless wall still standing and there were often small fires burning somewhere within what was left. In these photos there was almost nothing left. None of the walls were there above the ground floor windowsills. Even with the graininess of the print, Hogan could see that the force of the explosions that tore down the buildings had blown large pieces of them outward for quite a distance. There were lots of fires in the area well clear of the craters from near misses. There had been one whole hell of a lot more explosives going off there than one A-4 could carry. Five tornados in a trailer park would do less damage.

"What the hell did this? There's chunks all over the place."

Wilson spoke up. "What it looks like to me, X.O., is that the Vietnamese painted up a warehouse and stored some kind of munitions in it."

He turned to Taylor. "Drop the other shoe, Nick."

Taylor handed over one more set of photographs. These were just like the first set showing the undamaged buildings except that there was a five-car train at the loading docks in the rear and several canvas-covered trucks backed up to the front. There were no red crosses and no antiaircraft guns on the roof.

"Those were taken fifteen days ago, which was five days before this target was added to the approved list that came down from Washington. It would seem that the gomers are on the Pentagon's mailing list."

Cordella cleared his throat, getting Hogan's attention. "Sir, the secondary explosions were huge from these buildings. I caught a glimpse of the whole roof of that one there going straight up before it came apart. I've never seen anything blow up like that."

Hogan leaned back on the bunk. "Okay, Tony. Tell me what happened from start to finish."

Cordella looked trapped. Like all good junior officers, he really wasn't comfortable around the "heavies," especially when there was trouble. He looked over at Wilson, who gave him a nod of encouragement. Taylor stared at the floor.

"Well, everything was pretty normal really. We coasted in as planned and got to the target okay. The C.O. led us right there, and we all rolled in in order. There was a whole shitload of pretty nasty Triple-A around. The Skipper released a little early and his bombs landed short. I dropped on the target and hauled ass for

113

the join-up. When I got behind him, I saw that he was losing something. I joined up and looked him over. That's when I saw that he was streaming a little bit of fuel from some battle damage. He said everything was fine, so I dropped away when he was setting up for a straight-in. It surprised the hell out of me when he ejected."

Cordella looked relieved now that he'd told his story, but Hogan could see something else there. Maybe just a touch of defiance. It was as if he were thinking, "Okay, there it is. Try and find a hole in it." Hogan saw it but decided to let it pass for now. He turned to Wilson.

"Have you shown these pictures to the Skipper yet?"

"Tried to, but he said that he didn't give a shit, he was through. He said that his strike had taken out the target and that collateral damage was part of the game. That's when he told me he wanted to see you as soon you got down. I went and told you and here we are, havin' a good time."

Hogan was silent for a few seconds. He had a lot to think about and not a bit of it good. He looked up at the two lieutenants.

"Is that all you've got on this?" They nodded. "Okay, I'll take it from here, but I don't want either of you running your mouths about this. I'm not even sure what we've got here, but shut up anyway. Got it?"

Both J.O.'s agreed and left, not quite as fast as they would have from a burning building, but quickly enough to make Wilson smile. He closed the door behind them and sat back down in the desk chair. Hogan pulled up another chair and took out a deck of cards and a large wooden cribbage board. Both men were passionate about the game, but, curiously, they played only at sea. It also gave them a chance to talk about serious things without the formality that would have constrained the exchange of ideas. As they played they continued to discuss Blake's mission that morning.

"The problem as I see it, Jack, is that the Vietnamese could use that strike for some more of their propaganda. Missing targets is nothing new, but if they claim that we deliberately bombed their hospital, we'll have Washington on our ass in minutes."

"Yup. Ever since we got authorization to expand our target lists, we've been moving closer to the population centers. Things like this are bound to happen. You have to admit that it's really a pretty slick move, painting up buildings like that and then inviting in the press. At least half the world will believe them and the

President will be on the run again. Every time something like this happens he gets cold feet and puts more limits on us. I just wish he and McNamara's bunch of whiz kids in the Pentagon cared as much for the aircrews they're losing as they do for the enemy's opinion."

Hogan scored his hand and his crib, moving the pegs on the board. He was leading for a change.

"Well, what do we do?"

"Well, X.O., the way I see it, we've got three choices. One, we can shut up and hope it goes away. It very well could unless the press picks up on it and stirs the pot. Two, we can make a big deal out of it ourselves. We can throw ourselves on the mercy of the court, but that would make us automatically bad guys. It might also keep the Skipper around awhile longer, but it would mostly just make the squadron look like McHale's Navy again and the squadron morale couldn't take another hit like that."

Wilson picked up the deck of cards and began to shuffle and deal.

"Or, the third thing we can do is go to CAG, tell him about it, and make sure we have all the paperwork squared away. That way, if anybody comes down on us, we can say truthfully that we are aware and are investigating."

Hogan arranged his cards carefully, throwing two into the crib. "I think there's a fourth choice. We can take the offensive here."

"What do you mean? We've bombed a building that the Vietnamese are going to claim was a hospital and the world will believe them, which means we're the bad guys again."

"I'm thinking that we can take your third option and add a twist or two. Suppose we took those pictures and used them to show that the Vietnamese are playing games and fucking with the press. Suppose we came off like we'd discovered a new tactic. You know, strike them before they get us. I bet we could pull it off or at least cloud things up enough to take the sting away from them. Even Washington ought to know that you don't put flak sites on the roof of a fucking hospital. There's got to be a law against that somewhere."

"Yeah, but aren't we just a little low on the totem pole to do this?"

"Probably. Look, you're right that we're at the bottom here, right where whatever comes down from on high winds up, and we can never satisfy the people who have nothing to do but sit around and bust our balls. But suppose that when they came marching up with their briefcases and lists of questions we had all the answers already. Suppose we could turn the tables on them."

Wilson scratched his chin. He liked the idea.

"Okay. Do we have a plan already and can we all get in on the fun?"

"Well, my son, as soon as we finish this hand and you admit that you'll never be half the cribbage player I am, I'm going to go tell the Skipper that he's a hero and you are going to grab Taylor, Cordella, Chief Napier from Admin, and whoever else you think we need but keep it to the J.O.'s only. Fill the department heads in and explain that the J.O.'s need to do this. We are all going to meet in the wardroom in one hour and we're going to have a creative writing seminar. If we can get this done quickly, like maybe by tonight, we can beat the Vietnamese to the punch."

"What? You mean go public with this?"

"No. Of course not. That would be a breach of security. If we can get this at least off the ship and on the way to Washington, we'll have stolen their thunder and put the whiz kids on the spot. It'll be a small victory, but it will be a start."

Wilson laughed. "Of course, we'll have to have an all-officers meeting to explain this to the rest of the squadron. We wouldn't want them to be taken by surprise, would we?"

Hogan looked evenly at Wilson. "Absolutely not. What they know will never hurt them."

14

Tuesday, January 16, 1968

It took so long for Blake to answer Hogan's knock on his stateroom door that Hogan thought he wasn't in. He was just turning away when the door opened, and Blake quietly asked him in.

Inside, Hogan took his usual seat and watched Blake walk stiffly over to the bunk. He sat gingerly and leaned back with a grimace.

"Are you okay, Skipper?" asked Hogan.

"Yeah. My back's pretty stiff from the ejection. Funny, I didn't feel it before, but in the last couple of hours I've discovered lots of aches and pains. The doc says that there's nothing really damaged, just some muscle problems that will go away soon."

Hogan chuckled. "I know what you mean. Last time I had to punch out, I was inverted going through three hundred knots. It was three days before I could get out of bed without help, and it took me a month to walk right again."

Blake sat up and nodded, not smiling in return. "The worst part was when I was under the parachute. I couldn't get free and it kept getting worse and worse. I figured I was a dead man when that swimmer got to me." He shook his head abruptly, clearing away a reprise of the fear he had felt.

"What brings you down here, Jim?"

Hogan handed over the folder containing the photographs. "We might have a problem with some collateral damage from the strike you led earlier today."

Blake looked over the pictures carefully one at a time and then laid them side by side on the bunk. He looked at each view of the area with the "hospital" circled in white grease pencil, and then he took out the blow-ups and examined them, finally staring at

117

the last one, which showed the building after all of the strike aircraft and much of the smoke had gone.

Still staring at the last picture, he asked, "Who knows about this?"

"Pretty much just us in the squadron and the photointelligence guys. I would imagine that everybody will pretty soon and, if the gomers are smart, most of the world will in a couple of days.

"Cordella told Taylor that there might be a problem and Nick got the pictures developed on a rush job and brought them to me. He figured we ought to have a chance to get ourselves organized before this goes any further."

Blake spoke almost too quietly for Hogan to hear. "I didn't know about this. I didn't mention it in my debriefing." Then he remembered that he hadn't had a real debriefing. The questions had been asked of him down in sick bay by a jaygee who did only a cursory job, being as considerate as he could of a guy just hauled out of the Gulf of Tonkin.

He looked up at Hogan. "Do we know who the pilot was?"

Hogan drew a breath. "Yes, sir, we do. It was your bombs that hit short."

"How can you be sure of that?"

"Cordella saw them hit before his did. As your wingman, he was the second aircraft in on the target."

Blake closed his eyes and ran his hand over his face. There would be only one conclusion from all this. They would all know that he'd panicked and had simply dumped his bombs in the area of the target and hauled ass. There would certainly be an investigation, and there would be only one result from that. His career would suffer irreparable damage no matter what specific findings and recommendations would come out of the investigation. All his years of working and waiting were now gone uselessly, all because he had flown this one fucking last mission. He almost wished that the goddamn swimmer had taken an extra five minutes to get to him. If he had, Blake probably would have drowned and been done with it. To him, the loss of his cherished dream was worse than being dead.

"What's next, Jim?"

Hogan sat back in his chair. "What I intend to do is send this on up the chain of command as a 'lesson learned' and as an intelligence finding. It's obvious to me and to everybody else that the gomers are fucking with us and using the targeting restrictions in

118

our rules of engagement to their advantage. That probably won't count for much in our defense, but if we can show that we've taken some action rather than try to cover it up, we may be able to get out of trouble. I have Jack Wilson, Nick Taylor, and a bunch of other guys working up a report that I intend to take to CAG this evening. It's worth a try. Since you're the pilot in question, it'll have to go out over my signature."

Blake saw the only way out but hated to have a subordinate in charge of holding the door open. Almost automatically he tried to regain control of his own fate. "Okay. Make sure that you run it by me before you send it."

Hogan collected the pictures, and when he spoke his voice was hard. "No, sir. I'm not going to do that. It either goes out my way or not at all. If it were ever found out that you'd had a hand in it, what little chance of success it has goes away. I'll be damned if I'll lie about this."

Blake was unused to being refused anything by his subordinates, and his eyes flashed angrily for a moment until he realized that this was really his only choice. He nodded and smiled, but the smile never got as far as his eyes.

"You're right. I didn't think of that. But if there is anything I can do to help, let me know, all right?"

Hogan stood. "Yes, sir. And I'll keep you posted on how it's going too. Is there anything you need other than some serious pain pills?"

"No, Jim. I'm fine."

"Okay. I'll stop by later." Hogan turned and opened the door.

Blake's voice stopped him. "Jim, it's not me you're doing this for, is it?"

Hogan paused and looked back. "No, sir, it isn't. Not primarily anyway. No offense, Skipper."

Blake watched the door close and sat heavily in his chair. He wasn't sure which hurt worse, his back or Hogan's words. He stared at the bare wall, thinking about what could have happened over this incident. A picture of what it would have been like had the building been a real hospital crossed his mind, but he deliberately shoved that away. Still, it hovered just in the corner of his thoughts. He stood and began to pace the room, trying to divert his mind from the picture of dead and dying people buried amid the rubble of hospital wards, but he could not.

After a few minutes he began to win the struggle. His naval

aviator's ability to compartmentalize his mind was building a wall around those thoughts. But before he had successfully walled them off, he realized that they couldn't be put away forever. He knew that they would be back from time to time. And with a vengeance.

Blake looked at the small pile of folders on his desk. He pulled them over and began to look through them carefully, signing each and rejecting only two as needing some more fixing. At the bottom of the pile was one labeled TAYLOR WAIVER. He opened it and read through all the documentation and physician's report forms and endorsements. He looked it over carefully once more and saw that everything was in order.

He kept looking at that folder for an extra few minutes, thinking about Nick Taylor and his place in the squadron. He realized suddenly what would have happened both to the squadron and himself if Taylor hadn't bent Blake's cherished rules and procedures by intercepting the photos of Blake's last mission. There was no doubt that Taylor had acted not to protect his C.O.—he could have easily stepped aside and let things take their natural course and been quite right to do so. Instead, Taylor took action. He saw something wrong about to happen and took action.

He had made a choice to do something that was right but not necessarily legal. Blake wondered for a moment whether he would have, or could have, made the choice Taylor had. He didn't notice the folder drop back onto the desktop as he stared at the barren wall, his eyes unfocused and his brow knitted.

Hogan opened the door into the wardroom, spotted the men from his squadron sitting in the far corner of the room, and stood for a minute, almost peeking in at the group. From the eagerness on their faces it was obvious that Wilson had let them in on at least a small part of what was happening. One of the group, Chief Napier, was sitting quietly, listening carefully, and trying to be inconspicuous in the unfamiliar surroundings of the officers' wardroom.

Hogan realized suddenly that these younger men were just like all the others he had served with and that they deserved the absolute best he could give. He shook his head, remembering that he'd had this thought at least twice a day since he'd come aboard VA-262. What he didn't know was that it was in fact that he had had it more than once and wanted to keep having it that made him different from most of the other C.O.'s they'd had.

He stood for a moment longer just watching them, both saddened at the disservice that had been done them and marveling at the resilience that kept them going. Just like all the other naval aviators with whom he'd served, they were quite a bunch indeed.

He took a deep breath and put on his X.O. face, confident, prepared, knowledgeable and approachable. He walked into the room and closed the door behind him loudly enough to alert the others to his presence. When he turned back and approached the table, he could see that the expressions on several of the junior officers had changed. They were masked now, attentive, apparently open and respectful but guarded. Except, of course, for Nick Taylor, who probably wouldn't get respectful-looking unless President Johnson himself walked in and sat on a whoopee cushion that just happened to fall out of Taylor's pocket.

"Okay, guys. Have you all heard about our little problem?"

The J.O's looked at each other. "Little problem?" Blake would have spent an hour explaining the gravity of it all and another on making sure they all were suitably impressed.

Wilson spoke up. "I kind of filled them in, X.O., but maybe you'd better take it from the top."

Hogan sat at the head of the table. "All right. Nick, pass those pictures around."

He waited until everybody had a chance to see them. "What these pictures show is that the little commie bastards are going to try to get us in some serious trouble for setting off some high-explosive medical supplies. What we're going to do is take the offensive. We are going to have an investigation right here and now and then I'm going to take it to CAG.

"Actually, what we're going to do is send out a highly accurate and incisive report on an insidious new tactic the nefarious enemy has come up with to defeat us guardians of democracy. We've got somebody from each department here and, working together, we'll be finished with this by dinnertime. The reason you're here, Chief Napier, is that you and your yeomen are going to have this all typed up in the smooth by 1900 this evening so that CAG and the captain can endorse it and get it off to the admiral. Remember, the less time something like this sits on our desk, the longer it sits on somebody else's. Okay?"

There were nods all around and renewed interest in the photographs. Hogan watched them all as they examined the pictures as the level of conversation increased. They all seemed to have caught on to the general idea of what he had in mind, and he just let them go. Soon he began to hear chuckles and then a couple of voices got into discussions about word choices. They had caught it completely now. They as a group, and therefore the whole squadron, were going to put something over on somebody. He could see that most of them thought that it was about damn time.

As Hogan knew it would, it gradually dawned on the group that they needed more information and needed to draw on the expertise of others. After a few more minutes they had decided that they probably couldn't finish by the deadline that Hogan had established. Cordella, who had surfaced as sort of the informal leader of the group, asked if they could have an extra hour or so. Hogan pretended to think about it and granted the request, telling them that he wanted to see the rough as soon as possible. They all rose and left through the various doors, chattering eagerly about the project.

Hogan called Chief Napier back. "Chief, when you guys type this up, make sure it's for my signature 'by direction.' Okay?"

"Yes, sir. And you'd better be able to read faster than my guys can type, or you'll owe me a beer."

"Chief, if we can have this on CAG's desk by 1930, I'll buy your whole office bunch two cases, Deal?"

"Deal." Napier grinned and headed for the Admin Office.

Wilson leaned back in the chair across the table from Hogan. "You seem to have lit a fire under them."

"I sure hope so. They'll be fine if they can keep their sense of humor."

"If you don't mind letting me in on a trade secret, how about telling me what you said to the Skipper. I mean, you wouldn't try to pull something like this behind his back, would you?"

"No way. He's the C.O. and that's that. Despite what either one of us thinks, he is the man in charge. If I were to try and pull something without telling him that I'm doing it, then I wouldn't deserve to be in this job now or in his next week. He is well aware that today's mission is not one he should be putting in his résumé and is letting this go because he can't think of a better plan and because the significant ass on the line is his. I'm doing it this way because he's going to be gone soon, but we're all going to have to deal with it. If you think about it carefully, Jack, you'll see that there is nothing dishonest or illegal about it. What we're doing is simply using the system against itself. That, to me, comes under the classification of either fun or professional training, but that call depends on who's asking.

"Anyway, I showed him the pictures and told him what I intended to do. He didn't say much and he didn't fight it. But that doesn't matter. All we have to do now is sell CAG on it. What do you think?"

"Well, to be honest, I was worried that this was going to be one of those deals that seem like a good idea at the time but somebody winds up losing his career or going to jail. Then I was worried that you were not going to be able to get it past the C.O. Then I was worried that the J.O.'s would greet it as some sort of drill that benefits only the heavies. Then I was worried that they'd figure out what you were doing."

"And exactly what is it that I'm doing?"

"Not much. Just one of the better practical jokes on the system that I've seen in years. And one of the best leadership ploys ever. This is great."

Hogan stood. "Yeah, well, let's not count our chickens yet. We've still got to get this through CAG and the captain."

At quarter after seven that evening Hogan sat in the wardroom again as the group reassembled. Cordella handed him the final smooth version of the report. Hogan had already been through it once and had made only a couple of small suggestions, making some of the prose both less vague and more effective. Everyone was waiting for Hogan to go through it word by word once more. Instead, he flipped through it, making sure all the pages were there.

"Are you guys sure that it's all correct? You've got all the changes in?"

The J.O.'s glanced at each other and nodded resignedly. They were used to going through the editing drill five or six times under Blake, and so expected it again.

"Looks good to us, X.O.," said Cordella.

"All right, then." Hogan turned to the last page of the report and signed where Chief Napier had left the paper clip. Separating the original copy from the rest, he stuck it in a clean folder and headed for CAG's office. As he reached the door, he turned back to the group.

"You did a whole hell of a lot of good work here and only missed the original deadline by fifteen minutes. Not bad. Not bad at all."

At the knock on his stateroom door, CAG Andrews put down the folder he was reading and got up stiffly from his bunk. He wasn't sure whether the stiffness was from the beating he had taken as a halfback in college or from the three plane crashes he had survived back at the tail end of World War II. He supposed it really didn't matter much; the point was that he was getting old and his unconventional life's history was catching up with him.

He opened the door and found Jim Hogan standing there. He was a little surprised at that, since most squadron business with CAG staff was conducted by the C.O. but, on second thought, he'd rather deal with Hogan than with that lame duck, Blake, anyway.

"Come on in, Jim. What can I do for you?"

Hogan stepped in and took in the room. It was always amazing to him how an officer's private room took on the character of the occupant. Even though the rooms themselves were identical—small, spartan, and ugly—each man brought enough comforts from home to make it seem unique. CAG's room had brightly colored pictures on the wall, mostly of mountain scenes from his home state of Colorado, a state that he probably hadn't seen more than two dozen times since he joined the Navy. It also had a large, overstuffed chair and matching hassock into which CAG now sat gracefully despite the stiffness in his back.

Hogan handed him the folder with a small apology.

" 'Evening, CAG. I'm sorry to bother you with this, but we think it's kind of important that we get this off to the admiral's staff before we leave for Singapore tomorrow afternoon."

Andrews glanced up at Hogan and then back at the cover sheet of the report.

Now that he was presenting this to his superiors, Hogan felt that maybe he should have handled it in a more routine manner. He didn't know whether to feel foolish or not, but it was too late now.

"What it is, sir, is a report about the Vietnamese trying to gain what we feel to be a propaganda advantage. Right now they've got guys like that reporter we were briefed on a couple off days ago cruising around on a guided tour of their peace-loving country, looking to find stuff they can make into 'war crimes' in their papers. We figured it's important enough that the other air wings should get briefed about it as soon as possible."

"All right, fine. Have a seat while I look it over."

Hogan sat in the small desk chair and looked around the room. In quarters as small as this, it was difficult not to watch CAG for any sign of his reaction. To keep from that, Hogan picked up a copy of *Time* from a small pile and pretended to be interested in it.

It was actually only a couple of minutes, but it seemed a week before CAG put down the report and looked up at Hogan.

"You really think that this is that important?"

Hogan looked into the level blue eyes. "Yes, sir. I know that things like this come through you all the time, but we feel that it deserves some extra push rather than a standard endorsement."

"Uh-huh. And why this particular one?"

Hogan suddenly had the feeling that he needed to say something to CAG, there, then. Something that was off the point but very important nonetheless. He sighed.

"CAG, what you've got there is an attempt to pull a fast one. Those buildings were taken out by accident pretty much, and that's probably not going to go away quietly. I don't want the guys in my squadron taking any more crap from anybody because of what their fucked-up command structure has or hasn't done. They're good guys, all of 'em, and even though I haven't been here all that long, I'm tired of watching them live and work like there's a tiger behind *every* door.

"I haven't heard a single belly laugh out of any of them, and there's absolutely no togetherness. That scares the shit out of me because that's the last step before they fall apart completely on the ground and guys start getting killed in the air. If Washington decides to send another of their wonderful fact-finding gangs over here to find out who committed this atrocity and we wind up under the elephant's asshole again, that'll be the end of the squadron and the end for quite a few really good men who deserved a whole lot better from the Navy than leadership like they've had.

"If we can get that report into the system, we can deflect some of the crap. The farther up the chain it is when the trouble starts, the less bullshit there'll be for my guys to deal with."

Hogan sat back in the chair, surprised at his own vehemence. He had hoped to quietly slide this through, but that was impossible now. He looked down at his hands, which were moving nervously in his lap, and then up at CAG Andrews.

Andrews didn't say a word in response. He just looked at the pictures again and reread a couple of passages in the text. He closed the report and picked up the telephone. After dialing a three-digit number, he waited for an answer, and when it came, Hogan felt like the sun had just come up.

"Chief Conklin? This is CAG. I need you to type up an endorsement for me right now. It's to go on an urgent report from 262 to Commander in Chief, Pacific, via the captain and admiral. I want it saying that I strongly endorse both the conclusions and recommendations of the report. Then draft one for the captain's signature, saying roughly the same thing. I'll grease the skids with him while you're typing it up. Commander Hogan will be down in ten minutes for them. Okay? Oh, yeah, I want this done right the first time, and I want it tonight, so you do the typing, not your idiot son in there. Thanks, Chief, I'll make sure that Hogan contributes to your bail fund next time in port."

Andrews put down the phone and handed the report back to Hogan. He smiled as he saw the expression on Hogan's face.

"Jim, you're absolutely right. If I've ever seen a piece of paper crucial to the safety and security of our nation and our Navy, this is it. Now, you get down to my office and see the chief. Bring the endorsements to me here and we'll go see the captain so he can sign his. We'll have it on the first helo tomorrow that's going anywhere near the flagship. Fair enough?"

Hogan didn't know what to say. He just mumbled his thanks and started for the door, but Andrews's voice stopped him.

"One more thing. I agree with your assessment of your squadron, Jim, and I'll do everything I can to help you get it squared away. I'm going to give you a word of advice about that. You take credit for the success of this little adventure. They need to believe in you, not in me and not in the captain. Just you. Don't let 'em down. And you're right in that they don't deserve any more crap. They've certainly had more than their share. See you in a bit."

As Hogan closed the door behind him, Andrews picked up the file folder he had been reading when he had arrived. It was a set of pictures identical to the ones Hogan had shown him and an assessment of the strategic and political impact of the bombing. Andrews sighed as he read the recommendations of the ship's Intelligence Officer, who had charge of the entire effort down

126

there. It was a masterfully reasoned and professional piece of work full of the several ways that a defense could be mounted against the probable investigations to come. Andrews's gut told him that Hogan's way was better. It took the offense which, given the type of man Andrews was, was the only real way to go.

A little more than an hour later Hogan was sitting in the ward-room, absently sipping a glass of "bug juice." This was one of the delights of service in the Navy. You were denied a drink of scotch or bourbon when you wanted one but had every opportunity to enjoy as much of the nearly lethal simulated fruit drinks as your system could take. And it was free too.

Wilson came in and poured himself a glass of the purple stuff. He hated the red kind like Hogan was drinking. A while back he'd tried to mix in some of his antisnakebite vodka than he kept under the drawer beneath his bunk with the red kind, but even that couldn't kill the taste.

Carrying his glass with exaggerated care, he sat down next to Hogan.

"Well, how'd it go? You've got every J.O. in the squadron waiting for the verdict. Not to mention us experienced and jaded lieutenant commanders, who take things like this in stride."

"Jack me bucko, with my very own two eyes I watched the captain and CAG sign the endorsements. Here are the copies."

Wilson read the two pages, his expression changing to near wonderment as he finished the second one, the captain's. He read them both again.

"I expected you to sell it, X.O., but I didn't expect them to go for it like this."

"They didn't. The captain told me he was signing it out of respect for the Old Navy. He hadn't seen anything like it since he was a J.O. Why don't you take them down to Admin for me."

Wilson chuckled. "Good plan. As soon as Napier sees these, he'll have it all over the squadron in ten minutes. Even the enlisted troops will hear about it." He saw Hogan's level gaze. "That's what you have in mind, isn't it?"

"Yup. Even though the facts are interesting enough, Napier will have it all exaggerated by the time he tells the rest of the chiefs about it. If we let just the officers in on it, it'll never get down to the troops. This way it becomes a squadron thing. Now, get going. I need to write a letter home."

*   *   *

Gerry Carroll

Wilson decided to go to Admin by crossing the flight deck rather than through the brightly lit passageways. He felt that he spent too much time below decks in the first place and took every opportunity to get out and breathe fresh air. He stepped through the hatch and climbed the five steps to the catwalk. Flight operations had been secured for a while now, and all the aircraft were parked and ready for the first launch the following day. Most of the men who worked on the "roof" had gone below, leaving the deck almost silent except for the sounds of the wind passing through the rows of parked jets, flapping all the red "remove before flight" flags, and the hissing rush of the bow through the calm sea below, invisible in the darkness.

Wilson paused, leaning his back against the reel of a fire hose, and looked up, searching the sky for his old friend, Orion. The magnificent constellation was directly above the bow, its brilliant white stars shining with more dignity than all the others.

Jack Wilson loved that constellation. Ever since he was a small boy and his father had pointed it out to him one night and told him the myth behind it, Wilson had considered Orion an old friend who could be trusted with his most private thoughts. It may have been coincidence, but every time anything good had happened in Wilson's life, he had looked up that night and seen Orion's great pair of shoulders, square and strong, high in the darkness.

To the poets, starlight is cold and often forbidding. To Jack Wilson, Orion's pure white stars were as warm and reassuring as his father's large hand had been that night so many years and so many miles past.

Wilson smiled up at his old friend, certain that Orion was aware of what was happening in this small squadron of his fellow warriors now that Jim Hogan was aboard. He knew also that Orion was well pleased.

With a smile of near contentment, Wilson turned and climbed the three steps to the flight deck and threaded his way through the maze of invisible tie-down chains to the far corner of the deck. He was whistling as he climbed down the short ladders that led to the Admin Office and the gathered crowd, waiting to find out how things had gone.

128

15

Wednesday, January 17, 1968

★ Commander Chris Scott sat in his squadron ready room and read through the thick binder that told him everything he always wanted to know about Guntrain 206, the F-4 he was to fly this morning. The binder was known as the "yellow sheet" from the color of the form that the pilot had to sign accepting the aircraft. He finished going over all the maintenance discrepancies, or "gripes," signed his name in the acceptance block, and handed the binder to his RIO, Lieutenant Randy Norris. He looked down at his kneeboard and began to write down the information on the weather and frequencies for his flight to Tan Son Nhut airbase outside of Saigon, Republic of South Vietnam.

Two seats over was the flight lead, the senior man, CAG Andrews. He had to go in to the beach and meet with a couple of representatives from MACV, or the Military Assistance Commander, Vietnam, and with all the air wing commanders from the other carriers in the war zone. Scott had no idea what CAG's meeting was about, but he'd grabbed the chance to go to the beach, if only for a little while. He'd get to go to the base exchange while he waited for CAG to return. He hadn't been ashore for a while and had assigned himself for this mission.

The ship was about to leave Yankee Station for the transit to Singapore, and he and CAG would fly back aboard later in the afternoon when the ship was much farther south. Scott made sure that he copied the expected ship's position exactly, on the odd chance that the ship would be there when the two Phantoms were ready to land. It was not an unknown phenomenon for the ship to be someplace other than where a pilot was briefed she'd be. There was always a good reason given when the ship wasn't there,

129

usually some esoteric explanation blaming forces greater than the ship's crew, but the pilots had long ago learned to keep a reserve of fuel just in case they had to go on a carrier hunt because the fact that a ship was not where she was supposed to be was not considered an effective defense when a pilot ran out of fuel looking for her and was forced to eject. The fuel reserve was usually a given amount multiplied by the number of dependents a pilot had. Scott had had an Irish-Catholic C.O. once who swore that no Phantom ever built, even with full external tanks, could hold enough fuel to provide the reserve required for his wife and all the kids he'd sired.

On the far side of Andrews sat his RIO for a day, Lieutenant Nick Taylor. There was to be an intelligence briefing as an adjunct to the big poohbahs' powwow-type meeting, as Taylor called it, and Andrews had quietly but firmly arranged to take Taylor as the *Shiloh*'s representative. It seemed that the carrier's brilliant Intelligence Officer and Taylor's at-sea boss, a superb analyst marked for positions of much greater responsibility, had absolutely no inclination to fly to the meeting. He blithely admitted that flying from a ship terrified him, mostly because of the yahoos they gave gold wings to, including his old friend, Sam Andrews. He stoutly maintained that if he were going to fly at all, he'd do it with a stewardess at one hand and several very large vodka martinis at the other. Navy Phantoms and the ship's CODs were renowned for their lack of stewardi, thank you very much.

Scott was reasonably annoyed that Taylor was going along that morning. He'd mentioned his concerns to Andrews earlier and had heard them noted and dismissed. He felt that since Taylor was medically grounded, he had no business in the backseat of a high-performance fighter like the Phantom, especially a Phantom from Scott's squadron. CAG explained that according to the flight surgeon, all Taylor was precluded from doing was "DIACA," or duty involving actual control of an aircraft. Since there were no controls in the backseat of Navy versions of the Phantom, there was no risk of him violating that one. Furthermore, even the damn chaplain had gotten to fly in the back of an F-4 on the transit from San Diego, so it shouldn't be a problem.

Realizing that he was certain to lose the argument and that CAG was not going to listen to much more about it, Scott backed off. He was still chafing about the whole thing but now was beginning to wonder whether his objections were motivated more by his normal irritation at Taylor's attitude than by some true concern about flight safety. Whatever the cause, Scott was not in a particularly good mood that morning.

Taylor was unaware of the conversation between Scott and Andrews, but even if he'd known, he'd probably have put it in his "I-don't-give-a-shit" file. What mattered to him was that he was going flying. He was well aware that his presence in the back of the F-4 was going to fall decisively in a large gray area within the rulebook. The odds were that nothing untoward would happen that day, since it was essentially a milk run, but if something bad did happen, the whole flight, from conception to the final signature off the yellow sheet, would be scrutinized. If the interpreter of the rules was one of the increasingly more common types for whom things had to be expressly permitted before they could be done, then everybody concerned could get in some trouble. But if the interpreter was one of the older "it's easier to get forgiveness than permission" ones who firmly believed that one could do anything that wasn't expressly forbidden, then all would be well. Even though Taylor was relatively young, he'd been brought up right. He belonged to the latter group.

It had never seemed to Taylor that the rules were the tracks on which the system had to run. He regarded them, rather, as signposts that warned of danger or pointed in the right direction or were measures of progress, but nothing more. In his relatively brief career so far, he had had to work with many men to whom the rules themselves were the reason the system existed and not the accomplishment of the mission, and he abhorred that way of thinking. He always felt stultified when he was forced to deal with such men and at the end of the day he would go back to his room and wonder whether his latest exposure had drawn him closer to them. Somewhere deep inside him lurked a real fear of becoming a drone, of failing to make a difference. There had been a moment or two when he almost became convinced that he might be wrong in his attitude and he wondered whether in his iconoclasm he was being honest with himself or if it was just a way for him to get attention. In those times it wouldn't be long before he would run up against another stupid and mindless edict or procedure that would completely piss him off. He'd then automatically go get his lance and tilt at another windmill. But he would always end the day satisfied, possessing the feeling that he had done it right in not giving in. He knew that it would eventually lead to

131

his not becoming the Chief of Naval Operations, but he also knew that the CNO's uniform would cost too much anyway. So it was a wash.

Taylor listened to the brief with that small part of his mind that automatically remembered the important things. The rest of him was imagining what it would be like to once again sit in a ready room with the other pilots, preparing to fly their single-seat attack jets. He had been there many times before, but he was not sure that his absence had not colored and romanticized his memories. Recently he'd stood in those ready rooms and briefed others who'd gone out and flown the missions, but it was not the same. The fire was missing for him.

Twenty minutes after the briefing, when Taylor climbed the three short steps from the catwalk that surrounds most of the *Shiloh*'s flight deck, his bad leg caused him no discomfort at all. He was too happy to notice that his limp, which had been getting better all the time of late, was now almost gone. He made each step easily, and ducking under the wing of an A-4, he gently ran his hand along the slat on the leading edge of the wing, pushing it up a little on its rollers. The smooth paint and the rivets that were still barely noticeable to his touch told him that this was one of the newer Scooters on the ship and hadn't been beaten up too badly as yet. Soon the paint would begin to wear and the pilots who flew this jet would yank and bank and dodge missiles and fly through thunderstorms and then the endless battle between the maintenance people and corrosion would begin in earnest.

Taylor stepped over the tie-down chains and walked aft, dodging the tow tractors and the huffers, or starter carts, and the seeming millions of other pieces of equipment and people who were going about their jobs almost joyfully in the bright sunlight. There was always a sense of purpose to the movements on the flight deck and a consciousness that sometimes one false step could mean instant and messy death. It was best to be careful always, not just at the dangerous times, because the habit one wants is the one that will take care of the worst case.

The cheerfulness was due to the fact that very soon, in an hour or so, the *Shiloh* would turn her great bow to the south and leave Yankee Station for Singapore, leaving the small area of the Tonkin Gulf where the enemy was always just over the western horizon and heading for a place where there were all the things denied a man who sailed on a warship.

It would be a fine old time for the men of the *Shiloh*. It would be a part of the grand adventure most of them sought when they joined the Navy. It would be full of the smaller adventures that would be remembered for a lifetime and they could tell and retell, with little regard for accuracy, among their present and future shipmates. The stories would be told with somewhat lesser accuracy years later when they finally left the service and when they ran into an old friend from these days or when their sons asked them what they had done so long ago to earn the rows of colored ribbons that lay in the small box in the top dresser drawer. Few of them realized it then, in the middle of the great events, that they would someday take the greatest pride in the fact that when the events became just lines in books or images on a movie screen or letters on a black granite wall, they could know that they were there by choice. They could know that they had answered the bell. They could not know then that there were also many, many men who would profoundly regret that they had not been there, also by choice.

Taylor found the Phantom parked all the way aft, behind the arresting wires, with its tail nearly over the deck edge to starboard. Next to it, slightly farther forward, was the one CDR Scott and his RIO, Norris, would fly in to the beach. Taylor was the first of the four to arrive and stood there, just taking in the huge fighter. He'd never flown in a Phantom before but had spent nearly two hours the previous night down on the hangar deck with one of the pilots from Scott's squadron, an old friend, getting a sort of prebriefing briefing on the rear cockpit and all the knobs and switches and dos and don'ts. The last thing in the world he wanted to do was to look like a rookie on his first hop.

He was looking at the wingfold hydraulic plumbing, idly trying to figure out what did what, when he saw CAG Andrews step up onto the deck from the catwalk.

"All set, Nick?"

"Yes, sir. I was just looking at the size of this thing. I've never really noticed how big they are. I mean, they look bigger when you're about to get in 'em."

Andrews chuckled. "Yeah. Kinda make those A-4s of yours look like kiddie cars."

He led the way over to the left side of the nose where the skinny little ladder hung beneath the pilot's cockpit. They hung their helmets by the chin straps on the steps and Andrews performed the walk-around inspection with Taylor following along, listening carefully as CAG explained each thing he looked at. The younger man was struck by how similar the walk-around was to that of the A-4. There was just more of it.

When the two had gotten all the way around and back to the ladder, Andrews gestured for Taylor to climb up first. Taylor went up, moved aft along the fuselage, and then stepped nimbly into the rear cockpit, ducking under the raised canopy. The plane captain was next and squatted on the top of the intake to help Taylor strap in. As Andrews climbed up into the front, he had the thought that Taylor's leg didn't hinder him at all and made a mental note to check on how his request for reinstatement was coming along.

Once in the seat, with all the straps and hoses and wires hooked up, Taylor looked carefully around the cockpit. It was much roomier than his A-4, which had been designed for dwarfs. Aside from a very basic set of flight instruments and the radar, there was not much to it. Probably looks bigger because there're no flight controls back here, he thought. But what the hell, it goes up in the air.

He heard the Air Boss's voice come over the 5MC, or flight deck loudspeaker system, with the Start Speech, telling everybody to check all the chocks and tie-downs, to check that the intakes and exhausts were clear, to check that their protective gear was properly fastened and finally to start the aircraft.

The first engine he heard before his own Phantom's J-79s drowned out everything else was the chugging cough of the old reciprocating engine on the C-1 which was to fly its daily logistics run to Danang and back. The huge cloud of white smoke from the C-1's right engine blew aft down the deck and through Taylor's cockpit, bringing with it the smell of Avgas and engine oil, a smell from an era that was rapidly passing.

Over the nose of Scott's F-4 to his right he could see the rotor blades of the plane-guard helicopter begin to spin up on its parking spot between the two waist catapults on the angled deck. The catapult crews were hustling about the deck behind the helo, getting everything ready, continually looking over their shoulders to make sure that they were not straying too near the deadly tailrotor on the helo. Taylor saw the C-1, with its long narrow wings folded over the fuselage, taxi carefully past the helo, between the spinning rotor blades and the tails of the A-6s parked nose-in next to the island structure. The yellow-shirted taxi director guided the C-1 around until it lined up precisely with the number-three catapult, directly behind the helo, while two blue-shirted chockrunners kept pace, ready to throw their chocks against the C-1's wheels should its brakes fail.

"All set back there?" CAG's voice came through the built-in earphones in Taylor's helmet.

Taylor fastened his oxygen mask and reached down and turned on the oxygen flow. Taking a second to make sure he was depressing the intercom and not the radio foot switch, Taylor replied with a simple "roger," trying to keep his voice matter-of-fact to hide his excitement.

"Okay, here we go. Canopies on my command."

Taylor put his left hand gently on his canopy switch, ready to close it when CAG gave the word so that both canopies would close exactly together. It was a small thing, but fighter guys do like to look good.

To the right, Scott's Phantom eased forward, dipped as the pilot applied the brakes, checking that they were going to work, and then moved out onto the deck toward Cat 3. As soon as Scott's F-4 was headed up the deck, the yellow shirt in front began to signal Andrews forward and he moved a little and applied his own brake check. Making the turn toward the Cat, Taylor hit the canopy switch on Andrews's command, consciously checking to make sure he had nothing on the rails, like fingers, which would prevent the canopy from closing fully.

The helo lifted off and hovered for a second or two as the pilots made sure that everything was working properly, then dropped its nose and moved up and away from the ship, turning left to arc around the stern into the plane-guard pattern. Almost immediately two large white pinwheels of condensation steamed back from the propellers on the C-1 as the pilot applied full power. Within five seconds it was hurtling down the deck and into the air, its large main wheels retracting into the wells behind the engines.

The jet-blast deflector lowered back into the deck and Scott's Phantom taxied onto Cat 3. Taylor lost sight of it as Andrews moved forward because the view out the front of a Phantom from the backseat was lousy at best. Very soon he could hear the deep roar as Scott went to full power and then into afterburner. The roar abruptly diminished, and Andrews moved the fighter forward

Part Two

16

Saturday, January 20, 1968

★ "Parade the colors!" The command from the adjutant began the ceremony.

The color guard from the *Shiloh*'s Marine Detachment marched slowly across the front of the formed divisions of the squadron. As the marines reached the center point of the squadron, between the adjutant for the moment and soon-to-be X.O., Commander Terry White, and the two principals in the ceremony, Commanders Jim Hogan and Frank Blake, they turned to face the squadron and came to a halt. The squadron duty officer reached onto the small shelf built into the portable podium and pressed the play button on the tape recorder wired into the speaker.

The marine carrying the flag of the Navy lowered it until the staff was at about a forty-five-degree angle and the two marines on the ends moved their rifles into the vertical present-arms position directly in front of their upper bodies. Their precision was admirable because, after all, they were doing their thing in front of a bunch of goddamned swabbies and were not about to look anything but perfect. The marine holding the American flag kept it vertical as the scratchy, tinny sounds of the well-used recording of the national anthem were whipped around by the breeze which snapped the flags on their staffs. Many of the men standing at attention in the ranks behind their division officers could catch only snatches of the tune, but stood a little straighter as the officers saluted at the first notes.

Hogan heard the last note of the anthem followed by the scratching of the needle on the record from which the recording was made. He made a mental note to have a new recording made, one that would not sound so tired, so tattered, so typical of the

139

attitude of VA-262. As the marines marched slowly to the side, Hogan looked over the command that would be his in just a few minutes.

The men were in their blue dress uniforms, many of their "Dixie cup" hats at angles which, while not horrendously out of line, were close enough to show that they considered themselves experienced men of the sea—salty, in their words. They stood stiffly, relaxing their knees only enough to allow the blood to flow and prevent fainting. Their faces were carefully blank, except for the few younger ones who had never been through one of these change-of-command ceremonies before. The young ones tried to follow the movements with their eyes, allowing their heads to turn just enough to use their peripheral vision but not enough to appear to be "eyeballing," which was something their drill instructors had not too long ago taken great delight in punishing them for.

When the color guard had moved off to the side, the master of ceremonies, Lieutenant Tony Cordella, approached the podium and asked the adjutant to put the men at ease. Once the commands had been given, Cordella introduced Commander Andrews, who, as CAG, was not allowed to be there as a spectator but had to be the officer to preside over the ceremony and give a speech of praise for the squadron and the departing C.O.

Andrew gave the standard say-nothing speech filled with canned references to naval heroes of yesteryear and a small litany of the accomplishments of the squadron under Blake's command. It was vigorously middle-of-the-road, the sort of thing that fulfilled all the requirements but stopped far short of making Blake out to be Nimitz, Jr.

When Andrews finished and took his seat, Blake rose and approached the podium almost warily. He stood looking at the squadron, his squadron but not his squadron, for a long moment. He cleared his throat and began to speak in low, inflectionless tones, without the fire that departure speeches usually contain. It was mercifully brief and, with just a few small changes in wording, it would have seemed an apology. He paused at one point, looking about as if he realized that something huge and unseen were ending for him.

He seemed to discover, standing there in the sunlight, that he and his speech were holding something up. As if he were crossing the street in the middle of a block while all the cars and trucks and buses and life itself were halted, not impatiently honking their horns but just watching him cross their path, understanding that he was an impediment which would, in its own time, finally make it to the curb. They were waiting for him to clear their path so they could be on their way to the future. They would go on without so much as a glance in the rearview mirror. He was a memory that would dissipate forever at the next stoplight.

Blake finished and opened the folder that contained his orders and announced quietly, "I shall now read my orders."

The adjutant called the squadron to attention again. Blake read the single sheet of paper slowly and carefully, then turned to Hogan and said, "I am ready to be relieved."

Hogan approached the podium, took out another folder, and read his orders. He then turned to Blake and saluted. "I relieve you, sir."

They both turned to CAG, who was now standing behind them. Blake saluted and spoke the old words: "I stand relieved, sir."

"Very well." Andrews returned the salute and listened as Hogan saluted and said, "I have assumed command of Attack Squadron 262."

Andrew returned his salute and shook both men's hands. He and Blake sat and Hogan stepped to the podium to make his remarks. He kept them brief, laid out all the traditional bromides, threw in the obligatory quotes from Lincoln and Churchill, and challenged his new command to strive for excellence. This was not the place or the time for him to begin the reconstruction of VA-262. There was not a man standing in the ranks whose mind was on anything but the city of Singapore which served as the backdrop for the ceremony. Hogan finished his speech and went back to his seat.

The rest of the ceremony went quickly, and within two minutes of the final commands no one from the ranks except for the duty section clearing away the chairs and sound system was left on the flight deck. Hogan and Blake both received handshakes of either congratulations or farewell from the guests, mostly senior officers from the other squadrons or the ship's company.

At last Hogan found himself standing alone with Blake. Hogan repeated his invitation to attend the party in the hotel later in the day, but Blake declined.

"No, thanks. I've got a couple of people to see and then I've got to get to the airport. This is one flight I don't want to miss."

"Okay, then. Do you need any help with anything? Getting your gear ashore?"

"No, I'm fine." Blake paused, looking across the flight deck at the land beyond. He turned to Hogan and stuck out his hand.

"Good luck, Jim. I hope you get more from this squadron than I did. You won't have much fun in your new job. All you can do is try to hold things together until you get them all home. Things always seem easier back at Lemoore."

Hogan shook the proffered hand. "Thanks. I'll keep that in mind. Take care, Frank. Have a safe trip home."

Blake nodded and walked away.

Hogan watched him until he disappeared into a hatch in the island structure, then turned back to look at the shore. He stood for a long time, until he heard a voice behind him.

"Well, Skipper. You're in it now. You're officially Ghostrider One."

Hogan turned to find Terry White, the new X.O., standing there, still in his dress blues. He smiled a little.

"Hi, Terry. I was just thinking how long I've worked for this, and now all I can feel is nervous. They didn't tell me anything about that back in the Skippergartens."

White smiled at the reference to the various schools that prospective C.O.'s and X.O.'s had to go through before they arrived at their new commands. "Yeah. Well, I suppose it's like getting lessons on sex. There's no way you can really know until you're in the middle of it. Usually turns out to be fun though. Despite all the bad stuff that they warn you about."

"Yeah. I guess so. Oh, well, I think the first thing we have to do is make sure that everybody has a good time here in port before we go back on the line. It's always easier to get smiling guys to do things."

"Yup. Let's us go over too. I could use a beer or six after my long and dusty trip here."

Hogan laughed. "What do you mean, long and dusty trip? You sat in the hotel bar for two days, waiting for us to pull in."

"No. I'm talking about the ride out here in the liberty boat. It took almost fifteen minutes, and I had to worry about drowning the whole time. Look at my hands. My nerves are shot."

"Okay, you're on. Besides, there's somebody I want you all to meet. He's a marine aviator who got stuck as an Air Liaison Officer with the grunts."

Still talking happily about the places to go while on liberty, the two headed below to change and to catch the next boat ashore.

Blake found Andrews in his office, sitting behind his desk with his tie pulled down and his shirt collar unbuttoned. He knocked on the doorjamb gently and stood as a small boy would at the door to the principal's office.

Andrews looked up and smiled, gesturing Blake to the chair beside his desk.

"Come in, Frank. Have a seat." Andrews handed over a folder that contained a long sheet of green paper. It was Blake's departure-fitness report which was widely referred to throughout the Navy as "the good-bye kiss," mostly because the reporting senior officer usually inflated the report to try to help the guy's career a little. This was reasonably hard to do since the system was so incredibly inflated in the first place that the reports had become little more than an exercise in using a thesaurus.

Blake read through it expressionlessly and then read through it again. He half expected to see something about his bombing of the fake hospital, but it wasn't there. On the whole, the "fitrep" was better than he had expected. He had feared that Andrews would use his last fitrep to vent his true feelings and his disappointment with Blake's performance as C.O. of the squadron. Blake had seen it done often enough. But Andrews was better than that, Blake realized. He was being scrupulously fair. To cover his thoughts, Blake read through the narrative summary again. He was a little humbled by what Andrews had done. He looked up at Andrews when he was finished.

"Thank you, sir. This will help."

Andrews sat forward in his chair, placing his forearms on the desktop. "I think it will, Frank. As you can see, I strongly recommended you for promotion and for staff positions."

Blake referred to the block containing those recommendations. "Yes, sir. Thank you for that."

The old careerist in Blake showed himself just for a second. "I also see that you are not as strong in your endorsement for subsequent command."

Andrews sighed. "You're right. That was not an oversight, Frank. After our talk a couple of weeks ago, I thought at first that you were just burned out with command and would probably be eager for it sometime later on. But the more I thought about it and reflected on what you've said on other occasions and the way you've run your squadron, I realized that you weren't burned out. You really have hated this."

Blake said nothing. He just looked calmly back at Andrews, who looked down at his desktop and then back up.

"Frank, I think I've done you a disservice. The biggest problem you've had in command was that you really never trusted your people. You held the reins too tight and tried to force them all to think exactly like you did. When they couldn't, you turned your back on them. Looking back on all that now, I believe that I saw it happening and failed to take action. Why, I'm not sure yet, but I suspect I was a little chicken in that I hoped your problems and your squadron's problems would simply go away. It doesn't work that way. It never has, so why should I have expected it to this time?

"Your squadron has not been as bad as some I've seen. They've gotten the job done and the numbers are all acceptable. But there's none of the spark that should have been there. I know you used the leadership style that fit you best, but it's not the one I think would have been best for the squadron. I should have brought you in here and told you that and maybe tried to help you map out some sort of strategy. But because I didn't do that, because it was my job to help you lead your squadron as effectively as you were able, I failed in my own position of leadership and my responsibility to you. For that I'm sorry."

Blake was completely unused to frankness of this sort. He'd rarely gotten it before from any of his earlier superiors, who had often cloaked things in vagueness and counseled keeping everything close to the vest. Perhaps one of the things wrong with Blake was that he remembered only those men and not the other, more open, men with whom he'd served. Hearing CAG's words, he had no idea what to say.

Andrews broke the silence. He stood and offered his hand.

"Good-bye, Frank, and good luck. Stay in the staff jobs. You can do more in them than you could by coming back to the war. You'll be a hell of a lot happier too."

Blake nodded as he shook Andrews's proffered hand. "Thanks again, CAG, for the fitrep. And good luck to you too." He folded his copy of the fitness report as he walked out of the office.

Andrews sat back down wearily and leaned back in his chair. He rubbed his hand across his eyes and stared at the ceiling. He thought over the conversation he'd just had. One topic that had been avoided was Blake's mistake on his last mission. A thing like that would be like a bomb hidden in Blake's record. It would explode as soon as Blake showed up in a position of leadership again. Both men had known that something like that was known to too many people, and it would haunt Blake whenever he came near the operational Navy. He could lose himself in the bureaucracy in Washington and do well, but he was now professionally dead in any other arena. Andrews had thought long and hard about bringing it up but knew that it would serve no purpose. Those who should learn from it—Blake's, no, *Hogan's*, squadron—already had, and Blake would have to live with it for the rest of his life.

Andrews reached for his coffee cup and sighed. One of his biggest problems was gone now, so why did he feel so lousy, he wondered.

Blake looked back at the *Shiloh*, rising out of the water like a small mountain range. He stood on the coxswain flat of the "P-boat," or officer's launch, which was used to carry officers to and from the ship whenever she was in port and anchored out as she was now. He should have been feeling relief at that moment, but he couldn't muster any. All he felt was sadness.

As the great ship receded from him, this strange feeling grew. He wondered why he could feel that way when he was headed for a job he'd always dreamed of having, when he was on the very brink of success. He would be among the policy makers, right there in the halls of power, helping to decide the course of great events and shaping the Navy of the future. He'd be leaving a mark.

He'd never been a particularly gregarious man, so he was used to being by himself, and it was certainly not the prospect of traveling across half the world alone that was bothering him.

The fitness report CAG had given him held nothing negative—quite the contrary, for, when taken with his talents and his usual excellence at staff work, it would only ensure that he would remain in Washington. He would never again have to go back out and fly from the deck of a ship.

That thought brought a fresh wave of emotion through him. But it still was not one of relief, it was the terrible chill of loss. Blake almost staggered with the impact of realization. But why? After the soul-searing terror of his near drowning and the professional dread of what could have happened after the bombing of the fake hospital (until Hogan had come up with a plan to save his ass), he should have felt nothing short of giddy.

Along the edge of the *Shiloh*'s flight deck, he could see the tails of the jets hanging out over the catwalk. With the sun flashing on their wings, they achieved a beauty that was foreign to him. Or was it?

The sounds of youthful laughter came up at him from the forward cabin, where a group of J.O.'s were enjoying the prospect of some liberty and their usual blithe fun in port. And with their laughter came the knowledge of what it was that Blake had lost.

There had been a time when he had been just like those young men. Brave, immortal, confident, full of the fun of being a naval aviator, of flying the greatest machines ever designed by man. He had been just as irreverent and fun-loving as they, looking at the senior officers, the "heavies," as a teenage son looks at his father— full of old ideas and ignorant of the magic of modern things.

Blake looked around at the harbor and the pier fast approaching. He understood what he had lost now. It was Frank Blake himself. He had become something far different from what he had once hoped. He looked back at the *Shiloh* and saw her standing proud and magnificent in the sun, and a sob grew within him. Only the automatic restraint he had cultivated for so long kept it from breaking free. He turned his back on the ship and watched the boat approach the pier.

As he picked up his bag and placed the sling over his shoulder, two lines from a song he had heard long ago came back to him:

I knew a lad who went to sea and left the shore behind him.
I knew him well. The lad was me, but now I cannot find him.

Blake stepped onto the concrete pier and began to walk toward the cab stand. He glanced over his shoulder once more at the young men coming ashore and then at the carrier, floating easily in the harbor. The images started to blur, and he turned away once more and walked to the waiting cabs.

An hour later Hogan and White stepped from the liberty boat onto the metal float that prevented the fiberglass boat from beating against the concrete pier at Fleet Landing, and then up onto the steps of the pier itself. Fleet Landing was the traditional name of whatever spot in whatever port the liberty boats used to embark and disembark passengers. They climbed up the steps and stood, looking around the crowd of locals, all hawking something, like genuine $50 Rolex watches, or Cokes, or small snacks, some of which might not cause food poisoning. Others, farther back, were leaning on their cabs, waiting for a fare.

"Hey, Skipper!"

Hogan turned at the shout to see Nick Taylor approaching from the small beach-guard shack where the officers and men in charge of coordinating the orderly flow of men and materiel to and from the carrier were headquartered. The beach-guard shack also served as a focal point for the shore patrol efforts for the in-port period.

"Hi, Nick. How's it going in here?"

"Pretty good, actually. We've only had to send two guys back to the ship so far. Took them exactly two hours to get themselves in a fight with the locals. Seems they objected to the prices in one of the joints up the hill there. All they kept yelling was how these 'goddamned foreigners' around here tried to cheat people."

Hogan sighed. "They weren't our guys, were they?" If they were, his first official visit with the Shiloh's captain was going to be a one-sided conversation.

"Nope. They were bosun's strikers from the Deck Division. Ship's company."

"Good."

Taylor looked around at the sky as if checking the weather. His sunglasses couldn't completely hide the mischief in his eyes. "Look, Skipper, I'm really distraught that I had to miss the change-of-command ceremony. I'd have given anything to be there, but somebody had to be stuck here on the beach, preserving the dignity of our fine nation."

"Uh-huh. And you were the best man for the job. Right?"

Taylor scraped the toe of his shoe on the pavement in a parody of modesty.

"Aw, shucks, sir. My legendary humility forbids me to reply, but I do thank you for recognizing my wonderfulness in front of the X.O. here. Anyway, I did get Commander Blake off on his pilgrimage to the five-sided wind tunnel on the Potomac and I made sure that it was rose petals not dog shit that the peasants were throwing. You'd have been proud. Anyway, congratulations. And to you too, X.O."

Hogan turned to White. "I'm sorry. X.O., this is the resident wildman, part-time Intelligence and Powerplants Officer and full-time squadron conscience, Nick Taylor. He's managed to con his way into the shore patrol job. Again.''

White chuckled. "We've met. Two nights ago in the hotel bar.''

Taylor looked pained. He turned to Hogan. "Skipper, I was off duty at the time and was merely checking the town for tourist traps so the rest of the guys wouldn't get in trouble. You can never tell when somebody will slip inferior booze into the bottles.''

"Your dedication is commendable and fills me with wonder. I'm sure that it will be duly noted in your record. Now, where did you hide the Admin?''

"Suite 940 in the Hilton. Overlooks the pool, of course. My room's just down the hall, and we can use that for the overflow. There's also some marine asking for you. He said he'd either be out by the pool or in his room this afternoon.''

Hogan turned to White. "That's the guy I was telling you about.''

He turned back to Taylor. "When do you get off duty?''

"1800. Until then, I'll be right here, keeping a lid on things so that my shipmates can enjoy their time in the mysterious East without worrying about the fate of their great country.''

"Nick, that chokes me right up. You're a true hero.''

"Yessir, I know. Please let my mom know if I should not survive.''

Hogan chuckled and led White over to the fence and the gate that led to the taxi stand.

Singapore is much like any port in the world. The city is long and narrow as opposed to Hong Kong, for example, which is kind of short and fat. It is exceptionally cosmopolitan, much more so than the teeming morasses of many Asian ports. The population had a large Indian influence and the city itself had quite a few well-attended temples of many religions, always a good indicator of the tolerance with which the locals lived. The temples, for all their beauty and symbolism, were really not the main attractions for the men of the *Shiloh*. Those attractions were to be found at the end of the long cab ride from Fleet Landing.

The two took the first cab in the line, ignoring the other drivers, who bartered with each other and with the American sailors for the fares. Their driver left the lot and sped toward town, not even bothering to ask the destination. It didn't matter really: the fare would be more than the locals paid and, since this was the first day in port, the sailors didn't really care about cost—that would come later, when they had time to compare notes and were not so eager to spend the money they'd accumulated during the previous weeks at sea.

The Hilton in Singapore, very much like the other major hotels there, held fashion shows with great regularity. In accord with the basic sophistication of the city, these fashion shows displayed clothes from as many diverse cultures as were represented in the population, and one of these shows was taking place when Hogan and White walked in. Having been to Singapore several times before, Hogan knew that he'd find whichever of his squadron officers had come ashore, especially the one who had the key to the Admin suite, sitting around the room, ogling the models.

He knew also that no matter how it appeared, his guys would swear that they were simply looking for something that would make a good present for their wives or girlfriends or sisters back home. He'd spent many an hour at shows like this, searching for just such a gift. The fact that the sarongs and saris and *ao dais* were being worn by stunning young Eurasian models was, of course, irrelevant to the pure high-minded purpose of the young Americans. The drinks that were being served to them at their tables were, equally obviously, just there to quench the thirst built up from the long taxi rides from Fleet Landing.

White stood in the doorway, admiring the models as Hogan went over to the table and retrieved the key from young Lieutenant (j.g.) Tom Grant, who seemed annoyed that his C.O. had to block his view while he waited for the key. Hogan was grinning as he led the way to the elevators.

White punched the button for the ninth floor and turned to Hogan. "What's the plan? I need to call home and then I'll be all set. How about you? Gonna call your wife?"

"No. I'm not married anymore, and my kids are still too small for me to call. I just need to change and track down my friend."

White apologized for asking about the wife and phone call. Hogan smiled dismissively.

"No problem. She just couldn't handle the upheaval and worry of being married to a Navy pilot. Actually, there's no hassle between us. We're still friends and even lived on the same block.

"She had a real good job, vice president of a bank, and didn't want to give it up when I left Lemoore for Kingsville. But that was kind of the last straw. I got shot down once on my last tour, and they didn't wait before they listed me as missing. She had twenty-four hours of hell before I could get word back to her that I was okay and just got stuck in the weeds for a night."

The door of the elevator opened with an annoying little ding, giving both men an excuse to change the subject. They followed the signs down the hall and found the suite of rooms.

An Admin is the naval aviator's version of a crash pad. The officers of the squadron pooled their money and rented several rooms or a suite to serve as a headquarters for their time ashore. It was usually stocked with a bar and some beer, and the officers used it to store their clothes and as a dormitory rather than taking the long, boring boat ride back to the ship.

Since the Navy has never been famous for its democratic style, the C.O. and X.O. usually hogged the beds, graciously allowing the other officers to sleep on the floor. Smart junior officers bought an air mattress or a camp pad of foam rubber to sleep on. However, since most of the time everybody was suitably anesthetized, sleeping on the floor itself was not all that bad until the next morning, when it was difficult to decide which hurt more, the back from lying on industrial grade carpet all night, or the head from the hangover. Either way, a couple of Bloody Marys, administered in time, would fix the problem.

Hogan entered the suite and was surprised to find that it didn't look like a herd of buffalo had stampeded through. It was cluttered, to be sure, but apparently the J.O.'s had discovered the fashion show before they could sit around and trash the room. It would be only a matter of time though, so Hogan dropped his bag on one of the beds, staking his claim, and reached into the small refrigerator for a beer. He handed one to White.

"Nice room. Make your call and I'll meet you down by the pool. I've got to find my marine friend before he starts picking on unsuspecting navy guys and running up their bar tab. That's always been one of his favorite pastimes."

White chuckled as he sat down on the bed and picked up the telephone. As he watched Hogan pull out his bathing suit and head for the bathroom to change, he was glad he'd been assigned to VA-262. Between him and Hogan, they should have a lot of fun. A lot of work but a lot of fun too. The trick was going to be keeping a sense of humor.

17

Saturday, January 20, 1968

At the loud and insistent knocking on his hotel room door, Marine Major Dick Averitt rose from his bed with a groan. He stood for a few moments, making sure that his equilibrium was going to be up to the task of getting him all the way over to the door. When he felt that his gyros had squared themselves away well enough for the trip across thirty dangerous feet of carpet, he shuffled slowly over and pulled the door open.

All of four inches, that is. He cursed the lineage of the door, pushed it to, and pulled off the chain that held it. The effort proved to be about all his arms were capable of for the moment, so he allowed them to fall to his sides as he turned and walked back to the bed and lay himself gingerly facedown. It didn't occur to him that he hadn't bothered to look carefully at whoever was knocking. He was much more concerned with how much his head hurt. If he were lucky, he thought, it would be somebody who would quietly shoot him and put him out of his misery.

It was only Jim Hogan who greeted him far too loudly for his tortured brain to bear, his smile infuriating in its pleasantness. His hands held a paper bag that was wet in enough places for it to appear to contain cans of beer. Hogan pulled out two of the cans, opened them with a churchkey, and handed one to Averitt.

"Feeling a little poorly, are we?"

Struggling to a sitting position, Averitt managed a grunt. But he did accept the beer.

"And did we have fun last night?"

Averitt put down the now-empty can and reached into the bag for another. He opened it and took a long swallow.

"I don't know why I'm so thirsty this morning, I certainly had

151

enough to drink last night," he said through a belch that nearly made his stomach heave.

"Uh-huh. And what happened? You look like shit. I mean, even considering that you've been stomping around in the weeds with a bunch of grunts for two months. You even look worse than you did back at Danang."

"Well, I got in yesterday. Wait a minute." Averitt looked at his watch, moving it back and forth in front of his eyes until it seemed to be in focus.

"Yeah, it was yesterday," he continued. "Anyway, I ran into a guy from your ship and we went out on the town. We met a couple of girls and then went barhopping. It gets a little vague from there on, but I think we all wound up in the pool and the next thing I heard was you knocking."

Lights went on in Hogan's head. "This guy from my ship. Do you remember his name."

"Nick something. He was an Intell type. Good guy. He's the one who found the girls."

"I don't suppose that it was Nick Taylor, was it?"

"That was it. Taylor. Do you know him?"

"Yeah, I know him. In fact, I can't believe he can look as good as he does this morning and you look so bad. Actually, he's from my squadron. He's an A-4 pilot who got wounded and is trying to get back into a seat."

"He's got a hollow leg and a line of bullshit a mile long. I couldn't even stand up, and he was out dancing his head off and charming the hell out of the girls. I don't know how he does it."

"You used to be able to handle it too. But now you're old and slow, like me. It won't be long before we're both sitting in rockers on the porch at the old sailors' home. But we sure will have some stories to tell."

Averitt nodded slowly. "That's for sure. The liberty stories are always the best too. So what's the plan? If I'm gonna live, those beers you've got there won't do it."

"How about we go down to the market and get something to eat. I'll go get my X.O. and you take a shower. We'll meet you in the Admin, Suite 940. I'll leave these here." Hogan put the rapidly disintegrating bag of beer down on the dresser and walked to the door. He turned and looked back at his slightly out-of-focus friend who was rooting through his duffel bag, looking for some clean underwear and his shaving kit. He smiled at the picture.

Walking down the hall toward the room, Hogan thought back on his times with Averitt. The younger man had been a superb instructor back at Kingsville. His combat experience had been a tremendous influence in the Tactics syllabus and had gone a long way in preparing the young student naval aviators for tours in Vietnam. This had gone largely unappreciated at first, but as the word filtered back that the training had come in handy in later squadron assignments for many of the graduates, his reputation grew. The students would look at the ribbons on his chest and wonder what it would be like to be there, to be actually shot at, to do the job for real. To hear his stories and those of the few others, like Hogan, who had been in combat, was sobering for some, but most students were filled with all the glorious and heroic fantasies of youth.

Even though Hogan had seen Averitt only a couple of weeks before at Danang, he was surprised at how lousy he looked. He was much thinner than he had been back in Kingsville. He was deeply tanned on his neck and his arms, which were not covered by the camouflage utilities he wore in-country, but the rest of him seemed deathly pale in the clean confines of a beautiful hotel in a city far removed, culturally if not geographically, from the war. He had the dark circles around his eyes typical of those who spent long periods living in the presence of death and danger with too much fear and too little sleep, with too many body bags and too few moments alone. This was his two-week R&R period, and rather than go off somewhere where he knew no one, he'd jumped at the chance to spend some of his time with Hogan in Singapore.

Hogan was glad that Averitt had made that choice. It would give his squadron a chance to get a glimmer of what the war was like for those who did not get to fly home to hot meals and clean sheets after their missions. Not that flying into the teeth of the North Vietnamese air defenses was exactly a walk in the park, but there was the opportunity for some normalcy in a naval aviator's life.

The door to the suite was ajar and the too-loud voices of the officers from VA-262 came out through the gap. Hogan paused for a moment, listening to them as they raved about the models who'd been in the fashion show downstairs.

The voices were happy and boisterous, sending gibes and laughs flying about. He heard White's voice among them inserting his two cents here and there. Hogan was struck by the idea that White was rapidly being accepted into the squadron as the first "heavy" in the post-Blake era. He had the opportunity to begin with a clean slate while Hogan still was a part of something that had been psychologically painful for all of them and, knowing how the young are, best relegated to that part of the mind where one puts memories that might color or distort participation in the sheer fun of being alive.

What was normal and natural for White was going to take some work for Hogan. He was well aware that his next step, into the room, was the first of a long journey both for him and for his men. The road ahead for them all was clouded by chance and uncertainty. The final goal stood bright and clear in the sun on a hilltop in the distance, but the road ahead was vague and indistinct. He just hoped that he had the stuff to find the way.

Hogan pushed open the door and stepped into the room.

It was obvious from the raucous greeting he received that everybody had had a wonderful time at the fashion show. Hogan looked over at Terry White, who was sitting at the end of the large couch that faced the door. He had a beer in his hand, his feet up on the coffee table, and a large grin on his face. Next to him, one of the J.O.'s was speaking with alcohol-induced earnestness about some subject that had taken on the gravity of the search for Atlantis. White glanced up at Hogan and gave him a large wink, turning back to the young man with his expression once more serious.

Hogan walked through the open sliding glass door and onto the balcony. He reached into the cooler and pulled out a beer, opening it with the churchkey that hung from a string on the railing. There were no empty chairs on the balcony, so he got one from the room and moved it out into the sunlight.

The other chairs were occupied by the more senior pilots from the squadron who had been around long enough to want to just sit and look out at the view of the city and the sea for a while. When they were younger, they'd been the guys in the room, talking grandly and planning the operations that would place them in the closest possible proximity to manic fun. Now they knew enough to simply sit and decide where they wanted to roam. They knew that there was fun to be had and that they would find it without the expenditure of significant amounts of energy. They also knew that much later in the evening, when everyone had been at it for nine or ten hours, they'd be the ones to carry on and leave the younger ones snoring peacefully in the various nooks and crannies of the Admin.

Jack Wilson moved his chair over a little to give Hogan room in the row of pilots contemplating the view.

"Finally made it in, I see."

"Yep. A Skipper's work is never done. Sunup to sundown. But then, I figured that I'd dump it all on the X.O. and you guys. I believe I'll be the brains of the outfit from now on. You know, sort of wave the baton."

Wilson looked over in mock horror. "You don't mean we'll actually have to go to work, do you? I didn't join the Navy to work. All my contract says is that I have to wear my wings and impress the common folk with my wonderfulness and panache. I'll have to check the fine print, but I do believe that I have a clause in there somewhere protecting me from tyrants like you.

Hogan sighed. "I was afraid of that. I guess CAG and I will have to transfer you to Tierra del Fuego as the Lava Officer. Or maybe to the Recruiting Command. Yeah, that's it. You can go be a recruiter."

"Okay, you win. I'll see if I can find the guidebook on how to work." Wilson sipped his beer. "In the meanwhile, did you find your friend?"

"Yeah, he's taking a shower and will meet me in here. He's moving a little slow this afternoon. Unfortunately, last night he ran into Nick Taylor, who took him out on the town."

"That's a terrifying thought. It says a lot for your friend that he's not in intensive care."

"You should have seen him when I knocked on his door. Looked like somebody pulled him through a hedge backward. Nick, of course, looks like a recruiting poster."

Wilson smiled at the picture. "What are you guys gonna do? The J.O.'s are all heading for that new disco up the hill. They figure that the models from the fashion show will be there. Probably wishful thinking."

"I thought we'd head for the market and get something to eat. I hadn't thought much beyond that. Do you want to come along? I promise it'll be boring."

"Boring sounds perfect."

The sliding glass door opened behind them, and Averitt stepped through and onto the balcony. Hogan handed him a beer and introduced him all around. In the eternal manner of military aviators, once they found out that he was one of the brotherhood, he was accepted immediately and besieged with questions about how his war, the one in South Vietnam, was going. There were a few barbed references to his marine lineage, but Averitt would have thought something was wrong if there hadn't been. What he got from everybody was sympathy for being on the ground with a bunch of mud marines instead of in the cockpit of an attack jet. He felt instantly at home with these guys.

18

Sunday, January 21, 1968

Late the next morning Jack Wilson and Dick Averitt lay comfortably on two chaise longues that were strategically placed near the pool of the hotel. Strategically placed because there were four young, possibly Scandinavian, women sunning themselves about thirty feet away, and the two aviators had a wonderful view of the entire group. Through their dark sunglasses the two could watch each and every move they made. Normally, a group of women catching rays was no big deal, but this simple pleasure had been denied them for quite a while. The other attraction was that these ladies had obviously been cheated when they purchased their bikinis, because none of them had apparently come with a top.

The two pilots were playing the ancient military game of Do You Know? When Hogan had introduced them on the balcony of the Admin the day before, both men had had the disquieting feeling that they had met before. It didn't take long for them to figure out that they'd been in the same section back in flight school and had had a casual acquaintance then, about ten years before. From there it was simply a matter of catching up on and off throughout the evening. When they'd all gotten to the disco shortly before midnight, their attention had been diverted and the conversation didn't resume until they'd arrived at the pool about an hour before. They were now waiting for Hogan and White to join them as they talked about men they both knew and where they all were now.

It was surprising for them both how few of the men they remembered were still flying in the Navy and the Marine Corps. Some were now with the airlines, driving busloads of people through the sky. Others had drifted away to God-knows-where after their obligated service was up.

Many were dead, killed in combat or operational accidents or by the stupid vagaries of life itself. It seemed that there were only about one in ten or twelve still around, and that number was diminishing quickly. Here, close to the war, these thoughts had an immediacy and a closeness that would have been absent had the conversation been held in any of the clubs back home. They both felt it, and by an unspoken agreement changed the subject to something that would not cast a shadow on them on this bright, beautiful morning.

Several minutes later, another, bigger shadow was cast over them, but this time it was Hogan's. He stood over them, blocking both the sun and the view of the Scandinavians. Next to him stood Terry White, who was paying more attention to the girls than to Averitt and Wilson.

"With all due respect, Skipper, sir, would you kindly get the hell out of the way?" Wilson leaned to one side, trying to maintain his view while still remaining casual about it.

"You're going to ruin your eyes, Jack. That is, if you don't break your neck twisting it around like that." He pulled up a chaise and plopped down.

Wilson sat back and readjusted his sunglasses. "So how'd you make out last night? The last I saw of you was sitting there, talking to that blonde."

Hogan chuckled. "Fine. I've got a date with her tonight. Dinner somewhere she says is really good."

"Who was she with? One minute you were talking to us and the next you were over in a corner with her. You move quick, but if I'd seen her first, you wouldn't have had a chance."

"Actually, I was second in line. She came in with Johnny Greene. Or, rather, she brought him in. He was feeling no pain."

The others, always ready for a good liberty story, quit staring at the Scandinavians and gave Hogan their full attention. Greene was a lieutenant (j.g.) who had joined the squadron shortly before it left for this deployment. He had still not lost his youthful enthusiasm but was rapidly becoming an excellent combat pilot. He had gotten married only two months before the deployment began and, in the view of most of the others in the squadron, would probably be a newlywed until he was about seventy-five. For him to get slightly loaded and wind up with a blonde was a story that would amuse his friends for weeks to come.

"Well, the two of them came in with her doing most of the navigating. I was at the bar and they took a couple of stools next to me." Hogan told the rest of the story, choosing his details so as to minimize the damage to Greene's reputation and make the Blonde (It was obvious that the others thought of her that way. She'd never really have a name, just a title.) seem more ladylike.

Greene had waited until he thought the Blonde wasn't listening and leaned over and asked Hogan whether she was as homely as he thought she was. Hogan had glanced up and had seen her dancing blue eyes measuring him. He turned back to Greene, trying hard to keep a straight face, and told him loudly enough for her to hear that it was unfortunately true that he had hooked himself up with a real dog and that it was probably going to look bad for him in the morning.

Greene had drunk his beer quietly and then had a wonderful idea. He could flee and stick Hogan with the problem.

"Look, Skipper, can you cover me? I mean, if I say I'm going to the head and you keep her busy, I can make it back to the Admin before she knows I'm gone. You know, you can sort of draw her fire for a couple of minutes."

Hogan nodded in mock severity. "Okay. But give me a couple of minutes to go to the head myself."

Greene agreed and turned back to the Blonde. Hogan winked at her and went to the back of the bar, gesturing for Greene's roommate, Lieutenant Paul Miller, who was sitting at a table, to follow. Once out of sight he told the young pilot that Greene was going to head back to the hotel, and even though he had only about three blocks to go would most probably need a navigational escort. Miller peeked around the corner and saw Greene leaning on the bar next to an absolutely gorgeous woman, trying to hold both himself and his end of the conversation up. He laughed and agreed. This was going to give him unlimited material to pull Greene's chain with. He offered to help out Hogan with her, too, when he came back, but Hogan refused the selfless offer and walked back to the bar.

As soon as Hogan slid back onto his stool, Greene looked over at him and winked slyly, although his determined attempt to focus made it anything but conspiratorial. He looked back at the Blonde, excused himself, gallantly kissed her hand, and sort of walked back toward the rest rooms.

Once he was gone, Hogan moved over a stool and offered to buy the Blonde a drink. She laughed and accepted. It was not long before the two had moved to a quiet table far from the bandstand.

Averitt chuckled at the story. "So who is she? I mean, this town isn't exactly overrun with good-looking blondes."

"She's the fashion coordinator for that show that was in the hotel yesterday and sort of a chaperone for the girls. When our guys moved in on the models last night, she tagged along and wound up with Johnny. He was sort of the odd man out, and so was she. Anyway, when Johnny got loaded she stuck with him to keep him out of trouble. They finally got to the bar and she figured she'd drop him off 'with his own tribe,' as she put it, and then split. It seemed her girls were being well taken care of. She's a nice lady. Not like her models, who are sort of drifty, says she."

Wilson chimed in. "They might be drifty, but they didn't have a lot of trouble handling our guys. There was nobody missing when I got up this morning, and there were no shapely legs sticking out from under any of the blankets either. But on the other hand, it was the first night, and they can always claim that they were only doing a reconnaissance run."

Hogan asked, "Do you think they'll be in any shape to have a little meeting later?"

"What do you have in mind?"

"Nothing much. Dick and I figured we might be able to have an informal briefing about what is going on in-country South Vietnam. Sort of give them a picture of what it's like in there. It'd be kind of like a bull session. I thought maybe they'd get more out of it if we did it here on the beach rather than in the ready room."

"I like it, but day after tomorrow might be better. There's still a bunch of steam they need to get rid of."

Hogan thought for a minute. "Sounds good to me. That okay with you, Dick?"

Averitt grinned. "No problem. Maybe it'll be rainy and those honeys over there will be inside. For right now, though, I want to stay right here. After I get a waiter to bring us some beers, that is."

Hogan smiled and pulled a paperback novel out of his bag. He sat back and adjusted his sunglasses, but, since he was constantly looking over the top of the books at the Scandinavian girls, he didn't get very much read.

About five miles away, Commander Chris Scott was seething. He hated to lose at anything, really hated it. He was famous for playing Risk or Monopoly with as much intensity as he flew his jets. Nobody in the squadron would play acey-deucy with him anymore, and only his RIO, Randy Norris, would even consider playing him in cribbage, probably because Norris could usually win and loved to watch Scott get mad while he just sat back and gave him the needle until Scott became so enraged that he began to see how silly he looked. He'd then laugh at himself and all would be well.

That morning Scott had not yet reached the point where he could laugh. He was doing fairly poorly at golf, which was the one game in which he found no humor. He hadn't played in almost two months and his game showed it. It was only the fact he was teamed with CAG Andrews that was keeping the lid on his anger.

The opposition, Norris and that wacko, Nick Taylor, were doing everything they could to pry the lid off. They were both dressed in outrageously colored knickers with shirts carefully selected so as to clash blindingly with their pants. Each wore a pink Panama (naturally including the purple hatband) and rhinestoned sunglasses. Taylor had explained that they were both fed up with the basic drabness of their existence and had decided to spice things up. Norris added that it was unnatural for the male of the species to be the one drably accoutered, witness the peacock and the cardinal. Therefore they were beginning a revolution and these outfits were their new idea for a naval golfing uniform.

The topper was the fact that they showed up with their own caddies, two Eurasian women in extremely short skirts. Scott had fumed that the club would never allow this. One had to use the caddies that the club itself provided. He had been speechless when Taylor told him that the girls were the daughters of the club manager whom Taylor had met on his first day in Singapore, before the ship had pulled in. He figured that they would be invaluable, since they kind of knew the course, having lived on it all their lives, and none of the Americans had ever seen it before.

Andrews had roared with laughter and was having a fine old time with this round. The match was even through seventeen holes with Andrews making shot after shot and Scott only occasionally contributing to the score. The younger pair played easily, laughing and joking all the way and hitting prodigious shots at will. Scott had tried to outdrive them only once and had hooked the ball far out of bounds. Norris's comment that it had probably gone through Ho Chi Minh's window was the final straw, and he had finally blown up, but when he looked at the others, including the caddies, roaring with laughter at his tirade, he stopped and glared at them fiercely. Undaunted, the two younger players collapsed on the ground at his choice of curse words. "Sonsabitches-bastards" was the one that had been the best of them all.

Norris and Taylor began to refer to each other by the new name until even Scott saw the humor in it all. The final hole went well for him, and he beat all the others by a stroke, accusing the two J.O.'s of letting him win. Feigning indignation, they instantly challenged him to a rematch later in the week. He and Andrews accepted and led the way into the bar.

After a half hour or so Andrews excused himself to head back to the ship, and Norris, who had some work to get done, went with him. As Taylor went up to the bar to get a couple more beers, Scott thought over the events of the day. He found, somewhat to his surprise, that he had truly enjoyed them and was looking forward to the rematch. Young Nick Taylor had been his normal irreverent self and, away from the confines of the ship and the war, had been much easier to take. Scott had not really wanted to play with him that day, but Norris and Andrews had chivvied him into it. Now, watching Taylor wend his way through the crowd back to the table, he wondered why he could take him then and not before.

Taylor laid the beers on the table and sat, pouring his into the newly frosted glass. Scott waited until the foam in his glass had settled some and poured in the rest of his beer.

"Nick, tell me something. How come you're always so crazy on the ship?"

Taylor sipped his beer and considered the question for a moment.

"I'm not really nuts, Commander. I just remember how the briefings and things used to go when I was flying the missions. Most of the time the briefers didn't really have a feel for what the pilots needed. So they were all serious and professional and the pilots sat there and rolled their eyes and got bored. I figured that things needed a little livening up. It's also partly my way of keeping from going crazy while everybody else gets to go flying. The only way I can deal with some of it is to laugh at it, and I hate to laugh alone."

"Okay, but you're also the greatest balloon-pricker I've ever seen. That really grates on some people. Like me, for example. The other J.O.'s pick up on that, and pretty soon we've got an asylum instead of an air wing."

Taylor sipped his beer. "I get tired of seeing things done for no good reason. I don't mean everything, but it's just that nothing is more depressing to me than to see a bunch of people make everything that happens seem like it's the pivotal event in world history. Pretty soon you run out of sweat."

"What do you mean?"

Taylor leaned back in his chair. "Everything that comes down the pike is treated with equal gravity. Doesn't matter at all if everyone knows it's bullshit or a dumb idea or just a pain-in-the-ass visit from some dumb-ass congressman. The captain has to get on the 1MC and announce that we'll need a special effort so we'll look good. That makes everybody do a whole lot of extra crap instead of what they should be doing, which is fighting a small war."

"For example?"

"Okay. How about that request we got two weeks ago about the number of sorties flown versus revisits to targets. All the squadron operations officers had to break down each sortie as to where it went, whether it was an initial strike or a revisit, and then put that up against the total sorties flown to date. Us Intell types had to get out all the bomb damage assessments and try to figure out percentage of hits per revisit. That took almost five days, and when it was done, all we got was a snide comment about how long it took. As I recall, we were in the middle of two straight weeks of twelve-on and twelve-off operations. What was really stupid about it was that all that information had been submitted already to several different offices in two or three different forms. The whole drill was complete bullshit and a massive waste of time."

"Why was it bullshit? Isn't it at least possible that all that stuff would be put to a good use?"

"It's possible, but the point is that there is no relation between the numbers we sent and the answer to the question. It seems to me that all they have to ask is how badly we're hurting the enemy. If we blew up every building and vehicle in Asia, it wouldn't mean a goddamn thing if the enemy still had the troops and the bullets and the will to keep on fighting. You can't put a number on that stuff. He either throws in the towel, in which case we win, or he doesn't, in which case we lose. That doesn't seem to be all that difficult a concept to me.

"It's exactly the same with the sortie count. If we launch more sorties than the next carrier, we are therefore a better ship and air wing and therefore you guys, the squadron Skippers and CAG and the captain, are doing a better job, so you're better than your peers. That's all bullshit."

Scott was initially angry with Taylor for his comments about squadron C.O.'s but held back long enough to realize that there was some truth to it. He sipped his beer and signaled a waitress for another round.

"Okay. What do you suggest to fix the problem?"

"Somebody has got to have the balls to stand up and tell them that it's fucked up."

"Like who, for example?"

Taylor opened his mouth and closed it. He started to speak and then stopped.

Scott looked at him evenly. "It's a hell of a lot easier to criticize the system than it is to fix it, isn't it, sport."

Taylor nodded slowly and sipped his beer. He'd been so busy being pissed off at the system that he hadn't even started looking for a specific solution.

"All right, Nick. What do you suggest we C.O.'s do about it? How can we change the system?"

Taylor looked at Scott for a moment. It was not that they were the problem, nor was it CAGs or even the admirals who ran the task force. It was a whole lot bigger than that.

"I don't know, Skipper. I'm just afraid that if we don't start standing up to it, the whole thing will stick like my mom used to warn me about my face when I made an ugly one. You know, 'You'll be sorry when your face sticks like that.' "

He sighed. "It just bothers me that people really begin to lose sight of the whole purpose of things. Kind of like my ex-C.O. did."

Scott smiled. "Nick, you have pissed me off on a regular basis for a long time now, but I think I'm beginning to understand where you're coming from a little better. I doubt if I'll ever agree with you much, but I do understand you a bit."

He stood up and smiled ruefully. "This may surprise you, but, unfortunately for me, on this particular point I agree with you completely. I've never been able to figure out who should fix it either. Ready to head back to the hotel?"

Taylor stood also. "You're right, it does surprise me. I'll keep working on you, Commander. There's obviously some hope for you yet. Maybe, once you're completely converted to the gospel according to Taylor, we can come up with a generic reporting form we can just plug some random numbers into. They'll never know the difference."

Chuckling, the two walked out of the bar toward the lobby to call a cab, silently agreeing that it was far too nice a day to waste tilting at windmills.

19

Monday, January 22, 1968

Shortly after noon the next day Dick Averitt surveyed the group of pilots gathered in front of him. He was standing against the wall in one of the small meeting rooms in the hotel, idly rolling a piece of chalk in his hand as he would a pair of dice. The group of pilots were in various states of disrepair, some in imminent danger of bleeding to death from the eyes, some about the same shade as the chalk he held in his hand, a few were "bright-eyed and bushy-tailed," as his father used to say. Most of them were sitting up fairly straight in their chairs around the tables covered with white linen cloths. The hotel had provided pots of coffee and cups which were now going fast.

It had been intended that Averitt give this briefing in the suite that VA-262 had as their Admin, but when word got around, flight crews from other squadrons had asked if they could sit in and it soon became a better idea to get the larger meeting room. The hotel manager, a precious British-sounding fellow with a porno star's pencil mustache, donated the room. It would have been empty anyway, and he marked up the price of the coffee by only six or seven hundred percent, which everyone thought was generous indeed.

The crowd, sitting pretty much in squadron groups, included nearly all the C.O.'s and even CAG Andrews himself. Some concern had been expressed about divulging classified information in a briefing like this, and a few had suggested that the whole thing be moved back aboard the *Shiloh*. But wiser heads, who were well aware attendance would be cut sharply if the J.O.'s were required to go back to the ship, put on their uniforms and risked being caught up in actual work when they should be on liberty; they promised that nothing classified would be let loose among the millions of Communist infiltrators and agents who everyone knew infested the hotel.

Averitt blandly told the worried few that he could give the entire briefing without violating security. He knew that almost everything he could say would be available in the press within days and the information would pretty much be out-of-date in a month anyway, so it really didn't matter. He had absolutely no intention of actually holding anything from these men who shared the same dangers and goals as he and his fellow marine aviators did. Furthermore, he was damned if he would sugar-coat anything or lie just to preserve some distant beancounter's idea of what should or should not be told to the men on the spot. So he had simply agreed and made the concerned officers feel better.

There was a small commotion in the back of the room as one of the fighter squadrons wheeled in a keg of beer, claiming that they were only protecting it from the dreaded beer pirates who were known to ransack rooms in Singapore hotels and make off with the occupants' supplies. Scott, sitting at a table near the front, turned and momentarily was glad that it was not guys from his squadron. He saw CAG summon Commander Tony Pilaggi, the other fighter squadron's C.O., and speak quietly to him. Pilaggi smiled wanly, nodded, and walked over to the group of young tigers. He thumbed them to a table and placed a paper cup over the pump, signifying that the bar was closed for the moment.

When everyone had found seats and the conversations started to die a little, Jim Hogan stood and walked to the front of the room. He put his thumb and forefinger in his mouth and whistled to get the attention of the last few talkers.

"Good afternoon, gents. Welcome to today's effort in continuing education. Our speaker is Major Dick Averitt of the United States Marine Corps." He pronounced it "corpse" and had to wait for the catcalls to stop.

"He's taking time from his R&R to do this, so you should be really respectful to him. You guys have to admit that you're not anywhere near as attractive as some people he could be talking to this morning. Dick is here to tell us a little bit about what is going on in the South and what we can do to help the grunts if we're called upon. Let him say his piece and then you can ask questions. Okay?"

He turned to the tall marine. "They're all yours."

Averitt grinned and walked over to the center of the room. "Good afternoon. I'm the Air Liaison Officer for the 29th Marine Regiment. In real life I'm an A-4 pilot, but the Corps has decided that we aviators should get some experience with the grunts whenever possible so, in their infinite wisdom, they select some of us for these unique positions of greater trust and confidence.

"They say that every marine is first and foremost a rifleman, but there are those of us who do not enjoy sitting in the weeds, smelling like we've been dead for a month, eating C-rats and burning leeches off our dicks. I'm terribly ashamed to admit that I fall in that group. I prefer getting out of trouble as fast as I got in, which is about six hundred knots. I have discovered that I have an uncontrollable affinity for roofs over my head, a club nearby, taking a dump without leaves tickling my ass, and the odd letter from home uninterrupted by incoming rounds. I am also fully aware that my fetish for creature comforts limits my chances of ever becoming the commandant of the Marine Corps."

He paused while the laughter died down, and he walked to the blackboard. "Our organization is pretty simple. At the regimental level we have the ALO, which is me, and under that we have an airedale lieutenant in each battalion, and a couple of trained enlisted troops in each company as forward air controllers. Usually, the ALO is a captain, but I got a special deal, probably because I am relatively junior or because I stood still while all the other volunteers took one step backward. Anyway, I get to go back to flying in a month or so, and somebody else will take my place for some professional broadening."

He paused, taking a sip of coffee from a paper cup, and began to draw a remarkably good map of the Indochina peninsula. "Here we have the various countries with which you are all familiar; here's Laos, here's Cambodia, and here's that land of milk and honey, North Vietnam."

He drew in South Vietnam and divided it up into four sections. "These are the different areas of responsibility which are called 'military regions,' all of them under the overall direction of MACV, or Military Assistance Command, Vietnam. That's actually over-simplified, but it's all you guys need for now.

"Anyway, here in the northern part of the country, right below the DMZ, or demilitarized zone, is the area called I-Corps." He pronounced it "eye-core" and erased the map he had drawn, immediately beginning another one, a sort of a blow-up of the northern part of South Vietnam.

"Here, on the coast, is Danang, which is usually your primary shore divert field. Around that we've got a whole bunch of satellite bases, Marble Mountain and Chu Lai, for example." He made small dots on the map as he named them and explained their purpose. He drew in the five different provinces and their capitals, including a brief but surprisingly thorough history of the ancient capital city of Hue, and its almost mystical importance for the Vietnamese people on both sides of the war.

Listening to Averitt's easy and often humorous delivery, Hogan was struck by the depth of knowledge the marine had about the entire war. He blended a history lecture with a tactical and strategic assessment and geography primer. His explanation of the Vietnamese culture, going back hundreds of years, and his political depiction of the leadership of the North was better than anything Hogan had ever heard. He looked around the room and found nothing but rapt attention in the expressions on the other listeners, including the senior types who had heard something like this many times over the past four years or so. Hogan had to admit to himself that he had not known even a third of what Averitt was so magically giving to the pilots of the air wing.

Hogan heard a subtle change in Averitt's voice and sat up as the marine erased his map and began to draw a fresh one. It appeared to be the very westernmost portion of the I-Corps area.

"This is where we have one of our regiments placed to block the infiltration and supply routes from the North. It's called the Khe Sanh Combat Base, but it's really a system of units holding high ground. I was there about ten days ago, briefly, for a planning conference, and believe me, it's no garden spot. The main base itself is here, and the town of Khe Sanh is here, a little way to the south. We've just extended the runway with metal matting, which is sort of a portable runway surfacing, easily repaired or replaced. You can see that Highway 9 runs along here from east to west, so the base sits right next to the main drag."

He drew several small shapes off to the north and west of the main base. "These are some of the hills in the area that we have marines on. When I left, it was getting pretty dangerous to move men and supplies along on the ground, so most of the resupply is by helo. The main plan from the poohbahs down in Saigon, as far as there is one, is that this will be a set-piece battle instead of one of maneuver. The generals want to pin the gomer in one place and kick his ass. But I don't mind telling you that being in a place like Khe Sanh, in the middle of the enemy, is sort of like sitting in a well while somebody drops rocks on your head. Those guys may be holding the enemy in one place, but the gomers also have the advantage of being able to shoot at them with mortars, recoilless rifles, and heavy artillery from everywhere, even as far away as Laos in the west here. Except when we get real lucky with air strikes, there's not much we can do about the guns in Laos, since we're not allowed to go in there and get 'em.

"The other two big problems with this are that the entire complex and the marines in it are surrounded by main force regular North Vietnamese Army units and that the enemy has an easy retreat north back across the DMZ and west back into Laos."

Averitt placed the stub of his chalk down on the little ledge under the blackboard and tried unsuccessfully to rub the white dust off his hands. He frowned momentarily and then looked back at his audience. "That's a quick and dirty look at what's going on in there. I'm not really too familiar with much of the situation farther south, but I'll try to answer your questions. Okay?"

The room was silent for a long half-minute. Averitt was afraid that he'd been one of those guys whose lectures numb the mind to such an extent that the listener is completely unable to frame a coherent thought, let alone an intelligent question. He needn't have been concerned. Rarely had anyone in the room had a lecture nearly as good or as thorough. What was taking so long was that the listeners were trying to figure out which question they wanted to ask first.

Nick Taylor raised his hand. "I read somewhere that there's been a big decrease in the number of contacts with the Viet Cong recently. Is that true?"

"Yup. There's two schools of thought among the different commands on that. Some are saying that it proves that we have the V.C. on the run and we've hurt them badly enough that they need to be more selective in their operations. The other thought is that they have just pulled back to prepare for something really big in the next few weeks. Personally, I go with the second group. I think the little fuckers are setting us up, and whatever it's gonna be, it'll be nasty. But you guys have been hitting the Trail. Have you seen much reduction in available targets?"

Averitt looked around the room as the pilots thought that one over. They all knew that even though they had been bombing the hell out of the various supply routes from North Vietnam into the South down through Laos, known collectively as the Ho Chi Minh Trail, there had been little or no reduction in the flow of trucks, and the road repair efforts, especially around the famed Mu Gia Pass, had not slowed at all.

Taylor answered for them all. "Out on the ship, we still get lots of targets around that whole area. Most missions come back with some reports of secondary explosions. The BDA we get from the forward air controllers is significant."

Another pilot from the A-6 squadron stood. "Major, in a newspaper I was reading yesterday, one of the articles compared the marine base at Khe Sanh to a place called Dien Bien Phu. He made a pretty good case for the similarity. What do you guys think about that?"

Averitt smiled. "We've heard nothing but that from the press ourselves. For those of you who don't know, the French got themselves surrounded in a valley in western North Vietnam called Dien Bien Phu back in 1954. They lost, and that led to the defeat of their whole war effort up there. The differences as they were explained to me are that we have superior air power both from land- and carrier-based tactical air and from the helo resupply effort. We also have a great deal of fire support from these Army

169

fire bases out to the east." He drew in several other symbols in the area several miles from Khe Sanh. "I personally don't think that the similarity is anything other than superficial, but we shall see."

The questions went on for nearly another hour, with Averitt answering each one of them. Hogan was glad to see that he never once hid behind the standard "classified" shield when he was confronted with a difficult question. When the pilots were through with their questions, the mood in the room was thoughtful, and it was obvious that everyone had gained a much richer feel for where all the pieces fit in the jigsaw-puzzle war.

CAG Andrews stood and profusely thanked Averitt for his time and for the information he'd given. He turned to the room and saw that the pilots had reverted a little into their natural military mood even though they were sitting ashore in a hotel in civilian clothes. Few of them were still struggling with hangovers, since the first-day craziness had worn off, and even those few looked thoughtful. They were waiting patiently but not particularly eagerly for dismissal. Andrews noticed the keg in the back of the room.

"It was extremely thoughtful of the guys from Fighting 148, the world-famous Black Lions, to bring their own personal keg for us to share. I think it was one of the most unselfish acts I've seen in the past, oh, twelve or thirteen minutes. Speaking as a fellow fighter pilot, I must say that their amazing generosity fills my heart with pride. Bar's open." He ignored the stricken looks of some of Pilaggi's young pilots and, amid cheers from the others, walked to the keg, drawing a beer into a large coffee cup. The rest of the audience gathered around, waiting their turn at the tap.

Hogan laughed as Averitt came down and stood next to him. "That'll teach 'em to get cute. They'll never get their keg out of here with anything left in it."

Averitt chuckled. "Yeah, but they'll have a replacement in five minutes. Come on, I could use something stronger. Let's hit the bar."

In the bar the two found a table as far from the jukebox as possible and ordered a couple of Jack Daniel's and water apiece, figuring that it would be a while before the listless waitress got around to noticing them again.

When the drinks arrived, Hogan took a long pull and lit up a

170

Marlboro before speaking. "Nicely done, partner. I think our guys got a lot out of that."

Averitt nodded, but before he could speak, CAG Andrews walked up and sat down, signaling the waitress over. No one spoke as they watched her ooze her way over and disinterestedly take his order. Andrews shook his head. "Can you imagine being married to that? You'd starve while she got the roast out of the oven."

He looked at Averitt. "Good brief, Dick. I must say I'm glad as hell I'm not one of those guys sitting on one of those hilltops at Khe Sanh."

"Me too. In my job I really don't have to go out in the weeds that much. I freely admit that every time I've had to go it has scared me shitless from start to finish. I feel completely defenseless with just a flak jacket and an M-16."

Hogan was struck by the abrupt change in mood when Averitt spoke of going out in the bush. He changed the subject. "Do you guys figure that you're going to need the Navy for close air support if the gomers try to take Khe Sanh?"

"My friend, if they try to overrun the place, we're gonna need everything we can get our hands on. I didn't tell you guys really how far those grunts are hanging out. The gomers have built up their forces over the past weeks so that there are at least four divisions of enemy regulars out there, and all we've got is a little more than one regiment of marines and a few ARVNs, so it's about forty thousand to six thousand. Like the man said, it could wind up to be 'hell in a very small place.' I had to go there for a planning session and I hope I don't have to go back."

"Is it possible that you might?"

"Yeah. It's amazing what good deals come your way when folks figure out you know what you're doing."

He looked around the room, as if deliberately seeing something else to talk about. "But enough of this stuff. What are we doing tonight?"

Hogan grinned. "Well, I've got another date with the Blonde. But the good news is that she has a friend who is stuck way out here in the Far East and doesn't know anybody. We have reservations for four down at The British Club. 'We' includes you, jarhead."

The three continued for another half-hour, talking easily about the myriad things that fliers always talk about. From women to new aircraft to the age-old argument about who was better, fighter pilots or the rest of the underprivileged masses, which, of course, included the attack types.

The others from the air wing began to drift in, having polished off the keg in the other room, and the bar took on all the aspects of a stateside happy hour. Even the waitress began to move about more quickly. She almost got all the way out of first gear.

It was almost six that evening when the piano races began, but by that time Hogan, Averitt, and Andrews had wisely left the room.

Jim Hogan sat at the small round table in the pseudo-Hawaiian bar and watched the pseudo-Hawaiian waitress bring the flaming bowl of rum and floating slices of fruit over to the table next to his, which was occupied by four of the pilots from Hogan's squadron. The Blonde sat next to him with Dick Averitt on her other side. Averitt's date, a beautiful Eurasian woman named Sandra Worth, watched with fascination from her chair between Hogan and Averitt.

The Blonde, who really did have a name, Moira Donald, turned to him and asked if they could order one like that. She had had a couple of the drinks known as Sufferin' Bastards and was now feeling no pain at all. Hogan was regretting that he'd followed Sandra's suggestion that they try this new place for an after-dinner drink which had turned into two rounds and was probably going to get out of hand if they ordered one of those massive four-straw bowls of flaming rum.

The waitress bowed ceremonially as she stood at the edge of the other table, waiting for the pseudo-Hawaiian native barman to cease his obligatory gong solo in the corner. Every time anyone in the place ordered one of these special drinks, the same drill was repeated, complete with flames. Hogan sincerely hoped that the small bluish fire in the bowl would be confined there and not spill over and catch on to the waitress's pseudo-Hawaiian grass skirt. On the other hand, if that happened, the young Americans who were sitting at the table would probably climb all over each other, coming to her rescue.

Hogan turned to Moira and shook his head. "One of those monsters would likely kill us all."

She put her hand on Hogan's shoulder and looked at him with her slightly out-of-focus but still knee-watering blue eyes. "It looks fun. With four of us working on it, it wouldn't do much harm. Please."

Hogan nearly gave in when Sandra spoke up. "Moira, I think I've had nearly enough to drink and so have you. I am not going to touch one of those things. If you must have another, stick to what you already have. Don't mix your drinks."

Moira sighed theatrically and put her chin in her hand, elbow on the table. It had been a wonderful evening. For all four of them the dinner had been superb and, for Moira especially, the walk down the darkened city streets had been full of more laughter and fun than she could remember in a long time. She really liked this big, laughing American that she was with, and Sandra was somewhat taken with his marine friend too. She realized that she was in danger of getting herself really "bombed," as Hogan called it, and didn't want to look foolish in his eyes. Sandra was right.

The four pilots at the table next to them were getting a bit loud as they tasted the huge drink in front of them and she was beginning to feel that it was time to go. She looked back at Hogan and smiled. "You're right. That would put me well over the top. I think I'll just finish this one."

She put her hand on Hogan's and asked him quietly, almost shyly, if he wanted to leave now. The two of them could have a cup of coffee at her apartment.

Hogan looked into her flashing eyes, saw the invitation there, and simply nodded. Moira leaned across him and spoke quietly to Sandra, who blushed and nodded, turning to Averitt.

Moira stood, pulling Hogan up with her. "Well, we're off. It really has been quite fun and I hope we can do it again." She extended her hand to Averitt, who half stood and took it. "Good night, Dick. It was nice to meet you."

She smiled at Sandra and said that she'd see her tomorrow. Pulling Hogan by the hand, she stepped away from the table.

At the next table the pilots from Hogan's squadron saw them preparing to leave and began to tease him loudly. They were sitting there with no dates while their C.O. was leaving with a stunning lady.

They caused a bit of commotion and all the other patrons turned to watch and listen to the humorous jibes.

Moira turned to them and, still holding Hogan's hand, smiled like a cat about to eat the canary. Just as she began to speak in a voice a little louder than normal, there happened one of those silences when all conversations in a place reach a pause simultaneously so that her volume made her seem to be making an announcement instead of a simple statement.

"Say anything you wish, gentlemen. But I'm willing to wager that in twenty minutes, Jim here's going to be having far more fun than any of you will have this evening."

The four young men looked open-mouthed at each other as Hogan, equally stunned, was pulled gently out of the room by the Blonde. The four looked back at the pair as they strode from the room, one leading determinedly, the other, the one with the fire-engine-red neck and ears, looking straight ahead as he followed. The room was silent for quite a few seconds as the patrons digested what they'd just heard. Several patrons allowed their imaginations to run free over what the Blonde had just promised.

For Hogan, Moira's pronouncement turned out be accurate, but it was understated by miles.

20

Tuesday, January 23, 1968

Standing in the squadron ready room, Nick Taylor stared at the "Op-Immediate" message form in his hand and shook his head. He read it again slowly and then looked up into the tired eyes of Lieutenant Commander Sam Butler, the Air Wing Duty Officer who was from the RA-5C Vigilante reconnaissance squadron.

"Holy shit!" he breathed. Butler thought that that pretty accurately summed up his own reaction.

The message was curt and abrupt, as were most naval messages whose drafters always seemed to be trying for the title of who could put the most information into the fewest words. After the formatted beginning and the nearly two-page list of addresses, it simply summarized the events of the morning and untypically gave direction to most of those addressees.

Earlier that morning, a group of North Korean naval vessels had fired upon, boarded, and captured the USS *Pueblo*, an underarmed and essentially defenseless surveillance ship keeping station well outside Korean territorial waters. The story was a bit sketchy but, in the Navy, much of what would need to be spelled out for, say, a newspaper reader was already well understood. Taylor already knew about the legal implications of what could easily be considered an act of piracy or an act of war, depending upon the viewpoint. He was well aware of how badly things must have gone for the captain and crew of the *Pueblo* for them to surrender their ship on the high seas. He was also well aware of what lay in store for the crew when they were placed in the type of "confinement" so favored by the North Koreans.

The message went on to say that the USS *Enterprise*, a nuclear-powered carrier, was being diverted from Japan to the coast of North Korea in a show of force. The *Ranger*, another carrier presently on the line off North Vietnam, was being sent to join the *Enterprise*.

For the men of the *Shiloh*, it meant that they were being called from Singapore to go back to Yankee Station to replace the *Ranger*. Taylor had seen an emergency recall once before and knew that the next few hours were going to be an absolute zoo, trying to round up all the sailors and officers who were scattered throughout the port city. If things went true to form, there would be a bunch of stragglers and men who were nowhere near the addresses they had left with their units. There were going to be a bunch of musters taken, all of which would be inaccurate and all of which would further shorten the tempers of everyone in the chain of command who had any responsibility for the men at all.

The sheer logistical problem of rounding everybody up and getting them back aboard and then trying to collect the stragglers and fly them out to the ship after she had left port was going to tax everybody aboard. Unfortunately, as one of the Shore Patrol Officers, most of the hassle was going to fall squarely on Taylor's shoulders. He was suddenly unsure whether the good deal he had enjoyed in that job over the whole cruise was going to be worth what he was going to go through for the next few hours.

What Taylor regretted most was coming back aboard that morning to get some fresh underwear and then stopping in the ready room for a goddamn cup of coffee. Butler had caught him there and, since Taylor was the senior man aboard from VA-262, he had made him responsible for getting the squadron recall going. There were seven more squadrons to notify, and he was glad to have Taylor take some of the responsibility off his shoulders.

"Okay. We'll get started. I've got to go ashore and help out with the shore patrol, but I'll get somebody moving on this."

Butler nodded and headed for the door. "The ship says that they expect to get under way by 1900. That gives us about nine hours to round everybody up. Any bets?"

Taylor smiled. "Yeah. I'll give you seven to three against."

Butler shook his head as he left the room. "No chance. That'd be a sucker bet."

Taylor walked over to the squadron duty desk and asked the young sailor who was sitting there, waiting to answer the telephone, where his boss was.

"I believe he's down in the wardroom, Lieutenant."

"Would you please go find him? I'll answer the telephones while you're gone, but I need you to hurry it up. Tell him that lunch can wait; we have a problem."

An hour later Nick Taylor walked into the Admin in the hotel. He found several J.O.'s packing their gear and trying to figure out what to do with the extra supplies of liquor they had laid in. It was against regulations to have it aboard ship, and there was no way they could drink it all. It was decided that they would each have a drink while they discussed the problem. One of the newer guys asked whether they should be drinking, since they were supposed to get back to the ship as soon as possible.

The more senior lieutenants explained patiently that there was no specific requirement for sobriety on arrival—there was simply a requirement for arrival. When the young man looked doubtful, they asked Taylor about the recall.

He grinned as he stuffed some clothes in a bag for the squadron duty officer who was now marooned aboard the *Shiloh*. "There was absolutely nothing specified in the message about what condition you had to be in when you got back. There is also no prohibition whatsoever about carrying booze aboard internally."

That seemed to make sense, so somebody ran down the hall to the ice machine. Taylor looked around the room. "Anybody seen the Skipper or the X.O.?"

"The X.O.'s around here somewhere, but as for the Skipper, not since last night. He was out with the Blonde and left that Hawaiian place with her. That's the last we saw of him." Several nudges and grins passed among the pilots.

"He hasn't been back?"

More grins. "Nope. All his stuff's over there in a corner. Hasn't been touched since last night."

Taylor pointed to two of the more senior pilots. "Once you get your gear packed up, you guys try and track him down. CAG won't be happy if the Skipper misses his first departure since he took over."

"I'll take care of the Skipper, Nick. You two keep doing what you need to."

Taylor turned to the voice which belonged to the new X.O., Terry White, who looked just a little the worse for wear. White moved over to the low dresser that served as a makeshift bar for the Admin. He poured an inch of scotch in a glass and drank half of it, shivering as it went down.

"Hair of the dog. I think I'd have to get better to die. What's up, Nick?"

Taylor filled him in on as much of the events of the morning as he could, glad to have somebody in a position of responsibility to turn the problem over to. A half-speed Terry White was far better than one of the lieutenants operating at full power. Besides, Taylor himself had to hustle back to Shore Patrol Headquarters and help with the massive problem of rounding up 1500 sailors instead of just the few men from VA-262 who were still ashore. It seemed from the muster taken back aboard the ship that most of the men from the squadron had run low on money or had been partied out and so had stayed on the ship the previous night.

As Taylor finished the story, White refilled his glass, only this time he put in a quarter-inch of scotch and filled the rest of the glass with water. "Okay, you get going. I'll get these guys out of here and track down the Skipper."

White left the room and headed down the hall for Dick Averitt's room. If anyone could help find Hogan, it would be Averitt.

Averitt answered White's knock almost instantly. He had shaving cream on one side of his face and his razor in his hand.

"C'mon in, Terry. Have you heard what happened this morning? About the *Pueblo*? It was just on the radio." Averitt pointed to the box on the nightstand with his razor hand.

"Yeah. We've been recalled to the ship. We're supposed to leave port this evening and head back Up North. Do you know where Jim Hogan is?"

Averitt nodded. "Yeah. I think I can find him. Let me finish shaving and I'll make a couple of calls." He stepped back into the bathroom as White went over to the window and looked out over the city and the huge gray shape of the *Shiloh* almost out of view to the far left of the window.

He was thinking about all the small things that would need to be done to get the squadron again ready to fight an air war, when he heard Averitt's voice behind him.

He was speaking to a woman, conveying both deep interest in her and a sort of professional demeanor in trying to find Hogan, both in the same sentence. White felt he was intruding and stepped through the sliding glass door onto the balcony so as not to eavesdrop on Averitt.

In a minute or two he heard Averitt call him and went back inside. The tall marine handed him a slip of paper. "Jim and I were out with the Blonde and one of her friends last night. I just called the one I was with and she gave me that phone number and address. The Blonde called in sick this morning but Sandra says that she sounded fine. She figures that you'll be able to catch them there still. It's the Blonde's home number." He grinned.

White grinned back as he went over and picked up the telephone. He sat on the bed and sipped slowly on his drink as he waited for the hotel operator to place the call.

It was nearly a minute later when he heard the telephone answered on the other end and a sleepy female voice come on the line.

"Good morning, ma'am. Sorry to bother you, but I'm Commander Terry White from the *Shiloh* and I'm looking for Commander Hogan. Is he there?"

Seconds later White heard Hogan's voice on the other end. "Hello?"

"Mornin', Skipper. This is Terry. I'm sorry to disturb you, but we've just been recalled. The ship's going to get under way this evening. I can't say much more, but if you turn on a radio, you'll find out why. I've got all your gear packed up and we're closing down the Admin, so all you have to do is get to Fleet Landing. The last boat is supposed to leave at 1830. There'll be a meeting for all C.O.'s in CAG Office at 1930. I can take care of everything

178

for now, so why don't you catch that last boat and I'll see you back aboard?"

Averitt watched White smile a little as he listened for a few seconds. He shook his head as he continued speaking. "No, sir. We've got it all squared away. There's not a goddamn thing you can do right now, so keep on keepin' on and I'll see you back aboard. It's my chance to shine. Hell, if I do it all right, they'll make me CNO next week."

White listened for a couple of seconds, laughed, and hung up. He looked up at Averitt. "I hope he doesn't rush right back to the ship. That would be a waste of a beautiful day, but he probably will. He's one of those noble types who won't have his men working while he doesn't. I'd hate to see him miss out on a day with the Blonde."

"Me too." Averitt glanced at the glass in White's hand. "Do you guys have any more of that scotch down there? I'm out."

White led the way out the door. "I suppose we could scare some up for a poor dumb and lost marine."

Hogan hung up the telephone and swung his legs off the bed. He reached for his pants and slipped them on as he headed for the kitchen, where Moira was banging pots and pans around, beginning to fix breakfast.

Hogan walked up behind her and slipped his arms around her waist. She shoved her rear end against him, playfully pushing him away. "Stand back, sailor, if you want something to eat."

Hogan grinned and began searching through the cabinets for a couple of cups for the coffee which she already had perking merrily. Moira glanced at his back as he reached for the cups.

"Was that call trouble?"

Hogan put the cups down on the counter and turned to face her. "I'm afraid so. We've all been recalled to the ship. Apparently, she's getting under way tonight. Do you have a radio?"

Moira nodded and gestured with her chin to a corner of the kitchen.

Hogan moved over and switched it on. It was already tuned to the BBC World Service, and the sounds of two men discussing the effects of oil exploration in the North Sea on the wildlife on the north coast of Scotland filled the room. One of the voices sounded as excited as if he were calling a horse race and kept calling the other, apparently the host, "Reggie." Moira laughed.

179

"His name is really Reginald and he is veddy propah. It's probably killing him that he's being called Reggie, but that's the price of fame, I suppose." She looked up at the wall clock. "The news should be on in a couple of minutes, if that's what you're looking for."

Hogan poured the coffee and sat at the small table. He watched Moira move about the kitchen, completely taken with her grace. The sound of the chimes striking the hour on the radio brought him back to the present.

He stared at the radio as the BBC told him of the capture of the *Pueblo* and the reaction of the American government. He was not really surprised that few countries had issued statements condemning the action and that the predictable ones—China, Cuba, the Soviets—praised the tiny country of North Korea for standing up to good old American imperialism. There was no mention of military response and the details were still sketchy. It was about what he had expected.

He looked up as Moira placed the plate of ham and eggs in front of him and sat at the opposite end of the table. She began to eat, staring at Hogan with interest.

"That's why you have to leave?"

"Yes. There should be a lot of running around and screaming and yelling in Washington about now. They probably have no idea what to do, but moving forces around will send the proper signals while everybody tries to decide on some action."

"Will you have to attack them?" Moira's concern was evident in her wide eyes and quiet tone. She had little experience with military men and their profession.

"No. At least, I don't think so. The Koreans have about a thousand fighters, and we could probably only get ninety or so in the air to make the attack. Even if we were the best pilots on earth we couldn't survive long at ten-to-one odds."

He shook his head as if rejecting the idea. "Besides, Moira, we don't have the resources available to fight two wars at the same time."

Moira smiled a little as she went back to her plate. Even though she and Hogan had really only just met, she was beginning to feel strongly about him. She knew it was silly for her to consider flying against North Korea dangerous while considering what he did every day, flying against North Vietnam, safer.

She looked at Hogan, who was eating his breakfast silently, staring at a point somewhere in the middle of the table. He was with her physically, but his mind and heart were about four miles away, aboard the *Shiloh*. Moira was, like nearly all women, able to see through a man to his very heart, understanding the simpler motivations and reactions and drives that the male of the species always believed were well disguised and impossible for anyone else to read.

With a small smile she watched him eat mechanically, and when he was done she took his plate. Hogan was startled out of his reverie and blushed like a child caught daydreaming in class. She took his plate over to the sink and began to clean up the room. Brushing a stray strand of blond hair from her forehead, she spoke almost gaily.

"Well, we'd better get you back to your ship."

Hogan was torn between his promise to her that they'd have lunch and a walking tour of the open-air market area of Singapore and his responsibility to his squadron. He knew that White would get everything squared away and his presence would be superfluous to the squadron preparations. He remembered the days when he had been a J.O. and how much he had resented the C.O. coming down and looking over his shoulder while he was trying to do his job. He looked up at Moira, who was now standing next to the sink, looking at him evenly.

She spoke with more gaiety than she felt. "You'll be a complete bore all day because you'll be thinking about your men and your job. Besides, you're not the type to leave your responsibility to other people. Let me take a shower and put on my face and I'll drive you up."

Hogan gave her a sheepish smile. "You're right. I was trying to figure out how to apologize for having to break our date. Can I use your phone? I need to call Dick Averitt back and explain."

Moira put the dishtowel on the hook and headed into the bedroom to pick out some clothes. Hogan followed and sat on the edge of the bed, reaching for the phone. "I'm afraid that I'm going to have to go back looking pretty grubby since my guys have probably already taken my gear back to the ship."

Moira paused to give him a quick kiss as she headed for the bathroom. "I think you look wonderful for a man who has just gotten up. If you can look that good in the morning, you're all right with me."

Hogan grinned at her retreating back. That was a compliment he'd never received before. He kind of liked it.

Part Three

21
Wednesday, January 24, 1968

★ The little general sat in the cave just a few miles south of the demilitarized zone and only a few dozen miles south of the province of his birth and watched the morning mist drift by. His aides came and went, consulting each other and the large relief map on the crude table, issuing orders to the various units that lurked throughout the highlands the Americans called I Corps. There were well over four divisions of his troops lurking out there and surrounding the heights which the Americans were trying to hold with less than a tenth of those numbers. The general stayed aloof from the bustle, both remembering his triumph at Dien Bien Phu fourteen difficult years before and running through his plan for the triumph to come here.

The general had had a long, hard road getting to this place. He had been one of the early revolutionaries in Vietnam, and after years of fighting first the colonial French, then the Japanese, the French again, and now the Americans, he was still sitting in a cold and damp cave far from his family while his enemies in Hanoi plotted and schemed to bring him down once more. They had engineered his several falls from grace, and each time his devotion to the cause and his professional competence had brought him back. From next to nothing he had created the Army itself and its poor little brother, the insurgent force known as the Viet Cong.

The divisions he had surrounded the heights with were all from the regular Army, and in six days, during the customary Tet holiday cease-fire, the insurgents would rise across the whole of the South and strike dozens and scores of targets. While the American eyes were fixed on the heights of Khe Sanh, the unanticipated

185

uprising would galvanize the population of the South and finally crush both the Americans and their puppet regime.

He knew that there was no possibility that the Americans would allow the marines at Khe Sanh to simply be overwhelmed by his forces. So they would rush to reinforce and take the pressure off. The little general knew that his counterpart in Saigon had been praying for a chance to have a set-piece battle and considered Khe Sanh his chance. But, just as at Dien Bien Phu all those years before, his artillery and the heart of his troops would ultimately force the marines to either surrender or try to break out. No matter what they tried, he had them.

The general was not concerned about the advances in technology in the intervening years. Back then his troops had manhandled artillery into the high ground surrounding the French and pounded them into surrender. The French paradrops of supplies had failed, and no attempt at relieving the besieged men had succeeded. The French air power was equally useless in that it never could carry enough bombs to do any real damage to the general's men. The airplanes had been little more than an annoyance.

Here he had heavy artillery positioned in Laos which could not be attacked by the American ground forces and only rarely fell victim to air attack. He also had heavy guns in North Vietnam itself which could easily fire across the DMZ and into Khe Sanh. He had hundreds of heavy and light mortars which would pound the Americans into the very hills they sought so hard to hold.

The American aircraft would never be able to sustain air cover over Khe Sanh when the uprising began. They would be spread too thin after the planned attacks on their bases and even the weather itself would help the general's men, preventing the Americans from even attempting it most of the time. Even those maniacs in North Korea were helping by diverting two aircraft carriers to their own shores.

The general got stiffly to his feet, smiling a little to himself. It was all going according to plan. Everything had been anticipated and, if he and his men stuck to that plan completely, there was no chance of defeat.

And when the uprising of the population in the South, led by the cadre of forces he had created and trained over the past years, happened next week, again according to plan, the corrupt regime would collapse into chaos. The Americans would be pushed into the sea. Once again a smaller country would make them look like fools.

The general walked to the entrance to the cave and looked out into the gray mist which was beginning to thin even more. He could hear the concussions of his heavy guns firing in the distance from both behind him to the north and from his right, to the west. The concussions from their shell bursts all came from one direction, directly to his south. In the heavy and nearly motionless air he could hear the faint thumps as mortar rounds detonated within the American perimeter. But the mortars themselves were too far forward for him to hear them firing.

It was another morning in the final battle of liberation. It would not be long before the war was won.

He reached for the cup of tea an aide had brewed for him.

And when I've won, he thought, I will deal with my enemies in Hanoi as they heave dealt with me. He realized abruptly that he had far more respect for his enemies on the battlefield than for those in the offices and meeting rooms in his homeland in the North.

22

Friday, January 26, 1968

Major Dick Averitt jumped down from the back of the C-130 Hercules transport into the big aircraft's propwash and ran as hard as he could diagonally across the runway toward a group of holes and trenches dug in the rich red soil of Khe Sanh Combat Base. He threw his bag into one of the holes and dove in after it. He was trying to disengage himself from the bag and his rifle when somebody landed on his back.

Averitt struggled to get the legs and bag of the newcomer off and sort of sat up.

"Jesus Christ! Watch it."

He looked over and saw the pale face of an enlisted marine against the far side of the hole, a kid who couldn't have been more than eighteen. His fatigues were new looking and his rifle sling was as stiff as if it had just come out of the box. The marine looked at Averitt and saw the black embroidered oak leaf on his collar point.

"Oh, shit. I'm sorry, sir, but they said to find a hole and get down. I'll move." He began to gather himself to jump out of the hole and find another.

Averitt grabbed him and pulled him down again. "Stay down. There's mortars incoming. They always shoot at the airplanes here. That's why they just dropped the ramp and kept moving."

Over the whining of the aircraft engines and the cries of "incoming" from the marines nearby, Averitt heard several *car-rumps* as the North Vietnamese began trying to hit the Hercules which was now accelerating away on its takeoff roll. He looked over the rim of the hole and saw several tall clouds of dirt and smoke erupt behind the 130. The enemy mortarmen adjusted their aim but were too slow to catch the big transport as it lifted its nose and roared by barely ten feet overhead. Several more rounds landed dejectedly on the edge of the runway, and Averitt ducked again until he was sure that the hot shards of steel were through searching for an American to kill.

When it was apparent that the NVA had given it up until the next resupply aircraft came in, he climbed out of the hole and asked a passing marine where the regimental command post was. The marine wordlessly pointed to a low bunker about two hundred yards away and walked off without a backward glance. Averitt was nearly overpowered by the body odor from the man and abruptly realized how far he was from the relative comforts of his old command. It was obvious that the man didn't smell like that by choice—in this place, there was going to be no such thing as a shower for quite some time to come.

Averitt looked around and spotted what had once been a jeep moving past, driven by another extremely un-sharp-looking marine. He flagged him down and asked for a ride to regiment. The marine sort of smiled and indicated the passenger seat with his thumb. Averitt heaved his bag in the back and climbed into the ripped seat, noticing that there were several deep score marks and dents where pieces of shrapnel had hit the jeep.

The driver showed no inclination to talk, so Averitt passed the few minutes it took getting over to the bunker by looking around at his temporary new home. It looked like somebody had picked the entire hill up a mile or so in the air and then just dropped it. It had a crumpled look. Everywhere were shell holes and flat-topped bunkers piled with sandbags. Around the perimeter were trenches in which he could occasionally see helmeted heads moving carefully along. Most of the men who were moving about in the open walked with a characteristic hunched posture as if they were walking in a heavy rainstorm and seemed to pick their route so as to stay as close as possible to some hole or trench, where they could dive in at the first sign of danger. The gray clouds overhead diffused the light, giving both terrain and human features an odd shadowlessness. As far as Averitt could tell, there were only two primary colors here, the rusty-looking red of the soil and the desultory background green of the surrounding hills and forests.

It's odd, he thought, both colors appeared to mix in the marines besieged here. The marines were all covered with dirt, turning them a halfway brown and making them seem to have been created from the earth itself.

As the driver slowed from his already creeping pace at the entrance to the CP, he looked at Averitt and smiled a little. "Be sure to watch where you walk around here, sir. The gomers hit the ammo dump a couple of days ago and it blew up for quite a while. There's live rounds all over the place around here. The EOD guys have been cleaning it up, but you never know."

Averitt thanked him as he pulled his bag out of the back of the jeep. The marine drove away, leaving Averitt standing outside the sandbagged entrance to the CP and looked around the area for unexploded rounds. He didn't envy the explosive ordnance disposal types because, in that business, one false move often meant a loud and messy death. Averitt's personal plan for disposing of live explosives was to lie down about two hundred yards away and shoot at them with a rifle. Either that or head for the bar and let the EOD guys take the chances. Shaking his head, he headed for the L-shaped entryway, laid out so as to minimize the chances of enemy artillery or rocket fire going straight in the door.

Inside, there was a relatively large group of men doing all the things one would expect, making the place look very much like the command post scenes in all the war movies except that the

189

Richards, Widmark and Boone, had apparently taken this war off. Banks of radios and field telephones stood against one wall, manned by marines only slightly cleaner than their fellows outside. There were the obligatory charts and maps on the rough tables being pored over by groups of officers.

Several marines looked up from what they were doing at Averitt and, after making a quick judgment that if he had anything to do with them, they'd find out at the proper time, went back to their jobs. One burly marine, about five ten both in height and across the chest and looking both fierce and friendly, crossed the room and approached Averitt. He stuck out a hand.

"You look lost, so you must be our new ALO. I'm Sergeant Major Gorton. We heard you might be coming in today. Sorry nobody met you, but the schedules are just a little bit spotty and we don't really have your normal air terminal here. Did you have any trouble?"

Averitt dropped his bag to the plank floor. "Nope, aside from a twenty-one-mortar salute and a young marine trying to use me for a trampoline. Does everybody get noticed like that?"

Gorton grinned. "Naw. You're only a major. If you'd been a sergeant or a captain, they'd have greeted you with the heavy artillery. They don't shoot at second lieutenants or generals at all, since they figure they can do more damage to us alive and unharmed than an entire company of NVA sappers."

Averitt chuckled. He wondered idly what Gorton would have done if he had taken offense at the crack about officers. Probably couldn't care less, he thought. One doesn't get to be a regimental sergeant major without being far more competent than one's peers. Having reached the absolute pinnacle of the enlisted ranks, men like Gorton were treated as having almost equal status with the regimental commander himself and with at least equal respect. Many of these men are offered commissions, and it is an agonizing decision for them whether to accept the loss of status that comes with the commission.

In every officer's experience there is a painful memory of the one time he'd taken on a man like Gorton in an attempt to prove that an officer, and therefore he himself, was the true superior of the enlisted man. The disastrous consequences were always embarrassing when the C.O. wound up explaining the facts of life to the young officer, but even more humiliating was the fact that the young fellow nearly always had to seek the sergeant major's help in cleaning up the mess he'd made. It was a lesson that only the true martinet or a blithering idiot would have to have repeated.

It had been true in Alexander's day and it was just as true now—the commanders merely commanded but the sergeant majors ran the show. Averitt had no experience with how things were done in democracies like the Army and the Air Force, but he assumed it was pretty much the same.

Gorton turned and summoned a young marine. "Collins, take the major's bag over to the airedales' bunker. See if Captain James is there and, if not, find him and bring him here. The colonel should be back in a little bit and he might want to see both of them."

Turning back to Averitt, he smiled again. "The colonel is over at the ammo dump, which we now have to call the ammunition supply point. The NVA hit it a couple of days ago and they're still trying to get it all squared away. We lost a whole shitload of artillery and mortar rounds. We still don't know what we have to reorder, but getting it up here by helo is gonna be a lot harder than it was before we got surrounded a couple of weeks ago."

"Yeah, I've been warned about watching my step around here."

Gorton nodded. "The area still left to clean up is getting smaller all the time."

He led the way over to a chart table in one corner. Just as he was beginning to point out the ASP, a voice called out, "Attention on deck." Everybody snapped to, including Gorton, whose posture would have made any drill instructor proud. Immediately, another voice with a soft North Carolina drawl said "Carry on," and everyone relaxed. Gorton and Averitt turned and saw that the colonel commanding the regiment at Khe Sanh had arrived.

As the colonel greeted several of the people in the bunker and listened to brief summaries of what had happened in his absence, Averitt watched him appraisingly, reviewing what he knew of the man who was now his boss. Colonel James Aires was a tall, handsome, just-beginning-to-go-gray man with piercing blue eyes. His bearing made him stand out even though his fatigues were no cleaner than anyone else's in the room. He looked like he had stepped right out of a movie screen.

Aires noticed the strange new major standing with his RSM and broke free of the gathering knot of men around him. He came over and stuck out his hand.

"Major Averitt? I'm Colonel Jim Aires. Welcome to the bull's-eye. Sergeant Major Gorton will help you get settled, but first I want to fill you in on the situation."

He gestured to the chart on the small table, speaking in that abrupt and emotionless way that military men have when discussing professional things among themselves. He pointed out the various strong points in the defensive perimeter and the several pieces of "high ground," actually massive hills, to the northwest, outside the base itself, where smaller parts of the regiment were positioned—Hills 881 South and 881 North, Hill 861, the Army Special Forces camp down the road at Lang Vei and the fire support bases to the east, where much of the Marines' supporting arms fire came from. On the far side of all those positions lay the nearly invisible enemy. Aires finished with an assessment of where the North Vietnamese had placed their artillery in Laos to the west and the demilitarized zone to the north. The part that chilled Averitt was Aires's description of the trenching and tunneling efforts of the NVA, which were approaching the perimeter of the base itself.

He looked up at Averitt and grinned. "That's all the bad news. The good news is that we've had lots of warning. Back on 2 January, a platoon from Lima Company caught several high-ranking NVA officers scouting the base and killed them in a firefight. We've gotten lots of fragments of intelligence from our patrols that something big was going to happen here. Then, on the twentieth, we got an NVA deserter, a lieutenant, who has basically given us the entire NVA plan. So far they've run true to it, so if they keep that up, we'll stay a jump ahead of them.

"Now, to your part. You're here because we needed somebody extra with as much experience as possible to coordinate things from the air support standpoint. Seventh Air Force, Marine Air from all over I Corps, and the Navy's carrier airplanes are committed to supporting us here. We've got everything from B-52s to Hueys helping us. It's far more than normal, so I decided that we needed somebody else. The ALO and the various teams we now have are doing a superb job, but you are a fresh set of eyes and a fresh new brain on the situation.

"Now then, you're only on loan to us here, and the Regimental ALO, Captain James, is a good man. He's the most familiar with all the players, so he'll still be in charge. You will be his adviser. Any problems with that?"

Averitt, taken with Aires's breezy manner, smiled. "No, sir, not unless he snores."

Aires laughed. "Good, good. Sarn't Major, take him over to the airedales' bunker and get him settled. And you, Major, will attend all the staff meetings. The next one will be at 1800, right here. Okay?"

He didn't wait for Averitt's answer but simply turned and walked away to a table where another knot of marine officers was discussing something and pointing at the map a lot.

Gorton placed his hand on Averitt's shoulder and steered him toward the entrance. "C'mon, Major, I guess Cap'n James is tied up. I'll show you around."

Late that evening Averitt and James were sitting on the sandbags that formed one of the many layers of protection for their bunker. They were sharing a drink from the small store of scotch that Averitt had brought in, well wrapped and hidden, in his bag. James had been there for nearly a month and a half and, in that time, had discovered that booze was not the highest priority item on the resupply list. He was extremely glad to be having a drink, albeit a small one.

By unspoken agreement their drinks were extremely weak, just about enough to taste. It did not make a whole lot of sense for somebody in their position, either militarily or tactically, to go around smelling like a distillery.

The two had hit it off immediately, finding that they had many mutual friends and experiences. James was also on his second tour in Vietnam and was getting his disassociated tour with the grunts out of the way. He had an easygoing approach that reminded Averitt of Jim Hogan, who was now steaming around somewhere far to the east out in the Gulf of Tonkin.

So far, Hogan and his squadronmates had not joined in the nearly incessant bombing of the area around Khe Sanh or, at least, James hadn't remembered hearing their call sign, Ghostrider, among the many units participating in Operation Niagara, the air support off Khe Sanh.

According to James, tonight was unusually quiet. There had been no incoming mortar rounds for the past hour or so and even the marines who were sitting in the holes in the front lines had not opened up on the phantom noises coming in from the enemy positions.

The big excitement had been an arc light drop by some Air Force B-52s about an hour before. These huge bombers usually came over in "cells" of three and dropped their entire load of a hundred or so five-hundred-pound bombs by radar. They were normally restricted to bombing only outside two miles from the American trenches, but even that far away, an arc light was something to behold.

Averitt had stood behind James as he talked to both the Air Force EC-121 radar controller aircraft, called Hillsborough, and the B-52s themselves as they were switched to the Khe Sanh frequency. James had given them the specific grid position for the target, which was a suspected troop concentration, and then listened as the huge bombers talked among themselves, heading in on the run. As soon as he was sure that everyone was ready, he turned the radio over to an assistant and led Averitt outside.

He led him to a corner of the bunker and stood facing the northeast. The low clouds, characteristic of the area at that time of year, made it as dark as anything Averitt had ever seen. He bumped into several things on the way and finally into James as he stopped at the corner.

Averitt strained to hear the sounds of the B-52s' approach and then felt a little silly when he remembered that they flew at an altitude so high that their sound never reached the ground and no antiaircraft gun on earth could hit them. He'd never seen an arclight strike but had seen the ground after one had hit. He had never been able to convey the effects of one, except to say that whatever was under an arc light simply ceased to exist except for hundreds of smoking holes where the bombs had struck the ground.

Behind them Averitt could hear a voice counting down to the drop, and when he heard "zero," several more marines came out of the bunker to stand with the two officers and watch. For Averitt's benefit, James explained some of the salient factors of the strike.

"The bombs are on their way, but it takes a while for them to fall that far. The Buffs all drop by radar and sort of ripple the bombs off, so the effect is a long swatch as opposed to a larger cluster of holes. They ought to start hitting to the right and continue over and beyond the target point. There will be about three hundred bombs coming down which is, what, about thirty or so A-4 loads?

"These guys are out of Guam, so they've been flying half of forever to come all the way over for about thirty seconds worth of excitement and then get to fly the other half of forever on the way home. Tough combat tour, huh?"

Averitt thought about the last comment. It was quite true that the B-52s had it pretty easy for the present, but if they ever were to go over North Vietnam into the teeth of the surface-to-air missile defenses, it would be a whole different story. He had to admit, though, that compared to living in a bunker dead center in the sights of three or four divisions of enemy troops and artillery, the B-52 crews had a walk in the park.

A flash of yellow light off to the right caught Averitt's eye. It was followed instantly by dozens and dozens more. The flashes continued for what could have been one mile or five. There was no way in the now-flickering darkness that Averitt could accurately judge the scale, but it had to be horrendous.

There was a long series of shocks, felt through the feet, which made Averitt nearly stumble into James as he stepped to keep his balance. That was quickly followed by a long protracted rumble felt against the body itself as the shock waves from the detonations reached them through the air. It was as if a strong wind had come up and fanned him.

As suddenly as it began, the string of explosions ended, leaving small yellow spots in his eyes as if hundreds of flashbulbs had gone off. Here and there on the horizon, fires burned and several small secondary explosions momentarily lit up the bottoms of the clouds.

James spoke over his shoulder. "You felt the concussion through the ground first because sound travels faster through solid things than it does through the air. As to what was out there, whatever it was, it's not there now."

Averitt was still awestruck. "Do those happen much?" It seemed that "happen" was more accurate a verb than any other he could think of. Arc lights happened in the sense that an earthquake or a tidal wave or a Krakatoa happened. It was almost too huge an event to be caused by human agency. There really were no words he could think of at the moment to describe what he had just seen.

James chuckled. "They're more impressive at night. But you'll almost get used to seeing them. I know that they're doing us some good and all, but there's times that I almost feel sorry for whoever is on the receiving end. C'mon, let's go back inside and I'll fill you in on the rest of what we have going for us here.''

Averitt followed James by the dim light of the distant fires. Just before he went into the bunker, he glanced back at the flickering yellow flames and knew exactly what James had meant. That arc light strike seemed like a sort of portable hell, to be moved around and laid down whenever the gods got pissed off enough to destroy someone.

Now, an hour later, Averitt still could see that power in his mind. Even though the enemy had nothing like it, it still made him feel very small indeed. In all his life he had never been in a position like this.

As a pilot he could always take some action to protect himself. He could usually go on the offensive and take away at least part of the enemy's advantage.

Here he had to sit and take it, like everybody else. And like everybody else he was at the mercy of someone else's actions and the vagaries of chance. He didn't like that one tiny bit.

23

Friday, January 26, 1968

Commander Chris Scott rolled his head back and forth, trying to ease some of the pain out of his neck. He'd woken up that morning with a slight stiffness and a dull ache back there and it had progressively gotten worse all day. He remembered that his mother used to claim that one could get a cold in the muscles of one's upper body, and this felt like one of those. He doubted, though, that a flight surgeon would agree with the diagnosis.

He knew he probably shouldn't have gone flying with it tonight, but the habits of a lifetime are hard to break. When aviators are younger, like the ensigns, jaygees, and lieutenants, most wouldn't go to see a flight surgeon for anything less than the sudden and mysterious loss of a leg, because they all felt, and rightly so, that the flight surgeon would ground them until whatever condition they had was cured.

There's really nothing wrong with that. Quite the contrary, the flight surgeon's job is to make sure that the aviators are in peak physical condition so that they can do all the things they must with their aircraft, like bringing them back intact.

The real reason that aviators avoid burdening the flight surgeons with their problems is that when the flight surgeon grounds them and sends them to their room for recuperative rest, the aviators always run afoul of the squadron's Operations Officer, who gleefully seizes this chance to keep the seats of the aircraft filled with pilots. The poor, ill aviator, with his red grounding chit still damp from the flight surgeon's ink, is immediately assigned to the job of squadron duty officer for the duration of his grounding.

The SDO assignment is very much like being the guy at the department store returns counter the day after Christmas. The rules are that there must be one available twenty-four hours a day, three hundred sixty-five days a year. Having a grounded pilot handy to assign to this torture is great since it frees up a healthy pilot to go flying. If there's nobody grounded, the healthy guys have to do the job on a more or less fair rotational basis.

As the C.O., Scott was above having to stand this duty and was free to ask the SDO all sorts of questions which the poor guy would have no chance at all of being able to answer. He would then have to spend a half hour or so trying to figure out who might have the answer and then finally, somewhat embarrassed, track the C.O. down and give him the requested information. It was really not all that thrilling a game, but it did have centuries of tradition behind it and was a good way of whiling away idle hours at sea.

Scott brought his mind back into the cockpit and made the turn to keep his Phantom neatly in the racetrack-shaped holding, or "marshall," pattern far behind and above the carrier. There were only a couple of minutes left before his "push" time, when he would have to begin his instrument approach to the *Shiloh*. Stacked above him were the rest of the fighters, and above them were the A-6 intruders.

That night was the first night of operational flying after the ship had been hauled out of port. There had been a night and a day of high-speed transit during which everybody aboard had tried to anticipate where the poohbahs back in Washington were going to send them, Yankee Station or off the coast of Korea. The Korean possibility had caused some major chaos among the squadrons as they tried to find and dig out and clean up all the cold-weather gear that had been shoved off in some deep hole in the ship and forgotten.

The next day had been spent getting all the aircrews back up to speed on both day and night flight operations and the word finally came down that the *Shiloh* and the *Coral Sea* would stay off the coast of Vietnam. The men aboard both remaining carriers off Vietnam did not envy the men of the *Ranger* and *Enterprise* at all, freezing their asses off in the Sea of Japan. Worse than the horrible weather they were going to have to deal with was the probability that any strike into North Korea was going to be a one-way trip.

Scott and the rest of the fighters had been sent out tonight as Combat Air Patrol for the half dozen or so A-6s that had flown single plane, low-level interdiction missions all over the southern panhandle of North Vietnam. All the A-6s had gotten back out safely, and nobody had needed the protection of the fighters.

The weather, which rarely stopped the A-6s, was basically lousy over the Indochina peninsula but improved somewhat out over the Gulf of Tonkin. There was lots of clear air up high out here, but off to the west, Scott could see a huge bank of cloud lit from within by a constant series of lightning flashes. Both he and Norris had separate but identical thoughts as they looked back and saw the roiling storm—they were both very glad that they weren't trying to fly around in it.

"Shorten the next one up a little, Skipper, and we'll be right on the money."

Norris's voice from the back shook him from his thoughts. He checked the gauges, waited a few seconds, and turned to roll out on the proper heading. A "nice job" from Norris confirmed what he already knew, the turn and timing had been dead on. This was by no means unique for Scott, but naval aviators compete with themselves to see how close they can come to perfection every time. A pilot who begins to cut himself any slack at all usually doesn't live long.

Scott glanced out to the side and saw the blinking red anticolli-

198

sion lights of the other jets in their orbits as they all waited for their push times. He looked back in and watched as his bearing and distance indicators showed that he was at the right point at exactly the right time. He eased off some power and lowered the nose just a little to begin the descent as Norris made the radio call, giving the aircraft side number, position in the pattern, and fuel state in thousands of pounds.

"204, commencing. 6.5."

Below them was a thick cloud deck, which from the weather observations transmitted by the radar controller back aboard the *Shiloh*, went all the way down to four hundred feet. The visibility down there was supposed to be just a little less than a mile, but Scott would fly all but the last twenty-five or thirty seconds solely with reference to the flight instruments. The visual part of the approach would come inside three-quarters of a mile, when he had to use the lighted lens on the ship for his approach information.

Scott flew a gentle, controlled descent until he reached 5000 feet and twenty miles behind the ship, where he raised the nose a couple of degrees and retracted the speedbrakes to reduce his rate of descent and banked a little to set up a slight angling intercept to the final approach bearing. Norris made this call too. "204, platform."

The big jet flew on nicely, trimmed up unconsciously by Scott's right thumb on the little black "coolie hat" switch at the very top of the stick. Most pilots swore that in the training command nobody cared if you crashed as long as the aircraft was properly trimmed up at the time. Student pilots were yelled at so much about it that most guys were certain that they could hear their instructors screaming "Trim it up, dammit!" in their sleep for a year after graduation.

Scott banked again and rolled out on the final approach bearing, so he was now flying directly at the landing area on the flight deck and nearing his level-off altitude.

At ten miles and now 1200 feet, Scott "dirtied up," lowering the landing gear, flaps, and tailhook, once again trimming the aircraft for level flight, making sure that his angle-of-attack indicator was pointed at the three o'clock position, showing that the jet was "on speed" and flying at the most efficient angle of attack, or AOA. He glanced up and saw the small lighted AOA indexer affixed inside the left side of the windshield was showing a yellow circle, or "doughnut," confirming that in the last bit of the approach he would be able to use that and not risk vertigo by having to pull his eyes back into the cockpit. Inside the cloud layer now, he ignored the white glow from the fuselage lights and wingtip lights reflecting back from billions of tiny water droplets.

Giving the mandatory voice report, Norris checked in with the final radar approach controller down in CATCC, who gave a clipped acknowledgment and watched the small lighted blip on his screen approach the four-mile point, where the actual final approach would begin.

"204, approach. Ship's in a turn. New final bearing will be 096."

"204, roger."

"204, on final now. You need not acknowledge further transmissions. At four miles. Begin descent from below the glide path."

Scott held his power on for an extra few seconds, waiting to get well established on the glide path. Even though the controller had told him to begin his descent, Scott, like most pilots, hated to start an approach with a built-in error. The only voice on the radio should be the controller's from then on, while Norris in the back was giving him a confirmatory set of directions identical to the approach controller's but a split second earlier and over the intercom. As in the holding pattern and throughout the entire approach, Norris would do the talking on the radio so that all Scott had to do was concentrate on flying.

"Comin' up and on glidepath." At this, Scott lowered the nose slightly and eased off a little power. The Phantom began its descent, and once it was established, Scott eased the throttles forward to maintain a steady rate.

The Phantom flew out of the clouds into relatively smooth but unbelievably dark air. Scott resisted the temptation to look out and try to see the ship. Nothing is more dangerous than trying to fly visually at night over the water when your only reference is a small set of lights three miles away. The biggest light around will soon be the fireball created when you hit the water.

Scott continued the approach to just inside one mile, and at the controller's "three-quarters of a mile, call the Ball" transmission, looked up and saw the yellow visual landing aid, or "Ball," on the port side of the landing area. He peeked back in at the instrument panel to make sure that his rate of descent was still pegged at six hundred feet per minute, and said, "got it" on the intercom to Norris, who keyed his radio.

"204, Phantom, Ball. 5.1." "Five point one" was very close to

200

the optimum fuel state for landing—light enough to minimize stress on the aircraft and heavy enough to have sufficient fuel to go around and try again if they missed the arresting wires or had to wave off for some reason. They would still have enough to divert to Danang if necessary.

The Landing Signal Officer, standing on a platform next to the landing area, acknowledged the Ball call, giving the winds. "Roger, Ball, Phantom. Deck's steady. Twenty-six knots." The LSO, a specially trained pilot from the air wing, shut up then. His job was to give guidance to the approaching aircraft only if required. Too much talk was only a distraction, never a help. But if the pilot was having problems, his voice and advice could be a lifesaver.

Almost unconsciously Scott made the constant string of small control movements that kept the aircraft centered on the glideslope, occasionally dipping a wing to keep his lineup straight on the landing area on the angled deck which, because of the ten-degree difference between the final bearing and the ship's course, was constantly moving to the right as the ship steamed through the dark seas.

Scott guided the Phantom through the turbulence behind the huge carrier, crossed the fantail, and slammed down onto the deck. When he felt the jolt of landing, he shoved the throttles forward to full power in case the tailhook missed one of the wires.

He was abruptly thrown forward into his straps as the hook caught the arresting wire, and then he quickly pulled the throttles back to idle and killed the external lights when the big fighter stopped rolling forward. On signal from the taxi director to his right, he raised his hook, folded his wings, and taxied clear of the landing area so that the deck would be ready for the next jet which was now only about thirty seconds out.

Once the Phantom was parked on the bow, Scott and Norris shut down the systems and Scott yanked the engines to cut-off and watched the instruments wind down. They released their straps and climbed stiffly down to the deck. Walking toward the catwalk that led below, he glanced up to see another jet, an A-6, roar overhead at full power, climbing into the wave-off pattern.

A few minutes later, back in Ready Room 4, Scott and Norris sat down to fill out their postflight paperwork. The television hanging from a large metal bracket in the front of the room was tuned to the PLAT. The sound was loud enough for the several aviators sitting around to hear the voices of both the controllers and pilots talking on the radio.

They had just completed the last sheet when they heard one of the young men behind them speak to the pilot next to him.

"Here he comes again, Jake."

Scott glanced around the room and saw that it had fallen silent. All eyes were fixed on the television. Keeping his eye on the screen, Scott asked over his shoulder, "What's going on?"

"There's an A-6 having some problems. He got waved off in close for a foul deck on his first pass. Last time was a wave-off for technique because he was all over the place. This is his third try." There was true concern in the voice.

Even though all the pilots in the air wing competed fiercely to see who was the best at the incredibly dangerous task of landing aircraft on the decks of ships, each of them knew that the night landings held special terror. There was not a pilot or RIO in the room, or on the entire ship for that matter, who had not been scared to death out there in the blackness more than once, trying to bring tons of aluminum aboard a deck which in the dark looked no bigger than a postage stamp.

It is a fact of life that much of what a pilot is called upon to do goes against every instinct he has. He must force himself to believe his instruments and ignore what his body is telling him about what the aircraft is doing. The body normally uses the eyes and other senses to confirm what the balance sense is telling it. If the eyes can see features in the surroundings that confirm that one is indeed leaning to the left when the balance sensors in the inner ear say he is, the body simply goes about its business, accepting the tilt, and all is well. Many of the erroneous signals sent from the inner ear are automatically discarded when the eyes tell the brain that they are incorrect. This process goes on constantly, and even the feet get into the act by confirming that the earth or the floor of a building, say, are, in fact, level. One never notices the thousands of decisions this system makes every minute.

But if the body is strapped immobile into a machine which itself moves about on all axes, the eyes alone must take over the confirmatory responsibility. When that machine is driving around in the dark with no available visual reference, the pilot has to rely on his instruments to tell up from down.

Normally, this is simply a matter of training and practice. But every once in a while the body will decide that it is doing something it actually is not and will send almost overpowering messages to the brain, telling it to make some sort of correction in order to get rid of the leaning feeling. This phenomenon is called vertigo or, more correctly, spatial disorientation. If the pilot believes the incorrect feeling and not his instruments, he will probably crash.

When vertigo is severe enough, it takes a conscious effort of will for the pilot to deliberately disregard all the senses that have served him so well and so accurately his entire life, and rely on something artificial for his information. Added to this problem is the certain knowledge that one false move down close to the water will mean death.

All in all, it is one of the least fun experiences in a pilot's life.

Scott watched the A-6 approach and saw that the aircraft was well below the correct glideslope. He could hear the LSO's voice on the radio attempting to remain calm as he tried to talk the pilot into making the proper corrections. It soon became obvious that there was no chance at all for the pilot to save this approach, and the wave-off cue began to flash on the side of the TV screen, indicating that the LSO was flashing the red lights on the lens, or visual landing aid, on the deck above.

The pilot raised the nose of the A-6, and Scott watched it climb through the cross hairs on the screen as he executed his wave-off. Behind the disappearing Intruder, several more sets of aircraft lights could be seen as the line of approaching jets continued. Scott could hear in his mind the conversation between the A-6 crew and the radar controllers as the controllers tried to find another hole in the line to allow the A-6 to try again.

Scott got up and walked over to the duty desk. He dropped off the thick binder that contained all the paperwork for his last flight and then poured himself a cup of coffee. He walked back over to his seat and sat down.

Like all the other pilots and RIOs in the room, he had been in a position just like this before and knew exactly how the pilot was feeling. He knew that the Air Boss would allow one, maybe two, more tries before he ordered the A-6 crew to fly to Danang and return in the morning. That would be embarrassing but not nearly fatal. Scott leaned forward and asked the SDO if Danang was still the primary divert field.

The SDO looked back evenly and broke the bad news. "Danang's zero-zero in heavy rain and fog, Skipper. There are no diverts ashore tonight.''

"How about the Philippines? Clark or Cubi Point?''

"No, sir. They're down too. Same story with the weather.''

Scott sat back in his seat, staring at the TV screen. "Zero-zero'' meant that the weather was so bad that the clouds were right down to the ground and that there was no visibility at all so that an approach could not even be attempted legally. Whoever was out there in the A-6 had better get a grip on himself and the situation or there were going to be some busy rescue people tonight.

He knew that he could do nothing to help, but like all the others in the room, he was compelled to watch the next few minutes on the screen, pulling for all he was worth for the poor bastards out in the Intruder. In a surreal sort of way they tried to *will* any help they could from their ready room chairs to the men in the seats of the A-6 until, and if, they got safely back aboard.

24

Friday, January 26, 1968

The "poor bastards'' out in the A-6, Thunder 501, were both young lieutenants whose evening had been going pretty smoothly up until the past fifteen minutes or so. They had gone into North Vietnam on a low-level single aircraft strike and had hit their target nicely. Whatever antiaircraft fire they had encountered had been too little, too late: all the streams of tracer had arced into the sky well behind and above their Intruder. It had been almost as easy as the training flights they had taken back in the States.

The weather had been poor but not particularly dangerous, just some rain and winds that bounced them around a little but had never come close to putting them in a jam. Through very good fortune they had not encountered any of the huge embedded thunderstorms that were making a tremendous fireworks display out to the west. Once back out over the water, they had entered their marshall pattern and all had been well. It had almost been fun.

The pilot, sitting in the left seat, was Dave Nichols, who was on his first combat deployment and had shown quite a bit of promise so far. In the right seat, slightly behind and lower than Nichols, was the B/N, or bombardier-navigator, "Hoot" Gibson.

Gibson, who preferred his nickname to his real one, Emile, was on his second deployment to Vietnam and was considered one of the best in the squadron.

There is an unwritten but very wise policy in naval aviation that new pilots were teamed with older, more experienced B/Ns or copilots until the new guy had enough seasoning to be thought of as a veteran. Like most of these rules and policies, it had been learned at a very great cost in lives lost and destroyed airplanes.

Gibson was using his experience right now. Every bit of it, and some he was inventing on the spot. On their first approach, Nichols had told him that he was having a case of the "leans," which is pilot talk for everything from a mild case of disorientation to full-blown vertigo. The approach had not been pretty, but it would have been successful had they not been given a foul-deck wave-off.

Nichols had slammed on the power and set the optimum-climb nose attitude, but going around had tumbled his internal gyros badly, the lights of the ship passing beneath the Intruder adding another erroneous cue.

From the right seat Gibson saw that Nichols was tightening up, his arms and wrists beginning to jerk the controls around. His hand was squeezing the stick tightly and his forearm was no longer resting on his kneeboard. Turning downwind and reentering the overcast, Nicholas overshot the altitude and, instead of easing back the throttles and letting the A-6 settle back down, he pulled them back sharply, starting a much greater rate of descent than was necessary, or safe. Over the ICS, or cockpit intercom which was always on "hot mike" in the landing pattern, Gibson could hear the change in his pilot's breathing.

"C'mon, Dave. Settle down. We're okay. Concentrate on your scan. Get some power back on and hold the nose where it is."

Nichols nodded, saying only "'kay," which was another indicator of how hard he was making this on himself. Gibson watched the aircraft settle through the downwind altitude, but as he was getting ready to say something, Gibson saw it and pushed the throttles up to climb some. The correction was still a little too much, but it was smoother.

Nichols got the aircraft squared away finally, but his heading was a little off—he was angling in by about five degrees. Gibson deliberately made his voice relaxed.

"That's better. Come right five. We're looking good." Gibson kept his eyes on the instruments, watching the radar altimeter for any sign of descent and the altitude indicator to make sure that Gibson didn't let things get away from him again. He keyed the radio and made the mandatory voice reports to the controllers back on the ship.

They were given a turn back toward the final approach course far sooner than Gibson would have liked. It appeared that the controller had found a gap in the line of approaching jets big enough for Thunder 501 to fit in. It would have been better to give Nichols a little more time to settle down, but there were still a bunch of other aircraft out there, all of whom had to face the same sort of difficulties he and Nichols did.

Nichols turned the Intruder and concentrated on his instruments. As Gibson looked over at his pilot, it was obvious to him that Nichols's eyes were moving over the instruments more slowly than was usual. He was concentrating on each instrument for a second or so, mentally talking himself through the scan pattern his eyes should have been following automatically. This was the last-resort sort of scan, when a pilot took himself back to the basics and forced himself to start again. If he concentrated hard enough on making his scan work, he would not only get it right and not miss something, but he also might be able to almost trick himself into forgetting that he had problems in the first place.

All the way around the pattern Nichols continued fighting his disorientation while Gibson talked to him calmly and kept an eye on the instruments. Once established on final, the aircraft stayed pretty close to the center of the glide path. It wasn't until the aircraft was once again below the cloud deck and inside a mile that things went to hell quickly.

Nichols glanced forward, trying to see the welcome sight of the red and white rows of lights that marked both the stern of the ship and the landing area above. As he did, he waited too long and let the glide path get away from him again. His wings began to rock back and forth as he unconsciously pulled back on the stick to reduce his descent and slowed the aircraft. The Intruder began to settle toward the water.

Gibson recognized the error immediately and yelled at him to add power at the same time that the LSO saw the descent steepen and yelled the same thing into his radio handset. "Don't settle . . . attitude. Power. Power! *Power!! Wave it off!! Power!!*"

Nichols slammed his throttles forward and lowered the nose back to where it should have been. Through the rain-smeared right half of the windshield Gibson could see the large red wave-off lights to the left of the landing area flashing, and watched the rows of white lights denoting the deck shorten before the engines spooled up and began to shove the aircraft away from the waves. The jet climbed sharply and overflew the ship with now two badly shaken men aboard.

In the tower the Air Boss grabbed his radio handset and told the Intruder crew to climb straight ahead instead of attempting to follow the normal wave-off pattern. He had been in a situation like those guys and knew that what they needed now was a little bit of extra time to settle down. He was well aware that they had just scared the shit out of themselves, and abrupt maneuvers were only going to make things worse. To his right, his assistant, the Mini-Boss, grabbed the ship's telephone and called down to CATCC, telling them to make the next pattern as wide and as gentle as possible for Thunder 501.

He hung up the phone and looked over at the Boss. "Ready for some more good news? The tanker just went tits-up. Unless we launch the standby, we have no fuel in the air for those guys. The standby is an A-4."

The Boss nodded and spoke over his shoulder to the enlisted man standing behind him. "How many are left?"

"Including 501, four, sir. And 501 has fuel for two more passes before he'd usually have to head for the beach where, surprise surprise, the weather is still dogshit."

"Thanks." The Boss chewed his lip. With no tankers airborne, the other aircraft would not have enough fuel to stay airborne if the A-6 crashed or somehow fouled the deck. He looked forward and saw that all the aircraft that had been on this recovery were parked to the left of the bow, leaving catapult number one free.

"Okay. Tell CATCC to bring the others down first. Launch the standby tanker."

He thought for a few seconds and, as he did, he saw the plane-guard helicopter fly up the starboard side of the ship in its seemingly ceaseless orbit. Turning back to the Mini, he said, "You might call the helo guys and tell them to get another helo and crew ready just in case."

He picked up another handset which connected him directly with the captain on the bridge as the Mini-Boss spoke to CATCC. This is going to be one of those nights, he thought.

Down in his ready room, Scott watched the A-6 grow steadily larger on the TV screen. Distantly, he heard the thump and felt the shudder as catapult number one fired, sending the standby tanker up into the blackness.

This was the A-6 crew's fifth pass, and it was not a whole lot better than the last one had been. The little lighted dots that were the wing lights were waving all over the place, but the center one, which represented the nose, was holding pretty steady, moving only in response to the motion of the wings.

The room was quiet now as everyone watched the image of the A-6 wiggle its way down the glide path. It stayed pretty close to the center hanging just below the cross hairs. As the aircraft got closer to the ship, it began to grow rapidly, and Scott thought the guy had it made, when suddenly the nose dropped and the Intruder hit the deck hard and disappeared out of the camera's field of view.

The image instantly switched to the camera high on the island structure as it followed the A-6 up the deck and back into the night sky, with the LSO's radio call telling the crew that they had missed the wires and sparks flying from their tailhook as it scraped along the deck.

"Bolter, bolter, bolter."

There was a collective exhalation in the room as everyone saw the aircraft climb steadily ahead and its lights disappear into the overcast. Scott looked around the room and waited for the voices to begin professionally critiquing the approach. They did, but quietly and carefully with none of the usual humor they would have used if this had been daytime and the guy simply made a wild-ass play for the deck and gooned it.

Scott watched the image switch back to the centerline camera and pick up the lights of the E-2 which would normally be the final aircraft aboard. After that one there would be only two to go, the A-6 and the now useless A-3 tanker. Two fixed-wing aircraft and the plane-guard helo orbiting down low out off the starboard side of the ship. At least if they have to eject, they've got a chance with the helo there. That's better than it used to be, he thought.

Scott stood and walked over to the coffee urn, poured himself another cup of the sludge his squadron seemed to prefer, and then returned to his seat.

In the tower the Air Boss was speaking on the phone to the LSO, who was now almost invisible behind the sheets of rain blowing down the deck.

"I thought he had it that time. Well, anyway, he would have if he hadn't made that last-second play for the deck. What do you think?"

"I dunno, Boss. I can't really get a feel for what he's thinking. The B/N is doing all the talking. Since he reported aboard, the guy has been doing pretty well. He hasn't shown any unsafe tendencies before now. I think he can do it if we can get him to just calm down and fly the son of a bitch. Maybe we ought to send him up to the tanker now and get his mind on something else. When he gets everything squared away, we can give it another try."

"Okay, Paddles. Call him and send him up to the tanker. Talk to him a little." He looked out at the water but all he could see was occasional patches of foam as the waves broke over themselves. He would hate to be floating around out there, hoping that the helo could find him. There was one more thing that had to be said to the LSO.

"Paddles, if he gets wild out there again, don't wait until the last minute. Wave him off early. I'd rather see him eject than plow into the pack."

The LSO squinted through the rain and looked across the deck at the dozens of aircraft parked, many of them fully fueled. The A-6 crashing into "the pack" would be a disaster that would make the loss of one aircraft minor.

"Roger that, Boss. I concur."

In Thunder 501, Gibson looked over at Nichols, who was rubbing the sweat from his eyes. The last pass would have been successful had the young pilot not dumped his nose and dived for the deck. The Intruder had hit flat instead of main wheels first, which caused it to rebound and caused the tailhook to skip over the wires. Nichols had slammed the throttles forward and cursed loudly as he flew back into the clouds.

That was a good sign to Gibson's way of thinking. If Nichols was getting pissed at himself, he was getting away from the mind-numbing fear that vertigo could induce. That meant he was getting back to flying the aircraft as he was capable. The anger was properly directed—at himself rather than at some object over which he had no control. Anger like that could be dealt with, so things were looking up. He was about to speak, when he heard the LSO call on the radio.

"501, Paddles."

Gibson stayed silent, so with a glance at his B/N Nichols keyed the radio. "Paddles, 501. Go ahead."

"Okay, Dave. You had it made that last time until the very end. You were overcontrolling a little, but your attitude and descent were basically okay. You dumped your nose at the end and hook-skipped the three and four wires. If you fly the next one exactly the same way, only a little more smoothly, you'll be okay."

Gibson watched Nichols nod, unconsciously agreeing with the LSO as he answered. "501, roger."

"Okay, 501, your signal now is Texaco. Contact departure for the tanker."

Gibson switched frequencies to departure control and keyed his transmitter. "Departure, 501's with you level at twelve hundred."

"Roger, 501. Climb to and maintain angels fifteen. The tanker is Ghostrider 412."

"501, out of one-point-two for angels fifteen." Nichols shoved the throttles forward and eased the nose up, heading for fifteen thousand feet where the tanker was orbiting, waiting to give away some fuel which would in turn give the Intruder more time in the air and a few more chances at the deck.

In the plane-guard helicopter, Salty Dog 802, the pilot in command was Lieutenant Commander Ed Walker. He was sitting in the left, or copilot's, seat and his copilot, a new guy, Lieutenant (j.g.) Vic Valerio, sat in the right, or pilot's, seat. This was normal procedure for Walker's crew and most others in the helicopter Navy. The pilots would alternate seats for every mission so that the new guy would get as much experience as possible before he made aircraft commander himself. The right-seat pilot made all the landings and had the brakes but, once airborne, there was actually very little difference in the two positions.

In flight, however, there was one difference that might have had some significance that night. The right seat was the one that had to do all the hovers in rescue situations, and young Mr. Valerio had never done one for real. He'd had dozens of practice flights where the rescue evolution was *simulated*, but he'd never had to sit there and fly with a man's life hanging by the thin cable of the rescue hoist.

Psychologically, this is a difficult thing to do when the weather is bright and sunny, but at night and in the rain it is an absolute bitch to do smoothly, which is the *only* way it can be accomplished at all.

Walker was thinking just this as he listened to the voices on the radios. He knew that the A-6 crew was in real trouble just from listening to the clipped and slightly high-pitched way they were speaking. The LSO was being deliberately articulate, losing the calculated West Virginia drawl that most military aviators affected. The Air Boss was speaking quickly and carefully as he sorted out the seeming thousands of details that must be dealt with in getting ready for any eventuality.

There was silence on the intercom in Salty Dog 802. The crewmen in the back were listening carefully to the radios too, knowing full well that one of them could soon be in the water, trying to help the A-6 crew, while the other tried to talk a new and inexperienced pilot into a stable hover over the scene. They had a great deal of confidence in Walker but had never seen Valerio in a tight spot. He seemed to be a competent pilot and they were pretty sure that he wouldn't do anything stupid, but you never knew.

They had automatically prepared everything in the aircraft for a rescue, or "rigged" it, as they said, and so now had nothing to do but wait, which was the absolute worst part for them. The pilots could at least occupy themselves with driving the huge H-3 around the pattern, but the crewmen just had to sit and wait and think of the sixty or seventy million things that could go wrong.

Walker, for his part, was going over the mistakes he had seen before. Glancing over at Valerio, Walker saw that the red glow from the lights of the instrument panel gave his expression a look of harshness and age even though he had one of those faces which, in other light, would look sixteen until he was in his late thirties. Walker debated telling the young pilot just how serious the situation with Thunder 501 was but decided to wait until it was absolutely necessary. There was not much sense in giving him any extra time to think about what he might be called upon to do.

Walker keyed his radio. "Tower, Salty Dog's got two-point-oh to splash."

"Tower, copies."

Walker had given his fuel state to the Air Boss in the tower to let him know that one thing he didn't have to worry about was refueling the helo anytime soon. "Two-point-oh" for the helicopters meant two hours to fuel exhaustion so that 802 would have plenty for whatever happened.

The other reason Walker spoke was to let the Boss know that he had been listening to the situation and that he was prepared. The Boss would now be able to forget the helo's presence and concentrate on doing everything in his power to help 501 get aboard.

Walker looked out into the blackness and then down at the surface of the sea. There were long wind streaks of white foam all around, indicating that the wind was freshening some. That would help the helicopter's hover but would increase the difficulty in finding two bobbing helmets floating around out there. For about the thousandth time in his career, Walker was very glad that he was a helo pilot and not driving one of the jets around.

At least if something bad happened, it usually happened lower and slower to a helicopter.

25

Friday, January 26, 1968

Jim Hogan walked into his ready room and sat in his chair. In his hand he held a peanut butter sandwich which he'd picked up in the wardroom on the way. He looked at the group of pilots sitting in the row across from him and saw that they were engrossed in the drama on the PLAT.

"How's he doing?" he asked Jack Wilson.

"Not so good. The last one was a bolter, so they sent him up to the tanker."

"Who's in the tanker?"

"Jamison."

Hogan grunted. Jamison was one of the old hands who could be relied upon to have his jet exactly where it was needed exactly when it was needed. He also had been around long enough to know how to coax the finicky D-704 refueling package into working properly.

The D-704 was an add-on system that would be hung beneath the centerline of an A-4 along with additional external, or "drop," fuel tanks hung under the wings. The system could transfer hundreds of gallons of fuel to the receiving aircraft by pumps run by its own independent electrical power. The flight manual had a list of procedures that were supposed to be the definitive method of operating the system, but years of experience had taught the aviators that things didn't always go as designed. Over time the A-4 pilots gradually learned that if you did this before you did that when something didn't work, things might come out right. Jamison had been around long enough to have learned all the tricks.

Hogan stood and stretched his back and then walked to the rear of the room. He poured himself a cup of coffee and pulled the stack of folders out of his mailbox. He quickly shuffled through them to see if there was any personal mail stuck in there anywhere and, when he saw that there wasn't, he stifled a sigh and walked back to his seat.

He had gotten through about half of his paperwork when he heard the door at the back of the room open and the duty officer call out "Attention on deck!"

Hogan, for whom, as the senior man in the squadron, this call was usually reserved, half stood to see who had come in before he heard CAG Andrews's gruff "carry on."

Andrews walked up to Hogan and sat down heavily in the next seat. "Got any more of that coffee?"

Hogan sat and gestured for the duty officer. "Yes, sir, what do you want in it?"

"Nothing, thanks. Just black."

Hogan asked the duty officer to fetch a cup for Andrews and sat next to him. "To what do we owe this honor?" he asked with a smile.

Andrews smiled a little and handed over a folder. "I was on my way to my cabin when I remembered this message. I thought I'd drop it by personally since you're the one who started it all."

Hogan took the folder as Andrews accepted the coffee from the duty officer, who moved back to his desk and out of earshot. Hogan read the message and then read it again. It was the reply from CINCPAC, or Commander in Chief, Pacific, about Blake's bombing of the phony hospital. As he read it, Hogan felt that some distant disaster had been avoided, a disaster with no actual form or substance but capable of engineering apprehension nonetheless.

Stripped of its jargon and acronyms, the message asked for more information and any additional evidence of the enemy's "violation of the laws of war," including statements from the pilots involved.

Hogan let out a long breath and looked over at Andrews. "Does this mean what I think it does?"

Andrews sipped his coffee. "In the words of the great American Davy Crockett, as portrayed by John Wayne, 'It do.' Somebody up the line is using common sense and is willing to take this forward. So you and your squadron are off the hook."

Hogan sat back in his chair. His mind was already running through the requirements that this message was laying on the squadron. They'd already sent off most of their evidence, consisting largely of photographs. He wondered whether Nick Taylor had anything left. Abruptly, he realized that the pilot statement would now be impossible since the pilot, Blake, was back in the States and his wingman, Cordella, could add little except a nice description of the secondary explosions.

"Jim, how long would you say it would take your guys to get everything together and send it off to CINCPAC?"

Hogan thought for a moment. "We could probably have it out of here in seventy-two hours."

"If you did a very careful search of all the files and all the recce photos, I bet it would take closer to a week."

Hogan looked confused. "Why a week?"

Andrews grinned. "Because that's about how long I figure it will take the letter I just sent to Blake to get to him. I told him to expect a call from somebody in the Pentagon, asking him about the flight. I also said that all we would be providing would be the photos and damage assessments. He would be responsible for filling in the details of the flight."

"Okay, a week it is. Do you want us to send the acknowledgment to CINCPAC's request?"

"Already done. When you get all your 'evidence' together, draft up a cover letter for my signature and I'll send it all out. Okay?"

"Yes, sir."

"Good. Now, if you don't mind, I've gotta get back to my cabin in time to watch that young fella in the A-6 try again." Andrews stood and walked out of the room.

Hogan watched the door close behind the air wing commander. As he turned back to the PLAT TV, Hogan realized that he'd just learned a leadership lesson. Despite his certain concern for everyone in his air wing, Andrews was going to worry about the A-6 crew in his room instead of somewhere more visible. Hovering around CATCC or the A-6 ready room or the tower would do nothing to help the situation and might give the A-6 squadron C.O. the impression that his CAG didn't have full confidence in him.

As he reached for the pile of folders, he sipped his cooling coffee and heard the A-6 check back in with Approach.

26

Friday, January 26, 1968

Nichols eased the A-6 back and watched as his refueling probe disengaged from the basket. The lights on the little A-4 above him stood out starkly against the deep blackness of the sky. He backed farther away as Gibson made the required voice reports and switched frequencies back to the approach controllers.

The A-4 tanker pilot had given them half his available fuel and would stay around in case they needed more. Normally, the tanker would have been flying around at a much lower altitude, staying closer to the A-6, or "hawking" it as the term went, but with solid clouds nearly down to the deck it was far safer to stay up there where there was at least some visibility. In the tiny A-4 cockpit he stretched his legs as best he could and wiggled his butt, trying to get a little less uncomfortable.

He reeled the long hose and basket back into the removable "buddy" refueling store and trimmed his jet for the relatively low and easy orbit he would maintain until the controllers told him to start his own approach.

Gibson looked over at the intense expression in Nichols's eyes. The younger man had flown a beautiful rendezvous with the tanker and then had done the rest of the refueling procedure just as smoothly as if it were daytime. He seemed to have gotten himself squared away, but the danger now was going to come when they reentered the cloud deck below and began another approach. It was going to take a supreme act of will for Nichols to ignore what had gone before and fly this approach as if it were the first.

*   *   *

216

"Approach, 501's with you. Tanking complete."

"Roger, 501. Roll out on 270. Descend and maintain three thousand."

Gibson watched Nichols increase the bank of the aircraft, level out again on a heading of 270, and then pull the throttles back, starting their descent to three thousand feet. Gibson resisted the temptation to let out a long breath which would sound like a comment over the intercom's "hot mike." Here we go, he thought, but instead of saying it, he keyed the radio.

"Approach, 501's out of angels thirteen for angels three. Steady 270."

"Roger."

Down in the plane-guard helo, Walker began to have Valerio change the flight pattern. Normally during the day the plane-guard is restricted to a specific area off the starboard side of the ship in which it is required to stay during launches and recoveries for the fixed-wing aircraft. The area is D-shaped and is known as "Starboard Delta," or "Star-D" for short. The pilots just sort of fly around, keeping an eye on things and staying away from the approach and departure corridors for the fixed-wing aircraft.

But at night or in lousy weather the pattern has to be flown on instruments. The ship's lights are at best confusing at night, if one can see them at all, and using them as a reference is one of the more certain ways of getting into trouble.

The pilots fly out on specific bearings, arc around to another one, and then fly back, inbound, toward the ship on the second one. This process is repeated for as long as it takes for the fixed-wing operations to cease or the Air Boss sends the helo off somewhere or they run low on fuel, whichever comes first. Usually, it is the last.

Walker was coaching Valerio in lengthening the outbound leg some so that when they were ultimately flying back toward the ship at the other end of the pattern, they would have a longer time with their nose pointed at Thunder 501 and so could see how the A-6's approach was going and have visual contact in case something bad happened.

Another reason, which Walker had learned long before, was that it sometimes made a jet crew in trouble feel a little safer when they could see the lights of a rescue helicopter blinking along off to the right of their nose. It was not really all that big a help, but it was all the helo could do. He hoped that it was all they'd *have* to do for the A-6 crew that night.

The Air Boss took the cup of coffee from the Mini-Boss and sat back in his tall chair. He looked down at the flight deck and the sheets of rain intermittently blowing down its length. In the dim light from the few lights shining above decks he could make out the white forms of the other jets, most with their wings folded, sitting almost disconsolately as the wind blew the rain among them. There were few men visible on the deck. The ones who had to be out there were huddling as best they could in the shelter of the aircraft. There were at least seven of them hiding in the lee of the fire truck.

It was strange, he thought, how many men would have found some reason to be on the "roof" if the weather were bright and sunny. Tonight it was obvious how few were really required to get the job done. His thoughts were interrupted by the officer of the deck calling from the bridge on the silver bitch box at his left elbow.

"Primary, Conn. Doesn't look like this rain squall has an end to it. Do you want to hold the A-6 awhile longer?"

"Standby." The Boss looked around for the representative from the A-6 squadron but couldn't spot him in the dim light among the half dozen or so representatives from the other squadrons.

"Where's the Thunder rep?"

"Right here, Boss." It was the squadron's Executive Officer.

"Sorry, I thought that young fella of yours was still up here."

"He is, but I thought he might like to have an old fart up here too."

The Boss grinned. He knew that the X.O.'s answer was intended to ease any possible feeling in the young man that he wasn't good enough to do his job. The real reason that the X.O. had come all the way up there was that there might arise a question that would be beyond the scope of the young pilot's position or experience. Rather than wasting time calling down to the ready room to consult with the C.O. or X.O, or, worse, having him commit to something simply because it was somebody senior like the Air Boss asking for it, the X.O. had come up. The X.O. was there to protect both his young guys in the air and his young rep in the tower. The Boss also knew that the C.O. would be down in CATCC in case they needed something there.

The Air Boss liked that a lot. It reminded him of the way things used to run in his old squadrons. Even though this was pretty much routine, it was not written anywhere and it was one of those small extras that made the whole system work more smoothly and far more safely.

"Well, what do you think? Should we go hunting for a hole in this stuff or wait awhile and see if it gets better?"

The X.O. shook his head. "No, I don't think so. There's no way we could find a hole unless we stumbled on it. Our chances are just as good heading this way as any other, especially since we're heading generally toward the leading edge of the front. And it's still above minimums for operations."

"Would it maybe give your crew some more time to settle themselves down?"

"I figure the tanking has probably taken their minds off things for the moment. Personally, I'd hate to have a whole lot of extra time to get myself all worried and concerned. I'd rather just get on with it."

"Yeah, me too. That's about what I figured you all would say. But we'll keep the tanker up there until he's down. There'll be enough fuel for a couple more tries anyway." He turned to the bitch box and pressed the transmit handle.

"Conn, Primary. The squadron advises that they'd rather have him continue than wait on a possible hole. I'm gonna leave that tanker up in case he needs more gas."

After a few seconds the reply came back from the bridge. "Conn, roger. Concur."

The Air Boss sat back in his seat and stared out through the thick armored-glass windows of the tower. He was running the possibilities through his mind and hoping that he and his assistants had anticipated them all. To his right, the Mini-Boss was doing the same thing, all the while being very glad that his days of flying around in the dark and in shitty weather were behind him.

Gibson looked over and watched as Nichols rolled the Intruder out on the final approach course. The young pilot reduced power just a touch as the wings, now level, increased their lift slightly. The altitude, twelve hundred feet, stayed rock-steady. Gibson saw Nichols flex his fingers and his hand on the black grip on the stick, unconsciously forcing at least that part of himself to stay relaxed. He reached up and wiggled his oxygen mask a couple of times, trying to make it just a tad more comfortable, but each time he left it in exactly the same place it had been before.

Gibson was pleased to see that Nichols was at least appearing to be more in control. He was now ahead of the airplane, making control corrections almost before they were required instead of after, as he had been earlier. His eyes were quickly moving across the instrument panel in the long-practiced and ceaseless pattern all pilots must cultivate. The sweat that had been on his brow was gone, leaving just a trace of an oily sheen on his forehead.

He was not sneaking the peeks outside anymore for the reassuring but dangerously disorienting glimpses of something connected to the world below. His entire concentration was now on the instruments on the panel beyond his hand. Gibson stole a glance out into the blackness and smiled a little. He could peek without getting in much trouble, but the pilot could not. So what had the designers of the A-6 done? The pilot had the forced-air "windshield wipers" on his side and the B/N had none.

It didn't really matter much—there was nothing to see. It was like the old saying "darker than the inside of a cow"—so dark that he couldn't tell if there was any rain hitting the windshield anyway.

Gibson looked back inside and down at the instruments and saw that everything was as it should be.

"Lookin' good, Dave. Comin' up on twelve miles."

"Yup. I think I'm okay now."

"Yeah, I think so too."

Gibson hit the switch that lowered his seat a little and wiggled his butt on the cushion to get more comfortable as the approach controller's voice came back over the radio. "Thunder 501, approach. Ten miles, dirty up."

"501," Gibson answered as Nichols took his left hand off the throttles and moved the levers that lowered the tailhook, landing gear, and flaps. Both men watched as the indicators one by one showed that everything was down and that the Intruder was in the proper configuration for landing, or "dirty," as it was called.

Nichols trimmed the aircraft and adjusted the throttles to maintain altitude and airspeed in the new configuration. Now all they had to do was wait until they got to three miles and then begin their final descent. If it's so damn easy, why did I have so much trouble before, he wondered, and immediately forced that thought away. Dwelling on that could do nothing but cause problems.

He waited until his distance measuring equipment, or DME, said he was at three miles, and then reduced power and lowered the nose. Almost as soon as the descent began he readjusted the controls to maintain a seven-hundred-foot-per-minute rate of descent and the optimum nose attitude. With part of his mind he heard the approach controller's calls and Gibson's answers. They were all routine, so he simply concentrated on his flying and let them pass.

The Intruder flew like it was on rails, and Nichols resisted the temptation to peek. He still had a long way to go before he realistically had any chance of seeing anything, so there was no sense in stupidly risking getting vertigo again.

Walker, in the plane-guard helicopter, told Valerio to extend this, the outbound leg of the pattern, for a few extra seconds. He was trying to time this instinctively and felt he had misjudged the wind just a little. When the A-6 broke out on final, Walker wanted to be off the right side of the A-6's nose close enough to be seen easily but far enough away so as not to cause a distraction to the crew.

Walker looked across Valerio and, through his side window, watched the ship disappear behind the copilot. When he heard the approach controller tell the A-6 that they were at four miles, he counted to ten and told Valerio to start his turn. If he'd done it right, the A-6 would overtake them from the left and pass well clear just after they broke out of the overcast.

Out on his platform which extended almost out over the water, the LSO looked down at the wind indicator on the red-lighted panel beneath the deck edge and glanced over his shoulder at the lighted lens of the visual landing aid. He resisted the temptation to test them once more and turned back to face aft, where Thunder 501 would appear any second now. He hunched his shoulders against a sudden burst of rain and wished he were down below, where it was at least warm and dry.

The two sailors who took care of running the equipment for the LSO platform were wishing the same thing as they rechecked everything and made sure that their binoculars hadn't fogged up.

* * *

Nichols rocked his wings slightly to maintain his position on the final bearing. More precise corrections would come in a few seconds, when the A-6 broke out of the overcast, but the little wiggle he had put in would make the later corrections smaller and less difficult. They were almost out of it.

Gibson saw the slightly less-black tatters of the underside of the overcast whip by and glanced ahead of the aircraft. All at once he saw both the ship and the lighted Ball on the lens. It was only slightly high. Well off to the right, he saw the blinking red light of the rescue helo chugging along, ready if needed.

"501's at three-quarters of a mile. Call the ball."

At the approach controller's call, Nichols raised his eyes and spotted the yellow light to the left of the landing area. He eased a touch of power off and put it right back in, which placed the Ball back in the center and the Intruder dead in the middle of the glide path. "Got it," he said to Gibson. He immediately looked back at his instruments to make sure that the A-6 had not picked up an extra bit of descent while he was looking away.

Gibson keyed his radio. "501. Intruder, Ball. Two-point-five."

The new voice of the LSO came over the radio next. "Roger, Ball, Intruder. Twenty-six knots. Deck's steady."

The LSO had been listening to the approach frequency and had been trying hard not to stare at the spot where the A-6 should break out. One of his young sailors, holding binoculars, spotted the jet and checked its lights. He could see that the wheels were down and the light in the middle was steady, which indicated that the tailhook was down. If it had been blinking, the hook would be still up and there would be no way that the jet could stop on the deck. He checked the lights farther aft on the deck and saw that the deck status light was green.

"Intruder. All down. Clear deck," he sang out over his shoulder.

"Intruder. All down. Clear deck," the LSO repeated, and raised his right hand with the "pickle switch," which would activate the wave-off lights, showing that he had control of this landing.

He heard Nichols's voice as he called the Ball, and pressed the transmit switch on the radio handset in his left hand, glancing at the wind indicator as he spoke.

"Roger, Ball. Intruder. Twenty-six knots. Deck's steady."

He saw that the lights on the A-6 were lined up perfectly and that the middle one was amber, indicating that the jet's attitude

222

was right on. If it were fast or slow the center amber light would change to red or green accordingly, and the LSO would tell the pilot to make a correction.

Gibson flicked his eyes between the yellow Ball on the ship and the lights on his angle-of-attack indexer, which corresponded to the approach lights the LSO was seeing. The amber circle, or "doughnut," was glowing, with only momentary flickers from the red and green chevrons, indicating that the nose was moving a little but always coming back to the center. Nichols was ahead of the game on this one and was making all the right moves. This was actually a pretty nice approach and in another few seconds they'd be safe on deck, as long as the young pilot didn't make another play for the wires.

"Lookin' good, Dave. Don't get cute in close." A grunt was his only acknowledgment.

Down in his ready room, Scott discovered he was holding his breath as he watched the lights of the A-6 grow ever larger on the television screen. The room was silent as everyone else watched equally intently. There were no transmissions over the radio, which was also a good sign. When a pilot is trying to land on a ship, the last thing he needs is extraneous chatter. The LSO was the only one permitted to speak, and even he shut up unless there was something that needed to be said.

The lights grew brighter and separated as the Intruder got closer, until finally the dim shape of the aircraft itself could be seen. The large grayish tadpole shape slammed down onto the deck and there was a flash of a lighter color from the rear of the airplane as the tailhook snagged the wire.

Overhead the men in the ready room could hear the sound of the wire being pulled out of its drums and the groan as the hydraulic system took up the strain of bringing tons of metal to a stop.

The view switched to the island camera, and everyone saw the A-6 decelerate and finally stop. The pilot raised his hook and the wire fell away and moved aft as the arresting-gear crew reeled it in for the next aircraft.

Scott stood up in the still-quiet room. He walked over to the sink and poured his now-cold coffee out, rinsed the cup, and hung it on its hook with all the others. As he left the room, the voices began again. The fact that none of the conversations had to do with landing jets on a ship at night did not seem strange to him at all.

The Air Boss watched the A-6 taxi clear of the landing area toward the row of parked aircraft on the bow. He listened to the Mini-Boss tell Approach to bring down the A-4 tanker and the helo that there was one to go. There would be a few minutes extra delay until the A-4 came in, but that couldn't be helped. At least everyone was down safely and that last pass by the A-6 had been almost textbook.

The Boss hoped that the A-6 C.O. and X.O. would lay off the pilot. It was obvious that he was a pretty good man who had just had a bad night. He hoped that they'd remember their own bad ones and not embarrass the kid anymore. It was bad enough that everyone in the air wing already knew about it without him having to take any spare shit.

But that wasn't his problem. He took a last sip from his coffee cup, placed it down on the windowsill, and got back to the business of running the tower.

27

Saturday, February 3, 1968

The weather system that had caused all the problems for the aviators out at sea lingered in the area for the next eight days. As soon as one mass of lousy weather, low cloud, rain, and slow-clearing fog would dissipate, it was replaced almost instantly with another mass that was just as bad, if not worse. This was the deepest part of the monsoon season in Southeast Asia, which more than any human intervention worked to reduce the Americans' advantage of air power. There was a high percentage of days when the aircraft could not even find their targets, much less strike them effectively.

★ Ghostrider One ★

For the marines besieged at Khe Sanh, close air support strikes often had to wait until midday before the low fog that settled in the valleys and depressions of the surrounding highlands had burned off enough to give minimal visibility to both the controllers and the attacking jets.

For the pilots flying the missions in support of the besieged marines, letting down through the clouds, sometimes with less than a thousand feet between the bottoms of the overcast and the ground, was scary at best. So the Americans had gotten creative in their pursuit of the destruction of their enemy.

B-52s would fly over from Guam or Thailand and drop hundreds of bombs on either their own radar navigation or on the guidance and commands of radar controllers on the ground. These strikes, the "arc lights," were augmented by the "mini arc lights" in which four or five aircraft would join up in information with an Air Force or Marine jet specially equipped with a radar beacon for this mission, and everybody would drop at the same time.

This was not as precise as heart surgery, but it was reasonably effective, and if it scared the enemy as much as their artillery barrages did the American and South Vietnamese defenders of Khe Sanh, then it was doing some good.

Over the past four days the number of aircraft available for the defense of Khe Sanh had been diminished significantly by the Tet Offensive.

On January 30–31, during what was supposed to be a truce in honor of the Lunar New Year, the Viet Cong and the North Vietnamese Army had struck at hundreds of targets throughout the South. The attacks were not really a surprise (there had been ample evidence of *something* about to happen), but the scale of it had diverted assets from the defense of Khe Sanh to other, more immediate battles. At this point the offensive was still on but was being steadily and successfully beaten back nearly everywhere. Everywhere, that is, except in the ancient capital of Hue, where North Vietnamese regulars were holed up in the Citadel, the palace of the emperors. But even there the American forces were slowly gaining the upper hand.

It was a busy time for the marines throughout I-Corps.

Major Dick Averitt peeked over the top of the trench and watched the Marine Corps C-130 Hercules bank steeply and cross over the bands of barbed perimeter wire surrounding the Khe Sanh

Combat Base. He was torn between his instinct for self-preservation and his pilot's natural fetish for watching airplanes. Turning his back on the perimeter fence, he moved over a few feet so that his back was to a pile of sandbags that extended above his head. Now, reasonably protected from sniper rounds, he could watch the C-130.

The big prop-driven cargo plane slammed down onto the runway and decelerated quickly as the pilot reversed all four propellers. The aircraft moved quickly off the runway and spun around in the unloading area. Before the aircraft stopped, the rear ramp came down and two dozen or so dark figures ran out and either dove or were physically pulled into the various holes and trenches that served as the passenger terminal.

The first mortar rounds began landing just as the last man dashed out, their red-brown geysers of earth erupting fairly far beyond the C-130. Two large plastic-wrapped cargo pallets rolled out of the tail and stopped. The aircraft moved forward a few feet and three more pallets followed. Averitt could see one of the crewmen waving as several dark figures rose out of the ground and rushed toward the Herc, each pair dragging a darker body bag between them. As the men ran into the rear of the aircraft with their burdens, the mortar explosions moved inexorably closer.

As the last few figures, mostly wrapped with extremely visible white bandages, dashed toward the ramp, Averitt heard the engines spool up and watched the huge tail of the 130 begin to move forward. Two mortar bursts erupted about fifty feet behind the aircraft and two of the wounded men went down, only to be grabbed by a couple of brave souls and heaved into the back of the aircraft. At least, thought Averitt, when they get to a hospital, it won't be getting shelled five times a day.

The C-130 began to turn onto the runway as the mortar rounds followed, and as it had completed most of the turn, one round exploded directly under its left wing. The aircraft rocked slightly and fuel began to pour from the outboard tank between the number-one engine and the wingtip. As the aircraft moved out onto the runway itself, Averitt could see the ailerons and elevators move up and down through the full range of motion as the pilot did the fastest control check and damage assessment of his life. Even as he ran everything through, the aircraft straightened on the runway and the sound of the engines increased as they moved toward full power. It was obvious that unless the Herc was completely unflyable, it was going to get the hell out of there.

The big aircraft accelerated slowly at first, outpacing the mortars that pursued it, the mortarmen frantically trying to adjust their fire as quickly as they could. One of them, either extremely lucky or perhaps even well trained, managed to drop a round dead center on the runway ahead of the C-130 just as the pilot lifted the nose to fly it off. Averitt caught his breath, certain that the next thing he'd see was a huge fireball as the Hercules cartwheeled the rest of the way to the perimeter fence.

But the aircraft only wobbled a little and flew through the cloud of earth and smoke. It continued to climb steeply, banked away from the hills, and entered the overcast after about seven hundred feet of climb.

Averitt released the breath he was holding and stared at the exhaust trail that marked the spot where the 130 had disappeared into the gray clouds. Still marveling at the sheer courage and airmanship of the Hercules crew, it took him a few seconds to notice that the incoming fire had stopped. A couple of minutes later, so did the thumps of the outgoing return fire.

He reached into the pocket of his flak jacket and pulled out a crumpled pack of Marlboros. He took one out and fished in his other pockets for his Zippo with the rubber band wrapped around it. He lit the cigarette and inhaled deeply, thinking about the seventy yards he was going to have to run in the open to get to the holes and trenches next to the runway. Then he'd have to dash across the runway into another trench, wait a few minutes to get his heart going again, and then one more sprint to the command post. In all the days since he'd been there, he'd never been able to acquire the blithe disregard for danger that some of the other marines had.

This place still scared the living shit out of him. He couldn't figure out whether it was because he was subject to the impartiality of artillery or because he simply didn't want to die on the ground and be zipped into a rubber body bag like those who had just left on the C-130. At least, if he were in an A-4, he'd be able to get the hell out of trouble at five or six hundred knots once his job was done. And, in the A-4, he had an ejection seat to get him out of the airplane if need be. Since almost all the Marine missions were flown over the South, unless he was incredibly unlucky or unless God was thoroughly pissed off at him, he'd stand an excellent chance of rescue.

But sitting there, waiting to be turned into a collection of separate but indistinct body parts, was not the kind of thing he'd dreamed about in flight school. It seemed to take a lot of the shine away from being a Marine aviator.

Five minutes later Averitt leaned up against the sandbagged entrance to the regimental command post, trying to regain his breath. He raised his arms over his head and looked back at the way he'd come. There had been a time when several short sprints like that would have been no problem at all. He knew he could blame it on the boots and flak jacket he wore, but he also knew that the real reasons were that he was on the far side of thirty now and that he smoked too damn much. He decided once again that if he ever got out of this war alive, he'd give up cigarettes, but he knew that as soon as he got his wind back, he'd forget that vow.

Pushing aside the heavy curtain, Averitt stepped inside the command post and found the room as full of people as always, but quieter than it usually was. Colonel Aires was standing at the chart table in a knot of other officers, puffing on his pipe while another officer, a captain, was speaking to the group and gesturing at the chart with a collapsible silver pointer.

Averitt noted the pointer and shook his head. For some reason, he'd never been able to trust guys who used things like that. It had always seemed to him that they were striking for something, like general maybe. They were always trying to get noticed. All form and no substance would be the phrase, he supposed. He glanced briefly at the captain's chest and saw no sign of aviator's wings which meant that at least he'd not be professionally competitive with the captain.

Regimental Sergeant Major Gorton, standing next to the colonel, spotted Averitt, smiled, and leaned over and said something to the colonel.

Aires glanced up at Averitt and gently interrupted the captain. He waved Averitt over to the group. "Perfect timing, Dick. Come on over here. You're just the guy we need for this."

Averitt walked to the table and stood there across from Aires. The others made room for him in the way that told him he was genuinely welcome. He looked down at the chart and saw that it was a large-scale depiction of the area from which he'd just come.

He looked up at the captain as the colonel told him to continue his briefing.

The captain gestured at the area about a half-mile outside the perimeter wire. As he did, he spoke directly to Averitt, bringing him quickly up to speed on what he'd been saying. There was no trace of annoyance in his tone, which made Averitt begin to regret the snap judgment he'd made when he'd seen the pointer.

"Hi, Major. I'm Brad Cornell from Delta Company, Second Battalion. What I've been telling these gentlemen about are the certain trenches and possible tunnels the little bastards have been digging just outside the wire." He spoke with a gentle southern accent, North Carolina perhaps, thought Averitt as Cornell gestured with the pointer. "Here and here."

He looked up and, as Averitt nodded, he continued. "Okay, we've had all sorts of seismic gadgets around the area trying to find out if they've been trying to dig a tunnel under our trench line and do what the damn Yankee Army tried to do at Petersburg, which is blow a hole in the lines and charge through." Averitt could see smile lines appear around the captain's eyes as he remained looking at the table through the surprised chuckles from the group. A snort from Colonel Aires registered his approval.

"Anyway, either they haven't discovered anything or they've discovered a couple dozen tunnels, depending on how you read the graph paper. The equipment doesn't seem to work well in this climate or under constant artillery and mortar fire. Probably designed and tested in a nice lab in Southern California. Whatever. The point is that we can't really tell if they are digging tunnels."

Aires's Intelligence Officer, a tall major whose jet-black hair, deep sunken eyes, and pale complexion gave him a striking resemblance to Dracula, spoke up from the group. "We are all well aware that tunneling is one of their favorite pastimes, especially when they want to hide something. But it is not an offensive tactic that we've seen from them yet. In addition, the documents and tactical plans we captured back in January did not mention tunnels. Nor did either of the two defectors we've brought in. They were asked specifically about tunnels and couldn't give us any information about them. All of which points to the idea that there isn't any tunneling going on."

Aires nodded. "So far, they've followed their plan to the letter. Their next move is supposed to be assaults on the outlying hill positions. And you're right, tunnels aren't their style of offense. Go on, Captain."

Cornell gestured again with the pointer. "Yes, sir. What they have been doing is digging trenches toward our lines. They're zig-zagging them toward us every night, and in the morning they're a couple dozen meters closer. We've been trying to hit them with our mortars and stuff, but we can't seem to slow them down. They're now close enough so that their sniper fire is actually be-coming dangerous."

Averitt hadn't noticed that the earlier sniper fire had not been dangerous. In his own parochial aviator's way, he considered all bullets coming in his direction to be a threat to him personally, but he shoved that thought away and forced himself back to what Cornell was saying.

"What we need to do is pound the crap out of the trenches soon. We can't let them use the trenches to stage an assault and we can't let them keep sitting out there shooting at us. Worst of all, they can move in some 12.7mm and use them on our resupply helos and C-130s."

Averitt thought of the C-130 he'd watched just a few minutes earlier and imagined what it would have been like for those guys if the enemy had had some effective antiaircraft weapons, like the 12.7mm machine gun, close enough to concentrate fire on approaching aircraft. These thoughts brought the trenches out of the category of personal annoyance into the area of major tactical threat. If the gomers could shut down the resupply effort, Khe Sanh stood no long-term chance. This place had absolutely nothing in its favor when it came to supporting the many extra humans who had arrived with the war.

As he looked at the chart, he realized that there was something he might be able to do about the situation. He began to let an idea simmer on the back burner while he listened to Cornell.

"It would be suicidal for us to take a couple of companies out there and attack the trenches directly. We've been hitting the area with our artillery, but it hasn't slowed them down one damn bit. We can't use the B-52s to bomb them because they're well inside the safety zone for arc-light strikes. We also can't use radar bomb-ing from tactical air assets for the same reason—accuracy. We have no weapons heavy enough on helicopters to be effective. So it looks like it'll be up to the close air support to do the job."

Cornell fidgeted with the pointer, noticed that he was betraying his nervousness, and put it down. He briefly stared at the chart and then looked up at Averitt, who met his eyes evenly. For some reason Averitt realized that he liked this guy. He winked at Cornell as he spoke up.

"Colonel, you all have probably thought of this, but we have some ways we can fuse our bombs so that we can get them to penetrate the ground several feet before they detonate. I'm no expert, but I believe that we can deliver these bombs on a more or less continuing basis which will probably collapse the trenches and any tunnels around. It won't kill a lot of them, but it will keep them busy as hell repairing the trenches and digging each other out. If they're kept busy repairing what they've already dug, they won't have time to dig any new trenches. The danger will be that there will be a whole lot of bomb craters out there which could easily provide cover for them."

Aires stared at his pipe, which had now gone out, and then stuffed it in his shirt pocket. "True. But it will also provide rougher terrain for them to attack over. How long will it take you to get this organized, Dick?"

"I'm not sure, Colonel. I don't know what's available at Chu Lai or Danang, what with the offensive that's been going on. But I'll find out, sir."

Aires nodded. "Okay. Try to get it started as of tomorrow. The sooner we discourage them, the better off we'll be."

He looked at Cornell. "Brad, you give him a hand. It'll give you a chance to see how these damn aviators think. It'll also make you glad you're not one of 'em. I'll fix it with your boss. You two get back to me with a plan as soon as possible."

Averitt saw Aires's barely concealed smile as he made the crack about aviators and passed up a reply. He and Cornell both gave their "aye-aye, sir" and left the bunker. Averitt was pleased to see that the silver pointer stayed on the table.

Standing outside, Averitt offered Cornell a Marlboro and lit it and then lit one for himself. Cornell took a drag and looked out over the combat base. "Well, what do we do first, Major?"

"We can start with you calling me Dick. Then we can try to get to the Air Coordination bunker without getting shot. And then we'll get on the horn to the close air-support guys and find out what they've got available."

"What happens if they don't have what we need?"

"Never fear, my son. One thing you have to understand about us poor benighted airedales is that we always have a backup plan. If I can't get what we need from our guys, I'll get it from the Navy. After all, we've been stealing the Navy blind for almost two hundred years. They expect it and, if we don't steal from them, they feel hurt. You're gonna enjoy this. Trust me."

Cornell smiled and pointed to the left, away from the airstrip. "It's a shorter distance to your bunker than it is to mine, so I figure I'm ahead of the game already. Can we go now?"

Averitt stomped out his cigarette in the dirt and then picked up the remains.

"Yup. Unfortunately, I can't seem to think of any reason to stay here, nice and safe. Okay, let's go."

28

Saturday, February 3, 1968

Lieutenant Nick Taylor looked at the message form in his hand and then up at the weather forecast on the television screen over his worktable. It was now a little after 2200 and he was the only one still in the ship's Intell Center. He pulled down the clipboard that contained tomorrow's air plan and the individual squadron flight schedules.

The air plan was a sort of big daddy of schedules covering the ship and the air wing and each and every aircraft launch and recovery, including the helicopter missions and the logistics flights to and from Danang. It was created in a room known as Strike Ops, where the ship's operations officers and their counterparts from the air wing went over the requirements sent out from the overall commanders ashore and the longer-term schedule that came from the meddlers in Washington. They matched them with the noncombat requirements of each squadron—maintenance flights, ferry missions from the Philippines, pilot proficiency flights, and so on, and then tried to fit it all into the twelve hours of flight operations the *Shiloh* would fly the next day. Once they had a handle on all that, they would get out their grease pencils and put a rough plan together on the large Plexiglas board on the wall. They would then summon the operations officers from each squadron to come in and fill in the proper numbers and types of aircraft that would fly the missions themselves. When all that was done, the air plan would be published and the squadrons would put out their own individual schedules.

As often as not, somebody would say, "Oh, yeah, I forgot to tell you . . ." or "We now have a New Priority which means . . ." Then everybody would have to go back and start all over again. Usually, by the time it was finally finished, everyone involved was thoroughly pissed off and exhausted. They'd head for the wardroom or to bed, knowing full well that the following day would bring another set of identical problems. It was a very handy way for these men to go quietly, completely, and irrevocably crazy. But by the beginning of the second month of a combat cruise, everyone else on the ship was crazy too, so it really didn't matter much.

The message Nick Taylor was looking at had originated from the briefing that Captain Cornell had given the officers at Khe Sanh. Averitt had passed the requirements up the chain of command and the decision had been made to assign the task of bombing the trenches and possible tunnels to the Navy. Since the *Shiloh* was the carrier presently assigned to the dawn-to-dark schedule, her air wing was given the job.

The message specified the type of weapons and fuses that were going to be needed, and the ordnance divisions in the affected squadrons were now hard at work getting them all up from the magazines far below so they could be loaded on the jets for their launch. The pilots had been assigned and the briefing for the mission would begin at 0830 in the morning.

Jim Hogan, Terry White, and Jack Wilson, as the C.O., X.O., and Operations Officer from Taylor's squadron, which had been given this particular task, were due to arrive in a few minutes for the final mission planning.

Taylor laid the message and the squadron flight schedules down on his worktable and picked up another clipboard loaded with intelligence summaries concerning Khe Sanh. He'd read them all several times each, and whenever a new one came in, he added it to the stack, first checking the previous messages and making sure all the mental pieces fit.

He knew well that he might be getting just a trifle obsessive about the siege of Khe Sanh, but he couldn't help it. There were *real* marines there and *real* enemy divisions which were quite professionally trying to kill them, to shove them off the hills and to drive them back to the sea.

For months American aircraft had been pounding the hell out of the vast network of dirt roads in the Laotian panhandle known collectively as the Ho Chi Minh Trail in an effort to stop the enemy's flow of men and materiel to the war in South Vietnam. But it had been a waste of time and effort, not to mention the aircrews lost forever over the brutal terrain of eastern Laos and Cambodia. The beginning of the Tet Offensive, four nights before, had highlighted the failure of the effort, but the lessons were being lost on those directing things back in Washington. They equated tonnages of bombs dropped with the probability of supplies and trucks destroyed and came up with numbers that were considered facts and not estimates. The charts and graphs and glossy maps showed that it was working, therefore it must be. After all, formulae and numbers can't lie.

But the enemy's semi-surprise Tet Offensive had redirected the war abruptly. The attacks on forty towns and cities and military posts had been beaten back quickly and mercilessly in all but a couple of places. But those places, Hue and Saigon, were visible and accessible to the media so, suddenly, the major victory of the war was somehow now perceived as a crushing defeat.

Taylor got up and walked over to the huge wall chart and stood staring at the marks he'd made denoting everything he'd been able to glean about the situation there.

Khe Sanh was being compared to the place where the French suffered their humiliating and final defeat, Dien Bien Phu, nearly fourteen years earlier. Like Dien Bien Phu, Khe Sanh was an island in a sea of enemy guns and men, but there the similarity ended.

The French had no effective air power and no artillery support then. They had no resupply and no hope of relief. That was not the case here. There was no doubt in Nick Taylor's mind that the marines would hold out. There was also no doubt in his mind that aside from the fact that it was the marines with whom the gomers had tangled, air power would be the key.

For about the thousandth time in the past few months, Taylor cursed his wounded leg which was keeping him from being a part of all this. He felt like the guy who handed out the towels in the team's locker room, and he hated that feeling.

The pain in his jaw brought him back to the present. He had a habit of tightly clenching his teeth when he got "all intense," and intensity was not what he needed just then. To distract himself, he went over to the coffee urn to make sure that there was enough for everybody when they arrived.

He was back at the map board when the buzzer sounded at the door. With a quick, reflexive glance around the room, Taylor confirmed that no classified materials were lying about and then walked over and pulled the door open. He stepped back and held the door as Hogan, White, and Wilson walked in, and then pushed it closed.

By the time he'd turned around again, all three pilots were standing looking at the grease-pencil marks on the map. Taylor picked up the clipboards and joined them.

"You guys want any coffee? It's over there in the corner."

White and Hogan declined, but Wilson got himself a cup and rejoined them. Taylor waited a few seconds and fiddled with his grease pencil before he spoke.

"What I'd like to do is go over the area around Khe Sanh that you're going to hit tomorrow and to ask you to help me set up the briefing for the mission."

All three nodded and waited for Taylor to continue.

He sighed and handed the messages to Hogan, who passed them on as he read each one. When they were done, Wilson and White looked at him expectantly, but Hogan spoke quietly. There was something in Taylor's tone that he hadn't heard before. "What's on your mind, Nick? You don't need our help to set up a mission briefing. You do it better than any one of us."

Taylor laughed self-consciously. He was surprised at how easily Hogan had seen through him. "Okay. I know that tomorrow's mission is no big deal really. But I want to make sure that we can do the max damage possible to the gomers with what we have. That latest message you saw about the enemy possibly massing for an attack on Hill 861, which is right, um, here. The assessment from MACV in Saigon is that this is gonna be just the start of a major effort to drive the marines out of the place. If these trenches and

235

tunnels aren't stopped, it could be a real mess for the good guys. I just want us to do everything we can to help.

"The other thing is that I'm pretty sure that we are going to be called upon to fly a lot of close air support missions in the next few days, and I want us to have every edge."

Hogan broke in. "And you think that we might be a little rusty on the close air support? Is that it?"

Taylor nodded and Hogan continued. "Well, as far as I'm concerned, I am rusty. I haven't flown a real one since my last tour." He turned to the others. "How about you guys? And for that matter, how about the rest of the squadron?"

Both White and Wilson agreed that they hadn't flown the mission in a while, and Wilson added, "Most of the guys did some early on in the cruise, when we operated off South Vietnam, but not much since. We haven't even gotten involved against the latest attacks. That's been almost exclusively Air Force and Marines with a bunch of help from the South Vietnamese Air Force."

Taylor retrieved the stack of messages and pulled out a black three-ring binder. "Here's the air wing SOP for close air support. This one's completely up-to-date with all the latest changes. Jack, if you would, please have the flight officer check it against the squadron copy. In the back are the latest procedures from both the Seventh Air Force and from the Third Marine Division Headquarters at Dong Ha. I'll go over them in the briefing tomorrow, but I think we ought to rebrief them to everybody else as soon as we can."

Wilson thumbed through the binder. "Okay. Consider it done."

Hogan sat forward in his seat. "Nick, we're sending eight aircraft out on that mission tomorrow. Would you feel better if we had mostly senior guys leading each section?"

Taylor sighed. "Yessir, just this once. I know that everybody is qualified to fly every mission, but I think that this one deserves some special emphasis."

He stood and began pointing out little marks on the chart. "You can see that there are a bunch of hills around here that are a little bit higher than Khe Sanh itself. The enemy owns a lot of them, like Hill 881 North here. Nobody's seen any heavy Triple-A in the immediate area, but enough 12.7s can get you just as well. The mission itself shouldn't be too tough, but it does call for some extra care.

"If it were simply going to be a routine bomb-dumping job, it wouldn't matter, but this is going to take just a little more precision than that. We're going to mix in a few delayed-action bombs and a couple with fuses which will let them bury themselves deeply before going off. The delayed-action ones ought to really get 'em. If we mix these in with the normal loads, the next time those diggings get bombed, it'll make them slow the whole repair effort down. It won't be much, but it'll be something.''

White looked at the weather vision. "The killer is going to be the weather. If we're going to try to bury those bombs deep, we'll need a pretty steep dive angle, which means a fairly high ceiling.''

Wilson nodded as he looked at the flight schedule. "Skipper, we don't have to do much to this to get the right mix of pilots for tomorrow. I'll schedule an all-officers meeting for after flight ops to review the close air procedures.''

"Okay, sounds good. Nick, what about the other squadrons? We can't just do this on our own. They're involved too.''

"Well, I got with their AIOs earlier and we all talked to the CAG operations types. We're getting everything together for the follow-on missions and you can probably stand by for a C.O.s' meeting tomorrow. Since we're the only squadron going tomorrow, I thought we ought to get hot on it.''

"You're right. Okay, let's get with it.'' Hogan pulled the messages back across and began to look for the load plan for the bombs.

Averitt walked into the command post at Khe Sanh shortly after 2230 and found things almost relaxed. A few people were manning the telephones and radio consoles, but there was no one standing by the map table. The absence of the customary knot of men there made it seem as if the whole bunker was empty.

Sergeant Major Gorton was at a small table in the corner, staring into space as he chewed the end of a pencil. Averitt moved toward the chart table, and it was his movement that distracted Gorton. As Averitt bent over the table, he heard Gorton's voice.

"Evenin', Major. What can we do for you?''

Averitt grinned. "Not a thing, Sarn't Major. I was just coming in to make sure I had the area fixed in my mind for our little tunnel safari tomorrow.''

"Yeah, Colonel Aires liked your plan. The message from the *Shiloh* came in an hour or so ago. The Navy's going along with the delayed-action bombs. The colonel had me pass the word that nobody is to do any patrolling in that area until he gives the okay. Are you going to do the coordinating?"

"Nope. I'm just a fifth wheel around here. I'll leave that for the guys who do it every day. But I sure as hell am going to be watching."

Averitt nodded as he scratched a sudden and intense itch on his chest. "I'd kill for a shower right about now."

Gorton laughed. "I know. I haven't had one in, I dunno, three weeks at least. We can't spare the water. I'm just glad it's not summertime, because we'd be in deep shit here with only that little creek they call a river for a water supply. If the gomers ever shut off our water point or poison the supply, we're screwed, since, no matter how hard they tried, and they would bust their ass for us, there's no way the helos could keep us going."

Averitt nodded as he looked at the chart. Water parties were sent out daily to the Rao Quan "river" to bring in enough, but barely enough, to keep the base going. Water for washing or shaving was out of the question, and Gorton was right. If it were the heat of summer, men would literally be passing out from thirst. Still, it was better here than for the infantry companies on the outlying hills. Their water had to be flown in by helicopter, which was as dangerous for the men on the ground as it was for the helo crews.

When Averitt had first arrived, he was struck by how badly everyone else smelled. He no longer noticed now and knew full well that this was because he smelled just as bad.

"Sarn't Major, would you like to come out to the trench line and watch the show tomorrow?"

"I'd love to, Major. It'll give me something to write my grandson about."

"Grandson? You don't look old enough for that."

Gorton chuckled. "I got an early start, but my son was smart enough to wait and graduate from college before he got married. His name's Tommy, same as me, and he's almost five. My son is almost a doctor now, so the little one is going to have a full-time father."

Averitt watched Gorton's tough visage soften just a little as he talked about his grandson. Reaching into his helmet, Gorton pulled out a small photograph and looked at it fondly before handing it over. It was of a laughing black-haired boy who was riding on one of those ten-cent-a-ride electric ponies that sit outside department stores.

Averitt looked at it carefully and handed it back. "Fine-looking little man."

"Yes, he is. And when I'm done with this tour I'm going to retire and teach him how to fish. I've only got four months to go, and then it's home for keeps. Thirty years is enough."

Gorton shook his head and carefully laced the picture back in his helmet. In less than the blink of an eye he was again a regimental sergeant major in the Marine Corps. "Well, where are you going to be?"

Averitt pointed to a spot in the trench line at the closest point to the North Vietnamese trenches. "Right about here. The forward air controllers will be directing both the aircraft and the spotting rounds. Time over target for the jets will be 1100."

"I'll be there early, Major. I guess I'd better turn in. Good night, sir."

"Good night, Sarn't Major."

Gorton folded the paper he'd been writing on, gathered up his equipment, and left the command post, leaving Averitt to study the charts one more time.

It was just after midnight when Taylor's informal planning meeting broke up. They'd worked the tactics and rechecked the weapons loads on all of the eight aircraft that were to fly the mission the next day. They had even managed to have two spares manned and ready just in case. The fact that there were so many of the squadron's A-4s available and not mired in the maintenance effort quietly pleased Hogan.

It meant that a new attitude was taking over in VA-262. The sailors and their officers and chiefs were becoming a team. They were anticipating the demands of their jobs instead of reacting to them. New ideas were being tried, many of them quite successfully, and a few, well, they weren't so hot. But the key point for Hogan was that they were being tried.

He and White had made it a point to visit the squadron work spaces on a relatively frequent basis. The first few times had been difficult in that the sailors seemed to be waiting for a lecture or threats or something. When it became apparent that Hogan and White were genuinely interested in them as people instead of as cogs in a machine, they warmed up. They told their friends, and it was only a matter of a couple of days before the entire attitude of the squadron changed. Having ten A-4s available to fly the next day, where it was once a struggle to get six or seven, was an indication of just how far they'd come as a unit.

Hogan stood and stretched his back. "Well, I suggest we all turn in. There'll be time to double-check everything again in the morning."

The others stood also, and Wilson and White made their way to the door. Hogan hung back, saying that he had something he wanted to talk to Taylor about. When the door closed, he pulled an envelope from the leg pocket of his flight suit, handed it to Taylor, and watched as the young man read the sheet of paper inside.

When Taylor was finished, he looked up at Hogan, speechless.

Hogan sat on the edge of a table. "That's the first time I've ever seen you at a loss for words. Doesn't suit you."

Taylor looked back at the sheet of paper and read it again. It was a message from the Naval Aerospace Medical Institute in Pensacola to the squadron granting him a waiver and reinstatement, allowing him to resume full flight status. It was his ticket back home—to the cockpit of one of his beloved A-4s.

Never in his life had Nick Taylor had such a feeling as he did at that moment. Not when he'd first gotten his wings, not when he'd found out that he'd made all-American, not even when his sister had named her firstborn after him.

He looked up at Hogan again and tried to speak, but all that came out was a weak "Skipper, I, uh . . ."

Hogan smiled and stood up suddenly. He turned his back on Taylor and walked over to the coffee urn. He didn't really want any coffee, but he was having just a touch of trouble with his eyes at that moment. He sipped the half-cup he'd poured and busily stirred in some sugar. He spoke over his shoulder.

"Well, pardner. That's it. It says you can leave anytime. You'll spend a couple of months at Lemoore, getting yourself back up to speed in the aircraft, and then it's back to the fleet. You'll probably get your pick of squadrons too."

He turned around to face Taylor again. He grinned as he walked over and sat back down on the table edge.

Taylor very carefully folded the message and put it back in the envelope. The muscles of his jaw worked for a few seconds, and then he looked back up at Hogan.

240

"Skipper, it says that I can leave at the discretion of my commanding officer. If it's all right with you, I'd like to stick around until the cruise is over. When we get home, I can just step over to the RAG and I'll be handy enough to help out my replacement."

"Okay, Nick, it's your call. I'm more than happy that you want to stay for a while. We need you. But when you're ready, just say the word and we'll set it up for you back at Lemoore."

Taylor nodded. "Look, Skipper, thanks. I don't know how you did this so fast, but I'm grateful."

"But I didn't do it, Nick. Commander Blake took your packet back home with him and hand-carried it to the Bureau of Personnel. I imagine he saw to the whole process himself."

Taylor wasn't sure he'd heard it right. "Commander Blake? But he . . ."

"Hated you? I don't think he really did. He asked me for your waiver request packet just as he was leaving the ship. He signed it right there and we fudged the date on it so it would look as if he were still C.O. when he did sign it. He never said why he took it either, Nick, but I'm damn glad he did. It would have taken months longer from over here."

"Does anybody else know about this?"

"The Admin Chief handed it to me as I was on the way here. Judging from the way he and everybody else in the ready room was grinning, I'd say the whole damn air wing should know by now, so you can expect to take a lot of teasing in the next few days."

Hogan saw the light of combat come on in Taylor's eyes as he thought about the teasing he would be getting from those who were now, at last, his *fellow* aviators again. He knew that Taylor's briefings were going to be interesting from now on, to say the least.

Hogan turned and walked out of the Intelligence Center. What he had just been able to do filled him with amazingly good feeling. At least once in a while, even in the middle of a war, something nice and clean and *right* can happen, he thought. He wondered if Taylor would ask to return to this squadron when he finished his refresher training.

He hoped so. Men like Nick Taylor don't come along very often.

29

Sunday, February 4, 1968

Commander Jim Hogan looked out to the side and watched the last of his four aircraft join the formation. Terry White, in 410, was leading the second division of four which should have been joining up a thousand feet below. Hogan rolled out of the orbit and took up a course of 190 for the coast of South Vietnam. He keyed his radio and transmitted a curt "Ghostriders, switch."

Hogan rocked his frequency selector over to the one the Air Force C-121 radar control aircraft was on and waited a few seconds, giving everybody else a chance to get there too. He keyed his radio again, calling for the "ripple check."

"Ghostriders."

Immediately, the other aircraft came back in order, telling him that they were all on the same frequency.

"Two" from his own wingman.

"Three" from Joe Jackson, the leader of the second section.

"Four."

That's everybody, thought Hogan. He keyed his radio and called the Air Force controller. "Hillsborough, Ghostrider 406 is with you with a flight of four. Request radar following to Blackhorse. Level Angels 25 and squawking 4326."

"Blackhorse" was the call sign being used by the air control people at Khe Sanh. Hogan's flight was at twenty-five thousand feet and he had code 4326 set in on his radar identification transponder.

"Roger, Ghostrider. Radar contact. Make your heading, um, 195; that's one-niner-five for Ghostrider 406."

Hogan eased his jet a little to the right and steadied out on the

242

new heading. He signaled for the others to spread out some, which gave them a chance to fly without the intense concentration required in close parade formation. It was no more than thirty seconds later when he heard White's voice checking his flight in with Hillsborough.

Down below there was a solid deck of blinding white clouds that stretched out to the horizon on either side and through which his flight had had to climb separately and join up on top. The sky above was brilliant blue, the air through which they flew was completely free of turbulence, "smooth as a baby's ass" in pilot talk.

The weather-guessers had told them at the briefing that a massive high pressure system was about to move through the area, displacing the low cloud that had been hanging around for days. There should (words of certainty like "will" or "won't" are laboriously trained out of all weathermen) be a few days of reasonably good weather before the next mass of junk moved in.

Off on the western horizon to his left, Hogan could make out the ragged edges of this cloud deck. He hoped that there would be some clear air over the target, since two of these A-4s, Jackson's section, were carrying Mk-84 two-thousand-pound bombs specially fused to penetrate thirty or so feet into the ground before detonating. To deliver them properly, these two jets would have to roll in from about fifteen thousand feet and drop the bombs at five thousand or so, which meant that they needed at least that much altitude between the clouds and the ground.

The other six jets, Hogan's, his wingman's, and White's four, were carrying Mk-81 and Mk-82 "high-drag" bombs which weighed two hundred fifty and five hundred pounds respectively. These were fitted with tail fins that would pop out at release and slow the bomb's descent so that the dropping aircraft would have time to get out of the fragmentation pattern of the explosions. These "frag patterns" extended up to three thousand feet in every direction from the impact point so that not only did the pilots have to dodge whatever antiaircraft fire the enemy put up but also the chunks of metal thrown out by their own weapons.

The good news about the heavy bombs that Jackson and his wingman were carrying was that after detonating thirty feet underground, most of what went up in the air was dirt and smoke, and, of course, whatever bits of the enemy tunnelers and their equipment they happened to find.

"Ghostrider 406, Hillsborough. Blackhorse advises that the weather in their area is two thousand scattered, visibility unrestricted. The altimeter is 29.98 and rising."

"Roger, niner-niner-eight." This was good news. A rising altimeter setting meant that the high pressure area had arrived earlier than predicted and the weather was improving. The scattered clouds at two thousand feet would pose no problem at all for the higher level, Mk-84, bomb runs.

After ten minutes or so, the Air Force controller gave the flight a course change to the west. In a few more minutes he told them that they had crossed the beach line which was invisible beneath the clouds under them. Each of the pilots rechecked that all their armament switches were set and their sights were adjusted for the correct deflection. According to Hogan's navigation, they should be arriving over Khe Sanh in about eight more minutes.

"Ghostrider 406, Hillsborough."

"Go ahead, Hillsborough."

"Roger, sir. Blackhorse advises that they've got a resupply effort under way and several urgent medevacs coming. They got hit pretty hard last night. Can you hold for a while?"

"Roger. Any estimate on how long they'll need?"

"Stand by."

Hogan checked his fuel. They should be all right if the delay wasn't too long. One of the things they'd planned for last night was a longer than comfortable delay caused by the weather. There was supposed to be a tanker available on request from the ship that would meet them out over the water in case things ran too long. If the tanker went down for some reason, they could always land at Danang or Chu Lai and refuel there.

"Ghostrider 406, Hillsborough. Estimated delay is twenty minutes."

"Okay, Hillsborough. That shouldn't be a problem, but if it takes much longer than that, we'll have to make some plans."

"Roger, that. I'll keep you advised. Hold at present position. Maintain twenty-five thousand."

"410 copies." White had been following the entire conversation and was telling Hillsborough that he needn't repeat everything for his benefit.

"Roger, 410. You can hold at your present position. Angels twenty-four."

"410."

Hogan looked down and noted his position relative to the radio navigation aid, called a TACAN, at Danang, and set up an easy orbit around that position. He hated being stuck in holding. It gave him too much time to second-guess things.

Just after 1000, Averitt was studying the area outside the trench line with his field glasses, when he heard the sound of running feet, a thump, and an amazingly fluent string of curses. He looked down and saw Sergeant Major Gorton picking himself up off the floor of the trench. A younger marine was apologetically picking up Gorton's equipment and handing it to him as if he were afraid he'd pull back his arm and it would be minus a hand.

"I'm sorry, Sarn't Major. I didn't see you."

Gorton forced what he obviously felt was a warm and forgiving smile as he spoke. "That's all right, son. My fault. You're the one who has a job out here. Get on with it."

The young marine, a private who couldn't have been older than nineteen, backed around the sergeant major and, when his escape route was clear, ran off along the trench. The sergeant major laughed and picked up his helmet from the floor of the trench. Averitt noticed that the first thing the older man did was check the inside, where he kept the picture of his grandson.

He shoved the helmet back on his head and climbed up on the raised firing step next to Averitt.

"How're we looking this fine morning, Major?"

"Pretty good, but it looks like the gomers have moved their trenches forward another dozen meters or so." He handed his field glasses to Gorton and ducked below the edge of the trench while Gorton inspected the long zigzag scar across the front of this position. Gorton looked calmly out at the scene so long that Averitt began to worry about the snipers the enemy had placed everywhere. It was probably only fifteen seconds or so, but it seemed a lot longer.

The sergeant major finally dropped next to Averitt and sat on the firing step. "The colonel told me to tell you that they've got a large resupply effort coming in this morning. It's supposed to be here and gone by 1030, but you never know. There are also a bunch of wounded from mortar fire last night out on 861 and they'll have to be picked up too. None of 'em are critical, but we'll have to get 'em out of there soon."

"How'd it go out there? It looked and sounded pretty rough from where I was standing."

"Yeah, it was. Those little microphone sensors we have all over the place and all the intelligence we've seen say that something is going to happen soon. The gomers have to take those outposts before they can make a real try at taking this place. Last night was just the opening round, I'm afraid."

Averitt stared off at the distant hills. He couldn't see much beyond reddish scars on top of them from this distance. He hadn't seen any close combat so far, nothing except the impersonal and nonnegotiable death caused by mortars, artillery, bombs from the jets he controlled, and the odd sniper round that whined its way across the base toward the unwary. He couldn't imagine what it would be like to have the enemy coming through the wire at him. That thought brought back his long-standing belief that his fellow marine officers who were leading infantry companies and platoons were cut from a special bolt of cloth.

Suddenly, there was a *crack* and a sound like a slap, followed by a sharp *pow* from outside the perimeter wire. From the marines in the trench a bunch of curses and several shouts of "corpsman!" erupted

Averitt looked around and saw Gorton and the men from the communications section hunched down below the edge of the trench, looking around to see whom the sniper had hit. About forty feet down the trench, several men from the platoon assigned to this section of the perimeter were bent over a marine who was lying on the trench floor. There was a great deal of blood coming through his fingers as he pressed them to the wound in his neck.

Averitt was roughly shoved aside by a large young man in fatigues who was carrying an olive-drab pouch. "Make a hole. Comin' through."

The young man pushed his way through the knot of marines gathered around and dropped to his knees next to the now-groaning man. Surprisingly gentle for such a large man, the corpsman pulled the marine's hands away from the wound and examined it carefully, all the while keeping up a chatter about how soon he'd be on a medevac and how lucky he was that the wound was not serious. The corpsman pulled out a compress from his pack and tore it open, placing it over the wound and tying the strings around the marine's neck.

He got the marine to his feet, saying, "You ain't hurt bad. You're

246

going to walk because I'm sure as hell not gonna carry your ass."
The corpsman led him away, down the trench toward the aid
station known as Charlie-Med. His buddies cheerfully called after
him that they'd see him back there soon and urged him to enjoy
the round-eyed nurses back in the rear. They picked up his gear
and put it in their small bunker which connected to the trench on
the side away from the enemy.

Gorton walked over to the group, asked for their platoon sergeant, and when told that he was not immediately available, asked
them to go find him, please, and have him report to the sergeant
major here in the trench. Gorton walked back to Averitt, picking
up his rifle from the firing step where he'd laid it down.

"Fuckin' snipers. I wish we could spot them easier. That kid
was just trying to watch what was happening out there, I suppose.
Left his head up too long."

He saw the question in Averitt's eyes. "He's not really hurt too
bad. The round just tore up some muscle. He'll be a routine medevac at worst. If he's smart, he can probably take a month or so
healing before they catch him and send his ass back here."

Gorton called over one of the communicators and told him to
check with the command post and see if there was any word on
the resupply helos.

The man bent over his handset and spoke into it, but Averitt
couldn't make out the words. The marine listened for a few seconds and then spoke to Gorton. "Sar'nt Major, they say the fog
has cleared off enough everywhere now, so the resupply will be
here about 1045."

Gorton nodded. "Okay, thanks." He turned to Averitt. "Ready
for the air show?"

"Yup. But as soon as Captain Cornell gets here we'll make sure
that the mortars have the trenches registered for fire."

"That should already be done, Major. I don't think there's a
square inch around here that isn't registered by both sides. Even
Luke the Gook down by the airstrip is on the list."

Averitt chuckled. "Luke" was the generic name of a gunner who
stood in a deep hole just outside the perimeter with a 12.7mm
machine gun and shot at every aircraft approaching or departing
the combat base. He'd been hit with mortars, artillery, and even
air strikes. Every time they silenced Luke, he'd be replaced by
another gunner, who would immediately begin blazing away
again. Once, a Marine A-4 had dropped its whole load of weapons

247

on him as Luke simultaneously had put a burst of rounds into the Skyhawk. The pilot, enraged, had then whipped around for a strafing run. Apparently unharmed by the load of bombs, Luke popped up again just as the A-4 began to come apart. The pilot, with no options left, aimed the stricken jet at him and ejected.

The A-4 pilot had been retrieved from the perimeter wire by the grunts in the trenches, totally pissed off but only a bit the worse for wear and swearing he'd finally gotten the little son of a bitch. It was an even trade, he maintained, one slightly used Skyhawk to get rid of the gunner.

Just a few minute later a C-130 came in only to be met with a wildly inaccurate burst of fire from ol' Luke, who popped up again right next to the wreckage of the Skyhawk.

The marines in the perimeter gave him a standing ovation. Even the shot-down A-4 pilot joined in.

"Hey, Major. Good morning." Brad Cornell walked up behind Averitt and Gorton. "Good morning to you too, Sar'nt Major."

" 'Morning, Captain."

"Hi, Brad. Are the mortar guys ready?"

"Yes, sir. They've already got the targets registered and have their marking rounds all set to go."

Averitt shook his head at himself. He was used to working with mobile units who had to register their targets almost daily. Both Gorton and Cornell had gently reminded him that the mortarmen at Khe Sanh knew what they were doing. Once again he felt a little out of place here. He was essentially a spare air control officer, since each member of the regiment's normal air coordination team was in place and functioning. He'd not really have a job unless and until somebody became a casualty.

He could probably go to the colonel and get himself sent back to the regiment he'd come from to await the call there but something alien to his normal aviator's personality was making him stay. He wasn't sure exactly what that was, but he did know that he'd probably never again in his entire career have a chance to be with men like these, doing something as important as this. So he had avoided asking the colonel to send him back.

This was horrible and terrifying at times, but it was exhilarating too. He could almost understand why Gorton was still out in the weeds when he could probably be in a safe job somewhere in the rear.

The communicator suddenly called up. "Major, the Super Gaggle is about five minutes out. And the control bunker advises that your Navy A-4s are holding out to the east. Call sign is Ghostrider 406. Two flights of four with 410 leading the second flight."

"Okay, thanks." He was thinking that the Ghostriders were from Jim Hogan's squadron. He wondered idly whether Hogan was with them and whether he'd recognize his voice if he were.

Only a couple of minutes later the dull booming of the heavy artillery from the Army firebase at Camp Carroll out to the east could be felt as much as heard. Simultaneously, the coughs from the mortars and thumps from the smaller artillery pieces all over the Khe Sanh complex started up. In a matter of a second or so the entire surrounding landscape erupted in smoke and flying dirt. The marines in the trenches all opened up with their own weapons, putting out the maximum amount of fire into the enemy's hills and trenches. Almost lost in the din were the dull sounds of dozens of helicopter rotor blades beating the air as they approached from nearly every point of the compass.

This was the beginning of the "Super Gaggle." It had been learned that there was much greater safety for the helicopters and crews and for the troops who had to stand out and guide the helos into the landing zones if a maximum effort to suppress the enemy's ability to shoot down the helos was made.

The Super Gaggle would be timed so that all the aircraft arrived over Khe Sanh and the outlying hills at precise times. The helicopter gunships, the amazing UH-1E Hueys, would come from Quang Tri, the CH-46 cargo helos from Dong Ha, and the jets from Danang and Chu Lai. There would be a two-seat A-4, called a FAC(A), or Forward Air Controller (Airborne), overhead to coordinate the whole thing.

A group of A-4s would come in just a bit early and lay smoke mixed with tear gas on the hills and then climb out of the way. The artillery and mortars would be timed to land all at once everywhere, keeping the enemy's heads down with the gleeful help of every marine who could get his own weapon to the trenches.

A dozen or so twin-rotor CH-46 cargo helicopters would come in from every direction possible and land simultaneously on the hill outposts and on Khe Sanh itself. Accompanying the 46s would be some Huey gunships which would suppress whatever enemy weapons positions they could find.

As soon as the helos touched down, they would be unloaded

and the outgoing personnel would pile in. The helos would then get up and away as fast as they came in, leaving the jets, mortars, artillery, and marines' rifles and machine guns blazing away until the cargo carriers were once again well out of danger.

The enemy hadn't yet been able to figure out any effective tactics to counter the Super Gaggle, and by simply trying, he exposed himself to terrible losses for very little gain. It was just one more example of the Americans' awesome firepower.

Averitt had never flown on one of these missions; they had been invented especially for Khe Sanh. They seemed to take either hours or seconds, and he had tried on a couple of occasions to time them just to see how long they really took but, in all the excitement, he had never been able to remember to look at his watch. By the time he did remember, the whole thing was over, leaving just a ringing in his ears, the faint smell of smoke and gas in the air, and a couple of hundred new craters in the South Vietnamese countryside.

And some more citizens of North Vietnam who would soon get some very bad news.

The helos and jets had been gone for a minute or so and the mortars and big guns had ceased fire when Averitt felt a nudge at his elbow. He turned and saw the eager face of Brad Cornell.

"Okay, Major. It looks like we're ready for our little show now. Should I have the Navy called in?"

Averitt nodded. He glanced back out at the smoking hills. Bombing the trenches and tunnels was going to seem like an anticlimax after the past few minutes.

30

Sunday, February 4, 1968

"Ghostrider 406, Hillsborough. You are cleared to descend at your discretion but remain at or above angels fifteen. Contact Blackhorse on prebriefed frequency. If unable to establish contact, contact me again on this freq."

"Ghostrider 406, roger. At or above angels fifteen. Switching." Hogan reached down and changed over to Blackhorse's frequency and waited a couple of seconds after the channelizer tone stopped before he called for the "ripple check."

"Ghostrider."

All three of the others in the flight answered in less than a second.

"Two."

"Three."

"Four."

Hogan paused for a moment, making sure he knew exactly what he was going to say to the controllers on the ground at Khe Sanh. Then, "Blackhorse, Ghostrider 406 is with you twenty miles east, passing through angels twenty for fifteen. We're fragged for mission zero-four-dash-zero-seven. Weapons as briefed."

"Blackhorse has you loud and clear, Ghostrider. Hold east at five miles no lower than angels fifteen. The Super Gaggle should be passing south of you now at about your, um, left ten o'clock low. They're at four thousand."

Hogan looked down and saw the loose crowd of whirling circles of a dozen or so helicopters thrashing their way toward Dong Ha and Danang as they made their way out of the Khe Sanh area. He had seen the A-4s heading out while he was still holding.

"Tallyho the helos."

"Roger. We estimate we'll be ready for you in three minutes. Stand by."

"Ghostrider 406, roger. Standing by."

Dick Averitt took his position off to the side of the small knot of marines waiting for everything to get set and the strike to begin. The trench, just below the crest of the high ground that the combat base occupied, commanded an excellent view of the floor of the small valley between the combat base and the hills to the east. The enemy was using what was left of the distant forest cover to stage their troops, and the trenches began inside the treeline. Much of the vegetation had been blasted and burned away, but there was still enough left to hide literally thousands of troops.

The elevation of the American positions would give the spotters a good enough angle to judge the impact points of the bombs in relation to the target areas out beyond the perimeter wire.

The mortar section, with their 81mm mortars, would fire white-phosphorous, or "Willie Pete," rounds for the aircraft to use as aiming points. When these rounds hit, they gave off almost beautiful streamers of white and dense smoke. The bursts stood out quite nicely against the reddish earth.

"Major, the Navy is holding about five miles east at fifteen thousand. We're all set and ready to start. Do you want to spot the mortars?"

Averitt turned and saw the wiry black marine corporal from the air liaison section holding the handset out to him. The name on his fatigues said Simpson, and, like most of the other marines around there, the look in his eyes showed that he had been there far too long and had dodged far too many barrages of enemy fire.

It was obvious that they expected him, as the senior man present, to take over the show and do the talking. He remembered his section sergeant who had been frustrated nearly to tears by a few other officers who had shown up after the troops had made all the preparations, and run the targeting missions, sometimes with disastrous effects. It had been a lesson well worth learning.

He smiled at the marine. "No, thanks. This is your backyard and it's your football. Have at it, Corporal. I'll watch the jets and wish I was with them."

The corporal smiled widely. "Yes, sir. I wish I was with them too. Must be nice to be clean."

Averitt laughed as Simpson turned to his men and put the hand-

set to his ear. He could see the young man consulting his map
and hear him relaying the grid coordinates to the mortar section.
The corporal turned around again and stood on the fire step, peering out through a gap in the sandbags in front of the position.

Averitt was impressed with Simpson's double- and triple-
checking his chart. The man had been there for at least six weeks
and knew both the chart and its grid system, and the landscape it
represented, like he knew his neighborhood back home. He could
probably have called this part of it in from Guam and been dead
on, but he was a professional.

From somewhere behind and to the left, Averitt heard the cough
of the mortar and, with his field glasses, stared out at the land
beyond the perimeter wire, waiting for the round to come down.
When it did, he noted that it was a high-explosive round that left
little smoke, just exploding and proving that everyone was playing
from the same sheet of music. He liked that too.

If it had been a Willie Pete round and had been off, there was
a chance that it could have confused the jets. This one was pretty
much right on, so the corporal told the mortars that that was good
and to switch to the spot where the other suspected tunnel was
supposed to be. That one was perfect too, so that target was all
set.

Averitt moved over a little and stood closer to Gorton and Cornell but not so far away that he couldn't hear Simpson's half of
the conversation as he consulted a scrap of paper in his free hand
while he spoke to the A-4s.

"Ghostrider 406, this is Blackhorse 20. You are cleared into the
area. Present weather is two thousand scattered, visibility unlimited, altimeter three-zero-zero-zero. Wind's out of the west at about
ten knots."

"406, copies. Three triple-zero."

"406, Blackhorse, the target is on the east side of the perimeter.
There are two suspected tunnels and a system of trenches. There
had been reports of only light Triple-A in the area. Best ejection
is east and southeast. When you have the area in sight, we'll mark
it. Make your runs south to north."

"406 copies all and we're overhead at this time. We have the
target area in sight. Standing by for your mark. The Mk-84s will
be first. There'll be one run for each aircraft."

"Blackhorse, roger. Understand one run each for the big ones."

"Click-click." Keying the microphone twice and causing the clicks in the receiver was the pilot's universal acknowledgment.

Simpson's assistant, a huge white marine lance corporal who had taken over communicating with the mortars, turned to him and said, "Ready when you are, massa."

Simpson nodded and turned to Averitt. "That's Dugan. Can't get no respect from these guys once they grow up and find out they lost the damn Civil War." As Averitt and his two companions chuckled, the lance corporal said absently, "That's the War of Yankee Aggression, massa."

Simpson smiled weakly and shook his head resignedly. "All right, Dugan, you win. Call for the Willie Pete."

Dugan spoke into his phone and then turned to Simpson. "Shot out."

"Okay."

Out in front, almost exactly where the first spotting round had burst, a blossom of white smoke grew from the earth. Simpson studied it for a second or so and keyed his handset. "406, Blackhorse 20. Your first target is about twenty meters south of first smoke."

"406, tally. Break. 405, do you have it?"

Lieutenant Joe Jackson, who with his wingman was carrying the heavy bombs, answered immediately.

"Roger, 405's got it." There was a few seconds wait while Jackson adjusted his pattern. Then a laconic "405's in."

Everyone in the trench strained their eyes up and to the right to catch the first glimpse of the attacking A-4. Averitt knew that the minimum pull-up altitude for the kind of weapon and delivery that the first two jets carried was so high that the bombs would be well on their way down before anybody on the ground would either hear or see the tiny little white Skyhawk. He just glanced up and then turned his attention to the target area, where the smoke from the marking round was beginning to dissipate in the light winds.

In Ghostrider 405, Jackson rolled the jet nearly on its back and aimed it at the white smoke. He rolled it back over again and made a couple of small corrections with his wings and rudders to get the spot lined up squarely in the sight above his instrument panel. He eased his hands and feet on the controls and made sure that there were no pilot-induced errors that would throw his aim off. He glanced at his altimeter, and as it touched 4500 feet, he hit the release, feeling the aircraft shudder just a little as the two huge two-thousand-pound bombs dropped away. He waited for a two-second count and pulled back hard on the stick.

The G forces shoved him down in his seat, and he watched as the nose passed through the horizon and the G let off before looking over his shoulder to see his bombs impact. He knew that he really wouldn't be able to see the impacts, but he couldn't resist the old habit.

The jet rocketed back up, and he rejoined the circle behind his wingman, Dave Shays, who was flying 402 and was assigned the next target. He looked back down at the target again and saw a huge double-scoop of earth and smoke climbing out of the small valley among the hills.

Simpson gave up trying to watch the fall of the bombs and concentrated on their impact points. He didn't see the dark green bombs hit the ground and was surprised when the earth erupted almost directly beneath where the marking round had been. The dirt sort of bubbled up in slow motion until the bubble burst and smoke and clods of dirt went everywhere. He felt the concussion through the soles of his jungle boots before he heard and felt the protracted *whaaam* through the air. The shock wave could be felt as a strong wind on the exposed parts of the body.

He looked at Averitt and winked as he keyed the handset. "405, Blackhorse. That was a bull with both bombs. You couldn't get any closer if you carried them out there in a jeep. Stand by for next target."

"Roger, thanks. Next target will be for 402."

Simpson nodded at Dugan and watched him until he looked back and said, "Shot out."

The Willie Pete round exploded about a hundred yards north of the first one, just a little bit short of the actual intended target. "Okay, 402, your target is marked. Target is forty meters north of the white smoke."

"402, roger." A pause. "Tally the white. 402's in."

Averitt listened for the sound of the jet's engine as it pulled out of its dive. This time he distinctly heard a double *thwap* as the bombs hit and buried themselves in the earth which was immediately followed by the earthshaking blasts as the bombs detonated. Again, dead on the target.

Simpson watched the huge hemisphere of red dirt and brown smoke settle back. "Ghostrider 402, another bull. Whatever was there isn't anymore."

"Ghostrider 406, Blackhorse. You are cleaned in. Your target is the trench lines from one hundred meters north of the last hit to one hundred meters south of the first one. Make your runs from south to north."

"406, roger. We'll be making multiple runs."

Hogan led his wingman, Cordella, down to five thousand feet and broke away to set up the bombing pattern for his five-hundred-pounders. When he and Cordella were on the opposite sides of a rough circle, he began his first run.

"406's in."

He rolled the jet over on its back and pulled the nose through so it was lined up with the system of trenches. He rolled back out, waited a few seconds, and dropped his first pair, pulling up hard right to regain his altitude. He looked over his shoulder and saw the bombs detonate, shooting out a white hemisphere of moisture as the blast wave compressed the dense air. Simpson's call that he had hit twenty meters at nine o'clock told him that he had misjudged the wind and the bombs had struck 65 feet to the left, which was pretty close but not perfect. He told Cordella to take out some wind correction and was gratified to see that his wingman's bombs hit right at the junction of two arms of the trenches. Simpson's "bull!" brought a grim smile to his face.

His next run was better, and by the time all the weapons were gone, the two little Skyhawks had ensured that the North Vietnamese diggers were going to have a couple of days repair work to do before they could get back to inching toward the American lines.

"Blackhorse, 406 and flight are off target. Climbing out to the east and passing twelve thousand for twenty-five."

"Roger that, 406. We'll pass your BDA through Hillsborough, but it looks pretty good on first cut."

"Roger, thank you. 406's clear of your area. Switching." Hogan reached down and switched frequencies, then glanced over his shoulders and saw that the other three jets were hanging out there in formation, just as they should have been.

Simpson let his hand slowly fall to his side for a moment as he mentally shifted gears. The area which the A-4s had just pounded didn't really look that much different from the way it had twenty minutes before. There were a few fresh craters that looked like they had simply migrated over from a dozen yards away. Some tendrils of smoke, probably from bits of wood or pieces of enemy equipment, remained, drifting up a few feet and dissipating in the gentle breeze. The Skyhawks had done their job well, but Simpson knew that at nightfall the enemy would again be out there, digging with the mindless tenacity of ants.

He smiled a little at the comparison. The enemy commanders had little concern for their troops, considering them not much more than ambulatory tools, heedlessly discarded when damaged and easily replaced from a new levy of "volunteers."

Simpson shook his head and put the handset back up to his ear.

"Ghostrider 410, Blackhorse."

"Go ahead, Blackhorse."

"Roger, sir. You're cleared into the area. Weather remains the same except that the wind appears to be lighter than briefed. Altimeter is three-zero-zero-zero."

"Three triple-zero. 410 is a flight of four with Mk-82s now five miles east at eight thousand, descending to five. We copied the briefing."

"Roger. We observed no Triple-A against your playmates but there have been some 12.7s in the area. Do you require a mark on the target?"

"That's affirm. We've got a general idea but we couldn't see much."

"Okay, 410. We'll get some smoke out there for you. Call when ready."

"410's ready now." White signaled the others in the flight and peeled off. The others broke away from one another, forming a circle above the target, spaced so that each aircraft would avoid the fragmentation pattern of the bombs from the guy in front of him when they began their runs against the trenches.

Simpson was turning to tell Dugan to get on the horn with the mortars, when he heard "shot out" from him. Dugan was grinning and pointing mischievously at him.

"Us lowly assistants gotta be quick to keep up with you corporals, massa, so we can be like you when we grow up."

Simpson shook his head and turned back to the trench line. The white-phosphorous round burst almost in the trenches themselves. He keyed the handset.

"404, your target is marked. Anywhere for a hundred meters north and south of the smoke."

"Roger, I have the white smoke. 410's in."

* * *

257

White's wingman today was Lieutenant (j.g.) Will Crisp in 404. He was on his first deployment and was eager to make a good impression. Being assigned as White's wingman a few days earlier had been quite a thrill for him, and he was determined to learn from White and to look good whenever they flew together. The first of his goals was commendable. The second, while not inherently bad at all, was about to get him in some serious trouble.

Crisp followed White around the large wagon-wheel bombing pattern and watched as the X.O. rolled over and began his dive toward the target on the ground far below. He only glanced in at his gauges to check that his altitude was still right, but he didn't notice that he was angling in somewhat toward the center of the circle. When he saw White pull off target, he waited the last couple of seconds until he was lined up and began his own dive.

Since he had been angling in toward the target, he had begun his dive from a much closer point than had his leader. The dive itself, when he finally rolled out, was much steeper than White's had been. Increasing the steepness of the dive meant, in turn, that his pull-out altitude was going to have to be much higher for him to avoid hitting the ground.

Almost as soon as it began, Crisp was aware that the dive was steeper than it should have been and that he'd screwed up somewhat. Up to that point he was still okay, but when he rolled all the way out he was aimed off to the west of the target which was closer to the outer defenses of the American lines. He banked the jet to get himself lined up properly and then had to correct back the other way because he had overshot a bit. He was determined to put his bombs directly on the target just as White had.

All this took a few seconds, which normally would have been no problem. But the ground was coming up much faster than it should have been and he didn't have the extra time to fool around. By the time he noticed just how fast the target was growing in his sight, he was past the pull-out altitude he should have been using for this dive angle and was fast approaching the one he would have used if he'd done it right in the first place.

He realized suddenly that he'd put himself in a very bad position and, forgetting about hitting the target, hauled back on the stick. He felt the G forces pressing him down in the seat and his oxygen mask becoming heavier on his face. It slipped down his nose a little, and he felt a tiny stream of oxygen blowing into the corner of his left eye as the seal of the mask against his face was broken. He grunted against the G and pulled a little harder, trying to get the ground to stop coming up so fast. The faithful A-4, still laden with its complement of bombs, tried as hard as it could to help him.

The nose of the jet rose some, but the flight path was still down at a frightening angle. He felt the jet shudder as the efficiency of the wings decreased with the hard pull-up and it came close to aerodynamically stalling and departing controlled flight. He lowered the nose to get that back under control and saw the ground again, much closer now. He glanced at the VSI, or vertical speed indicator, and saw that his rate of descent was still horrendous. His barometric altimeter was useless because of an inherent system lag, but his radar altimeter showed that the VSI was right.

Crisp suddenly realized that there was absolutely no way on this earth that he was going to avoid hitting the ground. He raised the nose again to try to slow the descent and succeeded just a little, but it was a certainty that it was not going to be enough. With his left hand he reached down and grabbed the ejection handle between his legs and pulled up as hard as he could.

31

Sunday, February 4, 1968

Dick Averitt watched White's aircraft pull up from its run, little bursts of white vapor trailing back from its wingtips. He looked beneath and behind the jet and watched the pair of dark green bombs fall toward the enemy trenches in a rapidly steepening arc. They detonated and the shock waves struck him almost immediately.

He looked back up and picked out the small shape of Crisp's Skyhawk as it began its dive. He could see that this one was much steeper than the first dive had been. It didn't really strike him as anything dangerous at first, but as the little shape began to get larger he expected to see the pull-out begin. When it didn't, he realized that the pilot was now in big trouble, and all thought of the enemy and bombing his trenches went away.

Averitt watched with growing horror as the nose came up and then dipped again, the pilot frantically trying to get the thing flying away from the ground. He could see that the descent was shallowing very slightly but not nearly enough. Suddenly he knew that it was a lost effort and began shouting "Eject! Eject!" as if the pilot could hear him.

He could just begin to discern the individual markings on the Skyhawk when there was a flash from the cockpit and a dark shape flew out atop a brief burst of flame and a puff of smoke. The small drogue parachute popped out from the ejection seat, and almost immediately the pilot separated from the seat itself. His own parachute streamed out and inflated just before the pilot struck the ground nearly flat on his back almost directly in front of the position that Averitt and the others were standing in.

The aircraft itself had hit the ground off to the left, midway between the outermost perimeter wire and the enemy trenches in a huge earthshaking explosion of metal, high explosive, and jet fuel. The fireball went up at least two hundred feet before it turned into an ugly yellow-centered sphere of black smoke. Everyone in the trench ducked behind the sandbags as pieces of metal and clumps of dirt showered on the area.

Simpson stood back up and peered out at the wreckage, his mouth hanging open. Gorton stood next to him and said, "Ho-ly shit!"

There was an eerie silence after that. No one was sure that they could believe what they had just witnessed. Gradually, everyone became aware of the roaring of the fire and the occasional popping sounds of the twenty-millimeter ammunition from the Skyhawk's cannon cooking off.

Averitt shook himself free of his paralysis, unthinkingly climbed out of the trench, and began running out toward the pilot, who still had not moved. His parachute had fortunately become entangled in the barbed wire of the perimeter and was not dragging him along the ground.

Gorton saw Averitt jump out of the trench and turned to the others, who were still frozen. "I need five guys to help the major. You guys there. I need a corpsman too. C'mon."

He began to climb out of the trench and felt Simpson right beside him. He stopped and shoved the corporal back into the trench. "Not you, son. Stay here. We're probably gonna need some cover. Get some shit coming down on the gomers. Keep their fuckin' heads down! Got it?"

"Yeah. Cover comin' right up." Simpson slid back into the trench and rushed over to his radio.

Gorton chased after Averitt as hard as he could, but the younger man's longer strides were covering more ground. He could see Averitt reach the inner wire barrier and begin searching for a way through. The sergeant major caught up with him as he was attempting to climb over it and pulled him down.

"Wait, Major. You're gonna cut yourself to pieces going that way." He turned to the men who accompanied him and found the senior man.

"You, Sergeant. What's your name?"

"Clarke, Sar'nt Major."

"Okay, Clarke. Can you lead us through? This is your section, right?"

"Yeah. Over to the right about fifty meters. Come on."

Clarke got to his feet and dashed bent over to the spot in the wires he'd pointed to and dropped flat again. Gorton and the others followed as quickly as they could. As they lay catching their breath, another man ran up and threw himself down next to the group.

It was the corpsman named Lawson, who had treated the marine hit by the sniper. Averitt looked at his watch absently. He couldn't believe that that was only thirty-five minutes before.

Outside the wire, mortar rounds began hitting the area. Judging from the rate of fire, it seemed to Averitt that Simpson and Dugan must be getting everyone who could fire blazing away at the enemy. Scattered bursts from the machine guns cracked overhead as the gunners in the trenches added their weapons to the covering fire.

Gorton nodded at Clarke, who moved forward and led the way through the three barriers of wire. It seemed to take an hour for them to pass through and then move to the right the last sixty meters to the downed pilot, who still lay where he'd come down.

When they did reach him, he was semiconscious and breathing heavily, sounding as if he had a bad chest cold. His oxygen mask had been unfastened on one side, so Averitt unfastened the clip on the other side and pulled the mask away. He then released the fittings that held the parachute to his torso harness, absently noting the leather name tag that told him that the name was Crisp. That done, he sat back and watched the corpsman work, staying close enough to help in any way he could.

Lawson quickly checked the pilot over and looked up at Averitt. "Major, this guy is busted up real bad. I think at least one of his legs is broken and so is his left arm. It sounds like he's got a punctured lung. We gotta get him back to Charlie-Med most skosh."

He leaned down close to the pilot and looked into his eyes as he spoke. "Can you move your legs?"

The pilot moved his thighs, moaning as he did so. "Okay, good. How 'bout your arms?" Crisp moved his right arm weakly and then his left, groaning again as he did so.

The corpsman looked at Averitt. "His back seems okay. Probably because he hit flat on it and the ground is pretty soft around here. I'm gonna give him a shot that should knock him out."

He pulled his bag over and drew out a syrette. He jabbed it into Crisp's arm and threw it away. He continued inspecting the pilot's body as he waited for the morphine to work. It wasn't long before Crisp was out cold.

Gorton glanced around at the marines surrounding them, rifles pointed out toward the enemy. "Anybody bring a poncho or something we can use to carry him?"

Without taking his eyes off the distant trench line, Sergeant Clarke handed over a poncho. "Here ya go."

Lawson took the poncho and laid it on the ground next to Crisp. Looking the man over, he was glad that he was unconscious, because getting him back to the base was gonna hurt like hell. He called a couple of the marines over and they began to lift Crisp and slide the poncho under him. He had just about gotten it done, when there was a dull metallic sound and the corpsman's helmet flew off.

Everyone threw themselves flat and, after a second or so to check for pain, looked at one another to see if anyone else had been hit. Next to Gorton, Lawson was lying on his face. The sergeant major was reaching to turn the corpsman over and see if he was dead, when he heard a muffled "motherfuck!" from him. He put his hand on the man's shoulder and asked if he'd been hit.

This led to a long stream of cursing, the sense of which was

262

that the corpsman was still alive and absolutely pissed off at the sniper who had shot off his helmet, the goddamn Navy that had sent him to be a corpsman with a bunch of fucking jarheads in the fucking middle of nowhere, Republic of Viet-fucking-Nam, and especially the goddamn Navy again for sending pilots out who didn't have any fucking idea how to fly their goddamn silly-ass airplanes.

Gorton looked across the corpsman's back at Averitt and grinned. "Seems to be just fine."

"Terrific. But how are we gonna get out of here?"

Gorton scratched his ear as he surveyed the land outside the wires. "Well, I'd say we're either gonna have to wait until dark or hope that Corporal Simpson back there is smart enough to blow the shit out of those assholes so that we can make a run for it."

Lawson crawled back to Crisp and looked him over. "This guy ain't going to make it till dark unless we get him to Charlie-Med."

He lay down next to Crisp but between him and the enemy. "Just thought I'd mention it."

Averitt's answer was cut off abruptly by the roar of a jet engine and the deep thumps of two heavy explosions. He looked up and saw one of the other A-4s from Crisp's flight climbing away. There were two large balls of smoke and falling dirt at the head of the enemy trench. Seconds later, another A-4 roared overhead and dropped a few more bombs on the enemy's positions.

"Looks like Simpson's plenty smart enough, Sar'nt Major."

"Yup. I suggest we wait a while for the mortars to do some damage and then make a run for it. We can go from crater to crater in little stages. It'll take some time, but it's our best chance." He looked at Lawson. "What do you think, son?"

Lawson smiled wanly. "You don't want to know what I'm thinking right now, Sar'nt Major, but you're right. I just hope this guy can stand the trip. I suppose we don't have a choice."

Gorton called to Clarke's marines, getting them to crawl over and take up positions on the four corners of the poncho. One of the marines handed Averitt his rifle, but Averitt handed it right back and took the man's place on the poncho. "You're better with that rifle than I am," he said.

Averitt pulled the field glasses that seemed to have come with him and bellied around until he could see back toward the positions in the American lines. He saw several men looking back at him through their own glasses. He raised his arm and waved it over his head. One of the men—he was pretty sure it was Simpson—waved back.

Now that he could sort of communicate with the spotters, Averitt did his best to tell them what he and the others proposed to do. Simpson waved in acknowledgment, leaving Averitt hoping that he'd gotten the right message across.

"Hey, Sar'nt Major. I think we should wait a couple more minutes. I tried to tell Simpson to get us as much cover as he could. I think he caught on, and, if he did, it'll be starting soon."

"Okay. But not too long. The gomers probably have every sharpshooter in their army headed over here at the double."

White hadn't seen Crisp's aircraft hit the ground. He'd heard the third pilot in the flight curse and call out that it had happened, and when he looked at the spot, the fireball was already turning into black smoke. It had taken a few seconds for it to register and a few more for him to wonder what the hell had happened. Crisp had said nothing on the radio at all after he began his run. Not a damn word.

He was about to call Blackhorse, when Simpson beat him to it.

"410, Blackhorse. Your second aircraft hit the ground. The pilot ejected and we've got some people going out after him now. He came down outside the perimeter and we're probably going to need some air cover in a few minutes. What's your fuel state?"

White looked at his gauges and did some fast math. "Blackhorse, we can stick around for twenty minutes. If it's going to take longer, suggest you get some more fast-movers headed this way."

"Roger, 410. We're coordinating that now. Stand by, sir. We'll let you know how he's doing as soon as we know. We have no comms with the patrol out there now."

"Click-click."

On the ground, Simpson watched as the patrol finally reached the downed pilot. Through his glasses he could see the corpsman working and the other marines facing outward. He turned to Dugan. "Doogs, get some mortar rounds going out there. And we need to get the goddamn M-60s going too."

Dugan picked up his phone and began speaking quickly into the mouthpiece as he pulled the chart closer and placed his finger on the spot where the patrol was now trying to get the pilot back.

Captain Cornell jumped back into the trench from the ground

above. He'd climbed out and was going to follow Averitt out of the trench but abruptly realized that there was quite enough leadership out there already. He grabbed two marines standing nearby and sent them in opposite directions with instructions to get the M-60 machine guns going to try to pin down the gomers, wherever the hell the little bastards were hiding. The men out with Averitt and Gorton were perfect targets for any enemy who possessed a gun.

Dugan yelled that there were some Marine F-4s from Danang inbound with an ETA of ten minutes. Simpson nodded and turned back to watch the progress of the patrol. He was looking right at Lawson when he saw the corpsman's helmet fly off and everybody out there hit the dirt. He immediately picked up his handset.

"Ghostrider 410, Blackhorse. Request you put some bombs down on the treeline. Somebody out there's trying to pick off our guys. Make your runs south to north. Suggest you make as many runs as possible. We've got some F-4s inbound, but it'll be ten mikes."

"Ghostrider 410, roger. We'll be commencing in one minute."

Simpson clicked his mike switch twice and put his field glasses back on the small knot of men out in the wires. He could see one of them, apparently the major, gesturing back toward the lines. As best as Simpson could make out, he was gesturing that they would make a run for it as soon as the enemy's heads were down. It didn't seem like all that intricate a plan really, but he had to smile just a little at the exaggerated one-armed miming that the major was doing while lying mostly flat on his face.

He turned to Dugan and told him to coordinate some heavier stuff from the artillery batteries higher up the hill. Captain Cornell, standing next to Simpson, overheard and started passing the word up and down the trench for everyone to open up with their rifles when the artillery started coming down.

Up and to the left they could see the A-4s beginning their runs. Simpson called the jets and warned them of the artillery rounds that would begin hitting the area in just a few seconds. He received White's acknowledgment just as the first rounds hit out beyond the wire.

Averitt and Gorton looked at each other when the first rounds exploded in the enemy positions. Now, before the enemy figured out the targeting pattern of the American guns, was the best time to go.

265

Gorton pushed himself up to his knees. "Let's go."

Averitt grabbed his corner of the poncho and with the other three marines lifted it and began to run with Crisp's inert body bouncing and bumping inside the makeshift litter. Ahead, Gorton chugged along on his bandy legs and Lawson ran alongside, holding one edge of the litter as he tried to keep the two rifles he was carrying from sliding off his other shoulder.

Behind them, Averitt could hear the roar of the jets mixing with the pounding of the artillery and mortar rounds. He had no idea whether the enemy was firing at the small rescue party, because he couldn't discern the sharp cracks of rifle bullets going by amid all the other noise. He was staring at the ground ahead of his feet, trying not to trip, and so didn't see any stray rounds chewing up the ground around them.

After only a short distance, Averitt's arm and shoulder began to burn from the unaccustomed effort of running with such a heavy load. His breath came harder and harder, and he once again cursed the cigarettes he smoked. By the time they made it to the break in the wire, Averitt expected them to dive into one of the shell craters to rest for a few moments.

Gorton stopped and looked back. "Come on. We're halfway home. Keep going while their heads are down."

The marine on the opposite side from Averitt tripped suddenly and went down. Gorton dashed over and picked up the corner and with a shout urged the others on. They began to labor up the steepening incline, going to their knees two and three at a time as they got closer and closer to the trench. When they had about fifty yards to go, several marines jumped out of the trench and ran down to them. They relieved the four carriers, who staggered ahead and simply tumbled into the trench and lay gasping on the bottom.

Lawson, still breathing heavily, crawled over to Crisp and began checking him over once again. Captain Cornell came up and detailed four marines to carry the pilot up to the little all-purpose utility vehicle, or "mule," which immediately drove off toward Charlie-Med with Lawson kneeling on the back, holding Crisp's limp form as steadily as possible on the churned-up path.

Averitt pulled himself to a sitting position and fished for a cigarette in his pockets. He pulled one out and offered the pack to Gorton, who was sitting next to him, leaning against the trench wall.

The two of them sat there, smoking and trying to regain their breath. Around them the other marines who had gone out slowly recovered and began to accept the congratulations from their fellows.

Averitt looked at the hand that held the Marlboro and watched it tremble. All at the same time he was exhilarated, terrified, exhausted, and giddy. He chuckled at the relief he felt and the understanding that he and the others had put something over on the enemy, sort of tweaked his nose, and run away safely. It was almost as much fun as flying his A-4 was. He knew that this was not a particularly rational feeling, but it was there nonetheless.

Gorton stubbed out his cigarette and looked over at him. "Major, can I say something?"

Averitt nodded. "Yeah, go ahead."

"Well, sir, with all due respect, that was a pretty stupid thing for you to do, running off like that without a plan. You could have gotten yourself and all the rest of us in some big trouble. We could have gotten pinned down out there and the gomers could have blown the shit out of us. Then some more guys would have had to come get us. If you had waited, we could have coordinated it better. In case you don't get the point, we were lucky as shit, Major."

Averitt's first inclination was to argue, but he knew that the old sergeant major was perfectly right. He had acted unthinkingly, from his gut, and that was dumb. He had always trained himself to get colder and more controlled when the shooting started. In his A-4, the less emotion he allowed himself to feel when in combat, the more effective his actions were and the better were his chances for survival and those of the men he was leading. He'd let himself get away for just a moment and, even though the result was a good one, he had put himself and others in a dangerous position.

"You're right, Sar'nt Major. I got carried away. Shouldn't have done that."

Gorton smiled. "Glad you said that and didn't give me any shit. I'm too damn tired to argue."

Getting to his feet, he extended his hand to help Averitt up. "Come on. Let's get back to the CP. The colonel's gonna be pissed when he hears about this. It'll be better if we're handy for him to yell at when he does hear though. He's a real bear when he has time to work up a real good mad."

Averitt stood and glanced out at the place where they all had been just a few minutes before. Beyond, the artillery had ceased fire and the smoke was dissipating slowly in the treeline. The whole area didn't look a damn bit different than it had when he'd arrived in the trench only a couple of hours earlier. He shook his head and started off.

Gorton grabbed his arm and stopped him gently. "Major, I gotta say one more thing. I like your style."

The old marine slung his rifle and walked off, leaving Averitt to follow, his stride just a little prouder.

32

Sunday, February 4, 1968

Jim Hogan put the bottle of Bushmill's back in his small desk safe and spun the dial to lock it. He leaned back in his chair and put his feet up on the small pull-down desktop. He sipped the drink he'd made and idly stirred the ice with his finger. He was tired to the bone, not so much because of the strain of the past few days but more because of the events of the past few hours.

Up until that afternoon, being the C.O. of a squadron had been mostly fun. He'd immersed himself in the creation of a new squadron from the ashes of the old one he'd inherited from Blake and had truly loved doing it. As the C.O., he could be the guy who made the policies instead of the one who had to support and enforce the ones set by somebody else. He could be the good guy and rely on Terry White to do the supporting and enforcing. Hogan believed that the things he had set up were sound and thus easy for the squadron to follow. So far he hadn't heard anything to the contrary.

The squadron's performance had been improving dramatically. The rest of the air wing finally seemed glad to have them around instead of giving off the faint impression that VA-262 was nothing more than a passenger in the boat. Even the Air Boss had remarked on the difference in attitude. It was still far too early for the squadron to have fully proven their worth, but they were headed in the right direction. At least until today.

When White had checked in with Hillsborough on his way out of the Khe Sanh area, Hogan had been surprised that there were only three aircraft instead of the four there should have been. Hogan, who with his four jets was now far to the east, had asked White to switch up to the squadron common frequency and had then asked what happened.

White's reply that Crisp had gone down was a shock, but more disturbing was the fact that no one seemed to know why. The worst part was that other than the fact that Crisp had gotten out of the aircraft and was injured, no one really knew much at all.

The rest of the flight back to the ship had been pretty much silent and mechanical. Navy pilots try not to say much over the radio anyway but, to Hogan, the flight seemed unusually quiet. Perhaps it was because of the deafening sounds of the questions and second-guessing Hogan was subjecting himself to. From long experience, Hogan knew that he could be his own most brutal and least accurate critic, but by the time he'd returned to the ship, he'd ripped apart everything he'd done since the change of command. He'd found nothing wrong in his performance, but the sense of failure persisted.

The cold, unassailable fact remained that one of the men he was responsible for had gone down and been hurt badly, nearly killed. They had talked about this in the various schools he'd had to go to before becoming an X.O. but had very adroitly, he thought now, avoided telling him just how shitty it would feel.

Hogan had almost lost his temper in the ready room when all White had been able to tell him was that Crisp had hit the ground. The other two in the flight had not seen any antiaircraft fire, and no one had heard anything at all from Crisp after he had made his "rolling-in" transmission. The one pilot who did see at least part of the run said that he didn't see anything abnormal about Crisp's jet other than he looked a little steep in his dive. But that really shouldn't have been a problem.

White, accurately sensing Hogan's thoughts and feelings, went forward to the Combat Information Center to use the ship's radios to try to find out what he could from Danang but was told that there had been a large number of wounded brought in to the hospital that day and more were on the way. He would have to wait until the hospital was done with its real job before they would get all the administrative details squared away.

Hogan's mood began to turn to anger, the kind of heated frustration that comes when all one's powers and abilities can do nothing to affect the situation. Men like Hogan are not good at all at being powerless, at staring at a problem and doing nothing to fix it. It is sometimes possible for them to step back and let someone more immediately involved do something, but it's unbearable when the problem directly concerns them and they know that there is nothing they can do.

Hogan had nearly finished his drink and was debating having another when there was a knock on his door. "Just a second," he shouted through the door as he dropped his feet to the floor.

He shoved his glass into the small cabinet above his desk and lit up a cigarette, taking several huge drags and blowing the smoke around the room. He went to the door and opened it to find Terry White and Chris Scott, the C.O. of VF-147, standing outside. The two came in and White grinned annoyingly as he handed Hogan a message form.

It was from the hospital at Danang and was a report on Crisp's condition. All Hogan could understand was that the prognosis was good, but the rest of it was a list of the injuries suffered which were in a language that Hogan had never seen before. He was going to have to get the flight surgeon to interpret for him.

"Okay. So what the hell does all this stuff mean?"

White smiled just a little. "I had no idea either, so I stopped off and showed it to the Quack. He says that according to that message, Crisp broke everything but Mom's best china. He'll live and recover fully and will most probably even get back to flying, but that'll be a while. It also says down at the bottom there that he'll be shipped home as soon as he's fit to travel."

Hogan let out a long breath as he reread the message. "Okay. Who's his roommate?"

"Denny Hammill is one of 'em. They both live in the J.O. Jungle, but Hammill is his best friend. I've got him getting a bag of stuff together to send in for Crisp, but as beat up as he is, he won't use much of it. At least he can have his personal things, like his pictures of his family. The guys in the Jungle will pack up the rest of his gear tomorrow."

"Good. Terry, do we have any idea what the fuck happened?"

White glanced at Scott and then back at Hogan. "Skipper, if I were a betting man, I'd wager that Crisp got himself in a box. He probably waited too long to pull out of his dive. I have nothing to base that on except that he was too steep at the start and the fact that he didn't appear to drop any bombs. I saw no Triple-A at all, either before or after he went in, so I don't think he was shot down. That aircraft had no history of control problems and it had a relatively new engine. I flew it myself yesterday and it was fine."

Hogan thought that over for a moment. It was not altogether unknown for a pilot to be trying so hard that he left things too long. He'd done it himself once or twice and it was something flight students seemed to do quite frequently. From his own experience Hogan knew that sometimes the difference between one scared pilot rocketing away from the ground and a large fireball close to the target could be nothing more than pure luck. It was often said that there was one record that could never be broken, only tied, and that was the world's low-altitude flying record.

"It's happened before," he said. "I've come pretty close a couple of times myself. I guess the only guy who can tell us for sure is Crisp himself."

"Well, for now it's listed as a combat loss. I suggest that we leave it at that. We can always change it later. One of us ought to go in to Danang tomorrow and visit him if we can. We can take his personal stuff in then too."

"Okay, Terry. See what the schedule for tomorrow says and decide which of us, you or me, should go in. If at all possible, I'd like to go. I don't think there'll be a problem getting an add-on flight approved."

"All right. I'll see to it." White moved to the door. He started to say something but stopped and pulled the door open.

"Good night, Skipper. Commander Scott."

The door closed behind White, and Hogan looked at Scott and smiled. "So what's up with the fighters tonight?"

Scott pushed his leather jacket aside and pulled a flask out of his upper flight-suit pocket. "Not much really. Just turning lots of precious fossil fuel into speed and noise in our effort to hold back the Yellow Peril. Same as yesterday. But I figured you could use a drink."

"Just had one, thanks."

"No, you don't understand. You need another. I figured you also need somebody to talk to tonight. The absolute last goddamn thing on earth you need to be doing is brooding. Don't worry about how it'll look, Jim. Nobody's gonna call you the rest of tonight, Terry saw to that."

Hogan sighed as he reached into the cabinet and pulled out his glass. He got another from the little holder next to his tiny sink and then reached into the small refrigerator and pulled out some ice.

As he dropped a couple of cubes into each glass, Hogan spoke quietly. "You know, I have a friend on the *America*. He says the ship doesn't have the electric power for the officers to have refrigerators in their rooms. It must be awful to go to sea without a cold drink now and again."

He mixed the drinks and they both took a pull. "Good scotch," Hogan said.

"Yeah, it is. I figure with a name like mine I better never hand anybody any of that horsepiss most people drink. It's Glenfiddich or nothin' with me."

Scott sat up and put his drink down. "So how are you feeling, Jim? You look like shit."

"Thanks. Actually, I'm kinda pissed, but I'm not sure who or what to be pissed at. I feel like I've screwed up somehow."

"Like there is something you could have done that would have kept your boy from busting his ass?"

Hogan nodded. "Something like that. I imagine I'm feeling like you did after you guys lost that plane to the MiG."

"That's why I'm here. It's a shitty feeling, but it's one you're gonna have to get used to. No, that's wrong. It's something you're going to have to learn to deal with, 'cause if you're worth a damn, you'll never get used to it. Unless you're real lucky, you're gonna lose somebody else before we get home, but you can't forget that you still have a squadron full of young tigers to lead."

Hogan sighed. "I've been around long enough to see this happen a bunch of times, but I've never been the guy responsible before."

"Okay. Hold it right there. You've got to understand that responsibility stuff right off." Scott took a sip from his drink before continuing.

"You are responsible for giving your guys every advantage possible—the best training, the best-maintained airplanes, the least amount of hassle from their ground jobs as possible, and protection, as much as it is in your power, from stupid decisions and stupid missions. You are not and cannot be responsible for every mistake they make in their airplanes or in their paperwork or in their personal lives.

"If something happens because they weren't trained properly or their aircraft was a piece of shit or you busted their balls over their ground job, then, yeah, you are responsible and the Navy should hammer your ass. But that's not the case here.

"I suppose that you're very much like me in that even though you know that there is nothing you could have done, you've been sitting here, taking apart everything you've done since you got here.

"Well, what happened is real simple. Your pilot flew his jet into the ground. Unless you had a crystal ball, there was not a single damn thing you could have done to prevent it. And sitting here wondering about it will only drive you crazy. Or worse, make you spend so much time watching the others for mistakes *they're* about to make that you get your own ass shot off some sunny afternoon."

Hogan was staring into his now mostly empty glass. He remembered having lunch with Scott the day he had lost his wingman and how he had thought he understood. He knew that it hadn't been until that afternoon that he really did understand. It didn't make him feel any less lousy about what had happened, but it did make him feel a whole lot less alone. Still, there was nothing anywhere that could make his next few days easier, no guidelines, no instructions, no experience. He would have to go on what his gut told him was right, much like Scott had.

He looked up as Scott was heading for the door. "One more thing, Jim. If you start trying to see everything that your guys are doing before it happens, you're gonna wind up exactly the same kind of man your predecessor was. Neither you nor your squadron can stand that again. To be honest, I'm not sure the air wing can stand another C.O. like him for a while. Good night. If you need anybody to talk to, I'm around."

Hogan finished the last little bit of his drink and washed out the glasses. He was tempted to go down to the ready room and see how things were going, but instead he lay back on his bunk and picked up a book. He knew for certain that there was nothing

273

to do that night which White and the others couldn't handle, but he still found himself reading the same paragraph four times before he finally climbed under the blankets and switched off the light.

At about the same time that Jim Hogan had landed aboard the ship, Dick Averitt was recovering from the talk he had received from Colonel Aires. Sergeant Major Gorton had been exactly right in that Aires was furious.

The two of them walked into the command post and were greeted by a stony silence—one that blotted out the dull sounds of the artillery and mortar fire still sporadically coming in and going out around the combat base. The other officers and men who had been gathered around in some conference or other rapidly discovered that they had urgent business elsewhere and departed quickly to take care of it. A couple of the officers gave the two an I'd-like-to-stay-and-help-you-out-but-I-have-to-go-check-the-mail sort of look as they brushed by.

Very quickly the room was empty except for Aires, Gorton, Averitt, and the two young enlisted men who were required to man the communications and who did one of the more amazing fades into the woodwork that Averitt had ever seen.

Aires scowled at the two for a moment as he lit his pipe. Once it was going well, he spoke from the wreath of smoke he'd created.

"Come over here, you two."

The two men approached the colonel in their best professional stride, trying their damnedest not to show fear. Averitt had heard that Aires could smell fear in his prey. He'd probably heard that from Gorton, who didn't look too certain just then either. When they both got up to the table, careful to stay well out of arm's reach from the good colonel, they stopped and stood at a position as close to perfect parade-ground attention as they could remember.

"Stand at ease," the colonel said, inspecting his pipe to see if it was burning evenly.

"Sergeant Major, what were you doing down in the trenches?"

"Um. Well, Colonel, I went out to watch the air show."

"And were there any other marines out there with you?"

"Yessir. Lots of 'em. All doing what they were supposed to be. Good men we've got out there, Colonel. I think I'll spend some

274

more time out there with them. You know, command interest and all that."

"Good thought, Sergeant Major, good thought. Now, Major, I know what you were doing there. What I want to know is why you took it upon yourself to act like the Light Brigade and go charging off to rescue your flyboy buddy. Did he owe you money or something?"

"No, sir, Colonel. It just seemed like the thing to do."

"Major, that's bullshit. If you had stopped to think, you would have come up with a far sounder plan. Like maybe letting those marines of whom the sergeant major speaks so highly do their job.

"There are a dozen ways you could have gotten yourself killed out there. You had no idea where our claymore mines and trip-flares and all the various other nasty little surprises we have spent so much time and effort planting were. You had no idea even how to get through the wires. If it had not been for the others who went out there chasing you, you might still be trying to figure out how to get to that pilot. Do you understand that?"

"Yes, sir."

"Good. I understand why you did what you did. I really can't fault you for taking action. Even if it was kind of dumb and dangerous, it was a positive action. I have seen many other men who would have sat back and let somebody else carry the load, but you chose not to do that. The problem I have with it is that you *should* have let someone else do it, someone who does this infantry stuff for a living. I like what you did but I'm pissed off at you for doing it. I am going to need you, Major. Don't get yourself killed. Okay?"

"Yes, sir."

"Now, as for you, Sergeant Major, how long have we known each other?"

"I don't know, Colonel. Probably around twenty years, off and on."

"And in all that time have I ever chewed you out unfairly?"

"Offhand, I'd have to say no, sir."

"Do you think I would be justified if I chewed you out now, for your little foray into the wires under the leadership of this, this, pilot?"

"Actually, no, sir. I kept him out of trouble, didn't I? I mean, he didn't get shot or anything."

"All right, then. You're off the hook. But for your penalty, I

275

want you to continue to take care of the major. Until I tell you different, you will keep an eye on him and make sure that he doesn't take any more chances. Okay?"

"Yes, sir."

"Unless you two have anything for me, that will be all. I have to get back to the unimportant stuff now, like defending this place. Why don't you get over to Charlie-Med and check on the man you saved?"

"Aye-aye, sir." Both Averitt and the old sergeant major came to attention, took one step backward, did a sharp about-face, and headed for the exit. Just before they got there, Aires's voice stopped them.

"By the way, Major, I think that we owe something to those marines who went out there with you. You two will have to be satisfied with the thanks of a grateful nation. Are there any of the others whom you feel should be decorated?"

Averitt looked at Gorton and back at Aires. "The corpsman for sure, Colonel."

"Okay. Write him up and anyone who deserves it."

"Yes, sir."

Once outside, the two men stopped and lit cigarettes. Averitt looked at Gorton, who was grinning hugely.

"Sergeant Major, I haven't been so scared since I was in boot camp. I thought he was really gonna tear us a new one."

"Major, that man may be the finest officer I've ever known since Colonel Puller. He treated us the way he knew would get the best response. In amongst all that stuff he was saying is one message, he doesn't want us doing anything remotely like that again. He's proud of us but he was also dead serious."

Gorton looked at his cigarette. "One more thing. When anyone asks us what he said, tell 'em we were glad to get out of there alive. Not everybody needs to know what a good guy the colonel is. Some folks need to think he's Attila the Hun."

"Fair enough. Now let's get over to Charlie-Med."

The two men, one young and tall, one old and worn, both becoming friends, walked off up the trench past the dozens of marines filling the endless piles of sandbags.

Part
Four

33

Monday, February 5, 1968

The little general stared off into the distance as he half-listened to the dull sounds of his artillery pounding the American positions and the American artillery and aircraft pounding his in return. The sound seemed like a cadence to which he had marched for most of his life. He could almost hear his own heart beating in synchronization with the thumps and dull booms.

Behind the general, his staff was assembling the reports from the units out there in the jungles and forests. Tired men had been arriving in a seemingly endless stream, their faces deeply lined and their eyes glazing with fatigue and the horrors they'd seen.

Men had died, they said, gloriously, for the cause. Men had died, they said, standing against the storm of American weapons until they had fought to the last man and the last bullet. Men had died, they said, with joy in their hearts that the final victory would be that much closer.

Men had died, they said, following the little general's bold strategy.

The little general looked back over his shoulder at the knot of men deeper inside the cave and turned away. He walked down the narrow path to the small clearing below and sat on the log next to the tallest tree. He leaned his head back against the bark and closed his eyes. His aides, knowing that this was not the moment to be solicitous, hung back and avoided looking at each other. An intrusion, even so much as a whisper, was something to be avoided at any cost. Great men must have the time to think their great thoughts, they believed.

Feeling the rough texture of the tree through his now-shaggy

279

hair, the general wondered at the age of the tree. He wondered how many armies had been raised and sent off to battle and then buried and forgotten since it had been a seed fallen on the fertile earth. He wondered if the dead really knew who had won the wars and battles in which they died. And he wondered if they cared. He wondered what they would say to the commanders who sent them off to battle when they met in the afterlife, and, lastly, he wondered what the commanders would say to them in return.

Reluctantly, he put these thoughts away. As this endless war and his life dragged on, the little general was finding quiet moments fewer and farther between, and he resented that.

He stood and began to pace in the small clearing, letting his mind summarize the present situation before he would step in and make the decision he was dreading a little. His great offensive had been defeated as determinedly and as ruthlessly as any battle that had ever been fought. True, there was still fighting in the crowded parts of Saigon and in the ancient capital of Hue. His men were acquitting themselves well there, as they had nearly everywhere else. Just yesterday morning he had sent several more large units to reinforce those in Hue, but he knew now, this morning, that it was hopeless.

The general popular uprising in the South, so long planned for and hoped for and awaited, had not happened. The peasantry had stayed in their huts and houses and cellars while his guerrilla forces had been exterminated. They had not come forth and joined in the destruction of the corrupt puppet regime. From what the tired men had been reporting, he knew that the guerrillas, or V.C. as the Americans called them, had been crushed and no longer existed as an effective fighting force.

Last night, most of an entire regiment had been smashed by the combined artillery and air power of the American marines at Khe Sanh as it attempted to capture a hill overlooking the Khe Sanh base. Hill 861, the Americans called it.

He must try again, at least once more, to take that base and drive the Americans out. Or he must put the marines there in such jeopardy that the Americans would attempt to send a relief force down Route 9 from the coast to force their way into the base. A relief force would be easily destroyed and the victory he so desperately needed could be gained.

He had tried to build trenches close enough to the base so that a large attack could be carried out, but aircraft and artillery had cost him more men than he could afford to lose in the effort. The only thing remaining for him to try was to take a position on the high ground that would make the base indefensible. Last night he had tried for the second time to take the hill called 861 and his men had again been driven off.

In a couple of days he would take the southern crest of another hill, Hill 881, and then he would command the high ground. He would force the Americans to leave or he would destroy the relief column they would have to send. Either way he would have his victory which would, in turn, further damage the enemy's will to fight on.

He turned back to the path that led up to the cave. As he climbed, he smiled at the fragility and weakness of peoples, like the Americans, who seemed to be unable to accept the fact of a long and costly war of attrition.

The officers in the cave came to attention as the little general strode in and approached the table. With a light in his eye that had not been there thirty minutes before, he began to ask each of them to state the status of their units and to assess their ability to sustain a combined attack in two days.

He listened to the deliberate exaggerations from the commanders and their strong words about the victories they would win for him and the cause. Many of these men were replacing other men who had uttered the same kinds of words before they had gone out with their men and died.

The little general listened to their words with only half his mind. His trusted aides would make enough accurate notes for him to review later and make his decisions. He let them talk on, each in his own turn, speaking braver words than the commander before him. When they were done he excused them but told them to hold themselves nearby. He would have them back to discuss the plan in a little while.

He stared at the map on the table in silence. He had no choice now but to try a major assault on that hill. The Americans had foiled every other move he'd made, but it was very possible that they'd be unable to stop this one. He cursed the fact that he had four divisions of excellent troops here, nearly forty thousand men in all, but had not been able to overrun six thousand marines and South Vietnamese.

He shook his head and concentrated on his plan. He summoned

his aides and looked over the notes they had taken. He stared at the map for a few more moments and then asked his aides to go get the commanders. What this plan was going to require was superb leadership from them all. He hoped he had selected them well enough.

The little general, lost now in all the details, did not become aware for several minutes of the commanders gathered around him. The commanders were used to that, since it lately had become the normal thing.

34

Monday, February 5, 1968

At 1430 that afternoon Commander Jim Hogan walked down the long ward, looking at the wreckage of what had only shortly before been American fighting men from all the services. Most of the men in the ward had some part of themselves wrapped in plaster and suspended by wires, but the mood in the room was not as glum and somber as he had expected. Several of the wounded had groups of their friends and comrades gathered around their beds, laughing and joking quietly and doing all the silly things that one does in a hospital when one really doesn't know what to do.

Hogan found Crisp at the far end of the ward, laying back and staring at the ceiling. When he approached the bed he discovered that Crisp was not looking up in contemplation but because there was nothing else he could do. There was not a lot of his body visible outside the sheets that was not in bandages or a cast. His eyes were sort of hazy, so it was obvious that he'd been medicated, which in turn made Hogan feel worse for the pain his man was suffering.

Hogan placed the small bag of Crisp's personal effects on the metal nightstand next to the water pitcher and pulled the chair around so that he could sit facing the young pilot. He was tall enough that Crisp would be able to see him without moving his head.

"Hey, Critter. How are you doing?"

It seemed to take a long while for those words to break into Crisp's consciousness. His brow furrowed and his eyes focused. He moved them toward the sound.

"Hi, Skipper. What are you doing here?"

"We figured you'd need some of your stuff, so I pulled rank and brought it in. It gets me a chance to walk around on dry land for a while. Besides, it was time for a squadron booze run."

Crisp smiled. "I suppose the guys in the Jungle already drank mine. Just making sure it doesn't go bad or something."

"Yeah, probably so. But they'll have to pay you back when we get home, and at U.S. prices too, so you'll win in the end."

"The nurse told me that I'll be on my way to the States in a week or so. They've got me scheduled to go to Balboa, which will be nice. My fiancée works near there, so I won't be lonely. This is gonna postpone the wedding for a while, but I'll be damned if I'll get married in a wheelchair."

Hogan hadn't known that Crisp was engaged, which made him angry with himself again. What else did he not know about his guys? The thought made him feel small.

He forced a smile. "Well, if we have to carry you to the altar, that'll probably impress the hell out of your mother-in-law."

"Yeah, that'd be pretty cool all right."

"You still haven't answered my original question, Critter. How are you doing?"

"To be honest, Skipper, I figure I'm the luckiest guy in this whole place. When I ejected I must have been at the absolute edge of the envelope. All I remember is pulling the handle and then waking up with a bunch of marines around me. One of 'em was that Major Averitt friend of yours. I must have passed out again, because the next thing I remember, I was in a bunker with a bunch of doctors around and a little while later I was in a helo on the way here."

"What the hell happened? We still have no idea."

Crisp sighed. He knew that this question was going to come up sooner or later. He'd been more worried about answering it than he had his parents' reaction when they got the inevitable telegram.

He had relived every moment of his last flight a dozen times that day, and every time the result was the same.

"I screwed the pooch. My pattern was too tight and my dive was too steep. I got fixated on the target, and by the time I figured that part out, it was too late. I couldn't save it. So I jumped out."

Hogan nodded. He had been wondering what he would say to Crisp when this point came up. All the way in from the ship he'd been hoping that there would be another reason, but he knew that the chances were pretty slim.

"We kind of figured that. You're not the first guy to get target fixation, and you sure as hell won't be the last."

"Yeah, but I busted my ass and cost us a perfectly good airplane."

"That's true, but you didn't cost us a perfectly good pilot except temporarily. You'll be back to flying in a while and you'll go on. Mr. Douglas will build us another A-4 and that'll be that."

"You're not pissed? I figured you'd be standing there with a pilot disposition board all ready for me."

"Of course I'm pissed. But what the hell good would it do to make a federal case out of it. The absolute last guy in the world who's gonna make that mistake in the future is you, sport. I want you back in the squadron, and so does everyone else."

"There's gonna be a hassle, Skipper. Pilot error is still not forgivable."

Hogan thought that one over. What Crisp said was true. Pilot error was the one thing that could hang like a sword over Crisp's head for the rest of his career. There were other things far worse, but a pilot always looks back on a crash where he was the principal cause with a great deal of pain. In later years it assumes less and less importance, but the feeling always remains. Kind of like Lady Macbeth's spot.

"No, you're right. You're going to have to carry that one around for a while. It's your choice, though, as to how long you carry it and how heavy you allow it to be. You will have a blot on your escutcheon, but most of us have one or two of those. I figure it's sort of like a merit badge. Let's people know you've been somewhere. Don't worry about that, Critter. The hassle is only temporary. Okay?"

Crisp nodded. "Okay."

"Good. Because your job now is to get yourself back in shape and back in an airplane. Now, tell me what my idiot marine friend was doing dragging you out of no-man's land."

Twenty minutes later Hogan left the ward and stopped at the nurses' station. He waited while the nurse, who had told Hogan it was time to go, administered a shot to Crisp and came back. She looked at him expectantly as she disposed of the syringe she had used on Crisp.

Hogan waited until she was finished and gave her a smile. "Listen, um, Lieutenant, thanks for taking care of Crisp. We really appreciate all you people are doing. He's really a pretty good guy under all that plaster."

She forced a grim smile. "They're all good guys, Commander."

She stopped and shook her head. "I didn't mean that the way it sounded. I know he's your good guy and I appreciate your stopping by. Most folks don't bother. We've just been busy as hell the last couple of days. There have been medevacs coming in every five minutes, it seems, and as soon as these guys get out of surgery, they're sent straight to the wards. Which is probably a lousy excuse for saying something shitty like that, but it's the best I can do."

"No problem. To be honest, I wouldn't have your job for anything. I just wanted to thank you is all."

She smiled again, and this time her eyes joined in. "Well, you're welcome. Now I have to go to work here on some of the other good guys. And believe me, they are. But if you're ever back by this way, give me some warning and I'll let you buy me a beer or ten."

Hogan stuck his hand out as he looked at her name tag. "You've got a deal, Miss, um, Lawrence. Thanks again."

Before Hogan had reached the door, the nurse had turned away and begun filling out Crisp's chart.

It was almost 1900 when Hogan walked back into the ready room aboard the *Shiloh*. He was starved. He'd not had any lunch and had not had time to try to mooch something from the marines on the transient line at Danang.

He filled out his paperwork from the flight, went over to the duty desk, and dialed the number to White's stateroom. He asked White to meet him in the wardroom in twenty minutes for dinner and then walked out the door and around the corner into the squadron's maintenance control.

He found a chair over by the coffee urn and poured himself a cup while the maintenance control chief, a crusty old master chief metalsmith named Worley, finished yelling into the phone at somebody who was not saying much in return. The chief hung up the phone loudly and turned around.

" 'Evening, Skipper. What can I do for you?"

"Not a thing, Master Chief. Just stopped by to see how things are going and to make your life a little more miserable."

Worley laughed and picked up a can of Coke from his desk. He gestured at the phone as he took a sip. "You mean that? Hell, I was just keeping in practice. The Handler and his trogs in Flight Deck Control are trying to decide which airplanes we're going to fly tomorrow. I was just explaining that as much as we appreciate their help, they ought to stick to their real job of ramming planes into each other."

Hogan laughed. The age-old fights between squadrons and the flight-deck guys had never changed, probably since the day they put the first biplane on the first deck. Somebody, almost certainly a demented officer from the ship's company who'd been given the new title of Aircraft Handling Officer by the harried ship's captain, had decided to park the airplane on the other side of the deck, which led to the first argument. He was also certain that that first move had resulted in the first "crunch" when the airplane's wing was shoved into something harder than it was.

Worley put his Coke back down. "Anyway, if we can get a damned spot for a couple of low-power engine runs from the wizards in Flight Deck Control, we'll have enough up jets to make the schedule for tomorrow and we've got a replacement due in from Cubi for 411. That's supposed to be a brand-new one. You want us to paint your name on it?"

Hogan grinned. "Hell, no. I like 'em well broken in with all the bugs and gremlins worked out of them. Kind of like fine wine, Master Chief, A-4s need to age some."

"Wine maybe, but I'm glad beer doesn't."

Hogan laughed as he rinsed out the "guest" coffee cup and put it back on its hook. "I'm gonna go eat. If you have any more problems with the Handler, whatever the hour, day or night, feel free to call the X.O. He needs the experience."

Worley chuckled. "You mean you don't want to ruin your digestion with the problem, right?"

"That's about right. I'm too old for that crap. See ya."

Terry White was standing by the row of leather flight jackets hanging on the bulkhead outside the "dirty shirt" wardroom, the cafeteria-style eating area just below the flight deck, when Hogan appeared around the corner. The two men grabbed their trays and joined the other officers moving slowly down the line. The meal tonight was one of the rare ones that elicited actual eagerness in the diners. It was "surf and turf," which was served at odd and unpredictable times during the month.

Most of the reason it moved slowly was that there were two large groups of diners and one small one. The small one was comprised of the very few officers who actually ate both the small steaklike piece of beef and the long-frozen and overcooked lobster tail.

Most of the other officers were part of the other two groups who realized that there was incredibly agonizing, almost instantaneous indigestion lurking out there for anyone with a normal system, since mixing these two particular entrees was like combining a match with a glass of gasoline. Aboard ship these entrees simply didn't go together as they would at home, where restaurants that served food like this would be closed down in a week, either by the local health department or by a long line of lawsuits for killing some of the more delicate citizens, like Aunt Mabel. And on her seventy-fifth birthday too.

The other two groups were made up of the men who wanted either the steak or the lobster tail. Members of each group would try to hook up with a member of the other to trade entrees and thus get either two steaks or two lobster tails. And save themselves a long night of belching and groaning.

White and Hogan got their plates of entrees, spooned some of the less-brown green beans on them, and made their way out into the eating area. They each got two glasses of purple drink which one would expect to taste vaguely grapelike and found a couple of seats at a table in the far corner. They traded entrees, Hogan going for the steaks and White the lobster tails.

After they had dumped some hot sauce on their food, tasted it, grimaced, and continued, Hogan filled White in on his day visiting Danang. White was as surprised as Hogan had been when he learned that Dick Averitt had been involved in the rescue of their squadronmate. He listened to the story and, when Hogan had finished, asked him about the crash.

"He told me straight out that he'd gooned it. I had the feeling that he was kind of making a confession. I told him not to worry about it, that he'd be back to flying and that he probably hadn't hurt himself professionally to any great degree. I also told him I wanted him back in the squadron, maybe like we've done with Nick Taylor."

White nodded. "If that doesn't happen while you're still C.O., I'll make sure that it does when I get the job."

"Thanks. I appreciate that. So will he."

Hogan finished the last bite of his steak and pushed his plate away. "That was almost edible." He lit a cigarette.

"So what's been happening around here today?"

"They're gonna increase our close air support effort for the marines, just like Nick said they would. We did get some training in for the squadron in the procedures this afternoon. And we've got a new jet coming in from Cubi Point tomorrow. Aside from that, not much else."

White laughed. "Oh, I just remembered. One of the F-8 guys, a j.g. from the *Concord*, is in some deep shit. He diverted to Chu Lai yesterday and parked his jet on the transient line. The marines said they'd do all his servicing for him while he went and got something to eat. He had two of the new D-model Sidewinders on his aircraft and the jarheads simply stole 'em while he was gone. You wouldn't believe it possible, but he didn't notice until he got back to the ship, all fat, dumb, and happy, and the plane captain asked him where they were. Apparently, his C.O. and his CAG went ballistic and the messages have been flying back and forth. The marines swear that they had nothing to do with it, and he swears that he couldn't have lost them anywhere else. I see his Skipper's point: how in the hell can you *not* notice that someone has swiped your missiles?"

Hogan coughed as some of his purple drink went down the wrong way. "Jesus." He laughed.

"Yeah, now, here's the best part. The marines have the older B models. They don't have any of the support gear for the Ds, so they're completely useless to them.

35

Tuesday, February 6, 1968

Up in the tower of the USS *Shiloh*, Commander Chris Scott leaned back in the Mini-Boss's high-backed chair and put his feet up on the window ledge in front of him. To his left, the Air Boss was just finishing speaking to the Waist Catapult Officer and making sure that everybody had "the plan." One thing that people involved in working with high-performance aircraft hate is surprises. They never are pleasant and always seem to happen at the worst possible time. When those high-performance aircraft are involved in a war and are loaded with bombs, bullets, and fuel, surprises are not only unpleasant but can be spectacular.

Scott watched the cat crews pull the long rubber seals, which were supposed to keep foreign objects out of the tracks, out of the slot in the center of the catapult track and drag the heavy steel bridles out of the catwalk. For about the ten-thousandth time in his career, he was struck by the thought of how amazing were those kids who worked out on the flight deck. Their average age was about nineteen, yet they held more responsibility in their daily routine than millions of executives back home did in a week. Their job was as dangerous as any other in the world, yet they carried it out so quickly and efficiently that it appeared as if they were all working with one mind.

All over the deck the aircraft started to move from their parking spots as the great ship turned into the wind for launch. The Catapult Officers finished walking up the tracks, straddling the slot to make sure nobody had dropped a wrench down there, and when they were done, great gouts of steam rose from the catapults as the crews fired "no-loads," testing them just one more time. The

Air Boss held the microphone to the 5MC, or flight deck loud-speaker system, and made the "heads-up" calls which safety required whenever something particularly hazardous to the unwary was happening. But in a few moments, when the jets would be at full power for their launches, the 5MC would become useless amid the deafening noise.

When the ship steadied out into the wind, the Air Boss acknowledged the bridge's permission to begin the launch and flipped the switch that lit the green light on the "Christmas tree" hanging outside just below his windows in the tower. Instantly, the RA-5 Vigilante on catapult one on the bow came to full power and then its roar increased with a rush as the pilot shoved the throttles into afterburner. The black smoke blowing up above the steel jet-blast deflector turned into clear shimmering heat as raw fuel was poured into the exhaust of the A-5.

Scott could see the Cat Officer swing his arm down, touch the deck, and raise it again, pointing forward. Two seconds later, the big, sleek, reconnaissance aircraft hurtled down the track and into the air. Banking slightly to the right, the Vigilante flew away, its wheels retracting into their wells as the jet steadied out on its departure heading. Scott looked back at the bow and saw a Phantom go from cat two on the bow, following the A-5 by less than ten seconds. Before the Phantom had its wheels up, another F-4 was taxiing onto catapult one.

All over the deck, the rest of the aircraft were moving toward the Cats. To anyone not familiar with carrier operations, Scott knew that this would look more like a Chinese fire drill than what it was: an exquisitely choreographed ballet of man and machine. The differently colored shirts on the men hustling among the bravely painted aircraft fluttered in the wind and the steam and the jet exhaust. This was like no other scene in the world and, Scott admitted to himself, there was really nothing that he would rather be a part of. Or just watch whenever he had the chance.

Down on the waist, the crews from cats three and four were readying two A-4s for launch. Scott watched the Cat Officer down there take command of the launch and noticed something odd about the way he gave the signals to the pilot. And his clothes were a lot cleaner than they should be.

Every Cat Officer, or "shooter," has his own distinctive style, and pilots quickly learn to recognize them under all the gear they wear simply by the way they stand or move or do any of the dozens of things required of them. This guy was doing it all but had another Cat Officer standing right there behind him.

Scott turned to the Air Boss. "That a new shooter down on the waist? It's getting a little late in the cruise to bring out a new guy, isn't it?"

The Air Boss laughed. "Yes and no. It's Nick Taylor, that madman from 262. He's up here gaining 'fuller knowledge and enhanced experience,' as he put it. He conned us into letting him launch some airplanes, but he figured we would let him try it up on the bow, where it's nice and safe. You should have seen his face when we told him that he was going to the waist. I hope he remembers to duck."

Scott laughed too. The waist area, which was directly across the flight deck from the tall island structure where the bridge and the tower were, was not a whole lot of fun for the Cat crews. The two catapults, identical to the ones on the bow, angled toward each other because of space. The area in between, where the crews had to work, was a lot smaller and narrower than the similar area on the bow, where the catapults were more nearly parallel. So, depending on the size of the jet being launched, its wings with bombs and rocket pods and fuel tanks suspended below it sometimes went directly over the Cat crews' heads as they curled up in a ball on the deck. It was not altogether unknown for an aircraft to take some or all of an unwary crewman with it into the air. Only in the rarest of circumstances did the aircraft come out a loser.

The crewman *always* did.

Taylor raised his right arm over his head as he pointed to the A-4 on cat three, the inboard one, with his left. His right hand was rapidly moving in the full power signal. The pilot moved his stick to the limits of travel and shoved the rudder pedals back and forth as he did his control check. He placed his helmeted head back against the ejection seat and saluted with his right hand.

Taylor returned the salute and, after taking one more look down the catapult track, lowered his raised arm and touched the deck. As he brought his hand back up again from the deck, he curled up with one arm across the lower part of his face, peering over his arm at the now-departing A-4. When Taylor stood and turned to catapult four, Scott could see that he was no longer quite as clean as he had been, but his movements now had a lot of spring to them. He was almost dancing as he moved around, checking the weight board and looking at the steam pressure gauges in the hatch between the cats.

The second A-4 launched and Taylor jumped up and spun back to cat three. The real Cat Officer who was staying close and watching everything turned toward the tower and, shaking his head, spread his arms up and to the sides as if asking the gods for help before turning back to watch Taylor and everything else carefully. Even though Taylor was doing the "shooting," the Cat Officer was still responsible.

"He's having fun down there, Boss," said Scott, "and it looks like he knows what he's doing too."

"Yeah, it does. When he found out we were going to let him try it, he went down and borrowed the books and studied up on the whole system. Then he got the troops to show him everything they could. He doesn't know that I know that, so don't say anything. But you have to admire him, putting that much work into something he'll probably only do this once."

Scott sat back in the chair and watched Taylor and the cat crews launch the last aircraft and then hustle to stow everything before the recovery began in about two minutes. "You know, Boss, it wouldn't surprise me if that guy figured a way to get himself fully qualified to shoot airplanes on a part-time basis. Then again, there's not much about Nick Taylor that surprises me anymore. I've given up."

"I know what you mean. He loves to learn new things. Wouldn't it be nice to have that enthusiasm back for just a little while?"

Scott stood up. "Yeah, but I'm not sure I could handle it at my advanced age. See you later." He walked out and headed for his room.

After the recovery, Lieutenant Commander Brian Gill, the Maintenance Officer in VA-262, straggled into the ready room and dropped his overnight bag and helmet into one of the chairs at the rear of the room. Hogan spotted him and came over. Gill had just landed from Cubi Point in the Philippines with the new aircraft. He had been sent over early the day before on one of the ship's COD runs and accepted the jet from the maintenance detachment which the air wing kept at Cubi.

As Hogan approached, he noted that the pilot looked just a little green and the left side of his mustache was missing. "Hi, Fish.

Welcome home. How's the new jet? And pardon me for noticing, but you look like shit."

As he stepped out of his torso harness and unzipped his G suit, Gill looked up. "That bad, huh. Well, first, the aircraft's fine—all shiny and new. It even still has paint on the cockpit deck. It's been a long time since I've seen one so pretty. As for me, your poor, wandering boy, last night I fell in again with the evil companions my mom always warned me about. That goddamn warrant officer from the fighters and I started off at the club, having a nice, quiet dinner, and then we went down to the downstairs bar. There were a bunch of guys from the *Enterprise* and *Ranger* in there, so we got rolling pretty good. We got into the Flaming Hookers and I didn't get the fire out on the last one, so it burned off my 'stache. I did show enough sense to get out of there before they started to run Red Horse One, so I didn't get wet, which is definitely a first for me."

Hogan grinned. "Red Horse One" was a chair that ran on rails across the lower barroom in the Cubi Point Officers' Club. The occupant sat in it and tried to drop a hook attached to the chair as it passed over a wire so as to perform an "arrested landing." The penalty for failing to catch the wire was that at the end of the rails, through a usually open set of French doors, was a small pond of reasonably dirty water into which the rider was doomed to go. It cost a dollar a try, and after the daily party got rolling it was a sure money-maker for the club. Many a naval officer entered the bar, looked at the show, and swore smugly that he'd never be stupid enough to do that. Invariably, he'd find himself an hour later, after a few drinks, soaking wet but with a determined fire in his glassy eyes, sitting in that chair and handing the operators another dollar.

Hogan himself had contributed a few spare dollars to the fund. "Well, I'm glad you're here. And I'll be sure to write your mom and tell her you've been a paragon and a shining example for your men."

Gill squeezed his nostrils closed and blew gently, popping the last pressure bubbles from his ears. "Master Chief Worley told me about Crisp. Is there anything I can do?"

"No. Not really. It's gonna take a while, but he'll be all right. But even with that new aircraft, we're still short one."

"Not for long. There's another one due into the maintenance det in a few days. I'll be happy to go get that one too."

293

"Sorry, Fish. You've had your good deal for the month."

Gill turned to go back down to Maintenance Control. "That's okay. Just be sure to warn whoever goes about that warrant officer."

"I will. Oh, by the way, there's an AOM tomorrow at 0900. More close air support training. We're being fragged for Khe Sanh until further notice. The Navy is supposed to supply a thousand or so sorties a month in support of the marines, and we get a big part of the job."

"Okay. I'll tell the maintenance types what's coming. We ought to be able to handle it."

Shortly after 2300 that night, Jack Wilson looked over his shoulder at the lights of the three other A-4s in the small formation. He was taking them into a rendezvous with an Air Force Phantom that was to lead them in a "mini arc-light" strike against a suspected troop concentration in the forests to the west of Khe Sanh. The reason for the concentration had not really been made clear to the pilots, but apparently the marines suspected that the North Vietnamese were building up to something again and wanted to begin pounding them before they could really get going.

He glanced at the red-lighted instruments on the panel before him and wiggled his feet which rested lightly on the rudder pedals. Jack Wilson was a broader-than-average pilot and so had at first found the A-4 cockpit confining. His legs stretched all the way down the little tunnels under the instrument panel and his shoulders brushed against the sides of the cockpit. After he had spent a hundred hours or so driving the little Scooter around, he found that it seemed to fit him like an extra flight suit. His body soon became adjusted to the cramped confines of the cockpit and his butt quit aching on the normal hour and a half flights. But it was ready to protest painfully and immediately if the flight stretched much beyond that.

He glanced at his TACAN and saw that he was approaching the outer edge of the radar coverage from the *Shiloh's* E-2 and keyed his radio.

"Slug 771, Ghostrider 404 will be switching up Hillsborough."

"Roger, 404. Frequency change approved."

Wilson rotated the frequency knob and waited for the channelizer tone to quit. When it did, he got the ripple check from the other three A-4s and called the Air Force control plane. "Hillsborough, Ghostrider 404 is with you. Flight of four Skyhawks squawking 4202."

The Air Force had obviously been waiting, for the voice of the controller somewhere out in the dark came back immediately. "Roger, Ghostrider, radar contact. Come right to 235. Your lead aircraft with be a Fox-4 call sign Dancer 937. Estimating rendezvous in zero-eight minutes."

"Roger, a single F-4, Dancer 937. 404 is level at eighteen."

"Click-click."

Wilson sighed into his oxygen mask. All he was supposed to do was to join on the Air Force Phantom and allow him to lead the flight of now-five aircraft over a specific point in the night sky and everybody would drop all their bombs at once. Then they would all fly home. Simple as that.

And for the pilots, it was simple. There was an electronic beacon in the Air Force jet transmitting to a receiver on the ground which was part of a radar control system. The controller would guide, or vector, the five aircraft to a specific point, adjusted for altitude, airspeed, and the wind, and tell them to drop their bombs at that point. When the pilots hit the buttons on their sticks, intervalometers in the aircrafts' weapons systems themselves would release the bombs at a preset and almost invisible interval so that there would be an even pattern of hits on the ground covering a required amount of horizontal and lateral yardage.

Instead of the hundreds of bombs raining down from three B-52s, there would be a couple of dozen from four A-4s and one Phantom. The effect would be the same for the enemy troops, however. They would not know that the bombs were on the way until the world around them disintegrated into deafening explosions and flying metal.

"Ghostrider 404, Hillsborough. Dancer 937 is at your right one o'clock in a right-hand orbit. He's at angels nineteen."

"Roger, 404's looking." Wilson looked up and to his right, trying to pick out the lights of the Phantom a thousand feet above him. He quartered the area trying to catch a movement, something odd among the rigid fixity of the stars. At night, staring at a patch of blackness, is the surest way of finding nothing.

After a moment Wilson spotted the rhythmic red flashing of an aircraft's rotating anticollision light. It should be the Air Force, but it was best to check. "Hillsborough, 404 has an aircraft at my twelve o'clock high."

"Roger, 404. That's Dancer 937. Break. Dancer 937, the Ghostriders have you in sight. They're at your left eight o'clock low."

The Air Force pilot's West Texas drawl came back immediately. "Rojah, Hillsburra, cleahed for join-up."

"404 and flight will be joining port and starboard."

"Click-click."

Wilson eased his nose up a little and banked gently to cut inside the circle of the Phantom's orbit. He fixed the anticollision light in a spot on his canopy and watched as he drew closer to the Air Force aircraft. He knew that closure rates are almost impossible to judge accurately at night, so he was as careful as he could be. It may not have been as cool as it could have been, but it was definitely safe. He was also being careful to avoid getting himself in a position requiring huge corrective actions by the other three jets who were flying on him. Sudden, unexpected maneuvers could lead to a large midair collision that would definitely go down as a blot on his record.

Wilson eased his aircraft into formation under and slightly behind the F-4 and slid over into position on the right wing. The second section of two, led by Cordella, broke away and gently crossed under and took up position on the left. The formation now looked like an arrowhead with the Air Force at the tip.

Wilson clicked his mike switch twice to let the F-4 crew know that each man was where he was supposed to be, and concentrated on flying the proper formation. The F-4 was now the leader and, without looking, Wilson reached down and turned off his transponder. The only image the radar controllers would now see was the one given off by the beacon-equipped Phantom.

"Hillsborough, Dancer 937. Join-up complete."

Aboard the EC-121, the radar air controller had watched the two images merge and then become one as the Navy guy turned off his transponder. The F-4 was coming around in his orbit and almost on the proper heading.

"937, Hillsborough, steady out on 250. Descend and maintain angels fifteen. Khe Sanh altimeter is 29.97. There has been no Triple-A reported tonight."

"Dancer 937, roger. Steady 250. And we're out of nineteen for fifteen. Copy altimeter 29.97."

Wilson glanced at his altimeter setting. It was the same as the one they'd been given in the briefing, but he checked it out of pure habit. He again concentrated on maintaining his position, knowing that any correction he had to make in his position would be magnified for the A-4s on the outside tips of the arrowhead. He occasionally glanced in at his gauges just to make sure that his jet was still working all right and that the stranger in the F-4 had them where they were supposed to be. After a few minutes his confidence grew to the point where he was checking only his engine instruments and barely even noticing the others. He almost began to be comfortable.

"Dancer 937, Hillsborough. You are presently feet dry. Contact Blackhorse Radar on this frequency now. Hillsborough standing by." Not having to shift frequencies would save the formation pilots a little bit of hassle and delay.

"Blackhorse Radar, Dancer 937 is with you passing sixteen thousand for fifteen, squawking 3836."

"Dancer 937, radar contact. Blackhorse Radar has you loud and clear. Come right to 252. Make your speed three-fifty."

"Dancer 937, roger, right to 252. And we're at three-fifty. Arm 'em up, flight."

Wilson reached down and hit his armament switches as he followed the F-4's little wing dip that made the two-degree heading correction. He moved just a little bit away from the Phantom and just a little farther forward on his wing so that when the F-4's bombs came off, he would be well clear. He glanced to his right and saw that his own wingman had done the same.

"937 is steady 252." Normally, a two-degree heading correction on anything other than a ground-controlled landing approach would have been met with a subtle bit of sarcasm from a pilot, but the precision needed to drop these bombs reasonably close to friendly troops made it okay.

There were a few seconds of silence followed by the controller's calm voice again. "Dancer, come right to 255. There seems to be a little more wind than forecast."

"255." The formation eased a little right and steadied out again.

"937, Blackhorse. That looks good. Three minutes to drop."

"Click-click."

Wilson stole a glance into the blackness ahead. There were no lights to break the sameness of the ground below and only the lights of a couple of distant formations of aircraft to see. He didn't know what he expected really, maybe the searchlights and flak-bursts like they had in the World War II movies. After all, this mission was a lot more similar to the tactics used back then than it was to what he had been using—basic dive-bombing.

As the seconds moved forward, he began to see dim flashes on the ground pretty much in one area. He couldn't discern which were explosions of artillery shells and mortar rounds and which were muzzle flashes from the guns, but it didn't matter. He was now aware that even though this was a simple bomb drop for him, for the men on the ground it was only a small part of their nightly struggle to survive.

"Dancer 937, Blackhorse, twenty seconds."

"937."

Wilson checked his switches once more and resisted the temptation to caress the button on the stick. He concentrated on keeping his position as smoothly as possible.

"Ten seconds. Stand by to drop on my mark."

"Click-click."

"Five seconds . . . four . . . three . . . two . . . one . . . mark!"

Wilson jammed his thumb down on the red button on the stick and held it there, feeling the aircraft shudder as the bombs fell away in pairs. He pressed the red button once more to make sure.

"Blackhorse, 937. Bombs away."

"Roger, 937. Right turn to 075. Climb and maintain angels twenty."

"937, right to 075 and we're out of fifteen for twenty."

Wilson slid back into the normal position, reached down, and secured his armament switches. He wiggled his oxygen mask on his face, trying to make it more comfortable. As he followed the F-4 he was amazed at how easy that was. He had dropped a couple of tons of high explosives on a spot he couldn't even point to on a map and had never even seen the bombs explode except as a dim flickering glow reflecting from the underside of the leader. Nobody had shot at them, probably because they were gone before the enemy had even heard them coming.

"Dancer 937, Blackhorse Radar. The spotters tell us that your hits were dead on. We'll pass your BDA through the normal channels. We appreciate your efforts. Every time you guys show up, you make our job a little easier. Contact Hillsborough on this frequency now. Blackhorse out."

"Roger, Blackhorse, glad we could help out. Switching." Everyone in the flight switched frequencies and checked in with the leader.

"Hillsborough, Dancer 937 and flight are with you, level angels twenty."

"Roger, 937. Radar contact. You're coming up on feet wet now. You are cleared to separate. Dancer, take up a heading of, um, 175 and the Ghostriders take up 035. That's 175 for Dancer 937 and 035 for Ghostrider 404 and flight."

"Dancer 937 copies all. Break. 404, you have the lead."

Wilson keyed his mike. "404. I have the lead. Good night, Dancer. Thank you."

"Click-click." The Phantom accelerated upward and curved away to the right. Wilson relaxed a little, as he no longer had to work his ass off to keep a good formation. He flexed his fingers and wiggled his butt on the hard seat.

As he led his four aircraft away to the northeast and home, the thought struck him that he'd probably never meet the man who had just led him and his flight on a mission in the middle of a war. He pondered that for a little while, wondering whether it mattered to him and decided that it didn't. The man in Dancer 937 had been a fellow warrior and a fellow professional aviator, and that was enough.

36

Wednesday, February 7, 1968

At a little after 0400, Major Dick Averitt picked himself up from the muddy floor of the trench and leaned against the side, gasping for air. He resisted the natural desire to double over, and stood upright, forcing his muscles to stop trying to tighten up. The other marine picked himself up, too, and stood next to Averitt, unseen in the darkness, holding his nose which had hit Averitt's helmet at exactly the same instant that Averitt's ribs had hit the marine's rifle butt.

The marine groaned and said, "They oughta put some fucking stop signs around here. You all right?"

Averitt managed to grunt out that he was fine and, with no further apology at all, the marine moved off down the trench at the same high rate of speed with which he had approached. The major felt around himself, found that he still had all his gear, and moved away in the opposite direction—toward the command post.

As he moved along, the pain in his side lessened enough for him to again hear the thumps and cracks of artillery fire. None of it was hitting the combat base, but down to the southwest, well outside the perimeter, there seemed to be a major firefight going on. Averitt peeked out of the trench and could see nothing other than the dim flashes of exploding shells.

The other thing Averitt noticed was that after the adrenaline of the first three minutes of being awakened, he was conscious of just how tired he was. He'd been asleep for only an hour or so, and that did nothing to erase his sleep deficit. The last thing he remembered was listening to two of the enlisted men from the tactical air controller group arguing about their card game in the sleeping bunker.

He made it to the CP without further damage and, once through the curtains that formed the light trap, looked around the room. Over the past few days he had learned to judge what the situation was by the number of men standing around the colonel and the volume of the chatter from the men manning the radios. That night, or, rather, that morning, things looked pretty rough for somebody out there.

The colonel looked up, spotted Averitt, and acknowledged his presence with a nod before turning back to his staff. The major eased his way over to the corner, where he could be handy and inconspicuous and still listen to what was going on. In the dimmer light back there he could see that Sergeant Major Gorton was sitting astride a battered chair, already doing exactly what Averitt intended for himself.

Gorton looked as lousy as Averitt felt. Several times since their first meeting, Averitt had been struck by the old marine's ability, like his colonel, to be just as dirty and smelly as everyone else but still appear to be the brightest and shiniest of them all. But now in the harsh shadows thrown by the lights in the center of the room, he looked old. His broad shoulders were slumped above

300

his arms, which were crossed on the back of the chair, and an unlit cigarette dangled from the corner of his mouth.

"What's going on, Sergeant Major?"

Gorton sighed. He took the cigarette from his mouth and threw it down on the wooden floor. As he spoke, he bent down and picked it up again, rolling the filter between his thumb and fore-finger. "The fuckin' gomers have overrun one of the outposts. The last thing we heard from them was that there were tanks in the wire. They've been yelling for help and we can't do nothin' for the next couple of hours. Last night they took over the Vietnamese ville down the road, and now this."

"How about close air?"

"The bastards were in the wires before we could get anything overhead. Now we can't get them because they're mixed in with our own guys."

Averitt pulled up a battered chair, the twin of Gorton's, and sat down. "Shit," he said.

"Yup. We had an agreement with the Army, that's who's there, the Army, that we'd support them if something like this happened. We can't send anybody out in the dark to help. They'd be certain to be ambushed. We have to wait and, by the time we can do anything, it'll be way too late."

"Shit."

"You already said that, Major. This is killing the colonel, but sending a company or even two out there now would be suicidal. There's four divisions of the enemy, and if I were them, I'd have a real nice ambush all laid out for us. All we can do is wait for daylight and helicopter some help out there. The Army is going to hate us forever for this, but we can't risk getting two hundred more men wiped out in a futile gesture."

The old marine looked at the cigarette which was now nothing more than an unraveling filter. "The tanks are what worry me the most. This is the first time we've heard of them actually being used. There've been rumors and intell about them, but nobody's had to face them so far. This changes things a lot because if they've got enough of them and they use them right, they can shove our ass right off this hill. That would mean we'd be stuck in the valley among 35,000 or so bad guys and no way to protect ourselves."

Averitt only barely stopped himself from saying "shit" again. As he smiled at himself in dim embarrassment, the thought struck him that he no longer felt like an outsider, a visitor from the head office. Having spent the past few days taking the same chances and sharing the same hardships as all the other marines here at the combat base, he had come to consider himself part of the group. He felt the same concerns and fears that anyone who had been here awhile did, and he felt a huge loyalty to both the other marines and the regiment itself. The regiment to which he was permanently assigned felt like something from his past, much like his last squadron would when he was permanently assigned to a new one. He could share Gorton's feeling about being unable to help the men at the outpost and be just as frustrated. He knew that it was a sound military decision to wait until daylight, but he was learning quickly that sound military decisions are often extremely painful in that they are often in direct conflict with the emotional response.

A daring night march in force to the relief of the outpost would be emotionally satisfying, but totaling up the casualties from running into a massive ambush on the way would be militarily devastating. The colonel was right in his decision, but Averitt could only imagine the courage it must have taken. He was very glad he was not the colonel.

Averitt took out his cigarette pack and offered it to Gorton. The old marine took one with thanks and put it behind his ear "for later." Averitt knew that in a couple of minutes the new one would be lying shredded on the floor with the last one.

"Sergeant Major, do you have any idea why the colonel wanted to see me?"

Gorton looked at the major in surprise. "No, sir. I wasn't even aware that you'd been called over here."

Averitt nodded slowly. "I guess I'll find out soon enough. It doesn't look like he's got a lot of spare time right now."

"No, sir, it sure doesn't."

It was nearly six before Colonel Aires got around to summoning Averitt over. The intervening two hours had been full of comings and goings of marine officers and the constant drone of voices talking on telephones. It became mesmerizing for Averitt, and he found himself drifting off as his head rested on his arms on the back of the chair. He finally turned the chair around and leaned it back against the wall, where he dozed off several times for short periods. Each time he awoke, he would look around and see that the picture of the room had not changed at all except for a new face or two in the group around the colonel and one of the older ones missing, probably off somewhere getting his part of the Plan together.

He was almost back asleep when he thought he heard his name called. He looked up and saw Colonel Aires looking at him expectantly. It took a few seconds for him to shake free of the cobwebs and get to his feet. He walked over to the table, conscious of Gorton's presence a step or so behind him.

"Yes, sir."

"Major Averitt, I need a favor. I'd like you to go over to Hill 855 and take over the close air coordination for a few days. One of my air officers is on emergency leave and I have no one else to spare."

Averitt smiled and Aires caught it. "No, I didn't mean that you're the bottom of my barrel. I need someone out there who's got his shit together and you are the only one I have who is presently unassigned. There is a captain coming up from Chu Lai in a couple of days, but I need someone now, not next Tuesday. Do you want the job?"

"Yes, sir. When do I leave?"

Aires nodded at Averitt's willingness. There was no hesitation at all. No subtle weighing of the pros and cons of the assignment. There was only the simple agreement that he expected of all marines, even aviators. He had liked this big pilot on his first meeting and had had no reason to change his assessment since. He wished for a moment that Averitt could be permanently assigned to the regiment instead of on loan. He resolved to see if he could make that happen after Averitt got back from 855. He felt certain that Averitt would stay if asked.

"This morning. Sergeant Major Gorton will see that you get there. Now, there are a couple of things you need to get straight. First, you will be the senior man over there. I'd prefer not to have it that way, but I don't get to make everything happen the way I'd like. The senior man there now is one of the best company grade officers I have and I want it clear that he's in command and will remain in command. You are his adviser. Clear?"

"Colonel, no offense, sir. But the last thing on earth I want to be is in command of infantry. My family would disown me. I come from a long line of people who hate walking."

Aires looked at him, stunned at first, and then he began to chuckle. "I promise never to tell your folks. Now, the second thing. As you know, we captured what appeared to be the enemy's general plans before you got here. So far, he's not deviated much at all from them. He has to drive in our outposts if he's to push us out of here. So far he's not succeeded in doing that, but he has taken the ville down the road and last night he overran the army camp. We've got a force going out to relieve them in a few minutes."

He pointed to the map. "Even though the enemy's beaten the shit out of both 881 South and 855 with his artillery and mortars, he hasn't yet tried to assault either one. I expect that he'll take a couple of days to gather himself and then he'll try to take one or the other. It should be obvious that if he gets either one, we'll have some big problems here. 881S is in good shape, but I'm a little worried about 855. There have been no probing attacks on it in almost two weeks which means either he believes he's figured out everything he needs to know or that he's going to leave it alone and go for 881S. What I want you to do is to get over there and see what we can do to protect the place with air and supporting fire. I've already directed the commander over there, Captain Sam Demars, to do what he can to deceive the enemy. If the gomers have decided to bypass it, great. But if he figures that he's learned all he needs to and is just waiting for the right time to attack, Demars and you are going to have some surprises ready. Okay?"

"Aye, aye, Colonel."

Aires stuck out his hand. "Thank you, Dick. I appreciate this."

Averitt shook the colonel's hand. "Yes, sir. Don't forget me now, okay?"

"I won't. Three days at the most and you'll be back here in civilization."

Gorton stepped forward and spoke up. "Um, Colonel. If it's all the same to you, sir, I'd like to go over with the major. To keep him out of trouble, like. You told me to keep an eye on him and I ought to keep it up."

Aires looked at Gorton for a long moment. The last thing in the world he wanted to do was allow his old friend and teacher to put himself at risk in a place like Hill 855. He didn't really expect much to happen there, but it grated on him to think of losing Gorton, especially when he was so close to going home to his long-overdue retirement.

Aires knew that Gorton had managed to delay his retirement

304

until after this tour so that he could be the regimental sergeant major for Aires's tour as the regimental commanding officer. Aires also knew that Gorton arranged it that way not only because he wanted to do everything he could to help Aires succeed in command but mostly because he wanted to just be there to see the payoff for all the many years they had known and worked with each other. Aires knew that he would feel incomplete for the few days that Gorton would be gone. And he knew, should anything happen to his old friend, it would be a difficult thing for him to live with.

But as he looked at the weather-beaten face of the regimental sergeant major, he knew that there could be no crueler thing he could do to the man than refuse his request. Nothing would break the man's spirit more completely than to be refused a request to do his job as he saw it, no matter how fine or noble the motives for refusing. A man like Gorton, who has been a warrior for thirty years, cannot lay his sword aside until he, and only he, decides it is time.

Aires sighed and shook his head resignedly. "All right, you go too. But do not do anything stupid or anything heroic. Your entire purpose in life for the next few days is to sit on this airedale and keep him out of trouble. You are not going over there to run the show either. There are a bunch of perfectly competent noncommissioned officers on that hill who have been doing just fine without your help. And when the major comes back, you come too. Same time, same helicopter. No bullshit. If you let the major loose and he gets cute again, I'll bust you back to lance corporal. Got it?"

Gorton drew himself and squared his awesome shoulders. "Yes, sir. Nothin' stupid and nothin' heroic. Got it."

An hour later Gorton and Averitt sat in a bunker hard by the runway, smoking and looking out the door toward the east. There was a "Super Gaggle" scheduled in less than ten minutes, and one of the big CH-46 Sea Knights would ferry them and three others who, judging from their clean fatigues and their slightly wild-eyed expressions, looked to be nuggets, or new guys, who were to be replacements for casualties over on Hill 855. Averitt looked over at Gorton, who was carefully checking his rifle, an older M-14 which had been replaced by the new, occasionally troublesome M-16 like the one Averitt had.

"Where'd you get that?"

"I've always liked these things. They hit what I aim at, they

305

don't jam, and they shoot a real bullet. I guess I'm just more comfortable with 'em.''

"I haven't seen one since Quantico, but I liked them too. This thing"—he hefted his M-16—"is nice, but it doesn't feel like a weapon."

"Yeah. When we first got them they kept jamming and I just got so I didn't trust them. They've got a fix for them but I'm just more comfortable with this old gal. Besides, it looks realer than those little things."

A haggard-looking marine stuck his head in the bunker and asked who was going to 855 and who was going to 881S. He organized them into two small groups and gave them the briefing.

"Okay. When the helos get here, run, don't walk, aboard. Sit down, strap in, and shut up. When you get where you're going, get out as quick as you can and run, do not walk, to the nearest hole and jump in. We've lost eight guys in the past twenty-four hours who stayed in the LZ to get a look at the place. Don't be slow in getting out either 'cause the helo pilots will take off whether you're out or not. You don't want to fall fifty feet into your new home because it'll be a while before we can give you another helo ride to the hospital. Double-check that your weapon's clear, and if you have any grenades, make sure they're not hanging where they can snag on anything. Any questions?"

There were none, so the haggard marine disappeared from the entrance to the bunker.

Averitt checked his rifle, making sure that the chamber did not have a round in it, and watched as Gorton and the three replacements did the same except that one of the replacements pulled the handle all the way back and locked his bolt open. Gorton reached across, took the rifle away, ejected the magazine, and closed the bolt. He replaced the magazine and handed the rifle back to the embarrassed marine without a word.

Averitt watched the young man blush. He knew that, sooner or later the kid would have inadvertently released the bolt which would have automatically chambered a round. The weapon would then be ready to fire, and given the nervousness of the marine holding it, it would have fired at the worst possible moment, for instance, inside the helo.

Off in the distance Averitt could hear the dull throbbing of helicopter rotor blades. At first the sound was almost below the threshold of human hearing. It was more felt than heard, but it soon rose into a cacophonous drumbeat as the dozens of blades made their own sounds against the moist air. After a few seconds the sounds became distinguishable from one another. There was the sharp flat clatter of CH-46s and the slower, more rhythmic, thumping of the Huey gunships along as escort.

Averitt and Gorton stood up and moved out of the bunker into the short trench that protected the entrance. They peeked their heads up, trying to find the direction that the sound was coming from, but against the hills and forests the sound broke up so that it seemed to be coming from everywhere at once. The low morning sun made looking to the east where the helos should have been approaching from impossible.

All at once there was the roar of jets and the boom of exploding bombs as the Marine Phantoms and A-4s arrived early to keep the enemy's heads down. Several of the jets made low passes along the hills and valleys, laying smoke mixed with tear gas, while others strafed known or suspected enemy positions. The noise was incredible, so much so that the haggard marine couldn't be heard when he came to guide the passengers to the airstrip.

The marine gestured to Averitt and the others and dashed the fifty yards or so to the holes dug next to the airstrip. He jumped into one and motioned to the others. The small group of marines disappeared below ground as quickly as they had appeared from the bunker. Several CH-46s made high-speed approaches to the strip, hauling their noses up sharply when they were within a hundred yards or so to kill off their speed for landing.

Even before they landed, several marines from the Helicopter Support Department, or HSD, were running across the matting toward them. No sooner had their wheels touched down than men began running down the ramps in the rear of the helos, guided by the men of the HSD. The haggard marine gestured to Averitt's group of five and led them quickly to one of the 46s.

Averitt dashed up the helicopter's rear ramp past the last pallet of cargo that was going the other way. He found one of the worn fabric seats along the side of the helo and flopped down with Gorton right next to him. At the rear of the helicopter Averitt saw the haggard marine give the thumbs-up sign to the crew chief, who then spoke into the lip microphone attached to his helmet.

Averitt fumbled around on the seat and under his butt to find both ends of the lap belt. He found two and tried to hook them together, but they were the same—identical ends of two different

307

belts. He glanced over at Gorton and saw him having the same problem. Taking one of his ends, he swapped it with one of Gorton's so that each now had a functional belt. Before he could snap the belt together, the helo leapt off the ground and the nose dropped as the pilot did his best to get away from the runway as fast as possible.

Averitt had always hated riding in the back of helicopters. The noise, the weird vibrations, the feeling that the damn things were held together by hope more than bolts and rivets, never left him. When he was in an especially shaky one, like the average 46, he always gave himself up for dead. That way he was always pleasantly surprised when he actually made it to his destination.

Another trick he used was that he built up a mild case of hatred for the crew, who seemed to go about their tasks with blithe disregard for their proximity to eternity. When he was in a helo in combat it always drove him crazy how the crew seemed to act exactly the same as if they were on a sightseeing tour of the beaches in Southern California.

Averitt was concentrating on these thoughts to stifle his fear, when several large jagged holes abruptly opened up in the far wall of the aircraft and the pilot banked sharply to the side away from the holes.

37

Wednesday, February 7, 1968

The pilot banked the helicopter so steeply that Averitt felt that he was nearly lying on his back. He shoved himself away from the aluminum support on the back of the seat, rolled his head to the left, and looked out the circular window. The pilot had begun a steep climbing right turn and was now well above the stream of tracer from the gun that had hit the helo.

★ Ghostrider One ★

Averitt saw a couple of white streaks strike the ground just short of the spot where the gun apparently was. Two more streaks followed, and Averitt suddenly was looking at the Huey gunship that had fired the rockets. As the Huey went past, another pair of rockets left the pods on either side of the aircraft and two more after that. Several explosions blew the foliage around the gun to pieces and the tracer ceased, probably permanently.

The pilot eased the helo back into a more normal flight attitude, and the crew chief came back and inspected the holes in the left side. He looked at the overhead and checked the exit holes. He looked at Averitt and gave the thumbs-up, drawing his sleeve across his brow in an exaggerated sign of relief.

Averitt, still doubtful of this machine's ability to fly in the first place, checked for himself to see that there was no hydraulic fluid or oil or fuel leaking into the cabin. He couldn't tell if any of the moving parts had been hit. There didn't seem to be any change in the noise or vibrations, but then, he'd never been able to figure out the safe vibrations from the dangerous ones when he was in helicopters. He believed the old line that helicopters couldn't really fly—they just vibrated so badly that the Earth rejected them.

The crew chief gave another signal which Averitt interpreted to mean that they would shortly begin the descent into the LZ on Hill 855, but before he could do anything to get ready, the helo gave a sickening lurch and began a steep spiraling dive. Averitt looked out the window and saw the ground tilting crazily and moving across his view in a manner he could remember seeing only very rarely from the cockpit of his A-4. He watched fascinated as the individual trees on the ground grew larger and then they were over a cleared area of ugly reddish dirt.

The helicopter rolled out of its bank and the nose came up sharply. There was a huge increase in the vibrations, and the clatter from the rotor system became almost deafening. One of the young marines sitting across and farther aft from Gorton lost his helmet which slammed onto the deck with a thunk, causing the crew chief to whip around. He saw the marine pick up his helmet and relaxed, turning back to his door gun. Averitt smiled at the thought that even the helo guys worried about strange noises.

He felt the rear wheels bump almost gently on the ground and then the nose lowered a little. The crew chief moved quickly aft and gestured for the five passengers to follow. They all stood and

309

walked toward the rapidly lowering rear ramp and watched for their first glimpse of their new home.

When the ramp was down far enough, the crew chief thumbed them out the back and pushed the last man firmly in the small of the back. All five ran out and headed for the edge of the LZ with Gorton and Averitt bringing up the rear and urging on the three nuggets. Several marines passed them, headed for the helo, and the last two carried a litter with a wounded marine.

His legs were heavily bandaged but still present and he was holding his head up to see where they were carrying him. Even though he was in obvious pain, Averitt could see that his face held a great deal of eagerness to be away and gone from this hilltop.

The five jumped into holes dug below the LZ and lay panting. Averitt heard the sound of the rotor blades change and felt the air from the rotorwash blow over him as the helicopter lifted off. He waited for the inevitable mortar rounds, but they never came. By now the 46 was moving away and the enemy probably wouldn't bother firing, so Averitt stuck his head up and watched the helo depart.

The 46 lifted a very few feet off the ground and the nose dropped immediately as it sought to gain the speed that could be traded for altitude. Averitt could see the helmeted heads of the pilots as they passed nearly overhead and saw the crewman raise his hand in a small wave as he manned the gun sticking out of the right side.

The helo picked up enough speed and banked to the left, away from the positions the gunships were pounding as best they could with their 2.75-inch rockets and their mini-guns. The helo flew by the hill, headed the other way from its arrival course. Averitt looked around at the forests where the enemy now was beginning to increase its fire at the Super Gaggle and then looked back at this airborne Chinese fire drill.

He could see the helicopter climbing steeply away and the other helos from all the rest of the outposts climbing away from their drops also. In the background the Huey gunships still rolled in on the enemy positions but the jets were gone, probably still nearby but well above the altitudes the helos were using.

Averitt swung his gaze back to the helicopter that had just dropped them off. It was turning right, toward the southeast, and still climbing, when there was a large flash just beneath the rear rotor about where the engine would be. The aircraft yawed mo-

mentarily and steadied out. Averitt had just enough time to register approval for the pilot's response before a small plume of
brownish smoke began streaming out behind the helicopter.

An orange ball of flame burst from the area of the right engine
and the smoke streamer increased dramatically. The aircraft yawed
again but more violently before the pilot got it under control again.
The 46 was now descending and turning toward the large strip at
the combat base with the trail of smoke becoming progressively
thicker.

Glancing between the helicopter and the combat base, Averitt
judged that the helo should make it since the angle of descent was
shallow enough to intersect nicely with the end of the runaway.
He was just starting to breathe with relief when the helo pitched
up, slowly at first but gradually steepening. As the nose passed
through about sixty degrees, the helo bean to roll to the left until
it was nearly on its side. The roll increased steadily, the nose fell
through, and the helicopter plunged to the ground almost vertically and nearly inverted, leaving a huge black and orange fireball
almost directly on a line between Averitt and the landing strip
back on the combat base, where it had picked up Averitt and the
others less than ten minutes before.

"Ho-ly shit!" One of the new young marines was staring at the
crash. He climbed out of the hole to get a better look and stood
rooted as the billow of black smoke rose higher and higher.

Gorton saw the kid, grabbed him by the belt, and pulled him
back into the hole. "Get down, you idiot. This ain't a fucking
circus for you to stand around watching. There's real bad guys
with real bullets out here."

The kid stared ashen-faced up at Gorton. "Jesus Christ, Sergeant
Major, we just got off that helo. That could have been us."

Gorton looked grimly back out at the crash. "I know, son. But
it *wasn't* us. It was some other poor bastards. Now, get your gear.
We've gotta report in."

38

Wednesday, February 7, 1968

Nick Taylor placed his tray on the wardroom table and sat down next to several other men from his squadron. Across the table Jim Hogan put down his fork and tried to hide a smile as he saw Taylor wince.

"Are we in a little pain there, Nick?"

Taylor looked up. "Pain, sir? Agony would be more like it."

Hogan waited for Taylor to continue, but when he didn't, only sat there sipping his coffee, Hogan couldn't stand it. "Well, what the hell happened?"

Taylor looked up. "I was out on the roof, learning how to shoot airplanes, and a piece of one of the holdback bars came back and hit me in the thigh. I thought I was going to be crippled in the other leg. Hurt like a bitch."

"That's what happens when you try to play with somebody else's toys. Seriously, did you see the doc?"

"Yup. He said it served me right. What did you guys do, you and the doc, go to the same school?"

Hogan laughed and went back to his meal as the other guys in the squadron began giving Taylor the needle. He listened to the youthful laughter as Taylor told the story in much greater detail, pausing dramatically at the important moments before he went on. He knew that for Taylor this would become one of the stories he'd tell his kids someday when a movie came on TV about the Navy. He'd tell them all about the day back in '68 when he worked with the guy in the yellow shirt who stood *right there* and launched those big jets. The kids would marvel at their daddy and he would seem even bigger and more important than he already was to them. He'd probably get to tell his friends back home about it too.

312

Hogan thought back on all the times he'd gone home on leave and seen his old high school buddies. They were all lawyers and insurance men and such now, staring forty in the eye, much of their hair and most of their dreams gone, buried under the implacable glacier of stable responsibility. They were expanding slowly in the middle and aching some at either end.

For the first few years, when they were all still in their twenties, they'd kept some of the same exuberance that had made them friends in their teens. As time went on, he'd transferred from squadron to squadron and from coast to coast, shipping out to the exotic places they'd all dreamed of once, and managing to get home only once a year or so. In the meantime, he'd walked ancient streets and roads and met people who spoke languages that were old before Christ was born. He'd felt the sea breezes on his face and tasted the salt on his lips. He'd seen the Northern Lights and the Southern Cross. He'd sipped sangria on the beaches of southern Spain and eaten in the floating restaurants of Hong Kong.

When he went home, his face becoming gradually more deeply lined from squinting into the sun, he found that they'd remained the same but over time *he* had changed. Their interests now seemed trivial and boring to him. He couldn't really care about the new road linking the hometown and the new stretch of interstate or about how land prices had escalated since they announced the new shopping center. Most of the old classmates they'd told him about had receded into the mists of his memory and he knew that he'd have to pull out the old yearbook just to recall what they had looked like.

Most of his friends had married their high school sweethearts, many even willingly, and they would always ask him about what he'd been doing. He'd tell them a little and try to shift the conversation back to their interests, knowing full well that they could never understand what he did. In the early years they'd shift it right back to him, fascinated with the adventures he must be having.

As time went on, they asked fewer and fewer questions about his career and the Navy and talked more about their own concerns and their own small town. There were fewer and fewer gathered for the evenings at Jerry's Belvedere Tavern until there were only Hogan and two others going every time. It became a sadder and sadder experience for him and he'd not minded much when the last two had made their excuses and not met him in the old tavern next to the post office.

The last time he'd been home, he'd asked his father why it seemed he'd lost his old friends.

His father gently explained that he hadn't lost them at all. He'd just done something that they now wished they'd tried. They resented him a little because he'd had an adventure and, in fact, was still having one while they were feeling trapped in lives that to them had lost their color and become black and white. They knew that it was too late for them now and they had stopped going out because it hurt them to think about it, to go home down the same street to the same back door of the same house that once had seemed to be the dream beyond which there could be nothing grander. They'd lay awake nights and wonder what it would have been like for them if . . . They'd get up the next morning and leave the same house through the same back door and drive down the same streets toward the same job where today's problems were indistinguishable from yesterday's or last week's or last year's.

It was not that he'd lost them as friends, explained his father, it was that they'd lost him.

Hogan had looked at his dad and asked him how he felt, having lived in this town his whole life, much like Hogan's friends. His father had chuckled and then answered.

"Don't forget I was in World War II. I saw some of the world myself, mostly from about six inches off the ground, or below it if I could dig fast enough. For me, that was proof that this was all I ever really wanted. I've been happy here with your mother and your brothers. It was my choice to come back.

"I'm older now and my dreams are different from what they once were. I got many of them and the ones I missed out on don't seem too important to me now. I often wonder why they ever did.

"But your friends are here because they never got around to doing anything else or because, for some reason, they couldn't. The big thing, though, is that they're forty and that's tough if you suddenly realize you might have missed the boat. Thoreau said somewhere that 'the mass of men lead lives of quiet desperation.' So they're not unusual, you are. Who knows, someday you might even come back here to stay, once you get done flying your silly little airplanes."

Hogan looked up sharply and saw the smile in his father's eyes and then, chuckling, went to the refrigerator to get them each another beer.

But now, sitting here aboard a warship, Hogan wondered, if things had been different for him, if his wife hadn't opted (sensibly, he had to admit) to end their marriage, would he be satisfied with the type of life his old friends had?

It struck him, suddenly, that he'd had to make his own steep payments to follow his dream. He'd spent months and years at sea, fighting boredom and the Navy's own brand of routine. He'd lost a dozen friends closer to him than those old high school buddies. He'd had a family of his own for a while, but he'd lost that now too. But he had become what he'd always wanted to be—the commanding officer of a squadron of carrier pilots.

He thought again of the stability and order of the life back home, and even though he envied it in a way, he felt, for now at least, that who he was and what he was had been worth the cost. But he was smart enough to know he was still young and deeply committed to what he was doing with his life. He didn't know how he'd feel in ten or twenty years when he was no longer a naval aviator and was facing his final audit. He hoped he'd find that it all had been worth it. He truly hoped for that.

"Skipper?"

Hogan shook his head and dragged himself back to the present. "Yeah? Sorry about that. I was off somewhere."

"We were wondering if anything new came out of the C.O.'s meeting with CAG," asked one of the J.O.'s.

"Not much really. When we're not involved in normal flight ops, we've got to maintain some alerts for a while for close air support for the northern provinces. It seems that the I Corps commanders think we'll be needed. We are going to be pretty much devoted to that while the Concord will keep on with their normal assignments. The Ranger and Enterprise should be released from the Korean thing soon, so that'll help.

"Anyway, Jack Wilson and the other squadron operations officers are getting it all figured out now. As soon as we get finished with the UNREP, we'll be moving farther south."

The UNREP was Navy-ese for "under way replenishment," where the carrier was resupplied from ships steaming either alongside or close by. An oiler would pump across the thousands of gallons of fuel for the ship and her aircraft while helicopters would sling-load hundreds of pallets of bombs and food and the myriad of other items that kept a floating city like the *Shiloh* able to carry out her tasks. These operations occurred every three to five days, depending upon the carrier's tempo of operations. Lately, they had been happening at three-day intervals.

The best part of these UNREPs for the pilots was it gave them a few extra hours of rest unless the C.O. decided to spoil it with an all-officers meeting during which they would receive some more boring lectures from somebody. In the eyes of most J.O.'s, AOMs were about as exciting as watching all seventy-six acts of an Italian opera.

Taylor looked up from the remains of his dessert. "I guess I'd better get back to work so you guys can have some idea where the hell your targets are going to be."

Hogan answered a few more questions and left himself, headed back to the ready room.

Three hours later Commander Terry White climbed the four steps out of the catwalk and stepped onto the flight deck. He shoved his flashlight into the front pocket of his survival vest because there was enough light from the floodlights on the islands for them to get to their aircraft reasonably safely. He waited until Cordella stepped onto the deck and then turned and led the way aft toward the rows of aircraft parked like herringbones on the fantail aft of the waist catapults.

White and Cordella had been assigned the first four-hour alert from 2000 to midnight. Since they were the first, they got the good deal of stumbling around in the dark preflighting the aircraft and then turning it up and checking the systems out. It has been proven from long experience that the time to see if the jet works is not when men on the ground far away are screaming for help.

The two pilots turned their faces away from the rotorwash from one of the vertical replenishment, or VERTREP, helicopters bringing pallets of supplies from the ships farther astern, and continued aft, keeping one eye on the movements of the forklifts and men around the deck.

They found their aircraft without difficulty and hung their helmets and navigation bags on the boarding ladders. Pulling out their flashlights, Cordella and White began checking out their aircraft. The two young plane captains followed them around, keeping discreetly behind the pilots as the walk-arounds progressed. The young men had spent a good amount of the evening servicing their aircraft and making sure that they were ready to go. After the ordnancemen had loaded the bombs aboard, the young men checked that even that had been done right.

White looked over the right side and the wing, shoving the leading edge slats up and letting them fall slightly to make sure that when they were needed they'd drop smoothly and not hang up. One of the more thrilling experiences in flying occurs when the slats on an A-4 fail to come out together, causing a large differential in the lift produced by each wing. This results in a complete departure from controlled flight, when all the pilot can do is simply hold the stick in the middle, hope his harness is locked, slam the throttle to idle, and look at the trim indicator. He is merely a passenger for a few moments in a ride no amusement park could ever hope to duplicate.

Sooner or later the violent tumbling and rolling will stop, but the question then arises whether there is going to be enough altitude left to get the aircraft flying straight and level again. If the departure happens at too low an altitude, all that will remain is one of the famous smoking holes.

The pilots continued around their aircraft, poking, wiggling, and tugging everything they could see. They climbed up on the wings and looked into the upper recesses of the fuselage and checked their hydraulic reservoirs. Finally, they came all the way around again to the feet of their boarding ladders, climbed up, and settled themselves into their seats. The plane captains climbed up after them, helped them adjust the harnesses, and handed them their helmets. The plane captains climbed back down the ladders and prepared for the engine starts and the systems checks.

White and Cordella went through their engine starts and systems checks quickly and surely and then shut down their engines. Around the deck, the aircrew of the other alert aircraft ran up their jets and shut them down too. White sat in his cockpit for a few extra moments, just watching the show. After a few minutes he unfastened his straps and climbed down. Smiling, he thanked the plane captain and then he and Cordella went back to the ready room to sit and watch the night's movie, killing time for the next four hours until another pair of pilots came in to relieve them.

*   *   *

317

Up on the bridge, CAG Andrews walked in, in answer to the summons from the captain. He found him out in the small area known as "aux conn," where there was a sort of smaller bridge where the captain or the officer of the deck could drive the ship while it was alongside one of the oilers as it was now.

The captain was sitting in his chair, watching the goings-on apparently calmly while a couple of more junior officers "conned" the ship as it steamed along beside the old oiler with several thick black hoses stretching between the two ships. In between the hoses were lines and cables along which pulleys traveled carrying smaller packages of stores than those delivered by the VERTREPs to the flight deck.

Andrews walked over and stood beside the captain so he could be noticed when there was time. It took only a few seconds, for the captain glanced up at Andrews and swung his eyes back to the oiler only about seventy or so feet away.

" 'Evening, Frank. How goes it?''

"Just fine, Captain.''

"Good. Listen, what I wanted to see you about was the alert posture we'll be standing for the next few days. It may stretch on longer than that, but I need to know how long you can sustain it and still fly the normal schedule.''

"If we stay in a fifteen-minute alert posture and keep the normal schedule normal, we can go on for quite a while. If the schedule gets much more intense, we'll need to maybe go to a thirty-minute response time. If we start actually launching the alerts, then we'll probably only make it four or five days before we really start to get dangerous.''

"Okay. What do you have in alert now?''

"We've got two each from both A-4 squadrons and both fighter squadrons. We've got an alert tanker and, of course, one helo will be in Alert-15, but until this UNREP is over, they'll be in Alert-5.'' He was referring to the fact that whenever the ship was doing an UNREP, there was a rescue helicopter either airborne or, more commonly, sitting in a five-minute alert status with the crew strapped in and ready to be airborne in five minutes. Good crews could usually do it in less time, but five minutes was the standard. As soon as the *Shiloh* broke away from the replenishment ships, the helicopter crew would go down to their ready room and be in fifteen-minute status like everybody else.

"You know that if we get the call to go help the marines, there

318

won't be any time to screw around, trying to make decisions. If the aircrews start to lose their edge, you've got to let me know so I can tell the admiral. Don't let anybody screw around, trying to look good. If there's a problem, bring it up immediately. Okay?"

Andrews nodded. "Yes, sir."

The captain turned away again to watch his duty officers con his ship.

"Thanks, Frank. You're doing well. Keep it up."

Recognizing his dismissal, Andrews said, "Good night, Captain," and left the bridge.

He was smiling as he opened the door to the walkway on the side of the island and looked down on the deck and all the aircraft of his air wing. He had said exactly the same thing to the squadron C.O.'s at their meeting earlier that the captain had just said to him. Almost word for word.

The reason he was smiling, he realized, was that it felt pretty good to be on a team where everyone was pulling in the same direction. There'd been many times in his career when it hadn't been that way but, now in his last flying tour, he was glad as hell that things were working so well.

He looked far aft at the alert aircraft parked on either side of the deck and, in the dim light, made out the different markings on the tails of each pair of A-4s. The thought struck him that there was now small difference in the performance of the two squadrons, quite a change from how it was only a short while ago. That was pretty good too. He didn't have to worry anymore about VA-262, which, although only one of many problems he had to deal with, had been one of the most nagging.

Andrews nodded at the young signalman whose duties included standing out there on the walkway, searching the sea with his binoculars even in this modern age of radar and early warning aircraft. As he went below, he had another thought. It was also nice to work in an environment where tradition still counted for something.

39

Wednesday, February 7, 1968

Sergeant Major Gorton leaned his M-14 against the sand-bagged wall of the bunker. He shrugged off his harness and hung it on the muzzle of the rifle. Looking around in the dim candlelight, he found a cot that appeared to be unused and appropriated it for himself.

Averitt tried to hang his harness from his rifle muzzle but found that his M-16 was not heavy enough to support the weight and the whole thing fell over. He tried it again and the same thing happened, so he picked up his harness and dumped it on the cot next to Gorton's.

Gorton chuckled and offered Averitt a cigarette. "I told you that old M-14 was a hell of a lot better. More useful too."

"Okay, okay. What time is it?"

Gorton peeled the dark green cover off his wristwatch and looked at the luminous hands. "Almost midnight, but I wish you hadn't asked. It makes me tireder."

"Sorry. I'll try to be more considerate next time," Averitt said dryly.

"That's okay, Major. You're only an aviator."

Averitt grinned and plopped almost carelessly down on his cot. He leaned his head back against the sandbagged wall and sighed. It had been a long, exhausting day for him and now, just before midnight, he fell asleep before he remembered to loosen his boot-laces. He didn't even have time to review the events of his first day on Hill 855.

In the company of two of the three marines assigned to the fire control party, Gorton and Averitt had spent most of that afternoon touring the outpost and studying the surrounding landscape through their field glasses. Averitt felt that this was pretty much a very simple exercise. The land outside the perimeter of Hill 855 looked exactly the same as that outside the Khe Sanh Combat Base but with one very significant difference. The treeline was much closer here than back at the combat base, which meant that the enemy was nearer too.

What he could see of the once-dense vegetation had been chewed and shredded as if by a herd of huge cattle, and there were only a few spots between the perimeter wire and the mottled green treeline that had not been bombed and blasted time and again. Clods of earth and bits of metal lay among the innumerable shell craters. There were also small signs of the enemy who were there when the bombs and shells had fallen—a shattered assault rifle here and a bit of canvas there.

The low clouds that had rolled in again in the past hour or so eliminated the shadows and prevented Averitt from getting a true feel for the definition of the area. Off to the north, about four hundred yards away, Hill 881S climbed almost dejectedly from the small valley. With his glasses he could see only little bits of movement from the marines positioned there, and it struck him that those movements would not be presently visible to the enemy, but if the enemy held this hill, they'd be able to fire into that perimeter too. Now that he was out there among them, Averitt realized with a small flutter in his gut that this had the potential to be as big a mess as had been the Chosin Reservoir or Dien Bien Phu. He had read about both of them over the years, and now that he was hard up against the enemy, he had absolutely no desire to be a part of some fighting withdrawal that would go down in the history books. He preferred to stay right there, thank you very much.

Averitt watched as two more helicopters came in later in the day, dropping both food and ammunition and six bladders full of water. The marines of the helicopter support team ensured that the water was dealt with first and then the ammunition and finally the food, dealing with the shipments in order of their importance to their survival. The arrival of the water reminded Averitt that it had been quite a while since he'd had the opportunity to shower and shave, and he suddenly was reminded of just how dirty he felt. He'd been able to brush his teeth a couple of times a day, and that was at least some link with civilization.

They'd finished looking over that area outside the wire and were halfway through checking the outpost itself, when the clouds opened up and dumped a deluge of rain, turning the whole area into a sea of mud in three or four minutes of roaring sound. There was no wind and the rain fell straight down at a rate that would be seen only in a heavy thunderstorm back home. Gorton leaned under the shelter of the wreckage of a small above-ground bunker, a relic of slightly happier and safer days out here on Hill 855.

The rainstorm ceased as quickly as it began, leaving nothing of the express-train sound but a lot of mud in its wake. Gorton hoped that short rains like this would continue for a while because they would make the footing more treacherous for any enemy trying to climb the steep sides of the hill. But if the rain lasted too long, he knew that the little bastards could use it to cover the sounds of their approach. It would also soon rise out of the ground and form the fog that was so prevalent in the highlands during the monsoon season. It was a bitch, he thought, when even the elements seemed to have the ability to take sides.

Almost as he watched, the air filled with a dense white mist obscuring the distant treeline and shielding both sides from observation by the other. At least for the next few minutes, he thought, we can move about relatively safely.

He stepped out into the open, automatically checking his weapon to see that the rain hadn't impaired its ability to fire, and wiped the moisture off the front sight. He looked around and smiled when he saw the major doing the same. "Hey, Major, you're really getting the hang of this infantry stuff. Next, we'll be sending you out on patrol."

Averitt shoved the clip back into his rifle and looked back out at the forests and the mists now beginning to drift among what were left of the treetops. "Sergeant Major, I learned a long time ago that it's always best to leave things like that to professionals. I can't wait to get back to flying."

Gorton nodded. "You know, it's a funny thing. Most of us around here think it's you guys who're crazy. I never feel safe unless I've got my feet on the ground. Getting shot at is bad enough, but when you have to fall a couple of thousand feet to boot, that's more than I can deal with. But right now I've got another little problem to deal with."

He handed his rifle to Averitt, stepped to the nearest "piss tube" and relieved himself. Averitt suddenly had the same urge, and when Gorton was finished, handed him his rifle and then his own. He unzipped and stood over the cylindrical artillery shipping container and let fly, wishing he had been born with higher-speed pumps. Among the hundreds of things Averitt feared about serving in Vietnam was getting shot while he was standing outside, relieving himself.

When he was finished, he retrieved his M-16. "That one's getting a tad full, Sergeant Major."

"Yeah, well, the platoon responsible will deal with that and give the bad guys another present."

The piss tubes were a crude attempt at sanitation in a place like this, where over a hundred men were cooped up for a long time. Given the amount of human waste that they could produce daily, it rapidly became a serious problem to dispose of it and prevent the various possible debilitating diseases that could do as much damage to a unit as combat itself. The solution was to half-bury some of the containers in which artillery shells were shipped and use them. Some were for urinating in and others were used for depositing solid waste.

The problem then became one of disposing of the tubes when they became full. Someone, certainly one of the marines who had gotten stuck with the unpleasant cleanup detail, got the bright idea of simply replacing the tops of the things and rolling them down the hill toward the enemy. The rest of the marines thought it was hilarious, knowing that the enemy always crawled around out there, looking to scavenge anything he could. The image of one of those guys finding a full one and dragging it back to his unit and then proudly and dramatically opening it up in front of his officers always brought a smile.

Now, though, the enemy had gotten smart and there were dozens of these containers lying around down at the bottom of the hill. Several marines had decided that at the first sign of an attack, they were going to throw a couple of grenades down among the collected tubes and see if they could scatter the waste over as many of the enemy as possible. It would not be one of the more brilliant tactics they could use, but it would be somewhat satisfying.

Gorton had had that thought himself, but since his job was no longer to man the front lines, he wouldn't get the chance. He slung his rifle and moved off toward the command post with Averitt following close behind.

*　　*　　*

Captain Sam Demars, the commander of the marines on Hill 855, put down the radio handset and stared pensively at the wall for a few moments, drumming his fingers on the makeshift table. He looked around the bunker and saw the other marines in there trying their level best not to be interested in the conversation he'd just had with Regiment. He forced himself to smile as he called one of his men over.

"Corporal Jones, pass the word for all platoon commanders and sergeants to report for a meeting in thirty minutes. And make sure you include that major and his sergeant major too."

The corporal mumbled an "aye, aye, sir" and went out, leaving Demars to stare once more at the tabletop. He abruptly realized that he was giving the wrong impression to his men and stood, arching his back and grunting as he tried to relieve the stiffness. He picked up his helmet and headed for the door, once again forcing himself to smile.

"I'll be back in ten minutes. I'm going over to the third platoon positions."

Gorton saw Demars materialize like a wraith from the mist as he made the turn around the helo support team's bunker and stopped. He saw the expression on the captain's face, scratched his chin, and watched the younger man approach. Demars had sunken eyes and lines on his face far deeper than any twenty-seven-year-old should have. The way he was walking, head down and shoulders hunched, told Gorton that he was just about out of gas. He and his company had been there only about two weeks, but from the way Demars looked it could have been two months.

The constant shelling and fear and the loss of virtually all human comforts were taking a heavy toll. The marines hunkered down there and on the other hilltops around were suffering from a prolonged inactivity that drained them of the edge that marines should have had. Far worse was the incessant drain of manpower caused by the shelling and the snipers. Every day, it seemed, men were medevacked out either on stretchers or in body bags. It was hard on the men who had to watch their buddies bleed into the already red earth of the Vietnamese highlands.

Demars started when Gorton and Averitt greeted him, and stared as if trying to force his mind back from somewhere else. He looked at the two of them and attempted to speak, but only his lips were moving. The words finally came.

"Sergeant Major. Major. Finished looking around? What do you think?"

Averitt had seen the same things that Gorton had and so forced himself to be a little cheerier than he felt. "I think you've done a hell of a job setting your defenses. I'm no expert, but they look at least as good as any I've seen."

Gorton piped up. "Me too, Captain. I am an expert, or so they tell me, and they look pretty good."

Demars smiled with only one corner of his mouth. It was good to have independent sets of eyes looking over what he had done when he and the company had set up upon arrival. Then, he'd been certain that he'd done it right, but as time went on and the waiting got worse and worse, he began to doubt his own judgment. He wondered whether he'd left something out or whether he'd inadvertently created some weakness that he and his men had been unable to spot and the enemy could take advantage of. As the days passed, he found himself becoming increasingly obsessed with that one possible flaw in his preparations. No matter how hard he tried to keep his mind from dwelling on it, it seemed to jump into every vacant space in his consciousness, so that in between every mental move he made, the question stood there, staring at him. It hadn't been like that when he and his company were out in the bush, patrolling. Out there he'd at least had the option of movement. That was why he'd had to take a walk after talking to Regiment.

He sighed. "Well, it looks like we may find out sometime tonight. The gomers are definitely up to something around both us and 881. I just got off the horn with Regiment and they gave us a heads-up. I've called a staff meeting in about twenty-five minutes and Corporal Jones is looking for you to tell you. See you then."

He turned his back on the two visitors and walked away. Averitt, in other circumstances, would probably have been angered by the captain's abruptness. He knew that Demars had meant no disrespect—he was, after all, the man in charge—it was just that he'd simply had nothing more to say.

Gorton watched Demars walk away and turned to Averitt. "One of the reasons I never tried for a commission is that I never wanted to have to feel like that."

Averitt nodded. "Yup. But I'd rather be around a guy who worries than a guy who's got too much confidence. That's what gets people killed, at least in the flying business."

"You're right, Major. It works the same way in the mud marines."

Twenty minutes later Demars was rolling a short stick between his hands as he waited for the last of his senior people to arrive. He had spread a tattered large-scale map of the area on the table and had placed a mix of several items on the corners—two grenades, an M-16 magazine, and a full ration box. The chatter from those already in the bunker was minimal, far less than it would have been at a similar meeting back at the combat base. Averitt attributed this to the fact that the men had worked in much closer quarters on much smaller-scale problems and had probably said everything they needed to a dozen times already.

The last two men came in, a sergeant in his twenties and a lieutenant who would have looked like a teenager had it not been for the stubble on his face, the grime, and the old man's eyes he had. Demars acknowledged their arrival with a nod and began his briefing, pointing to the map.

"Okay. I was on the horn with Regiment a half hour ago and they're passing a warning to both us and 881 to expect an attack tonight. Before, they said only that they 'suspected' that something was going to happen, but now they're certain. There have been large troop movements detected in the area north and west of our positions. According to intelligence, the movements have been in a semicircular pattern and appear to be in at least regimental strength." He drew his stick across the northern part of Hill 881S and then down the western side of their own position on 855.

"Now, the best guess is that they want to take 881, since it seems that most of the enemy is deployed against it from about here to here. But the gomers are also facing our positions. Now, we don't know if they're going to just probe us to keep some attention focused this way, or if they're going to try to overrun us, or if they're going to ambush us if we try to help the guys next door on 881, or if they're going to be a blocking force for anyone trying to escape our way. All we know is that there's a shitload of gomers out there, up to no good.

"Tonight I want a hundred percent alert. All fighting positions are to be manned and there will be comm checks every fifteen minutes. Weapons Platoon, make sure that there are sufficient illumination rounds handy. For all you guys, don't send any listening posts out tonight. They'd be a waste of time since we already know that the enemy is out there and getting ready to attack. I also don't want anybody trapped out there among the gomers. If this attack is as big as everybody seems to feel, it may well last into the daylight and the LPs would have no chance to get back in.

"Now, we're going to have lots of H&I fire all night and there is lots of air on call, but unless the goddamn fog lifts, it won't do us much good. There will be some arc lights and some mini arc lights coming over, but with their distance limitations, all they'll be able to do is keep the enemy's supporting units at bay. We'll have to deal with the attack pretty much by ourselves."

Averitt stared at the map to cover his feelings. The H&I fire, or harassment and interdiction salvos fired by the artillery in the area, would help, but it was like shooting a rifle into the woods in hope of getting a deer. Close air support was going to be limited by the weather, and since neither of the arc lights, which were high-level bombing tactics, could safely bomb close to friendly lines, Demars was right. They were going to have to bear the brunt of any possible attack on the ground. That knowledge gave Averitt a cold lump in his stomach. He glanced at Gorton, who was standing next to him clenching and unclenching his jaw, which was the only sign of the emotion Averitt knew he must be feeling.

Demars looked around at the men standing and staring at the map with apparently the same intensity Averitt felt. "All right. You all know what to do. We've got a plan and it's a good one. This is going to be rough, so let your troops know exactly what to expect. Don't let them be surprised. Any questions?"

One of the lieutenants asked about the fall-back positions which led to a brief discussion and then there were no more questions. Everyone there knew that they were all in a very bad place and wished they could be elsewhere, but they were determined that as long as they were there, they'd get the job done.

There were no stirring speeches and no waving of the flag. There would be no famous quotes for somebody to engrave on a monument somewhere and no Chesty Pullers to be written about in the history books. Just a bunch of tired men with a job to do on a hilltop in a country far from home.

Demars looked at all their faces once again and dismissed them. They all filed out, leaving just the headquarters staff and Gorton and Averitt.

"Captain, is there anything you'd like us to do?"

Demars looked up and smiled wanly. "Yes, there is, Major. You can keep the artillery and air coming as hard and as often as possible. Other than that, stay low and keep moving."

"Okay. We can do that, especially the staying-low part. If you need us, we'll be in the airedales' bunker."

"All right, then. Good night, gents. Good luck."

40

Thursday, February 8, 1968

Major Dick Averitt sat on his cot and leaned back against the sandbagged wall of the bunker. He scooped the last of the peaches out of the tin and slowly sipped the juice, enjoying every drop.

It was quiet in the bunker. The other occupants, Gorton, two corporals from the Forward Air Controller Team, and their three privates, went about their business in hushed tones. Gorton was on the next cot on one elbow, writing another letter to his grandson. The five others were playing their standard card game on the makeshift table but without their customary enthusiasm. The room had the same feeling of cocked expectancy for Averitt that the alert shack back at Danang had when he and his flight sat around, waiting for the call to launch against the enemy somewhere out in the boonies.

Averitt got up and walked over to the small pile of paperbacks and selected one of the standard and omnipresent Louis L'Amour westerns. He glanced at the cover and wondered whether he'd read it before. He smiled as he realized that it really didn't matter because all he was trying to do was to get his mind off that which might happen at any moment. He also wanted to try to close out the thumps and bangs of the incessant artillery and mortar fire that often made the ground beneath his feet twitch and jump as if the earth itself were protesting the depredations of man.

The sound of the guns had never ceased since he'd first come to Khe Sanh and now had so established itself that it became a part of life and was noticeable only when it stopped. Or when it was directed at him. Or when it might be very soon. He had quickly picked up the trick that all the marines around there had learned—he could tell by the sound of an enemy gun's firing off in the distance where the round would hit. He would also know how long it would be before the round hit and could be a little more selective about the shelter he sought.

The sound of the jets of Westmoreland's Operation Niagara dropping their endless tons of high explosives and napalm for most of the others seemed to fade into the background, but not for Averitt. Pilots habitually let their eyes stray to the sounds of aircraft engines and, even though he was now "out of the seat," Averitt still looked up and absently judged each run made by the mess of fighters and attack aircraft that constantly screamed by. Even the old propeller-driven A-1 Skyraiders that the Vietnamese flew interested him.

Often he would wince as he saw how close to their targets the pilots flew before pulling up and away. It sometimes seemed that they were trying to hand the bombs to the enemy before they climbed away with long white streamers of condensation trailing behind their wingtips. But that night, there were no jet engines around with the weather as bad as it was.

There were bombs falling, but they were from Air Force B-52s that were so high that the sounds didn't reach the surface—only the long freight-train rumble of the hundreds of bombs that fell from their bellies.

Averitt walked back to the cot and plopped down, leaning toward the small light thrown off from the three candles Gorton was using. He opened the book just as Gorton spoke.

"I don't think that there's a single Louis L'Amour book ever published that I haven't read. I haven't seen a new one in months."

"Yeah. Me too. I think though it's been long enough for this one that I probably won't remember it all." Averitt closed the book. "I wonder if there's a single place in the whole damn Marine Corps that doesn't have a couple of them stashed away in some corner."

Gorton grinned. "I can't remember one, now that you mention it. But the light's too bad in here for my tired old eyes. This letter is hard enough."

"It kind of makes me wish for the good old days, like yesterday, when we had all those creature comforts back at Khe Sanh."

"Yup. All you have to do is look at Captain Demars to see *that* difference." Gorton got up and retrieved his gear from the far wall, stuck the letter in his "ass pack," and then laid the whole pile on the wooden-pallet floor next to his cot, rifle on top. He then did the same for Averitt's.

"You might want to keep it handier, Major." He lay on his cot and rolled over to face away from the light.

Averitt leaned back and opened the book again, but his mind wasn't on this particular episode in the trials of the Sackett family. He was thinking about something Gorton had told him as they walked back from the briefing with Demars earlier in the evening.

Averitt had said something, exactly what he couldn't remember now, about how he couldn't see where Demars got the energy to command his company given the pressure and exhaustion he was so obviously enduring. Gorton had chuckled a little and then said, "Captain Demars isn't commanding this company, Major, he's *leading* it. When you *command* a unit you wind up having to do everything since you have to have everything done your way. But when you lead it, you set the objectives and then allow the men to do their jobs as they know how and as they've been trained. All you have to do is step in when things go wrong or look like they're going to go wrong. The trick is in knowing *when* to step in.

"But when you command, you step in all the time because that's how you think. The men get used to being told what to do and sooner or later will get in some seriously deep shit because either the commander makes a mistake or they're afraid of using their own judgment. Sometimes the leader has to bite his lip, but the troops need it to be done that way. Any asshole can command—all you gotta do is have rank on your side and a loud voice. But it takes men like Captain Demars and Colonel Aires to lead."

As the two walked on in the darkness, Averitt could almost hear the old sergeant major blushing. He'd never been so forceful about anything with Averitt before and seemed a little embarrassed. Averitt shut up because Gorton was quite right and anything Averitt could say would force Gorton to add words to what seemed to Averitt to be the best and most succinct general explanation of leadership theory he'd ever heard. He knew that things worked pretty much the way Gorton described leadership in the aviation

330

marines, and he really hadn't meant the word "command" the way Gorton had taken it, but the response he'd gotten was something he hoped he would remember when the need came up in the future.

Averitt closed the book and lay back on the cot. As he drifted off, he imagined himself using the sergeant major's little lecture himself someday, assuming, of course, that the Marine Corps ever became so desperate that they put him in charge of a squadron.

Sergeant Major Gorton lay on his cot, running through all the possibilities of the next few hours. He heard Averitt's breathing change to a slower and deeper rhythm. The muted voices of the five young marines at the table continued both the voice reports required for their game and the discussion of exactly what one particular blade on the corporal's Swiss Army knife was for. Gorton smiled as he listened to the conversation, for he had heard it, or one very much like it, at least a hundred times before.

It always seemed that there was a large surplus of time in every military plan. After everything was done and all the movements of men and materiel were complete, the only figures that had yet to get themselves in position were the three hands on the watches on everyone's wrist. Depending on the spirit of the owners of the wrists, the hands could move with agonizing slowness or agonizing speed. Most men sooner or later learned the trick of diverting their minds, and one of the ways of accomplishing that was idle conversation like this one about the Swiss Army knife.

Gorton remembered one night in Korea just before his company was to push off for an attack, when he went behind the line to urinate and discovered that he was peeing on an extremely interesting tree. He was so taken with this tree, standing all gnarled and twisted in the moonlight, that he went and found two of his friends. They came over and found the tree equally interesting, and the three of them stood there, discussing its lineage and how it had gotten shaped as it was, so different from the maples and oaks and pines back home in West Virginia. The three marines never knew for sure how long they stood there talking about a lonely tree in the moonlight so early in a summer morning, but it had totally engrossed them by the time their platoon sergeant came by and ordered them back to their positions. Gorton did discover, though, that the hands on his watch had moved very much closer

331

to their own appointed positions by the time he had picked up his rifle from the firing step of the trench.

He resisted the impulse this time to pull the cloth cover back from the face of his watch and check the time. He didn't really care what time it was—only that it was nighttime again in Vietnam—another day gone in the long and inevitable parade of days that would soon bring him to the end of his career. And to the beginning of something even more wonderful—his time at home with his grandson.

The Corps had been good to Gorton, he knew. It had taken him from his father's cabin on company property next to the mine and had given him the whole world to play in. Sometimes that "play" got a little rough and dangerous and even painful once or twice, but mostly it was a wonderful tour through all the magic and mystery he'd dreamed of in those stark hills of his youth. He intended to teach his grandson, little Tommy, all about that magic and mystery, starting with the mystery of fishing.

He sighed when he thought of how much his wife would have loved to see the little guy, but she had died less than a year before he was born. And for Gorton, there wouldn't be another like her.

It was her death that made him stay in the Corps all the way to thirty years. When she found that she had the disease which was going to take her so swiftly, she made him promise to reenlist one more time. She knew her husband better than he did himself and thus made him promise to keep the only other anchor he would have once she was gone. She was right, as she always had been, but she also took out a little extra insurance by writing to Colonel Aires and simply and with irreducible logic convincing him to keep an eye on her husband.

The colonel had come all the way from Washington to be at her funeral at Camp Pendleton, California, and, after it was done, had taken Gorton out and gotten him drunk, much like they had done for each other in all those bad times in all the years before. The next morning, on his dresser next to his garrison cap, Gorton found a set of orders to Washington as a senior enlisted adviser to the Commandant of the Marine Corps, signed by the commandant himself.

Then, when the colonel got his regiment, Gorton got another set of orders as the regimental sergeant major, again with the commandant's personal signature.

Gorton closed his eyes and forced his mind away from Hill 855 and the cigarette-smoke-filled bunker and the sounds of young men going about their business of being young marines. He saw the clear mountain stream that ran through the valley in which young Tommy now lived with his parents, Gorton's son and daughter-in-law. It was only a hundred miles or so from the miner's cabin he had left so long ago.

As he drifted off to sleep, Gorton was debating whether he should take Tommy to see the little town from where his "Pop" had come. Maybe I will, he thought. Maybe I will.

Averitt would never be sure what woke him up, the sounds of the artillery barrage or the shaking of the cot from the concussion. He sat up, instantly awake but just about a half-second slower than the sergeant major, who was already standing and putting on his harness. The other marines in the bunker were in various states of dress but all were far ahead of him. He swung his feet to the wooden floor, grabbed for his own gear, and put his helmet on. As the radios came to life with frantic calls for fire support, he realized that none of the call signs belonged to anybody on Hill 855. The one marine, a corporal, who had the watch was already plotting the action on the map which apparently had been put back on the table after the card game broke up.

Gorton came over and stood behind the corporal, looking over his shoulder at the marks he was making on the acetate overlay on the map. The corporal was good, working quickly and carefully as he eavesdropped on the radio net. He was getting himself up to speed on the fight, wherever it was, so that he could join in if required. Gorton asked no questions, carefully not disturbing the corporal, but soon had enough of an idea what was happening that he strode to the door and went out into the trench.

Averitt picked up his rifle and followed. It would be quicker to get Gorton's assessment than stare at the map and figure one out for himself. He stepped through the blast curtain and into the trench. He was met with the dim white light from parachute flares and illumination mortar rounds and the huge assault of sound coming from Hill 881S right next door.

To his left he spotted Gorton standing on a firestep, staring at the hill with his field glasses, his elbows resting on the top row of sandbags. Averitt climbed up next to him and focused his own glasses on the battle for the hill.

Heavy shells were bursting all over the trenches near the top of the hill, and smaller mortar rounds were walking back and forth across the crest. From the low ground surrounding it, yellow sparks of rifle fire covered the dark ground halfway up the hill. Tracer fire from the trees farther out showed that the enemy was tearing up the place with heavy machine guns.

From the trenches just below the crest of the hill, streams of tracer reached out into the sea of sparks and occasionally ricocheted up into the dark sky as the marines' M-60 machine guns replied. Yellow flashes from the trenches on either side of the machine guns showed that the riflemen were definitely in the fight too.

Two parachute flares lit off overhead and, as they drifted below the cloud deck, threw a harsh white light on the whole area. Averitt got a good look at the sides of the hill, and it seemed as if the very ground were moving, so many were the enemy who were climbing toward the marines' perimeter. In two or three places at once, great fan-shaped flames burst out of the hillside and swept downward toward the enemy as command-detonated Claymore mines sprayed thousands of ball bearings through them. When the Claymores went off, the sea of sparks seemed to part for a few seconds as the enemy either were blown apart or simply ducked from the hail. Very quickly the sparks resumed and the enemy began to move forward again.

Averitt's mouth was suddenly very dry. He had been in ground combat before but only in a couple of firefights and those pretty much were at long range. This was something far different and far more terrifying.

It had the appearance of something from a horror movie where the audience could see the danger growing ever closer to its victim but was powerless to prevent it. They squirm in their seats, almost feeling the hot breath of evil as it moves inexorably toward its fulfillment. Averitt found himself staring, frozen, at the scene on the hill next door.

Summoning as much will as he could muster, he forced himself to look away from the wave that was reaching for the hilltop, and to scan the treeline below his own position. The enemy should be coming soon, but at least he and the others on 855 had had more warning than the men over on 881S.

Averitt turned back to the battle just in time to see two bright orange streams of fire come down from the sky and move over the ground at the base of the hill. Looking up, he could see a dark shape against the cloud deck in a slow left-hand orbit over Hill 881S. The Air Force's legendary "Puff the Magic Dragon" had arrived to throw its weight into the fight.

"Puff" was the term used for the AC-47 gunships that were constantly on call to help support troops under attack. The aircraft itself was a converted World War II–vintage C-47, commonly nicknamed the "Goony Bird," which had been dragged into one last war. Several rapid-fire machine guns or rotary cannon had been mounted in the sides, and the aircraft would orbit over a particular spot and unleash a flood of fire on the enemy. Using one tracer round in every four or five, Puff had the visual effect of touching the ground with a huge yellow-orange ray gun. The stream of bullets was continuous from the aircraft to the spot on the ground where no living creature could continue to exist. It was a real comfort, thought Averitt, that he was on the side that possessed a weapon like that.

He felt a man climb up next to him and glanced over to see Captain Demars staring across through his own glasses.

Demars lowered his glasses and looked at Averitt and Gorton, the dark circles around his eyes looking like caves in the harsh light of the parachute flares. "You guys all set here, Major?"

Averitt nodded.

"Good. There is some heavy supporting fire on the way from the fire base over at Camp Carroll and the combat base itself. We're gonna save our ammo until they hit us or until those guys over there really need our help. There's also a relay of Puffs up there— that's where those flares are coming from. Make sure that everybody you see has a helmet on, and no firing of weapons until they come at us. Grenades first."

Demars turned away to head down the trench but was stopped by one of the privates who had come out of the bunker to look at what was happening on 881S.

"They gonna come at us, Captain?"

Demars looked at him and answered before moving on down the trench.

"Yeah, they'll be coming pretty soon, son. If I was them, I would."

41

Thursday, February 8, 1968

At just about three-thirty in the morning, Commander Chris Scott dug the serving spoon into the gravy and spread a little of it on the two pork chops and the pile of rice he had taken from the steam table. The food was leftovers from the previous evening's meal and looked it. The pork chops seemed about as dry as a Las Vegas street and just about as tender. The gravy could easily have been used to hang wallpaper but, what the hell, he thought, it's better than the eggs they'd serve later on in the morning. He debated for a few seconds whether he wanted any of the wrinkled brown green beans and decided to pass. He took his tray out into the wardroom and, after stopping to get two glasses of "bug juice" and a couple of slices of bread, found a seat with several other pilots who were to take over the alerts in less than half an hour.

Across the table sat an extremely tired-looking Jim Hogan and a couple of other attack pilots. Hogan took a look at what Scott had selected for breakfast and nodded.

"Nothing like a little solid food to start the day, huh?"

Scott chuckled. "I've tried to get my wife to believe that pork chops and rice is a healthy breakfast, but she seems to think that cereal and juice is better for you. Silly woman."

"Well, at this hour of the morning my stomach's not awake enough to care."

Scott chewed a bite of his pork chop with a grimace and washed it down with the bug juice. "So how are things with the attack pukes?"

"Not too bad. The jets are holding up and so are the men. Mail

336

gets here pretty regularly and we're going home soon. What else could a man ask for?"

Scott's reply was cut off by the tinny but insistent sounds of the 1MC, or ship's loudspeaker system. "Now set the Alert 5. I say again, now set the Alert 5."

The pilots at the table looked at each other for a moment and began eating again at a somewhat less leisurely pace. The announcement meant that the alert crews would now be strapping in to their aircraft and spending their time waiting in the cockpits. Alert 5 usually meant that something was brewing that could require a faster response than Alert 15 which could be stood in the relative comfort of the ready rooms. One of the things pilots hated most was to spend four hours of alert time strapped into the uncomfortable seats of their aircraft, only to be launched within the last half hour. That meant that their butts were already numb before their flights even started. Most squadrons would try to shorten the time that a man would have to stand Alert 5 to two hours to prevent the certain loss of sharpness that always came with a prolonged period of boredom and ass pain.

Hogan finished the last of his coffee and stood. "Well, I guess we're going to have to change the entire plan again. See ya."

Scott waved his fork in farewell at Hogan and went back to his food. The other pilots at the tables finished theirs quickly and, nodding at Scott as they headed for their ready rooms, left him alone. He took a few more bites of his food and threw down his fork. Scott got up, carried his tray to the tall rack, and put it in with all the others. He glanced at the table that held the peanut butter and jelly. It was better than nothing, he thought, and made himself a couple of sandwiches for later, taking care to wrap the sandwiches in paper napkins. He was just turning to leave the wardroom when he heard the 1MC again.

"Now launch the alert aircraft. I say again, now launch the alert aircraft."

Before the command had been spoken the second time, the door was already slamming behind him.

Jim Hogan was reaching for the doorknob of Ready Room 5 when it suddenly was pulled open and two pilots dashed through on their way up to the flight deck. He stood back against the bulkhead and let them pass before he stepped into the room which was now full of ordered activity. The duty officer was on the phone with somebody and the maintenance chief was standing next to him, a scowl on his face. One of the squadron enlisted men was writing the weather on the blackboard along with some general target information. Off to the side, another officer, one of the J.O.'s from the squadron Operations Department, was writing a list of aircraft assignments and pilots, carefully consulting a sheet of paper in his hand. Hogan saw that his name was at the top of the list along with Cordella's.

Hogan resisted the temptation to walk over and demand that the duty officer fill him in on what was going on. He went forward and sat in his chair and pulled his kneeboard out of the drawer below the seat along with a couple of fresh briefing cards. He placed one of the cards under the top clip of the kneeboard just below where the stupid little light, which never worked after the battery cover cap was lost, used to be and began copying down the weather and frequencies. He reached forward and took one of the cards of the day, smiling at the title. *Carte du Jour*, they always typed on them. He carefully reviewed the daily code words and the frequencies preset into all the aircraft radios and then stuck it under his briefing card.

As he was reaching for his map bag in the drawer, Cordella came in and sat in the chair next to him.

"What's up, Skipper?"

Hogan gestured at the duty officer. "I don't have any idea, but those guys'll tell us as soon as they figure it out. From the speed that they launched the alert, I'd say that the shit has hit the fan, the balloon has gone up, or the game's afoot—maybe. Then again, maybe not."

Cordella shook his head. "Just what I need, Bill Cosby at four A.M. Looks like whatever happens, I'll be on your wing, so let's try to keep the crisis small until the goddamn sun comes up, if that's all right with you, Skipper, sir."

Hogan nodded. "No problem."

The duty officer hung up the phone and dialed another number, so it would be a few minutes before Hogan got the answers he was waiting for. He was again tempted to go over and interrupt in order to deal with his own curiosity, but he forced himself to remain seated. He knew that if he did interrupt the man on the spot, the duty officer, it would delay whatever action needed to be taken while the duty officer stopped what he was doing, answered Hogan's question and the inevitable follow-ons, and then forced himself back into dealing with the original problems. There was always the chance that the distraction would cause the duty officer to miss something, some detail in the planning which would turn out to be crucial and cause a much greater delay down the road. Hogan had always been angry when one of his C.O.'s barged into a problem and started giving "direction" which almost invariably turned out to be *exactly* what Hogan either had just done or was about to do.

It always angered him the most when it was something he had been about to do, because he resented the feeling that the C.O. didn't trust his judgment or thought him an idiot. He had always felt that if he wasn't qualified to deal with the problems, he shouldn't be given the responsibility of being the duty officer, and if that were the case, then the goddamn C.O. could just sit at the desk himself and eliminate the middleman.

Now that he *was* the C.O., he could understand the other's eagerness to get involved and take some action. He was feeling the same way himself, and it was all he could do to sit there and trust in the young man on the spot. He forced himself to concentrate on the fact that simply by sitting there he was helping by letting the duty officer know that he was handy in case something too big came up, and reinforcing the young man's self-confidence because Hogan was so obviously trusting his judgment. It was the proper thing for him to do, but for a man of action, it was often the one thing that would drive him crazy.

To occupy himself, he went back to the coffee urn and filled his cup. He kept his back to the rest of the room for a few extra moments, and when he heard the phone receiver placed back in its cradle, he turned around and walked calmly to his seat.

The duty officer picked up his clipboard from his desk and walked over in front of Hogan and Cordella. He pulled over the blue-painted ex-ammunition can that was now used for securing all the pilots' crypto gear and sat on it, facing the two pilots.

" 'Mornin', Skipper. Sorry it took me so long, but things are getting crazy suddenly. As you probably have figured out by now, we've launched the alerts and are getting some more ready. What's happened is that there is a major attack on Khe Sanh right now, and they've been screaming for air cover. The marines are sending everything they have and need more. There are several other big fights going on in other places farther south, and even the Air Force is up to their ass. We're the designated backup for the marines and they're yelling for help.

"As I said, we've already launched the first alerts, all of them, and we're pulling out the second wave. As soon as you're briefed and preflighted, you're to assume an Alert 5. The Ops guys are working up the schedule now. They've canceled the normal flight schedule for the day so that we can help out the marines when they call. Your aircraft assignments are on the board, and as soon as we can get the jets pulled out, we'll get the maintenance books down here for you. That's what I was on the phone about—the damn handler is trying to write our schedule again and the maintenance chief didn't have enough horsepower to do anything about it. CAG himself has gotten involved, so that should be the end of that problem.

"We haven't posted your weapons loads yet, but it'll probably be daisy cutters. The fighters and the other attack guys will be carrying whatever else needs to go. Anyway, for now hang loose, since we don't have much on the specific targets until Nick Taylor gets here, but it shouldn't be long."

Hogan looked at the aircraft assignments on the blackboard. "How are we fixed for airplanes?"

"Looking good so far. We've got a couple down on the hangar deck that we'd like brought up and a couple up on the roof that need to go below for inspections and stuff, but the maintenance chief says we're fine."

"Okay, John, it sounds like you've got it all in one bag. Let me know if you need my help."

The duty officer stood up and shoved the crypto box back to its place with his foot. "Yes, sir. You'll hear me hollerin'."

Hogan went back to his kneeboard and began copying down whatever information was readily available. He pulled out his chart of the I-Corps area and inspected the marks he had made earlier in the day when he'd updated it. He had outlined all the safe areas and the places where the enemy was the thickest, in case he had to eject, taking care to include the "suspected" enemy areas with the known ones. There was a great deal more of the area that was included in the bad guys' turf than there was held for sure by the good guys.

In the minds of most pilots, combat over South Vietnam was a hell of a lot safer than flying over the North. At least in the South you still had a far better than even chance of getting rescued. The flip side of that was that some poor bastard always got to be the guy who made up the bad part of the statistics.

Hogan scanned the chart carefully, trying to make up some sort of general plan of where to go if he got in trouble over the enemy territory. He had always believed that it was better to have done some thinking about disaster before it happened.

Just about two hundred feet aft of where Jim Hogan was sitting studying his chart, Chris Scott was fighting to control his anger. His ready room was as chaotic as Hogan's was calm and ordered.

Scott's squadron was having "one of those nights" which every squadron has occasionally and nearly always at the worst possible time. The flight crews had gone up and preflighted and turned up their aircraft that were scheduled for the secondary alerts, checking out the systems. Both fighters were found to have some problems that necessitated their being "downed," or considered unflyable, until the repairs were made. None of the other squadron Phantoms on the flight deck had been readied for flight yet, so the only two flyable jets the squadron had were the two that had just been launched. All this meant that there were no aircraft available, so if the next wave of alerts was to be launched, there would be two fighters missing from the effort.

It is one of the immutable laws of naval aviation that when a squadron is short of "up" aircraft and thus can't meet its commitments, people get totally pissed off and what follows is an amazingly unpleasant period for all concerned. This is precisely what was happening in Scott's ready room at that moment.

As Scott had walked in, he'd instantly noticed that few people would meet his eyes and several others oozed their way toward the exit. The duty officer, who is, simply by this temporary assignment, the recipient of everyone's problems, was on the phone almost begging maintenance to perform a miracle but was being told that the maintenance chief was sorry as hell but if Jesus Christ himself wanted to go flying, it would still take another hour to get a jet ready for him.

The duty officer replaced the phone on its cradle with all the deliberate care of a condemned prisoner who had just heard the warden tell him that his last appeal had been denied and the guys with the leg straps were on the way down. He turned and slowly walked over and stood in front of Scott, who was now sitting in his ready-room chair, watching him carefully.

341

"Good morning, Skipper. We, ah, have a little problem with aircraft at the moment, but it's being sorted out now. The first two alerts got off okay, but we don't have any aircraft for you yet. The two originally assigned as the alert backups both went tits-up, so we're trying to drag out the spares. 203 and 209 are 'comers,' and as soon as we can get them fueled, spotted, and turned, we'll be all set. The rest of the briefing info is on the board and the weather should be coming over the tube in a couple of minutes."

The young man finished and waited expectantly for a question. Scott took so long to frame one that the duty officer thought he'd escaped for now.

"Okay. It's now nearly three hours since the alerts were first set. Why has it taken so long for maintenance to get two backups ready?"

"Umm. Well, sir, I don't know. I'll find that out right away, sir." He turned to go back to the duty desk, but Scott stopped him.

"Just call down and get the Maintenance Officer in here."

"Yes, sir."

While he waited for the M.O. to arrive, Scott copied down all the relevant information on the board and listened to the weather briefing. He was angry at the delay in getting the aircraft fixed, and the more he dwelled on it, the madder he got. In just a minute or two he felt the first burning feeling in the center of his chest just behind his sternum. He wasn't certain whether it was from the lousy meal he'd wolfed down or his anger, but it didn't matter really. He was in for a grade-A case of heartburn, and he had nothing handy he could use to take care of it. He'd just have to suffer, which simply added itself to everything else that was pissing him off.

He belched several times and tasted the pork chops again. If anything, they tasted worse now than they had going down. He was searching his flight-suit pockets in the dim hope that he'd left some antacid tablets stashed somewhere, when the Maintenance Officer appeared in front of him.

"You wanted to see me, sir?"

The man showed no sign that he'd just been roused out of bed, as he undoubtedly had been. He stood easily in front of Scott, holding a clipboard which obviously was his informational armor against his C.O.'s wrath.

"Yeah. How come in three hours you guys haven't been able to come up with two flyable airplanes? That's question one. Number

342

two is why the fuck didn't anybody bother to tell me that they had a problem?''

The M.O. sat down in the seat to Scott's left. He inclined the clipboard so that Scott could see that it was a list of the status of each aircraft the squadron owned. The M.O. had also made sure that he wrote down the time at the top of the list so that Scott would see that the information was only five minutes old without being told. Scott had to admit it, this guy really had it together. And he didn't seem to be in the slightest bit intimidated at the moment, which told Scott that whatever he was about to be told was going to be the absolute unassailable truth. He felt his anger begin to ease somewhat. He had good troops and they worked their tails off for him. But what was the fun of being the C.O., he thought, if you couldn't get all pissed off once in a while?

"Skipper, what happened was we bet on the wrong horse. The two original alert backups didn't seem too bad at first, but when we tore into them, we found that the problem was far worse than we thought. 211 had a landing gear indicator go bad and we thought that it might be just the switch. We can get it fixed but we couldn't find the part right off. We would have cannibalized it, but we have to get permission for that. The other one, 207, was more serious; it turned out to be a bleed air valve. We tried all the games, but it was the valve. All that took more time than we figured. The deck spot, where the handler had put our airplanes, screwed us too since we couldn't get any fuel for a while for the other two, but that's nobody's fault.''

"Okay, if that's the case, why didn't you get the other two dragged out and spotted? Wasn't the maintenance chief thinking tonight?''

"That was my fault, Skipper. When we thought that the first two would be easy fixes, I told them to go ahead and work on them. While they were parked where they were, the other two were in a place where we couldn't do much—we couldn't get at the problem. We couldn't even fuel them. Like I said, we bet on the wrong horse.''

Scott nodded. "Okay, How long?''

"Skipper, by the time you finish your briefing, we'll have a nice shiny fighter all ready and waiting for you.''

"Fair enough. And you don't have to answer the second question. I've been there myself. Get out of here and go back to bed. Things may get interesting later on.''

"Yes, sir."

The rest of those in the ready room relaxed when they saw the smile on the M.O.'s face as he stood and left. The duty officer went back to filling out the log, knowing that the C.O., if not exactly pleased with how things were going, at least understood.

And that was exactly what Scott intended as he resumed his search for his Rolaids which he was sure he had left somewhere around there.

42

Thursday, February 8, 1968

Major Dick Averitt picked himself up off the floor of the trench and replaced his helmet. The smoke from the artillery round drifted over him and on down the hill. He stayed low in case another was on the way, but in all the noise from the battle on the next hill, he doubted that he'd be able to hear it coming any more than he'd heard the one that just hit behind him.

Gorton got to his feet and brushed himself off. "Son of a bitch!"

Averitt nodded. "I don't know if that was a short round or they're just keeping us interested, but I wish they'd knock it off."

"That could have been a ranging round too, Major. Sort of getting set for something later on."

Averitt hadn't immediately thought of that. He'd watched the fight over on 881S turn into a pitched battle in minutes and had let himself believe that that would be the only attack that night. He kicked himself mentally for the wishful thinking and went back to being scared. Gorton looked over his weapon and Averitt, reminded, picked up his own and checked that it hadn't been damaged.

One of the corporals from the Air Control Team came up and,

344

glancing at the battle across the small valley, shouted, "Major, Regiment wants you on the radio. Right now."

Averitt turned and hustled into the bunker, grabbing the handset the other corporal held out to him. He started to speak but looked at Gorton. "What the hell's our call sign?"

Gorton looked equally confused. "I don't fuckin' know. Make one up."

Averitt thought for a second and used his own, the one he'd gotten years before in his first squadron. "Oaktree, this is Spanky, over."

There was a pause and then a staticky answer. "Roger, Spanky. This is Oaktree Six. How copy, over?"

"Oaktree Six" was Colonel Aires himself.

"Oaktree Six, I read you loud and clear, over."

"Roger, Spanky. We've lost comms with the airedales on 881 South. They were calling for close air. What is the weather out there? Can we get airplanes in?"

"Stand by." Averitt went outside and looked carefully at the clouds now illuminated by the flares that were floating down. It was difficult to judge height, but he put his best guess on how far the clouds were from the tops of the hills as opposed to the surrounding flat parts, and went back inside.

"Oaktree, the cloud deck looks to be about eight or nine hundred feet AGL, but the visibility looks pretty good. Is there any chance that the gunship can tell you? They are overhead now."

There was a pause. "Roger, Spanky. Puff says that they're in and out at a thousand and they can't go any lower. They say it's good enough for them to shoot, but they're not sure about close air. What do you think?"

"Stand by."

Averitt realized that the decision to attempt to get jets down under the cloud deck was pretty much going to be up to him— the Air Liaison Officer closest to the action. He was by trade an A-4 pilot and thus knew the dangers and possibilites far better than would the colonel or anybody else around there for that matter. If the weather were any better or any worse, there would be little or no questions. But now it was right on the edge. He knew that if he were flying that night, he wouldn't like it a whole lot, but he would probably give it a shot. Pilots are like that. They first have a tough time believing that they can't do something and then are willing to try if they feel there's the most minuscule

345

chance of success. That little chance quickly gets magnified in their minds to near certainty. He keyed the radio.

"Oaktree, I think it would be very dangerous and possibly very costly. There would have to be a lot of coordination in keeping the numbers small. The major problem will be to get the jets down below the layer safely. If we can do that, we might, repeat might, be able to pull it off. The other thing to think about is that this will be right on the edge and the pilots ought to be told that."

"Roger, concur. If we can get them down, can you control them?"

Averitt thought that over. It was going to be dangerous as hell for the pilots but, on the other hand, being on one of these hilltops was not all that much fun either.

"Oaktree, this is Spanky. If you can get 'em below the layer and headed this way, I can control 'em. But only two at a time. There's an awful lot of shit flying around out here and airplanes are only going to make it worse. I also suggest that you tell Puff to go no lower than one thousand and to switch to my frequency for control."

"This is Oaktree. Roger, out."

Averitt was having some serious second thoughts. He turned away from the radio and stared at the wall. In all his time in Marine Air, he'd never heard of anybody trying something like this at night. During the day it would be dangerous enough, but at night was too much to ask. Now that he was on the ground and not strapped into a cockpit, he had a clearer perspective. He spent a few more minutes trying to think of an alternative to the plan but couldn't come up with one. He walked to the blast curtain and peeked outside, wishing things were different. He knew suddenly that to ask those pilots up there to try to come through the overcast into unfamiliar terrain at night in the middle of a battle and then have to find a target without hitting the ground was too much. The dumb bastards would try it too. He had to call this off.

As he walked back toward the radio, he was thinking of the marines on the hill across the way.

Colonel Aires put down his handset and looked up at his Air Officer. "Okay. Tell me how we're going to get some aircraft down here for Averitt to control."

The Air Officer, a captain named Butler, who hadn't been consulted up to this point, tugged on his ear. "Well, Colonel, we can do the same thing we do with the C-130s. We can give them a nonprecision radar approach or we can let them fly a TACAN approach down below the cloud deck and then they can go from there. We can give them an instrument climb out of here when they're done and turn them back over to the Air Force controllers."

"Great. Just what does that mean?"

Butler lit a cigarette. "Sorry. We can use our ground control radar to guide the aircraft down. We'll give them headings to fly to avoid the terrain, and the pilots will be responsible for their own descents according to the controller's guidance. The TACAN approach would use the aircrafts' on-board tactical air navigation receivers to give them the headings and we'll advise them on the descents before they start."

"That'll take a lot of time, won't it? I mean, how long will it take two planes to fly one of those approaches?"

"It'll be slow, Colonel. They'll have to come down two at a time in formation, and we can start the next two. The time will depend on how quick they can find the target once they get down here."

Aires nodded and turned away, but Butler stopped him. "Colonel, I have to say this. I know that the men out on 881 South could be in big trouble, but trying to get air down here under these conditions is not the best option. The weather is pretty much dog shit and there's a lot of bullets in the air over there. If the aircraft are armed with high explosive, there will be a thirty-second interval between runs because of the fragmentation patterns. We can't have the planes roaring around, trying multiple runs either—that's just setting them up. I strongly recommend we not do this. We've got a bunch of aircraft up there and I recommend we use them to hit the enemy's supporting troops so that those he has engaged will be on their own."

Before Aires could speak, the radio came to life. "Oaktree Six, this is Spanky, over."

Aires grabbed the handset. "Spanky, this is Oaktree Six. Go ahead."

"Roger, Oaktree. I recommend that we wait until first light to bring in the fast movers. It might be possible now, but I believe the risks are too great."

"Oaktree copies. Stand by."

Butler saw the pain in the colonel's eyes. Those were his men out there and he could see that there was little he could do for now except keep the artillery coming. He looked at his watch. "It's

347

about ninety minutes until first light, Colonel. We can bring the jets down then."

Aires's face fell. "Can we leave it up to the pilots themselves?"

Butler smiled just a little. "Colonel, what would you do if you were up there with them?"

Aires sighed. "You're right. How about helos?"

"We can try it, but it'll be at least forty-five minutes before they get here."

"Make the calls."

"Aye-aye, sir." Butler moved over to the communications equipment and began speaking to the marines manning the sets.

Aires picked up the other radio, which was on the company command net. He had worked all his professional life to earn the opportunity to be standing right there, as a Marine colonel leading a regiment. He was a little surprised when he realized that he would give anything to be somewhere else. He took a breath and let it out slowly, unconsciously squaring his shoulders as he began to speak.

Averitt listened to the colonel talk to the company commander over on Hill 881S. He felt rotten about having to tell the colonel what he believed to be the truth—that it was simply too dangerous to attempt close air support under these conditions. Listening, Averitt at first felt like hiding in a corner.

"Echo Six, this is Oaktree Six, over."

"Go ahead, Oaktree, this is Echo Six."

"Roger, Echo. Be advised we are unable to provide close air at this time. We are working on some helos and we're getting some mini arc lights in for you, over."

"Oaktree, Echo. Roger, understood. Be advised my air controllers are down. When you do send some fast movers in, we'll be unable to control them, over."

"Echo, Oaktree copies. 855 will coordinate for you, over."

"Roger."

"What is your situation, Echo?"

"Oaktree, we're holding them. They've tried three times so far to rush our positions, but we've held. They seem to be gathering for another try momentarily. So far they haven't gotten past the wire. What I don't understand is why they don't seem to be supporting their attacks with fresh troops. I'm concerned that this might be a diversion for something else."

There was a long pause. Then, "What are your casualties, Echo?"

"Very light so far, Oaktree. If they get past the wire, that'll change in a hurry. We still have ammo and water. If things don't get any worse, we'll hold."

"Oaktree, roger. Out."

Averitt turned away from the radio and looked at the small group of marines in the bunker. They were all just shaking themselves out of the trance they'd been in listening to the exchange between Colonel Aires and the company commander on Hill 881S. They turned their attention to their tasks which consisted largely of rechecking things they'd already rechecked five times. Averitt glanced at his watch and saw that it was almost four-thirty, the darkest and most deadly time of the night in Vietnam. He caught Gorton's eye and gestured him out of the bunker and into the trench.

Once there, he could see that the volume of fire directed against Hill 881S had diminished considerably, but the volume of fire going out from the marine positions had not. Apparently, the marines felt no compunction at all about filling the air around their hill with as much high-speed metal as possible. As he watched, the volume of fire began to slacken just a little and then finally stop, first in one section of the hill and then in the others, as the sergeants and lieutenants and corporals passed the word to cease fire.

After the din of the battle, it seemed as if the few rounds still going off were actually silent. There were only scattered *carrumps* of mortars exploding and the occasional drawn-out *brrrrrrrs* of Puff, the C-47 gunship, still orbiting at the very base of the clouds overhead. Averitt couldn't remember for sure, but he didn't think anything had fallen on this hill for a while.

He looked at Gorton in the dim light of the parachute flares that still ignited in the clouds and drifted down all around the area.

"Sergeant Major, what do you think? What did he mean, a diversion?"

Gorton leaned his chin on his arm on the top sandbag. "I think he meant that somebody is going to be in deep shit very shortly. And I have a feeling that it's going to be us."

"Why?"

"We have no intell that says that the gomers have built up their forces anywhere but around here. They've already tried 881 all by

349

itself and have everybody looking that way. We've put out a whole lot of ammo in the past few minutes, and I imagine that everybody who can walk is hustling more to the guns. If I was running the show for the gomers, I'd try 881 again and a few minutes later I'd try to take this hill."

"I was afraid you were going to say that. That's what I thought too. I was just hoping that you knew something I didn't."

"'Fraid not, Major. And I don't think it's gonna be too long coming either."

"Well, let's go see Captain Demars and find out if there's anything he needs us to do."

The two marines, one old and the other getting that way fast, moved out of the trench and across the crest of the hill toward the company CP.

The little general stood outside the mouth of the cave and leaned against the rough limestone. He was careful to stay out of the way of the messengers who dashed in and out of the cave, carrying the orders and the reports of the officers most directly concerned with tonight's attacks on the American hilltop positions.

The messengers reminded him of his childhood and the ants he used to watch that carried their tiny bits of food to the colony and then dashed out for more. The general wondered if the messengers would detour around him as the ants did when he put an obstacle in their path. Probably so, he realized.

In the distance he could hear only the bass sounds of the battle for the hilltops. The higher-pitched ones, the whine of ricochets, the cracks of the grenades, the shrill of the officers' whistles, and the hoarse shouts of the commands being given were all too distant to be audible. He was momentarily grateful that other high-pitched sounds—the shrieks of the dying and the keening of the wounded—were inaudible also. He'd heard enough of that in his life.

The thumps of the artillery and mortars and the rumble of the bombs from the American high-level bombers came to him as feelings, vibrations through his feet and gentle pressure of the moist air on his face, as much as true sounds.

His deputy approached from the dim yellow light of the cave, carefully, as if to rouse his master from sleep.

"Sir, the first assault has pulled back from the hill. Shall we proceed with the rest of the plan?"

The general nodded slowly. The first assault was merely to cause the Americans to waste their primary defensive weapons, their mines and deadly fire barrels, emplaced on the hills and to reveal their positions. Now his mortarmen had discovered and marked the American strong points and machine-gun emplacements. The second attack would begin with a concentrated barrage against the northern hill and would be followed by an assault on the southern hill.

The little general knew full well that this would be his best opportunity to capture the Khe Sanh complex. His great offensive had been crushed and he could see no further purpose in prolonging the siege of the complex. The Americans had managed to resupply the combat base by air and would soon mount a drive from the coast to relieve the complex. If he failed tonight, he would continue to pound the complex with his heavy guns but would have to begin to move his main units back north.

Tonight's attacks had been planned carefully and were being carried out by his two best regiments. If they took either one of these hills, he would drive the Americans out of Khe Sanh and would salvage something from the complete disasters of the past several weeks. He did not want to have to face his masters in Hanoi without something to show for all the losses of the past few weeks.

The little general looked up into the darkness and smiled at the heavy cloud cover he knew was there. Without their aircraft the Americans had no advantage. And without an advantage, they would lose.

He turned to his deputy and gave the order for the main assault to begin.

Demars was on the radio when Averitt and Gorton entered the CP. It was much quieter and more orderly than Averitt would have expected, and for a moment he wondered if only he and Gorton expected an attack soon, but Demars's conversation killed that idea.

"... yes, sir. We're on a hundred percent alert. I checked the positions myself, and we've done about all we can."

Demars listened intently and with a final "Lima, roger. Out" put the handset down on the makeshift table. He turned to the two

351

newcomers, and they were both struck by how exhausted he looked.

He aimed his thumb over his shoulder at the bank of communications gear.

"That was Regiment. The colonel says for us to expect to get hit right after the next try at 881. Are you all set down your way?"

Gorton nodded, shifting his rifle to his other hand. "Yes, sir. I'd feel a lot better if we had some air cover though."

"Yeah, I know, but it can't be helped. There's no sense wishing it. Maybe after first light. The colonel said that they're going to start an H&I barrage shortly. I'm glad you came over because I'd like you to coordinate the spotting from the trench. That okay?"

Averitt nodded.

"Good. We really need your help tonight, Major. I know it's tough for you, but you have my gratitude, for whatever that's worth."

Averitt had the irrelevant thought that the younger man would never know how much that was worth. "Okay. Give us a call if you think of anything else we can do."

"I will. But if the enemy comes up the hill in strength, I want you two to fall back here. You're the only two guys I have who really know how to get airplanes in close."

"The colonel said that I might be needed to direct strikes around 881 too. If he yells for that, you'll be able to get me over the air net."

"Don't worry, Major. We'll find you."

Averitt and Gorton climbed down carefully into the unfamiliar trench on the west side of the hill after finding a position from which they should be able to view the entire side of the hill, the treeline well outside the wire, and a good bit of Hill 881. In the dim light of the flares they tried to make out as much detail as they could, but various shades of dark was all there really was. The number of flares in the air had diminished to the point where there was just enough illumination to see but not enough to be wasteful of the flares that were certain to be needed later.

Averitt shook off the backstraps of the portable radio and carefully placed it out of the way. He picked up the handset and got a fast radio check with the C-47 overhead, double-checking that he hadn't damaged the thing either time he had tripped and fallen on the way over here. He placed the headphones on his head, leaving the ear closest to Gorton free, and replaced his helmet.

The sergeant major was sweeping the area outside the wires with his field glasses, trying to catch the smallest movement. He knew it was nearly useless, but it gave him some comfort to be doing something. On either side of them stood the marines of the regular line platoon covering this sector. Each man was peeking out and watching the small section to his immediate front and occasionally looking to either side, making sure that he wasn't facing this alone.

Averitt got another radio check with the Air Control Team back in the bunker and sat back to help Gorton stare into the gloom. He was almost comfortable when he heard the first rounds explode on Hill 881 to the north. He jumped up and adjusted the radio volume so that the hiss of the carrier wave was still audible over the noise of the barrage coming down on the marines next door.

From well behind his position he could hear the duller thumps as the artillery back at the combat base opened up in reply. Overhead several new flares lit off, bathing the scene outside the wires in the eerie white-green light of the magnesium candles beneath the parachutes and the slow sparklers of the mortar-launched flares.

He felt a nudge from Gorton and looked over the sandbags. Down below the hill was his worst nightmare. From the treeline came several lines of widely spaced men, moving in a crouch toward the base of the hill and the wires. Just as the first rounds of artillery and mortar fire began to land on his own hill, he picked up the handset and then stopped. There was no one for him to talk to. There were no aircraft overhead except for the C-47, and he was busy strafing the enemy preparing to attack 881S.

Averitt turned the volume on the radio up full and put the handset down. He picked up his rifle and chambered a round. He checked that the safety was still on and that automatic fire was selected.

Very quickly, large dirt geysers began to sprout among the lines of the enemy advancing toward him, but they came on anyway, now moving at a careful jog toward the beginning of the climb toward the marines' lines. Just as the first enemy reached the wires, several command-detonated Claymore mines went off, and all along the trench line American M-16s and M-60 machine guns began to fire. He aimed his own rifle at the enemy and pulled the trigger. He cursed, flicked off the safety, and began to fire short bursts at the lines of dark-clothed men coming up to kill him.

43

Thursday, February 8, 1968

★ Terry White eased the Skyhawk a little to the left and steadied it out again. The wind which had not been forecast was blowing him to the east, so his correction into the wind, called a crab, would put him right on the flight path he wanted. The word from the controller aircraft farther to the south and west was that the wind was increasing in intensity gradually to the point that it soon would have an effect on the layers of thick clouds, invisible in the darkness, that were causing dozens of aircraft to be placed in holding patterns all over the northern parts of South Vietnam.

White and his wingman had been launched from their alerts and gone tearing to the southeast only to be placed in holding off the coast as the controllers tried to sort everything out among the requests for help from the marines on the ground and the aircraft which had been launched to respond.

White looked at his fuel gauge which was dropping close to the point where he'd have to either head back to the ship or to one of the fields ashore. He could prolong his time if he refueled from one of the airborne tankers, but that was going to depend on what the plan was for the later launches from the *Shiloh*. He knew that there were two more *Shiloh* A-4s out there somewhere and four Phantoms too. The Phantoms would be in more urgent need of fuel than would the Skyhawks, so they'd get the priority.

Down below was one of the standard cloud decks that overlay this part of the world pretty much all through the monsoon season. White didn't like trying to bomb through a hole in an overcast. Dropping them straight and level on guidance from the radar guys on the ground was fine, but trying to dive through a hole over

354

unfamiliar terrain was suicidal. This entire mission was looking more and more like a loser.

He was tempted to switch frequencies to listen in on what was happening over the target, but that would mean his controller in the E-2 far to the northwest would have to use the special "guard" frequency to reach him and that would only cause a problem for somebody who might need it in a hurry. In the Navy, that frequency was called "Air Force common" because of the perceived overuse of it by the "zoomies." He was sure that the Air Force called it Navy or Marine common, too, from an equally obvious overuse by the "squids" or "jarheads."

White ran his eyes across his instrument panel again and noted that his fuel, despite his flying around at "max conserve," was getting near the decision point. His wingman, hanging out there just below and slightly behind White's right wing, was even closer because of the extra throttle movements flying formation on somebody required. He keyed his radio and called the E-2.

"Slug 771, Ghostrider 400. We're getting a little skosh on gas. Is there a plan yet?"

After a few seconds the E-2 controller's voice came back. He'd obviously been lulled a little by the inactivity of his mission.

"400, Slug. Stand by."

In the back of Slug 771, Lieutenant Doug McCarthy flipped up another radio switch and keyed the transmitter, calling the *Shiloh*'s operations types. "Zulu Two Charlie, Slug 771."

"Go ahead, 771. This is Two Charlie."

"Be advised that the Skyhawks and Phantoms are getting down on fuel. Request intentions."

"Stand by."

After another pause, the ship came back. "Slug 771, pass to all Two Charlie aircraft, RTB. Slug to remain on station. Say your state."

McCarthy sighed, another goddamn wasted mission. He called up to the pilots on the intercom and got the E-2's fuel state. He passed it on to the *Shiloh* and switched back to the control frequency.

"Ghostrider 400, Slug. Return to base. Pigeons to mother 038, at, um, 110."

White sighed disgustedly. All this for nothing. "Roger, 400 copies. RTB. Request you advise me of a safe area for jettison."

McCarthy looked at his radar scope carefully for anything under the jets' flight path. They could not land with their bomb loads and so would have to jettison them into the sea somewhere where there were no random ships or fishing boats.

"Roger that, 400. Looks like a clear area about halfway home. I'll call it out for you."

White clicked his mike twice in acknowledgment and banked around to take up a course of 038, or north-northeast. One hundred ten miles to home, he thought, about another twenty-five minutes until I can get out of this damn seat.

McCarthy called the other flights and sent them home too. He then called the Air Force EC-121 controller in charge of this sector and told him that he had eight fewer aircraft to bring to the battle for Hills 855 and 881.

"Roger that, Slug. We can't get anybody down through the weather to help anyway. Most of the strikes we can get in there are mini arc lights. We'll see what happens when the sun comes up. Hillsborough out."

McCarthy watched as the *Shiloh*'s aircraft closed the carrier, and called out the clear areas for them to jettison their bombs. He hoped that losing eight aircrafts' worth of bombs was going to be merely wasteful instead of fatal for the marines ashore. With a vague gnawing in his stomach, he settled back in his seat and reached for his thermos of coffee.

Back in the ready room, Jim Hogan watched as Nick Taylor drew black grease pencil arrows on the wall chart he'd taped to the blackboard. He drew corresponding marks on his kneeboard chart and listened as Taylor explained what little he'd been able to learn about the attacks on the hill outpost. Every once in a while his thoughts went to Dick Averitt, and his imagination put him right alongside his friend as he huddled in a bunker under the enemy shellfire or fired his rifle at the assaulting hordes.

Only one part of his mind was permitted to dwell on these horrors. Another part was running through the options and requirements his squadron had for the rest of this period. Still another was planning his own mission, should he be called upon to launch and help in the air support. On top of this was a small fire of anger at whoever had launched the original alerts prematurely and caused the waste of a good deal of ordnance. It never occurred to him that nowhere in all these thoughts was one of concern for his own safety.

One hundred and ninety miles to the southwest, Dick Averitt was neither huddling in a bunker nor blazing away at the enemy. He was holding a radio handset to his ear as he tried to direct artillery fire on the enemy approaching his hilltop. At first he'd joined in with all the other riflemen in the trench line but soon saw that the enemy had gotten through the curtain of artillery fire and were able to approach the wire barrier almost unmolested by the Americans' big guns far to the east. He put down his M-16, picked up the radio, and began to do his job.

He walked the artillery in closer to the wires and found that he had trouble at first figuring out which explosions out there came from which battery. The mortars were easiest, so he began with them, giving them a quick series of adjustments. Then he went to the larger guns and got their rounds all hitting in the right spots. He glanced over to his right at what little he could see of the battle for 881 South and wished that he could have all the artillery at his command instead of only half. He also wished that it was full daylight so he could get some jets in there.

When there was a lull in his yelling into the radio, he became aware that the enemy was shelling his hill too. They were a little long, though, since most of the shells were going off well up the hill from the trenches. He turned around again and watched as the first two lines of the enemy broke and began to pull back down the hill, leaving behind them still, dark lumps here and there. Several enemy were slumped over the barbed wire entanglements, but none apparently had made it through.

He called the batteries and told them to cease fire and very shortly there was what appeared to be almost a complete silence. As his hearing gradually returned, Averitt could make out occasional moans from the enemy wounded below and scattered cries of "corpsman" from the trenches on either side. He glanced at his watch and noted with a great deal of surprise that it had been only fifteen minutes since he had first seen the enemy coming out of the trees.

"You okay, Major?" Gorton was looking at him as he fished for another magazine for his M-14.

"Yeah, except that I really don't like this infantry shit much."

"Well, you did good with the artillery. Do you think we can get that C-47 back over there? I'm pretty sure that the bastards will try again real soon."

Averitt made the call, only to be informed that the gunship had had an engine problem and had departed, and that his relief was not due for another thirty minutes or so. He stared at the floor of the trench, thinking about what all of that meant to the situation. Without Puff the Magic Dragon up there, keeping the enemy's heads down, they would be able to regroup for the next attack all the more quickly.

Averitt glanced at his watch again. It was nearly two hours until sunrise but only about half that until first light. The enemy best liked fighting at night, when nearly all the technological advantages of the American forces were negated, and the cloud deck would keep that enemy advantage a little longer. Unless the marines had a lot of helicopter gunships handy, he and everybody else on these two hills were in big trouble.

He picked up the radio. "Oaktree, this is Spanky. What luck with the helo gunships?"

"Spanky, this is Oaktree Six. They're on the way, but it doesn't look good. They are having trouble with the weather too. The best guess is about twenty more minutes. If at all."

"Oaktree, this is Spanky. The enemy has pulled back into the treeline. Puff is gone, so I'd like to put some H&I fire into the trees to keep them guessing."

"Spanky, we've got some high-level bombers coming over in just a few minutes."

"Roger, understand. But the gomers are regrouping closer in than they can drop. Request some H&I."

There was a pause as Colonel Aires thought that over. Then, "Roger, Spanky. Use the battery back here. I want to save the heavy stuff for the next attack."

"This is Spanky. Roger, out."

Averitt called the fire support coordination people back at Khe Sanh and arranged for some more rounds to be fired into the areas where the enemy would be and then adjusted the fire as it dropped apparently randomly around the area. Concentrating as hard as he was, he didn't notice at first that the wind blowing in his face was getting stronger and stronger. When he did, he realized that it was coming from the west which meant that the layers of clouds above would be moving faster over the area and thus would begin to lose their solidity. That meant that there would be some holes for the jets to get down through and help out the marines on the ground.

He glanced up, and the parts of the clouds that he could see in the surreal light from the illumination rounds were moving now, but he couldn't be sure if the darker spots were holes or just shadows thrown by the magnesium. He was hoping like hell that they were not simply shadows.

He turned his attention back to the menacing darkness of the treeline and walked the few artillery rounds that the marine battery could spare into the more likely spots he'd picked out from his map.

There was a sudden roaring in the air above as one of the enemy's largest artillery rounds, 152mm, passed overhead and exploded on the far side of the hill. Several more followed, and the barrage from the other enemy weapons began again in earnest. Huddling in the bottom of the trench to avoid the flying shell fragments and feeling the ground shake, Averitt had the irrelevant thought that this felt as if the largest train on earth were rumbling past the trench.

From above the cloud deck the battle took on the look of a thunderstorm for Captain Ben Marzetti. Occasional flashes of light shone through the thinner spots and simply served as a constant reminder to Marzetti that he was accomplishing nothing more than burning fuel and adding flight time to his logbook. He was in a Marine Corps TA-4F and was supposed to be coordinating air strikes in and out of the Khe Sanh area. So far his contribution had been to periodically pass overhead and drop extremely bright-burning parachute flares.

Marzetti was a "FASTFAC," which meant that he was an airborne Forward Air Controller who was in an aircraft that moved a hell of a lot faster than the older propeller-driven FAC aircraft. His TA-4F was a new two-seat model of the same A-4 Skyhawk which the attack squadrons had. In the backseat sat a new pilot, First Lieutenant Bob Casey, who was almost finished with the mandatory local familiarization syllabus and soon would be promoted to the position where he would have all the responsibility.

When he had first been launched less than twenty minutes earlier from the Chu Lai air base sixty or so miles to the east, Marzetti had found that the predictions that the weather would break rapidly had been optimistic. The attack aircraft that had come up shortly after he'd arrived had been unable to get down and so had been turned over to the radar controllers, who had guided them in on level-bombing runs. There had really been nothing much for Marzetti to do except drive around and stay out of the way. And drop the flares which were now running pretty low. He hoped that the Air Force could get another C-47 gunship up there before he ran out completely.

Every once in a while Marzetti would ease his way over to the west just to see if he could find the edge of these goddamn clouds. He'd found as he orbited that it took a larger and larger wind correction to stay over the area, so he assumed that the weather-guessers were right—things were going to change, except that they hadn't gotten the timing down.

He swung the jet around to the west for a little weather reconnaissance, first telling the radar people on the ground what he was up to. In just a couple of minutes he was over the western border of South Vietnam and Laos. He knew that he wasn't supposed to enter Laotian airspace without expressed permission, but he pressed the limits a little, looking for the edge of the cloud deck.

He went about ten miles farther than he really should have and swung reluctantly back to the east. As the nose passed through due north, he saw a series of bright yellow-orange flashes below in the darkness, and for the first time in days clearly and not through the omnipresent layer of cloud. He leveled his wings, keeping the spot just to the left of his nose. He glanced to the east and saw that he was still about twenty miles from his assigned position over the combat base and then looked again at his instruments.

There were no air strikes supposed to be happening in this area, and it was too far west to be a ground action. He realized that he might have found the heavy guns with which the enemy had been shelling the marines. The Americans had known that they were out there somewhere, in complete disregard of the "neutrality" of Laos, and had been searching for them in equal disregard for convention. Despite the large number of missions that had been assigned to the job by both the Navy and the Air Force, they had remained completely invisible. Their shells had not, however, and the constant pounding was adding its toll to the casualties at Khe Sanh.

The best guess was that the guns were dug into hillsides in either man-made or natural caves and were pulled back underground whenever American attack planes showed up. At night the guns fired with somewhat greater security and ceased only when the American jets attempted to bomb them by the light of flares.

Their general area was pretty much known, but even pattern bombing by the B-52s had not slowed their fire. The Army had sent out several teams of Special Forces, who had yet to find them. Everyone on both sides knew that sooner or later the guns would be found and silenced. Well, maybe not silenced, thought Marzetti. The tenacious little bastards would probably just take them apart and carry them on their backs, piece by piece, to a new site and begin blazing away again.

Marzetti stared into the darkness ahead, trying to memorize the spot he'd seen the flashes come from, and soon gave it up. It is impossible to fix a spot with one's eyes in the dark, especially from a moving airplane. He keyed the ICS, or intercom.

"Hey, Bob. Take the controls for a minute. I think I saw something down there."

In the backseat Casey grabbed the stick gently and shook it. "I've got the aircraft."

Marzetti released the stick and leaned his helmet to the left until it was up against the canopy, trying to get as much of the land below in his field of vision as he could and praying that the enemy had not heard them coming. It was several seconds later that he saw four long flashes erupt from the darkness below. He punched out a flare and tried again to fix the spot with his eyes.

The flare took so long to ignite that he thought at first it was a dud. He had grabbed the controls again and rolled into a relatively steep bank, telling Casey to keep his eyes on the instruments. When the flare ignited, it was followed almost instantly by two more flashes from the ground. Apparently the enemy had tried to cease fire and at least two of the guns had not gotten the word quickly enough and fired one more round.

"Bob, I think we just found those fucking 152s everybody has been looking for. Back me up. We're going down for a closer look."

In the backseat Casey noted the TACAN position, heading, altitude, and airspeed on his kneeboard so that this could all be reconstructed later if need be. He glanced at the chart for a second or so to confirm what he already had memorized.

Over the ICS he passed the information to Marzetti. "Okay, partner. We're over Laos and there are several tall and rather hard mountains around here. The maximum obstruction altitude in this box is 4600 feet and six thousand to the east. The forty-six-hundred one is about fifteen miles north, so we should be good to four thousand anyway."

Marzetti acknowledged and swung the Skyhawk around, keeping his eye on the ridge line which the flare was now illuminating dimly. He lowered the nose and popped out his speedbrakes, steepening his dive. From the rear he could hear Casey calling out altitudes and rates of descent. It was very easy at night to misjudge distances, so pilots long ago learned to use the other guy in the aircraft to back them up with the readings from the gauges.

Marzetti shallowed his dive as he got closer to the ground and leveled off at four thousand. He was under the flare now and could see the ground much more clearly. He kept the speedbrakes out and slowed the aircraft to about two hundred fifty knots. He was gambling that at night the enemy would not be able to hear him coming or to fire their Triple-A accurately. One pass should be relatively safe, but a second or third would be increasingly dangerous.

They were approaching a ridge running roughly north to south that climbed sharply from a small valley. In the center of the valley was a small dirt road, which in these parts was probably considered the equivalent of an interstate. The road made an east-west jog right at the northern end of the ridge, so Marzetti decided to use that as a reference point and eased the Skyhawk lower and turned right, heading north. Casey called out the altitudes with increasing alarm until Marzetti told him curtly that he was aware he was going down but needed to in order to get a good look at the ridge. It was all Casey could do to keep himself concentrating on the instruments and not look outside.

Marzetti followed the road northward up the surprisingly wide valley until he came to the bend in the road. He banked a little, setting the jet up on a course that would be pretty much clear of rocks and things once he was past the ridge. He then flew as close as he could to the ridge, staying below the crest and staring into the trees that grew up the sides.

Now, at two hundred twenty-five knots, he had three impressions as he rolled the aircraft slightly to get a better view. The first was that the holes the guns were hidden in were a lot smaller than he'd thought they'd be. The second was that there seemed to be a lot more than four of them. The third was that there was suddenly far more antiaircraft fire coming at him than he'd ever seen around there before.

There were all sorts of streams of little lighted streamers flashing in front, behind, beside, below, and above the little TA-4. To Marzetti, it was as if they'd suddenly flown inside one of those mirrored balls they always used to have at high school dances, except that at the dances the lights all went in predictable directions and were not fatal.

He hauled back on the stick and shoved the throttle forward, simultaneously closing the speedbrakes. He banked around to the west behind the ridge and climbed away to the north.

He was trying to get his breathing under control when he heard Casey's voice from the back. "Well, now. That was certainly fun. Did we find what we were looking for, or do we get to go back and do it again?"

"Never fear, Watson. We're done with low-level practice for the nonce. If you'll be so kind as to take the controls, I'll phone this in."

"I've got the aircraft, and no matter what you say, we're not going down again until we get home."

Marzetti chuckled. The weather was finally breaking, and if it continued, they'd be able to get some close air down on the enemy for a change. When he smoothed his chart out to get the map coordinates of the guns, he was surprised at how much his hands were shaking.

44

Thursday, February 8, 1968

Jim Hogan folded the letter he was writing to his ex-wife and put it carefully in the leg pocket of his flight suit. He stretched, trying to get a kink out of his back. He'd been sitting in his ready-room chair for only thirty minutes or so, but the long hours of working and flying over the past few days were beginning to add up. He'd started the letter mostly to keep himself

363

awake on this alert, but he soon found his mind wandering to all the little problems of command, most of which were of no real significance at the moment, but the hour and his mental state were allowing them to magnify in his mind.

He stood, arching his back and then bending forward at the waist. The tightness seemed to ease a little so, just to get his body moving, he walked over to the coffee urn and reached for his cup hanging on the hook on the wall. He pulled his hand back when he realized that another cup of coffee would probably be far more than he needed. If he didn't have to launch on this alert, he'd be too wired to sleep and, if he did have to go flying, he'd probably be in agony from a full bladder about five minutes after he got airborne.

He walked to the duty desk and told the young pilot sitting there, reading a book, that he'd be down in CVIC if he was needed. As he left the room, he looked around at the other pilots sitting on alert and knew that they'd be feeling just as tired as he was. He resolved that the next standdown for replenishment would be a designated day of rest for the pilots of the squadron. No meetings, no paperwork—nothing. He made a mental note to tell Wilson and the X.O. not to schedule anything at all.

When Hogan walked into CVIC, the ship's Intelligence Center, he found Nick Taylor alone in the room, sitting on a tall stool and leaning over a chart table. He was carefully going over a stack of messages and comparing them to marks he'd made on a large chart spread on a table. Hogan walked up behind Taylor and stood, looking over his shoulder.

Taylor glanced up and grinned. Putting his pencil down, he turned on the stool.

"Good morning, Skipper. What are you doing roaming around at this hour?"

Hogan was surprised that he really didn't have a ready answer for that particular question. "I dunno. I've got the Alert 10 and I guess I got tired of sitting in the damn ready room, staring at the walls."

Taylor chuckled. "And getting a case of the nameless dreads?"

"The what?"

"The nameless dreads. That's what I call all those times when your mind starts magnifying little things into huge crises and disasters. The more you think, the worse things get, until you're doomed. Like when the curses of Egypt seem like a good deal. The dreads always get me in the middle of the night."

Hogan felt a little foolish having his case diagnosed by somebody so much younger. And so easily. He forced a smile. "Yeah, something like that."

He changed the subject. "What are you doing?"

Taylor waved a hand over the chart. "Just keeping up with the war. I couldn't sleep, so I swapped duties with the guy who was supposed to relieve me. There're some attacks going on all around the country, but it's Khe Sanh I'm watching mostly."

"What's happening there?"

Taylor picked up his pencil and pointed to the chart. "The NVA are attacking Hill 881 again. The marines are holding them, but most of the messages I've been able to get say that this will be a big one, so I don't think the jarheads're out of the woods yet."

Hogan leaned over the chart, inspecting Taylor's notations. He was about to ask a question, when the phone on the wall rang shrilly and Taylor hustled over to answer it. He saw Taylor nod slowly and wince as somebody on the other end spoke almost loudly enough for Hogan to hear. Taylor grabbed a piece of paper and began copying down a series of numbers. Without saying anything more, he hung up the phone and walked quickly to the front of the room, where he began marking the large wall chart while consulting the paper in his hand.

Hogan walked up and watched Taylor match coordinates on the chart with his notes before turning to Hogan. "Skipper, we have to launch the alert fighters for a strike into Laos here. Could you call down to Metro and ask the weather-guessers to give us an update for the area around Khe Sanh." He grinned. "When they tell you that it is the same as it was two hours ago, tell 'em who you are and that you'll have their ass if they're not up here in five minutes."

Hogan chuckled and walked over to the phone. Picking it up, he felt relieved. Even if it was only helping Nick Taylor get a brief ready, he was doing something. As he waited for the weathermen to answer, he decided to stay and listen to the briefing itself. He had a feeling that he and his squadron were going to get involved sooner or later and he might as well get himself up to speed now.

Averitt grunted as a heavy clod of earth struck him flush on the neck. He felt the impact but no pain, much as he had playing football. He ran his hand over the spot and looked at it and, seeing no blood, risked a peek over the sandbags at the bottom of the hill. The enemy had not yet begun their assault, which he was certain was coming any moment. He grabbed his radio, called for some illumination rounds, and tried to get some more heavy artillery fire down on the treeline.

All over the crest of the hill incoming rounds exploded, shaking the ground and throwing bits of hot metal in every direction. He huddled at the bottom of the trench for what seemed to be hours. Finally, he risked another peek over the sandbags and saw the small shapes moving from shell hole to shell hole as the enemy began another assault. There were many more of them this time than the last, and it didn't seem as if the marines could possibly have enough bullets to get them all. He wanted to run somewhere—anywhere—where the mass of men down below couldn't find him. He instinctively glanced to his rear, looking for an escape route, but forced himself to turn back and face the enemy. He looked for the radio handset and found it, with some surprise, still in his hand.

He looked over and saw Gorton climbing to his feet from the bottom of the trench. He had a gash across his cheek which was bleeding some and in the harsh light was giving him the appearance of something out of a horror movie. The sergeant major reached down and picked up his helmet. He jammed it on his head and pulled it right back off again with a curse.

Inspecting the thing, he found that the whole left side was smashed in with a large jagged hole in the center. He had jammed the sharp edges down on his scalp which was now beginning to bleed too. Averitt saw him reach inside, remove a small square piece of paper and stuff that in his shirt pocket, and then throw the helmet over his shoulder out of the trench. The old marine retrieved his rifle and began to fire measured bursts down the hill.

From the right came the shout "gooks in the wire!" All along the line the marines opened fire with their weapons, sending a curtain of small .223-caliber rounds screaming toward the small clumps of North Vietnamese Army troops. The M-60 machine guns spaced along the line opened up with their longer, heavier bursts. Averitt could hear the odd thumping sound of the grenade launchers sending out their high-explosive and flechette rounds.

Down the hill, small groups of NVA sappers had crawled toward the wire in several places. Waves of bullets washed over them, and they went down and mostly stayed down. A few flopped around, writhing in pain, and a couple dragged themselves across the broken ground. Others ran forward from the mass of men coming on and picked up the sappers' loads. There were too many with too much persistence to stop completely, and here and there the new sappers shoved their long pipelike Bangalore torpedoes along the ground under the concertina wire and pulled the fuse handles. Only one or two survived long enough to crawl away from the explosions which, seconds later, tore large gaps in the wire, providing avenues for the rest of the assault troops.

Averitt watched as the enemy began to get through the gaps with some throwing themselves on the wire so their comrades could step on their backs, using them as planks to bridge the obstacles. Averitt heard the enemy screaming and yelling as they charged up the hill, firing their AK-47s from the hip, completely undaunted by the heavy toll the American weapons were taking on them.

As he changed magazines, he glanced up and saw another wave of men break from the treeline and surge forward to support the first wave which was now tattered and torn and slowing down as its momentum spent itself against the steepening sides of the hill. He reached for his radio and called for more artillery, only to be told that he was already getting everything that they had.

He looked at the approaching enemy and the volume of fire that was raining down on them. He knew, suddenly and completely, that it would not be enough. There was no way on this earth that what the marines had to give was more than the enemy could take.

The phone rang in the ready room and the duty officer picked it up before it was finished with the first ring. He listened for a couple of seconds, nodding in agreement with the tinny voice at the other end. "Just a minute," he said.

He got up and walked over to the chairs where Scott, Norris, and the crew of the other alert Phantom were dozing. He gently shook Scott's shoulder.

"Skipper? You're wanted on the phone."

Scott came instantly awake and shook his head to clear the rest of the cobwebs. "Yeah, okay. Who is it?"

"It's CAG, sir."

Scott walked over and picked up the receiver. "Commander Scott speaking."

The voice on the other end sounded as tired as Scott felt. " 'Mornin', Chris. CAG here. We need to get the Phantoms airborne pretty quick, but we need to brief you guys first. Bring your crews down to CVIC, please."

"Yes, sir. We'll be there in a couple of minutes. Bye."

Scott replaced the receiver and turned to the duty officer. "Tell maintenance that we'll be launching in a few minutes. Probably forty or so. Oh, and thank them again for their hustle in getting them ready. Okay?" With a nod he turned and moved over to the alert crews. Norris was already on his feet and the others were sitting there waiting for "the word."

"That was CAG. He has something special for us to do and he wants us down in CVIC for a briefing. If you have to hit the head, do it on the way."

He reached down, picked up his gear, and put it on. He checked that he had all his charts in the bag, grabbed his helmet, and left the room, followed by the rest of his crews.

When Scott walked into the Intell Center, he saw that there was a small huddle at the front of the room standing near the map board centered around Nick Taylor and CAG. Jim Hogan was standing to the rear of the group, listening carefully. He pulled his kneeboard out of his helmet and placed the helmet on the front seat in the briefing chairs. As Scott approached the group, CAG Andrews turned and saw the fighter crews.

"Good morning, gentlemen. I think we have a real genuine target for you. As soon as the crews from the other squadron get here, I'll let Lieutenant Whiede here fill you in."

Nick Taylor turned around, and on his flight jacket was Velcroed a new name tag—"Dick Whiede." Scott chuckled, but Norris frowned at it until he figured out that Wheide was pronounced "weed," as CAG had said. He laughed too.

"That's one of your better ones, Nick, but I still like old Pat McGroyne."

Taylor grinned. "Pat's transferred."

He stopped as the crews from the other fighter squadron trooped in. "If you will all take your seats, I'll give you what we've got here."

CAG Andrews and Hogan moved to seats in the back of the

room and Taylor waited until everyone was as comfortable as they were going to get, which in steel Navy chairs was not at all. He picked up a wooden pointer from the chalk tray and placed the tip on a small dot he'd drawn over a spot just west of Khe Sanh.

"A marine FASTFAC appears to have found the NVA heavy guns we've been looking for for a while. We're sending you after them. The weather appears to be improving some this morning, at least for a few hours. Everybody else is still devoted to close air support, so you get the mission.

"The guns are located here." He pointed again to the chart and gave the range and bearing from the TACAN station at Khe Sanh. He pulled out a folder and passed around copies of detailed reconnaissance photographs of the area.

"These are various views of the ridge line where the guns are supposed to be, taken about a week ago. You can't see anything in those pictures because the little bastards are experts at camouflage. I gave you those just so you could get an idea of the terrain.

"Now, the plan is for you guys to arrive overhead just after six, local time, which is an hour and a half from now and pretty much first light, which means that your launch time will be in forty-five minutes. The FASTFAC, call sign Derby 009, will be waiting eagerly for your arrival. He's the guy who found the guns and is the only one who really can spot for you. The marines sent up a relief for him and called 009 back early so he could refuel and rearm. The frequency for the FASTFAC will be 336.6. After launch you will hit the tanker and top off, then check in through all the usual contollers—the Slug first, then Hillsborough, who will chop you over to the FASTFAC. Any questions so far?"

There were none, so he pointed at another large briefing board. "Okay, whatever weather in the target area I could give you will have changed by the time you get there, so all I've put on the board is what we have here for the next three hours. The rest of the briefing is the same as you got for the alerts. I don't have any real great words of wisdom for you except that lunch will be double-cheese sliders and I'll save you some unless I get hungry."

He looked around at the faces of the men who were going out on this one. They had heard what he had to say and were now waiting to get on with it. "I'll turn it over to the flight lead. Good luck, and if anything comes up, I'll be back in the corner there, going over recognition manuals."

Taylor walked back to his desk and picked up a copy of *Playboy,* being very careful to be no part of the rest of the briefing. Scott shook his head and smiled as he began his own briefing. He was going to miss the hell out of Nick Taylor when he finally left and went back to Lemoore.

The NVA made it almost to the trench line this time. Actually, they did get into the trenches in a couple of spots farther down the line from where Averitt was but were thrown back quickly by the arrival of a small reaction team that Captain Demars had organized from the headquarters and weapons platoons. The withering fire that the marines had laid down on the NVA had been just enough to break the assault.

Averitt remembered reading somewhere that in battle around a third of soldiers fail to fire their weapons, and of those who do, most are wildly inaccurate. The marines on either side of the position he and Gorton manned had fired slow, controlled bursts from their rifles or had fired single, if very rapid, rounds at the enemy. The first time the NVA had come at them, Averitt had blazed away merrily in between directing fire until Gorton had taken notice and gently cautioned him. The second time he had taken more care.

He had fired at many individual enemy and had seen some of them fall, but he wasn't sure how to feel about that. He wasn't sure yet that it was all real. Amid all the noise and smoke and fear, it seemed that the only reality was his own voice in his head, sounding like a cross between a coach and a play-by-play announcer. Everything else seemed to be happening to somebody else and projected on some sort of screen. Things had happened at double speed and were immediately followed by scenes at half speed and sometimes things seemed to be happening at both. There was no sense of touch, of taste, of smell, and sight and sound were of dubious validity. Once he had begun to actually do something, to take some action in his own defense, the fear evaporated for a while but came back as soon as the fight was over.

He could recall ducking once as another large bit of the hill was blown out of the earth it had lain in for a couple of thousand millennia and struck him in the back or on the helmet. He remembered calling for the artillery fire to be shifted a time or two, and he remembered grinning in satisfaction when his corrections dropped high explosives directly on the spots he'd wanted.

Now he hunched down in the bottom of the trench and puffed

greedily on a Marlboro. It was his turn, having insisted that Gorton get the first while Averitt kept watch. The smoke mixed with the coppery aftertaste of the fear he was only now remembering. He wondered if fear was like the tree in the forest: was it there even if you weren't aware of it?

He shook his head, knowing that he was letting his control get away from him a little, and forced himself back to the task at hand. He reached for the radio handset and keyed the mike button.

"Oaktree, this is Spanky. Radio check, over."

"Spanky, this is Oaktree Six. Read you loud and clear. Request sitrep, over."

Averitt paused. He'd drawn a blank and couldn't remember the format that situation reports were supposed to come in. There was a different one for every type of unit and action anyway, so he just made one up.

"Oaktree, this is Spanky. We've just repulsed a second attack. The enemy got into our positions briefly and have been thrown back. I have no idea of casualties or of ammunition supplies. Suggest you contact Lima Six for that, over."

"Spanky, we are unable to establish comms with Lima Six at this time. Request you investigate."

Averitt looked back up the hill toward the CP where "Lima Six," the company commander, Demars, was. He couldn't see anything over the mounds of chewed-up dirt. The heaviest part of the artillery barrage from the enemy had landed well behind the trenches, at least around there, so something might have happened to the radios in the CP. He might well have the only radio still functioning on Hill 855.

"Roger that, Oaktree. We'll investigate and call you right back."

Averitt picked up the radio and slung it on his back. He thumbed Gorton out of the trench to the rear and headed up the hill toward the CP. The two men moved as quickly as the broken ground, the weight of the radio, and the peculiar gait of men accustomed to being shelled would allow. Gorton led until they came to the crest of the hill, where he stopped abruptly. Averitt, looking at the ground to make sure of his footing, ran square into the sergeant major's back. He recoiled a step, then looked around the old marine's broad shoulders and froze.

Where the CP had stood only a short while ago there was now a smoking hole with bits of timber and sandbags strewn around. There were pieces of things, which Averitt remembered as having been part of the furnishings, lying in a jumbled mass against the part of the sandbagged wall still standing. The light from the flares and illumination rounds was too weak for him to make out exactly what had happened to the occupants.

Several wild-eyed marines were frantically pulling the debris aside and throwing it out of the hole in an attempt to find any survivors. Gorton grabbed one of them.

"Where's Captain Demars?"

The marine looked at him for a second. "He's dead. He got it up on the line."

"How about the other officers?"

"I don't know. My lieutenant is hurt pretty bad, but I haven't seen any of the others."

Averitt put the radio down and picked up the handset. "Oaktree, this is Spanky. Is Oaktree Six there?"

"Go ahead, Spanky. This is Six."

"Roger. The Lima CP took a direct hit. Lima Six is down and I'm unable to locate any of the other officers."

There was a long pause. "Is the Sierra Mike still with you?"

Averitt wondered what the hell a "Sierra Mike" was. Then he realized that the colonel was referring to S.M., which had to stand for the sergeant major.

"That's affirmative, Oaktree. He's right here."

"Roger, Spanky. I am directing you to assume command of Lima until relieved by my order. Organize the defense of your position and keep me advised."

Averitt was a *pilot*, for Christ's sake. He had only the very basic training that every marine officer gets, and that was years before in the relative sanity of northern Virginia. He was now in command of a company of marines fighting for their lives on a dark hilltop in the middle of Viet-fucking-nam. This was not the place or the time to learn how.

He looked up and saw the intense eyes of Master Sergeant Gorton staring at him. The old marine nodded and turned to the younger marine at his side.

"Son, find me as many of the platoon leaders as you can and bring them here to the major. Get with it. The gomers aren't done with us yet."

He turned back to Averitt and squatted next to him. He gestured at the handset Averitt was holding slackly in his hand. "You gonna answer the colonel or what?"

372

As if in a trance, Averitt spoke into the radio, "Oaktree, this is Spanky—I mean Lima Six. Roger out." He placed the handset back in its holder and looked at the sergeant major.

"Shit" was all he could think of to say.

Captain Ben Marzetti wiggled the rudder pedals and the brakes until the nosewheel was straight in the runway centerline. This jet, Derby 002, was a different airplane from the one he'd just landed in. He'd been all set to go once he was refueled and rearmed, but the plane captain had done his walk-around check of the Skyhawk as Marzetti and Casey had stopped at the entrance to the hot fuel pits and had noticed that there were a couple of pieces missing. Marzetti had not even felt the hits from the Triple-A that had taken off the tip of his tail and a piece of the tailpipe. They had been forced to get another aircraft which meant that they were now about ten minutes behind the schedule they'd planned on.

Marzetti shoved the brakes down as hard as he could and ran the throttle up to eighty-five percent RPM and watched it stabilize. He shifted the fuel control into manual and back again, noting that the RPM stayed within limits. He pulled the throttle back to idle and ran the controls through. Everything was nice and smooth. He switched the ICS to "hot mike" and told Casey that they were going flying. He keyed his radio.

"Tower, Derby 002's rollin'."

"Roger, Double-oh-two. Contact departure."

Marzetti shoved the throttle forward and released the brakes. He kept the nosewheel straight and the TA-4 accelerated nicely. He felt the controls become effective and eased the nose back, waiting for the airspeed to increase enough to get the Skyhawk off the ground. He glanced in at his instruments and then back out at the rows of runway lights which seemed to pass by in an increasing blur.

The little jet lifted off and he slapped up the gear handle, waited for the airspeed again, and raised the flaps. He banked around to the west and shifted frequencies.

"Departure, Derby 002 is airborne. Climbing to twelve thousand, squawking 4166."

"Roger, 002. Radar contact. Continue climb to fifteen thousand on a heading of 275. Contact Hillsborough on 334.7 now."

"Roger, Hillsborough on 334.7. Switching."

As he completed the post-takeoff checklist, turned off the spoilers, switched the ICS to "cold mike" and rotated the frequency knobs, Ben Marzetti had the thought that departure had switched him to the new frequency pretty quickly. Something must be up.

45

Thursday, February 8, 1968

Commander Chris Scott watched as the last of the three other Phantoms he led pulled back from the KA-3 tanker and slid over into formation with him. As Norris in the back made the radio calls, Scott eased the formation into a gentle climb away to the southwest. Off to his left he could see that the stars had begun to lose a little of their sharp brightness as the sun, still well below the horizon, threw the first rays of the new day across the skies farther east. It wouldn't be long before he and his flight would be in full daylight while the earth below would, for a few minutes, still be shrouded in blackness.

Scott had always loved to fly at dawn. It cheered him with the promise of something new and unknown. He felt that he got to see something first before anyone else chained on the planet below had the chance. The old feeling was present that morning and receded only when he forced himself back to the task at hand—fighting a war from the cockpit of a jet fighter. The morning remained beautiful, but the mission did not.

Norris checked them in with Hillsborough and released his shoulder harness lock. He looked out to the sides and just watched the other fighters become rapidly more distinct. There was not much for him to do, so he just enjoyed the ride.

* * *

374

★ Ghostrider One ★

Aboard the *Shiloh*, Commander Jim Hogan leaned his head back against the headrest of his A-4 and for about the millionth time in his career wished that either he were a couple of inches shorter or that the designers had raised the metal "headknocker," or safing handle, on the ejection seat those same couple of inches. The thing stuck out and hit him right below the curve of the back of his head. He couldn't really get comfortable like some of the more diminutive pilots in the squadron. The headknocker was raised right before takeoff, arming the seat, and so when the pilot was leaning forward, actually flying, it was out of the way, but when he was on deck, sitting in Alert 5, it was an annoyance. They should have reversed the positions, he thought.

As soon as the fighters had launched, the word had come down that the weather over the whole I-Corps area was expected to improve rapidly, and in the immediate area of Khe Sanh it was soon going to be possible to get in close air support. The Marine jets were already on the way and Hogan's four Skyhawks would be next to go. The move to Alert 5 was one way of ensuring that there would be minimum delay in getting additional weapons down on the enemy.

Hogan looked off to his right and saw the same weakening of the starlight that Scott had seen fifteen minutes before, and was glad that even if he launched now, at least part of his mission could be flown in some sort of daylight.

Averitt looked at the men surrounding him near the wreckage of the CP. None of them were officers, except one young second lieutenant who seemed much the worse for wear. He was bandaged in several places on his upper body and was staring at the ground, occasionally shaking his head, as if trying to clear it. One of the large 152mm rounds had exploded just behind his position, and it had taken several minutes to dig him out of the collapsed trench wall. Averitt knew that even at a hundred percent, the lieutenant would not be any more effective than Averitt, who'd had had at least a couple of months with a line outfit although never in command. He grinned at himself. Nothing like accentuating the positive.

The other members of the small huddle were telling Averitt a tale he really didn't want to hear. There had been far more casualties than had been apparent to him at the outset, and the ammunition supply, while still adequate, would not last against many more attacks like the one they'd just fought off. There was enough water to last the day and food was not a problem. There were simply not enough men to go around.

The reaction force with which Demars had reinforced the line in the last attack was the last of the reserves. The only option now was to weaken the line in some spots in order to strengthen it in others, where the enemy was most likely to strike. Which raised another question—would the enemy hit the same place he had twice already or would he attack somewhere else? Averitt tried to put himself in the place of the enemy and think like him, but he soon realized that that was going to be a waste of time. There was no way on earth he was ever going to outthink the NVA commander. He just didn't have either the training or the experience.

Gorton, sensing Averitt's dilemma, asked his opinion. "Major, the way I see it, we ought to pull one man in four off the back side of the position and reinforce the line where the enemy came last time. They're pretty rigid in their tactics and they'll probably do the same thing again. If you and I stay here and coordinate, and we get one of the guys from the Air Control Team to stay with us, we should be able to keep control of the situation. What do you think?"

"Okay. Who will we have spotting for the artillery?"

One of the sergeants piped up. "I used to be with the cannon cockers, Major. I can direct fire."

Averitt handed him the radio, pulling a sheet of paper from his shirt pocket. "Okay, you've got it and here's the comm plan. Take what you need and give it back to the sergeant major. The regiment's call sign is Oaktree and the batteries are Bravo and Charlie, both over at the combat base. If we need fire from the Army, call Oaktree. They'll set it up. Who'll replace you in your platoon?"

"I got a couple of good squad leaders over there. I'll get one of 'em going." The sergeant, finished noting down what he needed, shouldered the radio and walked quickly off to his platoon.

Averitt asked the remaining men what they had left in front of their positions. Most of them had set off all their Claymores already and in many places the perimeter wire had been breached so that it now merely had the effect of funneling an attack as opposed to slowing one down. On the other hand, placing the machine guns at the narrow end of the funnels might do some good until the enemy figured out a counter to it. He mentioned the idea and Gorton eagerly added a few personal touches.

376

When the meeting broke up minutes later, Averitt was struck with the realization that planning on the part of the besieged was very simple. You had nowhere to maneuver for advantage and, once you were in position, all you could do was shoot and hope. Despite his inexperience, he deeply wished that he had a lot more things to plan. Not only would there be more options, but he would be able to keep himself occupied.

He looked at his watch under the red flashlight Gorton held and was very surprised to see that it had been well over an hour and a half since the first shells had fallen on Hill 881 South and that it would be only about twenty minutes until first light. He looked up into the eerie blackness above and hoped that he wasn't just imagining that the clouds seemed to be getting more ragged. The C-47 gunship was due in twenty minutes also, and if the weather was really breaking, he'd at least be able to see his targets.

As the first thumps of the enemy's renewed barrage came to him from the west, he hoped that those twenty minutes would still see American marines standing on this hilltop. He and Gorton hustled over to the new CP which had shortly before been a platoon's sleeping bunker.

Captain Ben Marzetti glanced to his right and saw the shells falling on Hill 855 in the distance. Closer and below his altitude he could make out the dim shape of the new FASTFAC overhead as it banked around to begin the northern leg of its orbit, or "anchored on top Blackhorse," in the pilot's brevity code. He keyed his radio. "Hillsborough, 002 has the traffic in sight. Well clear to the north."

The two aircraft were on different frequencies, so the airborne controller had to make sure that they saw each other even though they were separated by two thousand feet vertically. One of the certain ways to ruin a perfectly good aircraft was by having a midair collision. They didn't happen often, but when they did they were usually fatal for somebody. He was very glad Casey was in the back, scanning the sky too.

"Roger. Your traffic is now northbound. Come right to 295 and resume own navigation. You're cleared to operate surface to twenty thousand outside of ten miles west of Blackhorse."

"002, roger."

Marzetti banked around to the northwest and eased back the throttle, descending to an altitude where he could see the ground and still be difficult for the enemy gunners or their Triple-A supporters to hear. When he was nearly due west of Khe Sanh he switched off his exterior lights and craned his neck forward to stare at the black ridges below.

The cloud deck had dissipated in this area and it seemed to be breaking up over Khe Sanh too. There were wide holes beginning to develop, and the wind at this altitude promised that the day was going to be vast improvement over the past few.

He banked around again and began flying east-west legs, keeping the area where he'd earlier seen the guns well to the north. To make sure he stayed far enough away from the guns that they wouldn't hear him, he set the indicators in his cockpit so that he would have an electronic reference. In a little while the ground would be visible and he would be able to use landmarks to keep his position, but the problem with that was that the muzzle flashes would be far less distinct than they would be now so that his chances of finding the guns again would be drastically reduced.

He called Blackhorse and asked if they knew whether the outposts were still receiving fire from the big guns. An exasperated radio operator told him that they were and that he would let Derby 002 know if there was a change. That basically meant that Blackhorse was busy and would Derby 002 please not jog his elbow.

Marzetti for a moment felt angry with himself that he was letting his impatience get the best of him but stuck the feeling away in a small compartment for later thought and went back to the business of trying to find the guns. There was intelligence that said that the enemy also had some larger weapons north of the DMZ, and he had the sinking feeling that perhaps those were the guns that were firing on the outposts while the ones in Laos were playing possum. If that were the case, this whole effort would be wasted and the Navy Phantoms that should be checking in any minute were not going to have a target.

The ridge lines were beginning to become distinct now. He wasn't sure just when he'd first been able to pick individual terrain features out, but they were finally becoming visible. The tips of the ridges were just a couple of shades less than black, but the valleys beneath them were much darker and still hidden. The sky to the east was now that milky gray that always made Marzetti think that the day was somehow reluctant to begin.

He was just turning to start his westbound leg when he saw a ripple of long orange-yellow flashes erupt from the still-indistinct side of one of the ridges. He fixed it in his mind's eye and continued the leg, turning back when he was just starting to lose a good view of it.

"Hillsborough, this is Derby 002. Have you got an estimate for the Phantoms that are coming to me? I believe I've got the target and we'll have to hurry."

"Roger, 002. They're about thirty out at this time. We've got to bend 'em around Blackhorse, but they'll be there ASAP. Stand by this freq. Their call sign will be Guntrain 207, flight of four."

"002 copies. Standing by."

Marzetti resisted the temptation to get closer for a better look, to get that one perfect peek at the target, knowing that as soon as he gave any indication that he'd spotted the emplacements, the gunners would pull their weapons beneath their camouflage or back inside the tunnels and he'd never be able to get them. By the following morning they'd be well on their way to new sites and the whole drill would begin again. All he could do now was to wait for the Navy to show up.

"The Navy" in the person of Scott and his flight were less than twenty miles away and coming fast. They had to "bend around," or detour, the invisible bubble over Khe Sanh below, and to their left as they passed they could see the vast number of orange flashes that looked like fireflies in the lessening darkness. Norris in the back remembered the first time he'd seen them on the night he'd arrived in Vietnam aboard an Air Force C-141. He'd peeked out the window and seen the landscape below dotted with little lights. He'd thought that they were quite pretty until the loadmaster told him what they really were. That was the first time Norris could ever remember being frightened in an aircraft.

"Guntrain 207, Hillsborough. Derby 002 is at your ten o'clock low at ten miles. Report him in sight."

Both Norris and Scott peered out into the distance, trying to find the tiny A-4. They couldn't and told the controller so. There was a pause and then, "Guntrain 207, Derby 002 has a visual on you. Maintain this altitude and contact him on prebriefed freq now, over."

Norris keyed the radio. "Roger, Hillsborough, 207 switching."

Norris spun the knobs on the radio, and when the channelizer tone on the radio quit, he stepped on the foot switch. "Guntrains."

"Two."

"Three."

"Four."

He heard them all check in and called, "Derby 002, Guntrain 207."

"207, 002. Loud and clear. Say your loads and state."

"207 is a flight of four Phantoms. We have ten Mk-82s each and we're zero-plus-five-zero on the fuel." Fifty minutes of fuel ought to be enough, thought Norris.

"Roger. Understand zero-plus-five-zero and Mark eighty-twos. Stand by."

In Derby 002 Marzetti told Casey to wake up and quit being along for the ride and give the brief to the Phantoms. Casey laughed and keyed the radio.

"Guntrain 207, 002 has a target of several 152mm artillery emplacements dug in on the east side of a ridge about fifty meters down from the crest. We believe that there are two three-gun batteries there. The weather in the area is clearing rapidly and the altimeter is 29.96. The highest terrain elevation in the area is six thousand to the east and forty-six hundred to the north. Best ejection is to the southeast. There was considerable light Triple-A in the area earlier but we did not see anything heavier than thirty-sevens. How copy, so far?"

"207 copies all. 29.96 for the altimeter."

"Roger. You'll be making runs from east to west as shallow as possible. When you have me in sight, I'll mark the target. Pull off to the south and call Derby and target in sight." Casey told Marzetti to switch on the top red anticollision light and in less than three seconds the Phantoms called to say that they had him in sight. Marzetti turned the light off again, knowing that he'd been able to angle it away from the guns on the ground. He armed his smoke rockets.

"207, tallyho, Derby."

"Roger that. I'll be marking the target now. Commencing."

Marzetti had maneuvered so that he was about two miles to the southeast of the ridge, headed east. He rolled hard left, pulled the nose around, and lined it up on the center of the ridge. As he did, the guns let go another salvo. He involuntarily hunched his shoulders, half expecting to fly directly into one of the big shells, but when he didn't, he got right back to business. He made little control movements, adjusting for the drift, and, when he had the altitude right, he hit the switch on the stick and fired a pair of white phosphorous rockets at the ridge.

As Marzetti hauled back on the stick and banked to the north, Casey looked over his shoulder and saw the two white balls of smoke hit just about exactly where Marzetti had aimed them. He was also surprised at how many details he could make out about the ridge now that the light was growing. The ridge looked an awful lot craggier and uglier than it had in the velvet of the darkness earlier.

He keyed the radio. "Guntrains, the target is marked. Place your bombs one hundred meters on either side of the smoke. There was no Triple-A that time but I'm sure that was because they were taken by surprise. Call your runs."

Scott's flight separated into the proper intervals and looked at the forbidding ground below. Everything down there was now a dark gray, which left relative height and depth very deceptive. Most of them hated bombing in this kind of light, but if they were to get those guns, they couldn't wait. In all four cockpits the pilots and RIOs wiggled their shoulders against their harnesses and got their tailbones hard up against the backs of their ejection seats.

Scott and Norris automatically double-checked everything in their cockpits and waited the almost interminable time it took to fly to the roll-in position. When they got there, everything began to happen at a vastly accelerated pace. Scott shoved the stick over to the left and pulled it back toward his gut. Rolling the big Phantom over on its back and pulling the nose toward the ground, he waited until the target was generally in the sight and rolled it back over again.

Norris transmitted "Lead's in. FAC and target in sight" and tried to see over Scott's shoulder and around the pilot's ejection seat to the target but, as usual, he couldn't, so he went back to watching the altimeter and looking around for trouble.

In the front Scott watched as the ground approached rapidly. He shallowed his dive a little so to reduce the angle at which his bombs would strike the ridge. He noticed several dark openings among the trees and with a little wiggle of the controls put the pipper on his sight directly on one of them.

He hit the release and pulled up and away, half hearing Norris's "lead's off" transmission. He had the impression that he'd seen the guns themselves as the ridge flashed underneath. He called it out.

"Guntrains, the guns are there. The gomers are pulling them back inside. Try to hit the openings."

The next Phantom called "Two's in. FAC and target in sight" and began his dive just as Scott's two bombs detonated on either side of the opening in the hillside.

In Derby 002 Marzetti and Casey watched the lead Phantom climb away, the characteristic white vapor trails streaming from its wings. They half heard the second jet's roll-in call as they waited to see if they'd been right. Scott's bombs struck and must have hit a ready ammunition store, because there was a massive secondary explosion immediately following.

Marzetti couldn't decide which he wanted to do most—sit up there and just watch the Navy jets pound the shit out of those goddamn guns or join in and shoot whatever he had at them too.

But he did neither. He simply sat there in his orbit and kept control of the mission.

46

Thursday, February 8, 1968

"Slug 771, Ghostrider 411's with you. Flight of four. Level sixteen thousand. Squawking 3357."

"Roger, 411. Radar contact. Come left to 250. Feet dry in sixty-eight miles."

"411. Two-five-zero."

Hogan wiggled his tail on the seat for about the fortieth time in the past hour and a half. His left leg was burning and tingling, as if trying to decide whether it should be asleep or not. Hogan had long believed that the designers of these seats simply sat in them for a minute and then got up, pronouncing them comfortable, and then went off in search of that pretty lab assistant they'd just hired. Most pilots endure the pain long enough to develop a "1.5 ass" and can bear sitting in them for about one and a half hours, but one minute later their tails begin to protest and become increasingly uncomfortable and thus let their owners know that it's time to land this thing and get out. When the pilot fails to heed this dictum, their butts simply turn up the pain.

The other problem is that the seats are alleged to be designed for the anthropomorphic average. In all the years he'd been flying, Hogan had never met anybody who was close to being the average. So everybody had to sit in the jets and suffer, while, on the other side of the world, the designer got to try his luck with the lab assistant.

Hogan looked around at the other three Skyhawks hanging out there in loose formation in the low sunlight. The dark green Mk-82 five-hundred-pound bombs with the pipelike fuse extenders protruding from their noses hung menacingly under their wings. The extenders would detonate the bombs just above the ground, turning the weapons into "daisy cutters," which would send out their fragments over a wide swath and into any "soft" targets, like maybe troops they found nearby.

Down below, the cloud deck looked just as solid as it had the day before, but the weather-guessers swore that it was clearing overland. Hogan hoped that they were right, because he did not want to have to waste four more loads of bombs, dumping them into the sea.

"411, Slug. Right turn now to 265. Contact Hillsborough on 334.7 now. Feet dry in five miles."

"411, roger switching."

Hogan rolled out on the new heading and waggled his wings as he changed frequencies. The other aircraft spread out into a much wider tactical formation and assumed the general course of 265. There was actually little threat of antiaircraft fire in the South, but there was no sense banking on that, so the pilots spread out and began to move up and down and left and right, never flying straight and level for more than ten seconds. It was a good habit to cultivate and, when the air wing eventually went back to flying over the much more dangerous North, it was a very bad habit to forget.

Hogan looked down at his TACAN indicator and noticed that

according to the needles, he was now crossing the coast. He keyed his radio and got the "ripple check" from his flight.

"Ghostriders."

"Two."

"Three."

"Four."

"Hillsborough, Ghostrider 411 and flight are with you at sixteen thousand. Four Skyhawks fragged for Blackhorse."

"Roger, 411. Radar contact. There are two Marine flights ahead of you, one coming overhead Blackhorse now. Current altimeter is estimated to be 29.98."

"Roger. 29.98."

Hogan glanced down at his barometric altimeter and saw that it was set at 29.96. He left it alone, since what he'd gotten was an estimate and thus probably off a little. If what he had set was a lower value than the real one, any altimeter error would be in his favor—if it were wrong, the instrument would read lower than he really was. Errors the other way could be fatal.

He sat back and wiggled his tail again. Damn these seats!

Averitt lasted less than five minutes in the new CP. He sat there, listening to the noise of the battle for the hill and felt the ground shaking around the position. Sand continually leaked down on him from the layers of bags that made up the improvised roof, greater or lesser amounts of it according to the size of the shells that were now coming down on the small hill as rapidly as anything seen so far all night. Or at any time since he'd come out to the Khe Sanh area.

He got up and, carrying his radio, moved closer to the entrance, turning his back on the close confines of the bunker. He turned the volume up as high as it would go and tried to get a picture of what was happening, but the noise of the barrage overwhelmed any sound he might get from the small set.

He turned to Gorton and shouted over the din. "I can't figure out what the hell's happening from here. I'm goin' outside into the trench. You stay here with the radio."

Gorton just started at him, and when the major got outside, he found Gorton right next to him.

"I said, stay inside, dammit!"

"You think you're the only one who can't stand waiting for the fucking gooks to knock on the door?"

Averitt turned back and tried to make some sense of what little he could hear from the CP. Off to the right there was a tremendous amount of small-arms fire going on, rising and falling almost rhythmically. In front and to the left the fire was much more intense, interspersed with the dim *thoom*-pause-*blamm* of the grenade launchers and the heavier chugging of the M-60s. There was also the flat sound of many AK-47s.

Averitt, overwhelmed for a moment by the chaos, didn't notice that he could now see a little definition in the darkness. It was definitely getting lighter but the enemy didn't seem to notice that their ally was deserting them.

He turned to Gorton. "See if you can get a hold of that gunship and get him to hit the perimeter. I'm going up to the line."

Averitt climbed over the sandbag wall and ran as hard as he could the forty yards to the main trench line on the west side of the hill. He saw the trench almost clearly and jumped for it. His forward momentum carried him hard against the far wall, and he slammed his ribs into the sandbags, knocking the wind out of himself. He lay for a moment on the wooden floor of the trench amid the spent rifle cartridges and the legs of the marines firing at the enemy.

He dragged himself to his feet and looked over the sandbags just in time to duck under a body that fell half in and half out of the trench. He stood back up, and saw the last few seconds of an enemy charge against the position. On either side of him the enemy had reached the line and were either tossing in grenades or jumping down, rifles blazing. Most of the early few were quickly cut down but more kept coming. For every one who got into the trench, a marine went down, reducing the defensive fire and ensuring that the next group would come in to stay.

Averitt could see that there was no way that the few marines left could hold the position, so he yelled for those close by to pull back. The marines passed the command down and climbed out over the back, most flopping down behind the rear sandbag wall and continuing their fire into the enemy.

Averitt grabbed the man next to him, who had been hit trying to climb out, and threw him bodily over the wall. He put his foot in a crevice in the wall and tried to haul himself over but felt a blow to his left leg followed by blinding pain. He rolled onto his back and shoved the muzzle of his rifle into the helmeted face of an enemy soldier who was just beginning to climb over the sandbags, and fired. The soldier rocked back, then fell forward into the trench at Averitt's feet, and lay still, leaving his helmet lying on top of the wall.

Averitt slumped back against the trench wall as he examined his leg. The leg of his fatigues wasn't torn and there was no blood, but his thigh throbbed as if he had been kicked by a horse. He glanced over at the face of the enemy he'd just killed. His eyes were half open, showing just the lower third of his irises. There was a blackened hole just under his left cheekbone where Averitt's bullet had gone in and the muzzle blast had destroyed more of the skin. This was as close as Averitt had ever come to the enemy, and he was surprised that he felt nothing at all for the dead man sharing this small part of the trench with him. He wondered for a moment at that but put it away for later, when his humanity had time to come back into the open.

He crawled over to the firestep and pulled himself up, finally getting himself out of the trench. He became aware again of the shouts and sounds of battle. Reaching down, he picked up his rifle and checked the action for dirt. He replaced the now-empty magazine and let the bolt slam forward. He was ready again.

For what seemed like hours but really was only three minutes, the fight went on, the two sides separated by the width of the sandbags. Occasional grenades flew over the wall but either went too long and exploded harmlessly or were thrown back by the marines. Whenever an NVA stuck his head up to take a peek, it was met by M-16 fire or by a clubbed rifle stock. It was apparent that things could not stay this way for long—either the enemy would figure out a new plan or he would receive reinforcements that would flank the unprotected marines. Either way, Averitt knew that they were screwed if they stayed there any longer. He gave the order to fall back to the secondary trenches around the bunkers.

The enemy fire slackened a little and the marines withdrew by turns farther back toward the crest of the hill, covering each other carefully. Averitt got to his feet and found that the best he could do was a fast hobble over the broken ground. He stepped on something soft and his leg gave way. He fell forward, halfway between the marines in their new positions and the enemy now trying to climb out of the trench, and began to crawl as fast as he could. He was nearly to the new position when he felt himself lifted off the ground and heaved forward toward the marine line. Hands reached out to pull him in, and he dropped nearly on his face among the small group of marines. Gorton landed right next to him and, still panting, looked him over.

"You all right?"

"Yeah. Thanks, Sarn't Major."

Averitt twisted around and looked out at the enemy. They were still halted at the old trench line and seemed to be regrouping for another try, and the artillery fire seemed to have eased up since the enemy had taken the first trench line. He looked back at Gorton.

"Did you get the gunship?"

"Should be here anytime now. I told 'em to hose down this side of the hill."

"Any idea what's going on anywhere else?"

"I still hear a lot of firing, so there's still gotta be somebody holding out. I called for the platoons on the back side of the hill to get over here, but most of 'em had to go off to the right because the gomers had broken through there first. It looks like it's just us for now. I got a hold of the colonel and told him what was happening. He says to hang on; he's trying to get us some help. There's some reinforcements being heloed in."

"I hope so." Averitt looked around at the few men he had with him. "I sure as hell hope so."

Just as Scott hit the bomb release on his fourth run at the guns, he felt a series of jolts deep in the airframe. The aircraft shuddered a little but kept on. He pressed the release and pulled up and away, slamming his throttles forward. He could hear Norris breathing over the intercom as he grunted against the G forces.

"Are we okay?" asked Norris.

Scott scanned his instrument panel and saw nothing wrong. "Yeah. I don't see anything. There's no lights on."

Scott guided the big fighter back up into the pattern his flight had established over the target. He again looked his instruments over and still saw that everything was normal. He keyed the radio.

"Guntrain Flight, lead took some hits on the last pass. Heads up."

The second aircraft in the flight came off its run without incident and the pilot, Lieutenant Art Van Metre, looked up and ahead at Scott's jet leaving a white trail behind.

"Skipper, you're losing something. Stay high and I'll look you over."

"Click-click."

Van Metre cut across the circle and slid into formation just to the left of Scott's Phantom. He stabilized in position and looked carefully at the underside of the aircraft and saw nothing. He slid smoothly down and under, crossing to the right side. What he saw chilled him.

"Skipper, you've got some real ragged holes in the belly. Your tank is pretty chewed up too. Pickle it."

Van Metre eased out to the side a little ways and moved forward a few feet. "I'm clear."

Scott jettisoned his centerline external fuel tank and watched Van Metre's F-4 ease back down and aft.

Van Metre looked again at the belly of Scott's Phantom. With the drop tank out of the way, he got a better look at the damage.

"Okay. You've got three large holes. One is to the right of your starboard forward Sparrow bay, around the front part of your right engine. There's also a bigger hole about halfway back to the tail-pipe, which is streaming something white. The last hole is about six inches across, in the center of your right stabilator. I think we oughta call it a day."

Scott looked hard again at his instruments and still saw nothing wrong, but there was no sense pressing his luck.

"002, Guntrain 207's heading out with 202 as escort. Request permission to jettison the remaining bombs."

Marzetti looked around at the area underneath Scott's two aircraft and saw nothing but green-sided ridges. "Roger. Go ahead and drop where you are."

Van Metre moved out and forward again and waited for Scott's command. He jettisoned his own remaining bombs when he got it and slid farther out to a reasonably safe escort position.

Scott returned all his armament switches to safe and keyed his radio, telling the other two Phantoms in his flight to continue with their remaining weapons runs and then to return home to the ship. He glanced at his TACAN indicator and thought about his options. He could head for Danang or Chu Lai and land there if he had any further problems. If everything was still okay, he could then decide whether to pass up landing ashore and continue on to the ship. It was the white stuff coming out of his aircraft that worried him. He had no idea what it was—oil, fuel, hydraulic fluid, or smoke—but whatever it was, it certainly wasn't good. The more he thought about it, the better the idea of landing ashore seemed. He called Norris in the backseat.

"Randy, I think we're going to put it down at Danang and check it out. I don't like the leak."

"Sounds like a plan. Do you have any indications up there?"

"No. Nothing. Everything looks fine and it's handling all right."

"Yeah, Danang's a good idea. It might be tough to explain how come we had to jump out halfway to the ship after having over-flown a couple of easy landing sites. Besides, we can get a beer or five while we wait for them to fix it. Overnight of course. We can use some of your Skipper pay."

"Right. Okay, check us out with the FAC and in with the Air Force."

Norris depressed his radio foot switch. "Derby 002, Guntrain 207's departing your area in company with 202. Frequency change."

Marzetti was watching the last runs by the two remaining fighters. "Roger, frequency change approved. I'll pass your BDA through my Ops people, but for now it appears that you've taken out the guns. Contact Hillsborough on, um, 265.8 for radar following. Good day and thanks for your help."

"You're welcome, Derby. 207 and 202 switching two-sixty-five-point-eight."

Marzetti turned his attention back to the target. He watched the last Phantom pull up and away from the target and saw the two large brown-black explosions erupt from the hillside as the twin shock waves spread out for a hundred yards or so on either side of the explosions and their smoke was added to the already impressive cloud drifting off to the east. He wondered idly for about the hundredth time where all the smoke from this war went. There had to be a huge cloud of it drifting around the planet somewhere.

He shook his head as he heard the lead Phantom of the remaining pair call.

"Derby 002, Diamond 112. We're Winchester at this time. Request BDA and clearance out of the area."

"Winchester" was the pilot's word for out of ammunition.

"Roger, 112. I'll pass your BDA through my Ops people. You're cleared to depart to the southeast and contact Hillsborough on 265.8 for radar following. Thanks for your help this morning."

"265.8 and you're welcome. 112 switching."

Marzetti eased his orbit over to the east a little and looked down at the ruined ridge below. He set himself up for a run out of the north to check the effectiveness of the strike. One of the chief jobs of the FAC was to assess that effectiveness, which meant diving through the gunfire from the now thoroughly pissed off enemy gunners for a look at what had been the target they were charged with protecting. It was not something you did blithely or a second time.

"You ready for this?" he asked Casey.

"Yeah, sure. I can't wait."

"Okay, here we go."

Marzetti rolled the Skyhawk over and pulled the nose toward the ground far below. When the red scar on the ridge was generally on the nose, he rolled back upright and aimed the flight path a little to the left. It was only a couple of seconds before the gunners on the ground woke up and shifted their aim from where they expected the next aircraft to approach to Marzetti's A-4.

In the backseat Casey didn't have the benefit of being able to control anything, so he tried his best to peer around Marzetti's seat at the ground. He rhythmically shifted his eyes back in at the altimeter and called out the altitudes which were passing by at an increasing rate. He felt the nose come up and the dive shallow out and looked out to the right in time to see the target pass by. He was pressed back in his seat as Marzetti rammed the throttle to the stop and hauled back on the stick, simultaneously banking the aircraft right over the crest of the ridge.

The climb and bank gave Casey an extra couple of seconds with a good view of the shattered side of the ridge. He could see several of the holes in which the guns were supposed to be sheltered with their entrances deformed and, in a couple of instances, the ridge seemed to have collapsed over them.

At least four guns were completely dismounted from their carriages and were lying on their sides. Two others looked almost intact from this distance, but their wheels were flat, so at least some damage had been inflicted. There was no sign of any others, so either they had been successfully pulled back underground or they hadn't been there in the first place.

Except for the Triple-A, which was now falling well behind, there was no sign of life. It looked pretty much like the other hundreds of scars of war that were left all over this part of the world.

"Well?"

Casey wiggled his oxygen mask on his sweaty face. "I think it'll be a while before that battery is back in action. I'd say we got most of 'em anyway."

"Okay. We'll see if we can get reconnaissance overflights to get some pictures. Let's go home. You have the aircraft. Going cold mike."

Casey took the stick and shook it gently. "I've got it."

He pulled his dark visor down and turned the little A-4 eastward. He switched the radio to the frequency for Hillsborough, and when the radio channelizer tone stopped, the first thing they heard was an emergency beeper, the kind that was installed in the seat pans of military jets and are activated by the ejection of the crew.

47

Thursday, February 8, 1968

"Skipper, you've got black smoke coming out of that hole now!"

Scott whipped his eyes across the instrument panel and still saw no indication of trouble. He banked the Phantom a little and looked in the mirrors attached to the canopy bow. Behind the aircraft he could see a thin stream of black merging with the exhaust from his engines. A flash of red caught his eye and he looked back at his instrument panel just in time to see the fire light come on. He reached over and pulled the inboard throttle to idle and then all the way to the cutoff position. Then he turned off the engine master switch which shut off the fuel, and hoped.

In the back Norris had checked his own mirrors and had seen

the same thing as Scott. He felt the jet decelerate as Scott shut down the right engine, and checked that his shoulder harness was locked. He glanced down at the ejection selector and saw that it was in the proper position, "single" for now, and touched the black and yellow handle between his thighs. If things got very much worse, he would have to remember to switch to "both," because with Scott wrestling with a dying aircraft, it would be Norris's responsibility to eject both men from the aircraft. It looked like that very well might happen. Norris wasn't really enthusiastic about ejecting and finding out if all that bailout training actually worked.

When Scott's aircraft slowed abruptly, Van Metre had to make a couple of quick moves to stay in position. Once he had everything back to normal, he looked up and cursed as he watched the smoke continue to pour out of the right engine. He knew that Scott had shut the thing down and that should have taken care of the fire. The smoke should have rapidly diminished in intensity, but as Van Metre watched, the smoke actually became thicker and blacker.

The Phantom was easily capable of flying on one engine so if Scott could get the fire out and if nothing else went wrong, they should be able to make it to the long runways at Danang. But the Phantom was not equipped with on-board engine fire extinguishers, so the only thing that could be done was to try to remove the fuel from the fire and let airflow blow it out. That didn't seem to be working at all.

"Skipper, the fire's still burning. It looks like it's getting worse."

On the instrument panel, the fire light continued to glow with the intensity that only that one particular indicator seems to have for pilots. Scott cursed the goddamned little ignorant gomer son of a bitch who had hit him with a lucky shot and put this hugely expensive aircraft and two infinitely more valuable asses, his and Norris's, in this jam. Although somewhat personally therapeutic, the cursing did nothing about the fire.

Norris saw the TACAN needle which pointed to the low-power transmitter at Khe Sanh swing past the 270-degree relative position, telling him that they had passed south of the combat base and were now clearing the area to the east. He switched channels to 77, which was the station at Danang, and watched the needle swing around the dial a couple of times until it found the station and then point directly to it. The mileage window, or DME, stopped at 95. He looked at the chart on his kneeboard and then at the terrain below them which was about to be swallowed up in the trailing edge of the cloud deck. He didn't like what he saw and told Scott.

"Skipper, Danang's on the TACAN and bears 135 at 95. If we go direct from here, we'll be over mountains for most of the way. There's also a lot of gomers down there. It's a little longer if we head direct for the coast and then go south over the water, but if we have to get out, we'll have a better chance."

Scott thought that over. Norris was right, and judging from the fact that the original problem was showing no signs of getting better, the key was that he would much rather eject into a rice paddy or the sea than onto a forested mountainside.

"Okay, straight for the coast it is. Coming back left to 090."

He eased the Phantom to the left and settled back on his original course. He reached down and tugged on his lap harness and then moved his tail up against the seat. Things could go wrong very quickly, and he wanted to reduce the number of small things he would need to think about. Proper body position for ejection was one of them.

"Randy, put the selector in 'both.' If we have to go, I'll either tell you to do it or give you a count. Stay ready."

"Roger that, Skipper. Selector's in 'both.'"

Norris reached down by his left knee and moved the selector handle to the forward position. Now when either crewman pulled their handle they would both go in sequence.

Well out over the water, Doug McCarthy had been following the Guntrain flight through all the frequency changes. He hadn't anything else to do really. The only aircraft from the *Shiloh* that were airborne were Scott's four fighters and Hogan's Skyhawks. He was now listening in on the frequency Scott had switched to.

He watched his radarscope and followed the Phantom's progress. He saw the heading change to the southeast and then change back again due east. That small maneuver told him that a decision had been made in the cockpit to head straight for the coast and the sea beyond, which in the minds of naval aviators equated with relative safety. It also told him that the aircraft was in enough trouble to be thinking about a possible ejection. The hit 207 had taken had to have caused a problem which was getting worse. He told the other two radar officers sitting on either side of him that he'd be monitoring 207's progress and that they should handle everything else for a while, and then keyed his radio.

"Hillsborough, Slug 771 on 265.8."

"Go ahead, 771."

"Roger, sir, I'll be up this frequency if you need any help with 207."

"Hillsborough copies. Thank you. Are you aware of his situation?"

"That's affirm. I've been monitoring."

"Roger that, 771. Remain this freq."

"Click-click."

Major Dick Averitt ducked as a burst of rifle fire tore into the sandbags next to his head. He popped back up and emptied his M-16 in the general direction of the source. He wasn't sure that he'd hit anything, but there was no answering burst of fire.

Alongside him were the remnants of the marine platoon that had held this section of the line. He had no idea how many of his men were still on their feet, but he had seven men here not including himself and Gorton and there was still a pretty good volume of fire coming from the other positions to the right and left.

One of the men with him was the platoon sergeant who had volunteered to be the artillery spotter earlier. He was now trying to fire his rifle one-handed because his left arm hung uselessly at his side. Seeing that reminded Averitt of his own leg which was now throbbing heavily. Whatever had hit him caused a small gash on the side of his thigh and a huge bruise. He found he could use it to stand and it would support a sort of gimpy walk.

He ejected the magazine from his rifle and fished in his bandolier for another, becoming acutely aware that he was running dangerously low. He yelled at the marines to conserve ammo and was met with a couple of "no shit, sir" glances. The marines went right back to the measured bursts they had been using in the first place.

He peeked through a chink in the sandbags at the old trench line and saw that only a couple of the enemy were firing as if to keep the marines occupied while the rest did something else. He yelled at the marines to watch the flanks of their position and moved over to Gorton.

"They're up to something over there. I think they're gonna either flank us with grenades or try another charge like they did last time."

Gorton thought for a moment and nodded. "Yeah, you're right. I'll post a man out a little ways on both sides and we'll start throwing grenades of our own over toward the trench. It ought to slow 'em down some."

Averitt leaned back against the sandbags and reached for the radio. "I'll see if the fucking Air Force is finished with breakfast yet."

Gorton smiled. "Don't tell me you're getting pissed off at the flyboys like the rest of us."

Averitt growled. "I'm against anybody who's not trying to hold this hill right now. I'll sort 'em out later. Let's see if the gunship is back yet."

He keyed the radio. "Spooky, this is Lima Six, over."

"Six, this is Spooky. We're about two minutes out. We're starting to get some decent visibility down there. Can you mark your position with a smoke?"

"That's affirm. Stand by."

Averitt looked around frantically for a smoke grenade and couldn't find one amid the debris and population in the trench. He yelled, "Anybody got a smoke?"

There were horrified glances from everyone who heard him, and it dawned on him that they thought he was asking for a cigarette.

"No. A smoke grenade. We gotta mark out position for the gunship."

One of the marines fumbled around and handed Averitt a dark green cylinder. Averitt looked at the yellow writing on the side. He noticed that he could now read it easily in the morning light and that the color of the smoke was supposed to be purple.

He pulled the pin and got ready to toss the thing over the sandbags but stopped himself. He leaned back and threw it as hard as he could toward the enemy trench and then picked up the radio again.

"Spooky, the enemy position is marked. Put your fire down on the other trench line. We've been driven back to the interior. We still hold the bunkers, but the gomers have got the trench."

There was a pause. Then, "Spooky has your purple."

"Roger, purple it is." One of the little rules in combat is that you let the aircraft call out the color of the smoke. That prevents the enemy from heaving out captured smoke grenades to match the color you just announced you were going to throw.

The enemy suddenly burst from the trench in two places to either side of the marines' small position. Gorton yelled a warning and opened fire along with the rest of the marines.

Averitt could hear the bullets cracking overhead as he lay the forestock of his weapon on the top sandbag and fired it in short bursts at individual enemy soldiers. Most went down, but he had to swing back to two who were coming in from the right. He ejected one magazine and shoved in another, his last.

He fired a few rounds at another group of the enemy who burst out of their trench as a sort of second wave, but they were quickly cut down by M-60 fire from a neighboring position. With nothing left to do for the moment, he grabbed the radio and was about to call the C-47, when he saw the ground between him and the enemy position erupt in hundreds of small brown geysers from the gunship's miniguns.

Averitt turned, put down the radio, and looked up just in time to see a khaki-clad figure run toward the position from the left rear. Before he could raise his rifle, he heard the heavier sound of Gorton's M-14 as the sergeant major shot the man. But as the NVA fell, he heaved a dark object that looked very strangely like a purse.

The bag struck the ground about ten feet from the position and bounced toward the Americans twice, the last landing only about four feet away. Averitt realized what it was just in time to drop to the floor of the trench and scream, "Satchel charge!"

The charge detonated with a roar that was more felt than heard, and Averitt was aware of the sandbag wall flying in on him before he lost consciousness.

At first Scott thought that his eyes were lying to him. It took what seemed to be seconds for their message to be accepted by his brain. There were now *two* fire lights on his instrument panel glowing. The fire had bled across to the other J-79.

At the same instant he realized that, Van Metre confirmed the worst—the fire was now out of control. He chopped the throttle to the left engine and turned off that engine master switch, then deployed his emergency ram air generator and got back some electrical power. But the big fighter was dying. It would either explode when the fire reached the fuel or would become completely unflyable when one of the control cables burned through. It was time to go and, for the first time in his flying career, Scott was going to have to bail out. A loud "shit" was all he could muster.

"202, we're ejecting."

Van Metre had slid ahead of Scott's jet when the thrust from the second engine disappeared, and accelerated up and around the stricken fighter as his backseater, Lieutenant Jake Lamb, strained to keep 207 in sight.

Scott leaned back against the headrest and lowered his chin so as to keep his spine in the proper position for the huge kick he was about to get. Norris knew what was coming even before Scott said anything and had gotten himself into the right position and brought his hands across his body so they wouldn't hit anything on the way out. This is *not* what I want to be doing, he thought.

Scott raised the nose, slowed the Phantom to nearly 200 knots, and grabbed the yellow and black handle between his thighs. He announced over the intercom the last warning. "Okay, Randy. Ejecting. Three ... two ... one ... now!"

He grasped his right wrist with his left hand and pulled up on the handle. He heard the air charge blow the rear canopy off and then the heavy bang as Norris's seat fired.

The time expanded so much for Scott that he was wondering what the hell was wrong with his seat and why the hell hadn't it fired and was he really gonna die trapped in this fucking airplane, when his canopy blew off and his seat fired exactly four-tenths of a second after Norris's seat had blown him clear.

The windblast even at a paltry 200 knots slammed into him and jogged him around. He didn't feel himself separate from the seat and thought it was taking an awfully long time, when the parachute opened with a hard jerk at both his crotch and his chest. He let out the air he'd been holding, and when he tried to inhale found that he couldn't breathe because the emergency oxygen bottle in his seat had failed to activate. He reached up for the fittings on his mask and noticed that he still had the ejection handle in his hand.

He threw the handle away and frantically unfastened the fittings on his mask, pulling it free. As he gulped in some air, he cursed himself for throwing away the handle that he'd always sworn he was going to keep for a souvenir if he ever had to eject. His next thought was that he'd better check his 'chute, and when he looked up and found that to be working as advertised, he looked down to see where he was going to come down.

Below was a thin gray layer of cloud, the last remnants of the weather that had nullified the American advantage at Khe Sanh. Scott was trying to see through the holes in the cloud, when he drifted into it and felt the cool water droplets caress his face. For just a moment the sound of Van Metre's F-4 circling above faded out as he fell through the gray mist. He was aware of a strange clinking sound from the parachute above and of his own breathing. It was as if he were suspended in another dimension.

Abruptly he was through the cloud and could see the land below. It appeared that he was still about six or seven thousand feet above the dozens of clearings and rice paddies that stretched ahead of him as far as he could see. He realized that in noticing the clearings with so much hope, he was ignoring the larger percentage of the terrain that was still covered with forests.

Scott looked over his shoulder and could see Norris's parachute below and behind him. In the far western distance the sun shone down on the highlands with that special gold that only the morning sun after the rain seems to have. He looked back to his front and judged that he was headed for one of the larger clearings, which was part dry pasture and part rice paddy. The only question now was whether he was going to land in the muck of a paddy.

Scott looked back at Norris and saw his raft drop from his seat pan and inflate. Good idea, he thought, and released his own. The raft would give him an idea of how high he was from the ground, and he no longer needed that stuff since he wasn't going to land in the sea. On the other hand, releasing his raft wouldn't really do much to improve his situation, but it was something to do as he drifted along toward the ground pretty much powerless to help himself for the moment.

Scott was alternating between looking around for anybody who looked like an enemy, trying to figure out where he was going to land, and trying to remember the procedures for making an injury-free landing. It was now apparent that he was going to land in one of the paddies, and he had a moment of panic when he remembered snatches of survival school lectures about the enemy seeding the paddies with poisoned bamboo stakes known as punji sticks.

For a moment he let that fear carry him away, and he unconsciously tried to climb up the risers of his parachute. He stopped and forced himself to calm down by calculating the odds of this paddy being seeded by punji sticks and then his landing on one and receiving a bamboo enema. He had almost succeeded, when he noticed that the ground was coming at him much faster, an illusion caused by his proximity to it. He grabbed his risers and twisted his body around so as to be facing away from his direction of travel and thus avoid smashing his face into the ground when he hit.

Scott felt the raft strike the paddy and had enough time to get his knees and ankles together, slightly bent, before he plunged into the brown muck of the paddy. He struggled to the surface of the water and stood up, releasing the parachute fittings on his torso harness as he did. He looked around and saw that he was pretty far from any treelines and so should be fairly easy to find and rescue. He spotted Norris hobbling toward him along the dike that separated this paddy from the others.

Scott looked up, saw Van Metre's Phantom approach from the west and fly over, wagging its wings, and waved that he was all right, fumbling in his survival equipment vest for his portable radio.

He was having a lot of trouble with the zipper when Norris came up and stopped on the dike. He looked down at Scott and laughed.

"What the fuck is so damn funny, Norris?"

"Skipper, you look like you're trying out for an Al Jolson movie. And if you don't mind, I'll try to avoid being downwind of you."

Norris moved away a few feet and Scott looked at himself for the first time. He was completely covered with a black-brown muck from the bottom of the paddy, and then he smelled the stuff. It struck him that this was the product of thousands of years of human and bovine excrement, as it had been so delicately described in survival school, and now he had been thoroughly dipped in it. He looked at Norris's laughing face and still failed to see the humor.

"Get out your radio, goddammit, and get us some help. And help me out of here."

He reached his hand out to Norris, but had to wait while, with exaggerated care, the young RIO put his flight glove back on and pulled him out. Norris chuckled and, before Scott could ask, said, "Skipper, I want you to remember this for my next fitness report. I was the guy who pulled you out of the shit."

48
Thursday, February 8, 1968

✦ Hogan was completing his fifth—or was it his sixth—lap around the holding pattern he'd established. The other three Skyhawks hung out there off his wings just following him around until there was room for the four Ghostriders to join in the close air support of the combat base.

There is an amazing hypnotic effect to holding patterns and listening to an aircraft radio. There are all sorts of sounds, hisses and pops and clicks, that one doesn't really hear consciously and tend to become only a sort of background. When the radio fails, the silence of their absence invariably becomes astonishingly loud.

Over this background are dozens of transmissions on your frequency, from somebody to somewhere else, none of which are really relevant to you or your future so you kind of tune them out, leaving a small part of your mind on sentry duty in case the combination of sounds which is your own call sign comes by. When it does, the small sentry runs round, giving the alarm and rousting out the rest of the parts that are engaged in pursuits far more useful, well, more pleasurable, anyway.

As he flew around the holding pattern, Hogan had been thinking about the Blonde from Singapore, an occupation that was beginning to draw quite a crowd of other mind parts that happened to be passing by and, attracted by the whistles and cheers of the growing crowd, stopped in to watch the picture show. Many of the good parts were shown over and over, just so they could be examined more thoroughly and enjoyed more.

Lots and lots of mind parts had made themselves comfortable when the sentry came tearing into the theater, blowing his horn and yelling something about an aircraft in trouble. In Hogan's

400

mind there were very disciplined parts indeed—they were taking action even before the sentry ran out of breath and wound down.

"Mayday! Mayday! This is Guntrain 202. Guntrain 207 is down on the Peacock TACAN's 350 degree radial at 66. Two good 'chutes. Request RESCAP and a helo."

Van Metre's transmission had been on the guard, or emergency, channel which all military aircraft monitored. Hogan glanced at his TACAN indicator which was tuned to the small lower-powered station at Khe Sanh. He spun the selector wheel to Danang's, or "Peacock's," Channel 77 and watched while the needle and the DME stopped spinning. He noted his position from Danang and spun the selector back to Khe Sanh, remembering to select the proper position so as not to damage the system. When the needle was again pointed at Khe Sanh, he switched on the distance mode and began his outbound leg in holding. All this took less than thirty seconds.

"Hillsborough, Ghostrider 411 is available for RESCAP if required. We're presently about thirty miles north of 207's last position."

"Roger that, 411. Stand by."

In the back of the Air Force EC-121 radar aircraft, the controller ran his hand over his face. He'd been up there for seven hours, doing his thankless job, and was getting very tired. There had been no letup in the number of sorties flying around the embattled country of South Vietnam for the past week, and even now, with the enemy on the run, every controller in the 121 was up to his ass in aircraft. He himself had about a dozen under his control and the rescue effort was going to be an even further demand. With the weather breaking, the remainder of this mission was going to be a zoo. He looked eastward out over the Gulf of Tonkin and saw the little lighted blip of the Navy E-2.

"Slug 771, this is Hillsborough. Request."

McCarthy had been watching the whole drama of Guntrain 207 unfold and was itching to do something to help. The Phantom was from his air wing and, as such, was one of "us."

"Hillsborough, Slug. Go ahead."

"Roger. Guntrain 207 is down with two good 'chutes. The only possible RESCAPs I have are four Alpha fours, Ghostrider 411 and flight. Can you take over the SAR coordinator? I have nobody available at this time."

McCarthy fiddled with his scope and found the Ghostriders and Van Metre's Phantom. "That's affirm, Hillsborough. Request you switch the Ghostriders to this freq and I'll coordinate. How 'bout a helo?"

"There should be a Super Gaggle passing by pretty soon. I'll do what I can."

"Okay, Hillsborough. I've got it."

"Hillsborough, roger. You have the airspace surface to twelve thousand within six nautical miles of the site. I'll keep that clear for you except for the helo. Out."

McCarthy asked the pilots over the ICS to move the E-2's holding pattern farther south and to contact the *Shiloh* and tell them what was going on. He waited a couple of heartbeats, drawing up his own plan before he keyed his radio.

"Guntrain 202, Slug."

"Go ahead."

"Roger, 202. Slug 771 is now the SAR coordinator. I have you in radar contact. Request sitrep."

In the backseat of Van Metre's Phantom, his RIO, Jake Lamb, consulted his kneeboard and keyed the radio. He had forgotten the format for this particular kind of situation report and had no desire to take the time to pull out his "gouge book" and look it up, so he made up a format. "Slug 771, Guntrain 202. Sitrep follows. Guntrain 207 is down on the Peacock TACAN 350 at 66. There were two good 'chutes and both survivors appear to be in good shape. They have joined up on the ground in an open area of rice paddies. There has been no hostile activity so far. How copy?"

"Slug 771 copies all."

"Roger. 202 has no comms with either crewman so far. 202 has one-five mikes left on station and will have to divert to Danang for fuel."

"Slug 771, roger. One-five mikes. We've got some relief for you on the way."

Lamb looked again at his fuel calculations. "One-five mikes" was fifteen minutes. At the low altitude they were flying, the huge J-79 engines were gulping fuel, and a quarter hour was slightly on the optimistic side of a strict interpretation of the endurance charts.

*　　*　　*

Hogan waited impatiently for somebody to get back to him. He was torn between his desires—to both help out the marines and a shipmate. He was pretty sure that 207 was Chris Scott's jet, but in any event, it was a *Shiloh* aircraft, so he decided to compromise—he'd take his wingman down to help out as a RESCAP and leave the other two to press on to Khe Sanh. The area down below was filled with small detachments of the enemy, but after the crushing defeat they'd suffered in their Tet Offensive and their disorganized retreat, there was absolutely no accurate intelligence on who was where with how many. In any event, it was far less dangerous for the crew of 207 than going down in the North would have been.

"Ghostrider 411, Hillsborough. Are you RESCAP capable?"

"That's affirm, Hillsborough."

"Roger. Switch 265.8 and contact Slug 771 for control."

"Hillsborough, 411, roger. Do you want me to split the flight and leave a section with you for the original mission?"

There was a pause. "That's negative, 411. On my scope here it looks like the world's longest conga line heading up this way. We'll be able to cover the gap. Hillsborough out."

"Roger, 411's switching." He spun the selector and waited a few seconds.

All three of his charges checked in instantly, so he called the E-2 and was given a steer toward the position where Scott and Norris now sat glumly and increasingly more tiredly, munching on Charms candy from their survival packs and trying to conserve water from the baby bottles they'd stashed in their gear and various pockets.

Norris screwed the top on his bottle of water and stuffed it in his vest. It was his second of the four he always carried and was less than a quarter full. He had been surprised at how thirsty he had been when the adrenaline of the mission and the ejection had ebbed. He was slipping into a mild depression sitting there in the early morning sun, and kept looking at the distant treeline for the hordes of enemy he knew were lurking there, just waiting for fifty or sixty thousand reinforcements to come out and shoot him and then drag his ass off to Hanoi.

After their initial first few passes over him and Scott, Van Metre and Lamb had climbed to a more reasonable altitude and had throttled back to conserve fuel. Norris knew that Van Metre didn't have much more time left to stay and cover them, and he hoped that somebody would get there most skosh to take over. The thought of being on the ground all alone did little to ease Norris's mood.

To his left on the dike and downwind sat Scott, who was feeling even worse. The muck was drying fast on his exposed skin despite his best efforts to wipe it off, and as it dried it smelled worse than it had in a liquid state. He didn't remember this being covered in any of the survival schools.

Norris's radio sat silently between them. After the initial bursts of chatter between them and 202, they had all quickly run out of things to say, and now everybody was waiting for something—anything—to happen. Well, not anything, thought Scott. He'd prefer to sit there for days if the other choice was capture by the local enemy, who would probably be in a very foul mood, given the ass-kicking they'd recently received and the failure of the rest of the population to join in their "great revolt."

Scott looked over at Norris, who was sitting there, working another candy from the roll of Charms. Spread on the ground next to him was some of the other gear that had been carefully packed in the small survival kit. Scott looked at a red and white foil package that contained one Trojan rubber contraceptive and chuckled.

Norris turned. "What's so funny?"

Scott held up the package. "This. The survival instructors call it a 'waterproof receptacle' and it always struck me as funny."

Norris took it from Scott and examined it. "Why? It seems to work. I mean, it does hold water and it comes packed small enough."

"Yeah, I know. But can you see yourself stomping around with a rubber full of water? I consider it a survival tester."

"What do you mean?"

"Well, I figure that as soon as I found an opportunity to use the damn thing for what it was designed, I would no longer be in a survival situation."

Norris laughed. "I see what you mean. On the other hand, you could always use it as an extra weapon. It would make a dandy water balloon, but it might just piss off the enemy. Your idea is better. Maybe we can submit it as a 'beneficial suggestion' and get some money for it."

The radio came alive with Lamb's voice, and Norris grabbed it. "Go ahead, 202."

"Okay, 207, we got four Scooters headed your way for RESCAP and they're trying to scare up a helo for you. It might be a while for that though, since most of 'em are committed right now. It was a bad night out in the hills. The call sign for the A-4s is Ghostrider 411. We'll stick around until they have you in sight, then we gotta go."

Norris looked at Scott. "Roger, understand Ghostrider 411. And, uh, be advised the Skipper says that you'd better have enough gas to make it to a runway or your ass is grass. Don't push it. We're fine down here so far."

"202 copies. We'll be okay until RESCAPs get here."

"Click-click."

Norris was just putting the radio down, when something splashed into the water near his left leg. It took two more for him and Scott to realize that the splashes were being caused by bullets. They rolled away to the opposite side of the dike and lay flat. Norris reeled the radio down next to him by the lanyard with which the parariggers had secured the easily lost pieces of survival gear to the pilots' vests, very much like the "idiot mittens" their mothers used to make them wear.

"What the fuck was that?" asked Norris a little unnecessarily.

"It appears to have been rifle fire."

"Well, where the hell is it coming from? Jesus Christ!"

"I don't know. Let me take a look." Scott poked his head over the edge of the dike and scanned the far treeline and the dikes surrounding all the other paddies. He couldn't see anything different from the peaceful scene it had been only seconds before.

"Gimme the radio." Norris began to hand it over and stopped, staring at the large hole in the thing. Scott looked at it too, and pulled his own out of his vest. He switched it on and listened for the shrill hiss of the receiver. It was working as advertised despite its dunking in the muck. He peeked over the dike again and thought he saw a couple of dark figures about halfway between him and the distant line of trees. Whoever they were, they were definitely coming this way, and judging from the way they were deployed, they were from somebody's military.

Gorton pulled his legs from under the pile of sandbags and sat up. He shook his head to clear the deep ringing sound out of his ears and looked around for his rifle. The sandbag wall on this side of the small trench was completely collapsed, and several marines were frantically pulling the sandbags off the pile and throwing them over the side toward the enemy. There were several arms and legs protruding from under the pile and, as he watched, the marines pulled their buried comrades hurriedly from the pile and stood them up. They all were conscious and a little bit dazed.

They searched for their weapons and, one by one, went back to manning their positions. Gorton looked around and couldn't find the major, and he got to his knees just as the diggers pulled the major from under the pile.

They laid him down on the floor of the trench, and one of the marines knelt over him while the other diggers picked up their weapons and got back to work. Gorton crawled over to the major and took a look. He was still breathing and almost immediately began to cough heavily and then rolled over on his side. Gorton looked at the other marine and told him to get back to work, he'd take care of the major. All around the pair, marines were again blazing away at the enemy.

As he looked back down at Averitt, whose eyes were beginning to flutter, Gorton was once again impressed with the discipline of the average marine. They'd taken a major hit from a large satchel charge, recovered enough to dig out their buddies, and then resumed defending themselves, all in less than a minute.

The major groaned and tried to sit up. Gorton helped him and leaned him against the back of the trench, pulling his canteen from his web gear and helping him drink. Averitt coughed and took another drink.

"Where does it hurt, Major?"

"Pick a place." Averitt tried to get to his feet but couldn't even come close to making it.

He looked at Gorton. "Help me up."

Gorton lifted the major to his feet and leaned him against the trench wall.

"Okay, get back to it. I'll be all right."

Averitt looked around as the sergeant major moved to the other end of the trench. He still had as many marines manning the position as he had had before, but these guys looked really beat up. They were covered with red dust, and where they were sweating the dust turned to streaks of mud. Averitt had the wild thought that they'd probably kill for a shower. He looked around for his rifle but couldn't find it, so he pulled his pistol from its holster, checked it over to see that it was relatively clean and undamaged, and then painfully climbed up on a sandbag so he could peer out at the enemy.

Between his position and the old trench line, the ground had been chewed up as if by a giant Vegematic. The passage of the deadly fire from the gunship had, for the moment, blunted the enemy attempts to capture the second line of defenses and however many of them were left were now firing accurately from the old trench line. As Averitt watched, an A-4 came roaring past from the north and two long cylinders of napalm tumbled away from its wings. The jet pulled up and turned away. A horrible red and yellow and black ball of fire climbed slowly into the air outside the wires. Averitt wondered who was controlling the air support and then decided it had to be the FASTFAC overhead.

Gorton came back over to Averitt and pulled him down into the trench.

"Major, I think the gomers have spent themselves, and those guys in the trench over there are just pinning us down while the majority escape. Now, we can either wait here and put up with their sniping and get more guys hurt, or we can take back our trench and throw what's left of the sonsabitches out."

Averitt looked at the sergeant major's fiery expression. "I take it that you'd rather we took the position back?"

"Yep. We can charge from two angles, here and the other position over on the right there. I think we can do it, Major. We'll prep with two volleys of grenades and go right after the second volley. We've still got a couple of M-60s for cover."

Averitt nodded. "Okay. I'll lead this bunch and you can go get the others."

Gorton smiled. "As soon as you see my signal, everybody heaves two grenades and charges." Gorton climbed out of the rear of the trench and dashed across the broken ground to the other position.

Averitt realized that he had no idea what the signal was going to be, but he supposed that it would be obvious. He turned to the other marines in the position and briefed them on the plan. One of them ducked into what was left of the bunker and came out with most of a case of fragmentation hand grenades which he distributed to everyone else. Several marines kept up a harassing fire on the trench, and Averitt alternated between watching the enemy position and looking for Gorton's signal.

407

Suddenly there was a wave from the other trench, and several objects flew toward the enemy. Averitt yelled "Now," and heaved his first grenade.

Before it even landed, he'd pulled the pin on another, and as he cocked his arm to throw, let the spoon fly off. He threw it as hard as he could and felt the muscle in his arm give as it had when he'd tried to play baseball years before. Everybody ducked as the grenades detonated in two ragged waves of sound and flying fragments.

With a shout Averitt led his tiny attack force out of the trench and straight for the enemy position. He could hear the chugging of the two M-60s and the shouts of his few men. Averitt reached the edge of the trench and jumped in, landing on something soft. The next man jumped down beside him and faced the other way.

Neither man saw any enemy, so they made their way cautiously toward the part of the trench where Gorton's men had attacked. There was a sudden burst of firing, which went high over Averitt's head, from a bend in the trench ahead, and he ducked back as one of the marines behind him threw a grenade around the bend. The grenade detonated with a thump, and the marine charged past Averitt and around the corner. There were several quick shots fired, all from M-16s, and the marine came back and gestured to Averitt.

"Position's clear, Major. The gomers're running away. Looks like we held 'em."

Averitt stepped past the man and moved on until he ran into the men from the other wing of the attack. "Where's the sergeant major?"

The marines looked at each other. "Don't know, sir. He was right with us a minute ago."

Averitt pushed past the marines and looked over the back side of the trench. There was a dark bundle lying in the dirt right at the edge. As Averitt watched, the bundle stirred, and, before he could give it another thought, completely forgetting the pain in his leg, Averitt was hobbling toward the sergeant major with as much panic as he'd ever felt.

As he dropped to his knees next to the old marine, he didn't even hear the sound of the helicopters that filled the air behind him.

49

Thursday, February 8, 1968

Hogan spotted Van Metre's Phantom as it climbed away from the rice paddies and banked around to the right.

"202, 411's with you at your five o'clock high."

Van Metre craned his neck and searched the sky above and behind him. He heard Lamb's voice straining against the force of the turn. "I got 'em. Keep your turn in."

"411, 202's got you in sight. We have both crewmen holed up on the side of a dike and they're taking sporadic small-arms fire from the west. Stand by for a mark on top."

Van Metre flew the Phantom around the circle until he was due north of the position of Scott and Norris, then, banking steeply, he flew over the two on the ground. As they passed overhead, Lamb transmitted, "Marking on top . . . now . . . now . . . *now!*"

Hogan watched the Phantom and on the third "now" he scanned the ground below the fighter. He spotted Norris's white helmet and then the two men waving frantically. "411 has a visual."

"202, roger. Be advised we're departing to the east. Low fuel."

"411's got it. Arm 'em up, Ghostriders." Hogan armed his weapons, banked, and flew directly over Scott and Norris, and then broke sharply to his left, followed in sequence by the other three. They set up a wagon-wheel pattern overhead, one jet spaced every ninety degrees of the circle. Now there were always two sets of eyes on the men on the ground, and the enemy would have to expose themselves to the Skyhawks if they made any attempt at capturing them.

For now things were a stalemate. The enemy couldn't get to Scott and Norris as long as the jets were overhead, but the jets were powerless to get the two crewmen out. The only advantage lay with the enemy, since the amount of fuel the jets had, and thus time-on-station, was finite.

Hogan made a couple of relatively low passes, saw nothing threatening the two on the ground, and told them so.

Scott and Norris relaxed a little at that, but only seconds later heard the flat crack of a bullet passing close overhead. Scott grabbed the radio.

"411, somebody's shooting at us! It's coming from the west—the trees, maybe?"

Hogan made his next pass directly over the treeline and saw nothing.

"202, I can't see anybody. Stay low." Hogan mentally kicked himself for saying something that stupid.

"Roger, that. Us and whale shit are the lowest things on earth right now, Hog."

Hogan smiled at Scott's gentle needle and was glad somehow that Scott also knew who was flying cover for him. Now, where was a goddamn helo when you needed one?

He was tempted to call Hillsborough but decided to wait another couple of minutes. He called 771 instead and filled him in on the situation, knowing full well that the information would be passed directly back to the ship and the anxious members of Scott's squadron.

When he heard the emergency beeper, Ben Marzetti had followed the drama across the frequencies. He was now passing just south of where Scott and Norris were sitting, and was having a great deal of trouble staying out of it. He was looking for a reason to help without being meddlesome.

There is an amazing need among military aviators to get involved in things like rescues and searches. It probably stems from the deep and well-concealed knowledge that someday it could well be them in trouble and, if one member of the fraternity let another down, the next guy to be left dangling might be the guy who failed to help. Mixed well in this equation is the quite rational knowledge that too much assistance usually makes things worse, so most pilots will call up and offer to help, and if accepted will be there in a flash but if not, will leave reluctantly, their radio tuned to the on-scene frequency as long as possible.

Marzetti listened for a moment and realized that he had a perfect reason to get involved—he was a professional searcher-outer of hidden enemy. You couldn't expect some Navy bomb taxi driver to know all the bad guys' tricks like a Marine forward air controller.

"411, this is Derby 002, currently an unemployed FASTFAC about two minutes south of your posit. Do you need any help?"

Another characteristic of military pilots is that sometimes they hate to admit that they need help. This is usually a dumb way to be, but it does happen. Hogan was not suffering from that. He knew that an expert, even a jarhead bullet magnet like a Marine FAC, would help.

"002, that's affirm. If you can find these guys, we can take them out. You're cleared into the area and when on station request you assume control."

"Roger, Derby's inbound at ten thousand."

"The Ghostriders are at four."

"Click-click."

Marzetti made his first pass along the treeline as slowly as he could and still leave himself options. From long experience he knew that the average enemy found it impossible to resist taking a shot at an airplane if he had a chance. Sometimes the unit on the ground, to avoid premature discovery, would be disciplined enough to pass, but usually once they started shooting, they'd figure that they were discovered and open up on anything flying close by. They'd apparently already opened up on the two Phantom crewmen only three hundred yards away, and so it should have been relatively easy to draw their fire.

This time the enemy was smart enough to know that they hadn't been discovered yet and refrained from taking potshots at Marzetti's A-4. He shoved the throttle forward and closed his speedbrakes, climbing up and away from the ground.

"Did you see anything?"

Casey looked back at the trees. "Nope. But if I was a betting man I'd give you three to one that they're in there."

"Yeah. What did you find out about the helo?"

"The marines are diverting one and an escort from a logistics run. Should be here in about fifteen minutes."

"Okay. When the helo shows up, we'll have 411 prep the area. That'll keep their heads down or piss 'em off enough to start shooting. Either way, we'll win."

* * *

Norris listened to Marzetti's plan and felt a great sense of relief. Even though it was still early in the day and there was no real threat of capture, he was feeling as exposed and defenseless as he ever had in his life. Here, in this goddamn rice paddy, he had absolutely no control over his fate. All he and Scott had between them for self-defense were two lousy .38-caliber issue pistols loaded with tracer ammunition, and the only thing they were good for was marking their own position or maybe starting a fire. It had been about two years since Norris had qualified with the thing, and that was the general-vicinity shooting one had to do to qualify to fly with a nuclear weapon hung on his jet. Thinking about it, he wondered just what the hell he was supposed to do with a six-shot .38 pistol from inside a supersonic jet fighter.

He rolled over and looked up at the sky which was now turning a brilliant blue as the west wind blew the clouds closer and closer to the far horizon. He could hear the engines of the A-4s above and, for about the tenth time in the past hour, wished he were with them instead of down there. They were not even a mile away, but the gulf between them and him was as wide as the Pacific Ocean. They were safe, all strapped into their familiar and comfortable cockpits, and he was lying in somebody else's shit with a pretty fair chance of getting shot if things went badly.

If that happened, he'd be dead ten thousand miles from home and the pilots above would regretfully fly back to the ship and tell the story over a cup of hot coffee. They'd honestly feel pretty bad about the whole thing, but the next day they would strap back into their aircraft and fly another mission and another and another after that until the ship finally sailed for home. For most of the five thousand men aboard the *Shiloh*, he'd be nothing more than a name on the In Memoriam page at the end of the cruisebook and a face dimly remembered in an O'Club bar.

To divert himself, Norris picked up the radio. "Derby 002, Guntrain 202. What luck with our helo?"

Marzetti smiled. He'd never been down in the weeds himself, but he'd coordinated several rescues, and each time the crewman would ask the same question about every minute and a half. "202, the helo's about ten minutes out. Have you taken any more fire?"

"That's negative, but we're a little hesitant to take a peek, since every time we do they give it another try."

"Roger. We'll start hitting the trees when the helo is a couple of minutes out. Stay down until the helo gets to you because you're right in the outer part of the frag pattern."

"202, roger." That was something he'd forgotten about. The fragments from five-hundred-pound bombs spread out 3000 feet or so in all directions, and he and Scott were right at the edge of that. Some of the fragments were big enough to kill even at this range.

Norris looked at his Skipper, who was grinning. "What's so funny?"

"You sound like my kid. 'Are we there yet, Daddy?' "

"It's not that I'm particularly eager to be leaving this place. I just can't wait for a ride in a helo."

"That's good, Randy. If you were home, you'd have to pay for one. Who says being in the Navy isn't fun?"

"Yes, sir. You're absolutely right, Commander. My fun meter is pegged. Just thought you'd like to know."

"All right, since you're having so much fun, you can buy the beer tonight when we get to Danang."

The radio at Norris's side came to life. "202, Derby."

"Go ahead."

"Okay, the helo is holding just north of your posit. We'll start hitting the trees in about one minute. Stay down until you see the helo approaching, then pop a smoke."

"Roger that." Norris looked off to his right and spotted two small black dots in the sky moving slowly left to right. They had to be the helos. It was a relief just to see them. He reached in his vest, pulled out a day/night flare, and made sure he had the right end. He put his finger through the ring at the end and waited.

In the helicopter, Jax 541, a "slick," or lightly armed, UH-1E Huey, the pilot, Captain Bill Chapin, looked at the area in which the Phantom crew was lying low. He'd been flying over this part of South Vietnam for nearly a year now and knew it pretty well. Over that time he'd inserted several patrols and sweeps of varying size near there and knew it to be one of the less dangerous areas in all of I Corps. He'd never been shot at there, but the Tet Offensive had changed a lot of the rules. He briefed his crew on what to expect, looked out at his escort helo, an almost brand-new Huey gunship, and then sat back and lit a cigarette.

Marzetti looked over all the players and adjusted his pattern so as to line up on the treeline. In the back Casey announced that

002 was commencing a marking run, and sat back in his seat, his hands near the controls. Marzetti rolled the aircraft nearly on its back. Rolling back over, he lined up on a specific clump of trees that seemed to be about the center of the area that needed to be hit by the bombs, based on his best guess as to where the enemy would be.

He made a couple of small control movements and fired two smoke rockets into the trees, pulling up and away. He looked back and smiled when he saw that his rockets had straddled the clump of trees.

"Okay, 411 and flight. The target is marked. Request you put your bombs one hundred meters on either side of the smoke. Call target and FAC in sight and you're cleared."

"411's in. Target and FAC in sight."

Marzetti watched as Hogan dove, released two bombs, and then climbed away. The two MK-82s detonated with the white shock wave almost dead on the northern smoke. Damn good work, he thought, for the Navy.

The second Skyhawk followed the first by just about fifteen seconds but from a slightly different angle. This time the bombs straddled the other smoke so that anything in the immediate vicinity of the spot Marzetti had marked was now gone. He made a mental note that if he were ever in a serious tight spot, he'd try to get guys from this squadron to come help. They were good!

Marzetti watched the A-4s pound the area and then called them off when it became obvious that there was nothing left to threaten the helo.

"Jax 541, Derby. You're cleared in to the survivors. Call the smoke."

"541's inbound. 202, pop your smoke."

Chapin broke away from his 2000-foot orbit and dove toward the ground. Above him, the gunship weaved back and forth, scanning the ground ahead for any threat to its charge. Chapin leveled out only a few feet above the dikes and headed straight for Scott and Norris, who were now nicely marked by an orange burst of color. He banked around to the left, climbing a little to compensate for both the loss of lift and to keep his rotor blades from striking the ground. The smoke was drifting from west to east, so he gauged the turn and brought the Huey directly into the wind. He hauled the nose up and slowed, finally dropping the few feet to the top of the dike and catching the drop in a perfect no-hover landing.

The crewman in the back reached out, grabbed both Scott and Norris by the backs of their harnesses, pulled them in, and shoved them flat on the deck.

"They're in. *Go*," he shouted, and Chapin pulled up the collective and the Huey sprang away from the ground, banking immediately to the right and flying away with his tail pointed at the enemy positions.

Before his turnout, Chapin had a glimpse of several white and brown geysers in the water a couple of paddies away but waited until he was well clear and climbing back to 2000 feet before he asked.

"539, what was the shooting about?"

"A couple of guys popped up and fired at you, so I hosed 'em."

Chapin had not even seen them. "Roger that. Let's go home."

He looked over his shoulder at the two Phantom crewmen who were staring up at him with stupid grins and extremely wide eyes. "Derby 002, Jax 541 has two aboard. Both are okay but they smell real bad. We're outbound for Danang."

Marzetti grinned. It was not even eight in the morning, and it had already been a successful day. "Roger, 541. Nice job and thank you. Break. 411 and flight, you're cleared to depart the area to the northeast. Contact Slug 771 on this frequency now."

"411, roger. And, uh, 541, thank you."

Norris lay on the deck of the helo, suddenly as tired as he could ever remember being. He got to his knees and then sat on the troop seat that stretched across the back wall of the tiny cabin. He found a couple of lap belts and fastened them across his middle, hardly noticing when Scott took the seat next to him. He looked out the open cargo door past the crewman who sat with his legs dangling into the airflow. He felt a nudge and turned to see Scott smile and give him a thumbs-up. He nodded and wiped his hand across his face, feeling the dried spots of rice-paddy muck flake off as he did. He looked at his hand, saw the gray-brown bits of mud, and shook them off into the breeze.

Looking back out the door, Norris wondered how long it was going to take him to wash South Vietnam off.

McCarthy had watched and listened to the whole little drama and reported the success to the ship and then steered the A-4s back toward the *Shiloh*. He watched the little blips of the helos

and the FAC head back to their bases on the coast and told the
pilots of his E-2 that they could return to their original holding
point. He slid his seat back on its rails, unfastened his chin strap,
and, pulling off his helmet, scratched his head all over. He replaced his helmet and reached for his coffee thermos, nodding as
one of the other controllers in the back told him that the *Shiloh*
was beginning another launch and he should stand by for the
departure calls.

He sipped his coffee, now just lukewarm, and switched his radios just in time to hear the first fighter off the deck check in.

50

Thursday, February 8, 1968

Colonel Aires jumped to the ground before the helicopter's skid touched down. All around him other helos were
landing and disgorging small groups of marines who
moved off at the double to the outer parts of the small hilltop. As
one helo lifted off empty, another would take its place until the
entire 100-odd members of the relief force and the resupply had
been dropped off. The helos climbed away to hold until called
back down for medevac. Aires looked around to orient himself
and saw with some approval that the other force was nearly finished arriving on Hill 881S.

All along the treeline and beyond, the jets in support of the
Super Gaggle strafed and spread their gas and smoke on the
enemy. Aires was distantly aware of the feeling that the only humans within miles were the American marines. The enemy
seemed to have spent himself in the past few hours and was not
even sending sniper fire across the marine positions. From long
habit Aires moved as quickly and as defensively as always toward
the forward positions.

As he did he found small knots of men from the relief force moving through the area, searching out the wounded and cleaning up the detritus of battle. Aires forced himself to remain a marine colonel and not, as he wished to be, a friend of the men who'd fought for this little outpost of the combat base. He accepted the reports of the young corporals whose platoon leaders had sent them over as messengers, and occasionally sent back another question or request for more information.

Somewhere in all this mess were Gorton and Averitt. Aires knew that if they possibly could have, they'd have greeted his arrival. Either they were up to their ears reorganizing their command or they were wounded. Or worse. He fought the temptation to seek them out himself.

Once in the forward positions, he watched the marines carrying their comrades back to the collecting point and checking over the enemy dead for booby traps and anything that would have intelligence value. Aires found it strange that there were no enemy wounded around, but he shouldn't have—the enemy would drag their wounded away for whatever crude medical care they could provide or to simply let them die away from the Americans and their idiotic body counts. It was a rare thing for the Americans to find a wounded enemy.

Aires was listening to two of the slightly wounded platoon sergeants from Lima Company explain what the enemy's tactics had been and generally how the battle had gone from their own admittedly limited perspective, when one of the lieutenants from the relief force dashed up and told Aires that they'd found Averitt and Gorton. Aires excused himself from the sergeants and followed the lieutenant.

When Aires arrived, two corpsmen were working on Gorton's bloody form in the shade of one of the few remaining intact bunkers. The lower part of his body was covered in battle dressings and his left arm was a mess. Averitt was kneeling by Gorton's head, holding a canteen of water to the old sergeant major's lips. Aires looked down at Averitt and saw that he was covered in blood himself. He waited until Averitt removed the canteen and laid Gorton's head back down on the poncho liner being used to keep him off the dirt.

"Major, how is he?"

Averitt looked up and saw the colonel standing there, but it took several seconds for who he was to register. He began to get to his feet, but Aires placed a hand on his shoulder and knelt with Gorton lying between them.

Averitt sat back on his heels. "I don't know for sure, Colonel. The doc here says he'll make it, but we shouldn't keep him away from Charlie Med too long. Most of the wounds in his legs are from shrapnel and his arm has a bullet through it. He's lost a lot of blood."

Aires looked at the face of his old friend, gray beneath the red dust, and then back at Averitt's bloody form. "And how are you? Where are you hit?"

"I'm not. Well, not bad anyway. Most of this is the sergeant major's. I got hit with some flying sandbags and stuff. I've got a gash on my leg and a busted rib, I think. Aside from that and a hell of a headache, I'm okay."

Gorton's eyes opened and he looked up at the colonel. It was evident he was having a bit of trouble focusing. "Colonel?"

"Yeah, it's me, Tom. How ya doin'?"

"All things considered, pretty shitty. The morphine is nice though."

"We'll have you out of here soon. Hang on."

Gorton smiled and then cursed as the corpsman put a knot in one of the dressings. "Three wars, Colonel, and they finally blow my ass off in the last year. Kinda figures. Listen, this airedale here did fine. We owe him."

Aires stood and made way as two stretcher bearers arrived and helped the corpsmen gently slide the sergeant major onto the canvas. "I'll make it good, Tom. And I'll see you in the hospital. Take care."

Aires nodded and the marines lifted the stretcher and carried Gorton to the landing zone and the medevac helos that were now beginning to shuttle the wounded off the hill. He looked at Averitt, who sat back against the sandbag wall of the bunker and was struggling with his cigarette pack. He reached down and took the pack, pulled out a cigarette and then his own Zippo, and lit it for Averitt.

"You all right?"

"Yeah, pretty much. My leg is hurting some, but I seem to have forgotten all about it in the last little while. The pain is coming back with a vengeance now."

"Let's get you to a corpsman."

"Not yet, Colonel. I'm only beat up. There's lots of men who need help more. I can wait."

Aires considered the younger man. As if making a decision, he nodded once to himself and sat down next to him, leaning back. He spoke as he looked across the area, littered with the detritus of battle.

"You all did a fine job here, Dick. Believe me, it looks a lot worse than it is. There are sixteen dead and thirty or so wounded, and that's bad. But most of your company made it through in pretty good shape. You held the hill and 881 held out too. From what I can gather, it was a regimental-size assault, but they split their forces so that they weren't able to concentrate enough strength on a single point."

Averitt nodded. "Thank God for small favors. It was a pretty bad night, Colonel. I'm sorry about the sergeant major; he got hit when we charged the trench the last time. I thought he was right beside me all the way, but when I looked around he hadn't made it. The corpsmen say he'll keep his legs and arm for sure and they'll probably work, but he'll never be the same."

Aires looked sidelong at the major and pulled out his own Marlboro. "I know he won't, Dick. And neither will you. It wasn't your fault that he got hit any more than it was your fault that the others did. You did what you could in a bad situation and you made it. Don't feel guilty that you're here and others are not. Those choices aren't ours to make. You have no more control over things like that than you do over the color of your eyes. I want you to remember that I said that, because when you can look back at this with some distance, you'll need to know that it wasn't your fault and that you did your best. Which was enough. I'm grateful for that."

"Yes, sir."

Aires sighed, exhaling slowly. "Tom said that we owe you. I'm putting you in for something for taking over here and leading the defense of this hill."

Averitt groaned. "Colonel, don't do that. If anyone deserves a medal for this, it's him and the others. I didn't have a whole lot of ideas about what to do. The sergeant major led me by the damn hand through the whole thing."

Aires smiled. "I know that. But I put you in charge because the men needed an officer to look up to and you were here. I made you responsible because the men needed the confidence that came

419

from knowing that someone was in charge, and majors, to marines anyway, usually are in charge.''

The colonel took a drag and stubbed out his cigarette, beginning to field-strip it as he spoke again. ''Look, you're going to be recognized and decorated because you were responsible for what happened here, and that was because I put you in charge of a damn fine and effective group of marines, my marines. You're going to think that you don't deserve it, which is okay. I hate guys who are always after medals for doing their job adequately. You're not that type.

''Medals are simply a device to recognize good work and to give others something to see and try to emulate. Napoleon once said about medals something like 'nothing means so much yet costs so little.' So enough about that.''

Aires stood up and brushed the dirt off the seat of his fatigues. ''Now, part of the wise use of the authority that goes along with leading men is knowing when to listen to your subordinates, who often know more than you do. You did that, and it saved this hill and most of your command.

''I want you to think about something else. I would like it very much if you finished out your tour with my regiment. Don't answer now, but please think about it. And again, thank you for this.''

He stuck out his hand and Averitt, with nothing to say, shook it.

Aires looked around at the marines going about their tasks. ''Okay. I've got to go get your relief company settled in. Now, go find their commander and brief him on what he needs to know. Then catch a helo to Khe Sanh and get back to work. Your relief should be here tomorrow and, if you want, we'll ship your airedale ass back to the O'Club.''

Aires spun on his heel and walked off. Averitt watched him go and then inspected the last of his cigarette. He flicked the butt away and got to his feet with a grunt—his ribs were hurting like hell now, almost as much as his leg. Looking around, he painfully bent and retrieved his rifle and then walked over and picked up the cigarette butt. He thought over Aires's offer as he absently field-stripped the butt and stuck the last little bit of paper and the filter in his shirt pocket.

Averitt looked slowly around at what remained of his first command. He heard a loud sound and looked up in time to see an

A-4 scream overhead and drop a stick of bombs on the retreating enemy. His eyes softened as they followed the little jet as it arced back up into the clean blue sky and banked away to join with the others from its flight.

Commander Jim Hogan climbed down from his A-4 and tried to stretch his back. He bent forward at the waist and then leaned as far back as he could. The flight-deck chief came over and Hogan greeted him with a smile. "No gripes, Chief. It's good to go on the next launch. I think the others are okay too."

The chief grinned and walked away. Hogan did his post-flight walk-around, ensuring that at a quick glance all the parts he'd left with were still attached with the exception of the bombs. The young plane captain came up and handed Hogan his helmet and nav bag and then moved the boarding ladder forward so that the flight-deck crewmen could prepare the Skyhawk for towing back to its spot down the deck for the next launch.

Two ordnancemen, their red jerseys pulled off and tied around their waists, were removing the arming wires from the bomb racks and talking about some bar they'd frequented back in San Diego. Hogan stood behind them, listening to their youthful chatter and the sure movements as they prepared the racks for their next loads. He smiled and walked away toward the catwalk, wondering if he had ever been that young.

Hogan dropped his helmet in the ready-room seat and picked up the thick book containing the yellow sheets. He filled in his time and all the other data pertaining to his flight, and made notations on the maintenance parts of the sheets. He was just finished filling in the other squadron-created forms, when he noticed four khaki legs standing just at the edge of his vision.

He looked up and saw Terry White and Jack Wilson standing there. "And what can I do for you this fine morning?"

White handed him a cup of coffee and several folders. "You have a meeting in CAG office in an hour. Here are the reports you'll need to know about. Also, there is a letter in there, a personal from that admiral in San Diego about the truck caper. He says he'll be satisfied with your handling the matter, so Taylor can quit planning on disguises for when we get home."

Hogan looked at Wilson, who handed him two other folders. "Those are the flight utilization figures for January and the pilot summaries for the year. You'll be happy to know that every pilot in the squadron met his minimums, including you. That might come up at the meeting too. You also are scheduled for the midnight-to-four alert again, so try to get some sleep in there somewhere."

Hogan put the folders in a pile in the seat next to him and asked what was for lunch. White grinned. "Looks like there might be a mutiny among the J.O.'s today. The wardroom ran out of sliced cheese, so we may not be able to have our double-cheese sliders like we do every Thursday. They've sent a helo over to the *Potomac* to try to get some, but there's no word yet."

Hogan chuckled as he stood up. "I hope they make it. I've gotta go down to CVIC and then to the Guntrains' ready room and fill them in on Scott's rescue. I'll see you in the wardroom in a half-hour."

White and Wilson left the room, and just as Hogan was about to leave himself, the phone rang and he looked over to see the duty officer holding the receiver out to him. "Skipper, Maintenance Control needs to talk to you about signing some request. You want to talk to them?"

Hogan sighed. "No, not on the phone. Tell them I'll be down in a couple of minutes." He left the room, closing the door behind him. He looked at the large squadron insignia painted on the outside of it and noticed that there were a couple of large chips of paint missing. I'll have to remember to get the first lieutenant to have that fixed, he thought.

Epilogue
Monday, March 4, 1968

The little general sat on the hard wooden bench outside the large meeting room. He was waiting for the Politburo to finish with their morning meeting so he could be admitted to the room to give his report on the failed Tet Offensive and siege of the American combat base. His hands on his lap held a thick folder that contained his written report and was identical to the ones he had forwarded to these men the day before. Even though he knew they'd all read it thoroughly, he still had to go through the formality of standing before them as they once again displayed their power and reminded him that he was their subordinate.

Next to him his aides fidgeted, nervous at the thought of standing in front of such an august body and having their commander defend himself. The little general knew that part of their nervousness was due to the fact that if he were to be found lacking, they would be tarred with the same brush. He did not envy them that.

He leaned his head back and thought the whole report through, making sure that he had everything straight and in its proper order, beginning with the early mistakes and poor execution. It had all been his idea, and it had all happened at his orders. True, the Politburo had unanimously applauded the plan and had enthusiastically sought to insert their own wrinkles so as to take credit later on. But there was slim chance that any of them would be eager to accept any part of the responsibility for failure.

There was no denying that the past six weeks had been a mili-

423

tary disaster. The "great uprising" which was to coincide with the beginning of his Tet Offensive never happened, and, as a result, nearly the entire guerrilla infrastructure that had been so carefully built up over the years was gone, wiped out as if by a sudden plague. What few insurgents remained would be powerless to continue their efforts for at least the next two years.

His own army regulars had been completely unable to overwhelm the American and South Vietnamese positions at the Khe Sanh Combat Base both because of the tenacity of the defenders and the awesome weight of their airpower. He had sent units from his four divisions to reinforce other units that had seemed to be making progress against the enemy, but they had been destroyed too. His largest assault on the combat base, this time against the South Vietnamese part of the perimeter, had been ruthlessly thrown back. He had had to order the retreat and give up his great plan. As a sort of over-the-shoulder parting shot, the general had ordered his men to fire at the combat base all remaining ammunition from the artillery and mortars. It was an act both of rage and of simple military logic—it was simpler to shoot the rounds at the enemy than to laboriously carry them off.

The little general sighed and bowed his head. There was no way of avoiding it—he had just suffered the greatest defeat of his long military career. He and his forces had been crushed and the future for the war was grim. If the Americans made a concerted effort to cut off the flow of supplies coming in to North Vietnam and continued to bomb what few targets were left within the country, there was no chance of the little general and his people achieving victory.

He was just beginning to wonder what it would be like to have a small farm and retire to growing flowers, when the door opened next to the bench and a stone-faced functionary gestured for him to enter.

The little general was stunned when he walked into the room and was greeted heartily by nearly everyone in the Politburo, who sat around the table and made the decisions. They shook his hand and told him how glad they were to see him. There was even a small smile on the face of the chairman, who still sat in his place at the head of the conference table.

He felt the thick report taken from him and reached after it, only to be told that everyone had read it and it was an excellent report. It was placed carelessly on the table and he was steered to a seat facing a small movie screen. He looked around in confusion and saw that his aides were equally befuddled.

He caught the eye of one of the ministers who had been friendly toward him in the past and began to ask him what was happening but was told to just wait, it would all become clear in a moment. From the background voices it was clear that some great victory had been won that had changed things for the better, but he couldn't understand how that could have happened in the thirty minutes since he'd left his office.

Someone drew the curtains and the room darkened. The light from the projector splashed on the screen, and in a second or so the little general was watching a terrible filmed copy of an American newscast. He recognized the newsreader as the one America thought of as a sort of uncle because of his sincerity and acumen. He did not understand the language but did recognize the maps in the background as representing the area in the South which he'd just left. Several points were highlighted as the newsman's voice droned on in its soft-yet-hard tone. The newsman said something and held a few sheets of paper in his hands, which rested on the desk. It was evident from his eyes that what he was saying caused him some pain, but there was also a hint of anger in his expression.

The film ended and the curtains were pulled back again. The little general blinked against the sudden sunlight and the minister of information handed him several sheets of paper. He began to read but was interrupted by the minister. "You can read that later, my friend."

He looked up and saw the others taking their places at the table. The minister of information continued. "That was one of the Americans' national news broadcasts from several nights ago. In short, their most respected newsreader has just told them that they have lost the war and that they should negotiate to save their honor. Other of their broadcasts and publications are saying the same sort of thing."

The little general looked again at the papers in his hand and then at the minister. "But they have completely defeated us. How can they think that they have lost?"

The minister nodded. "I wish you had paid more attention in the propaganda training sessions all those years ago. It is true that they have prevailed on the field of battle over and over again. But your attacks have shaken their confidence. Their people are being told what their information people have decided is the truth, so what is actually true is no longer important.

"There are demonstrations already beginning, and a careful reading of their newspapers tells us that even their leadership believes that defeat is inevitable. We must keep up the pressure on them; we must not show them that they have hurt us. To plan for that and to accept our congratulations are why you are here this morning, my friend."

The little general listened as the meeting descended into the nuts-and-bolts planning for the future. He listened with only enough of his mind to be aware that a response would be required.

The rest of him went back to the many days in the small cave north of the American combat base. He remembered all the planning meetings he'd had with his men over those days and suddenly he missed that camaraderie. He dearly missed all those men who had been lost, but he realized now that their sacrifice was not in vain. He winced inside at the terrible irony that the victory they could not achieve by their fierce courage on the battlefield had been achieved on the television sets in a country ten thousand miles away.

The little general shook off these thoughts and forced himself to concentrate on the list of ships entering his country's ports with replacements for all the equipment that had been lost in the past month.

It was quite an extensive list.

Saturday, September 13, 1969

The water flashed in the small beams of sunlight as it flowed by the grassy spot that jutted a little ways into the stream. The gentle breeze moved the tall grass just enough to tickle him behind his ear as he sat next to the old oak tree. He brushed the grass away absently, watching the nearly invisible fishing line move slowly and inexorably back toward the end of the rod. The boy was definitely getting the hang of this, the old man thought. He was bringing it in just quickly enough to keep the lure off the bottom and just gently enough so that the line wasn't jerking.

He looked at the boy and saw his face set determinedly, his eyes squinting into the reflected sun and just the tip of his tongue protruding from the corner of his mouth as he reeled in the line using only his fingertips on the crank, as he'd been taught. The boy's back was straight as only a child's can be, and his feet were firmly planted in the grass. For him, the whole world was centered in this little bend of the stream in the mountains of West Virginia. And that's as it should be, thought the old man. He straightened his legs and winced a bit at the little pain he still felt in them.

The boy saw it and asked him in his small voice if he was all right. Former Sergeant Major of Marines Tom Gorton smiled at him and looked up at the bright blue sky through the green leaves of the trees above his head. He chuckled a little as he thought about the question.

Carroll's
Glossary II

(More stuff you probably either never heard of or cared about. But if you did run out of important things to ponder and then blithely blundered into concerning yourself about things *militaire*, you couldn't find an answer because the guy you asked told you it was classified. This is a conditioned response that normally meant he didn't have a clue either. On the other hand, I've heard that using the classified-information gambit is also one of the more effective ways of impressing ladies with how dangerous and technical your job is. I never used it myself, you understand, but I know guys who did and it always seemed to work.)

Official Anti-Lawsuit Disclaimer: *These entries have been submitted by strangers from all over the world. I am merely an instrument in bringing their words to you, the reader. Since these items have been sent anonymously, the submitters' names are unknown. However, in the event of a lawsuit, I will furnish the courts with names, addresses, social security numbers, shoe sizes, videotapes, photographs, audio recordings, and whatever else is required to get me off the hook. Some of it might even be accurate.*

Aircraft Handling Officer (The Handler) This is the man in charge of moving aircraft around on the flight deck. He has a group of trolls who work for him and who are expert in taking the best aircraft a squadron has and running it into another squadron's best aircraft so as to damage both of them *almost* beyond repair. This causes a great deal of giggling and laughing in Flight Deck Control because there is no punishment the Navy can mete out to a man that is worse than a tour as a Handler on a carrier.

AIM-9 Sidewinder This is the Navy's premier heat-seeking air-to-air missile. It came out in the era when the military mistakenly decided that fighter aircraft would no longer need a gun or a cannon to fight with, only missiles. The 'Winder did its job nicely and even today is the weapon of choice in air-to-air combat. The Iraqis found it quite effective also. Just ask them. I'll give you the address of their Air Force. It's in Iran.

AIM-7 Sparrow This is a radar-guided air-to-air missile that came out in the sixties. The early versions of them had many teething troubles, but they were all eventually worked out. In Vietnam, fighters often carried two to make sure that they got one that worked properly. An old friend of mine swears that it was his favorite missile because, if he got in trouble, he could always jettison his Sparrows into the sea and significantly and instantaneously reduce his gross weight.

Battleships Even though these great warships do not figure in this novel at all, I can't resist commenting on them. From the earliest days of naval warfare, even the dumbest commanders have known that the thing which is the number-one most important gotta-have-it asset in a fight is weight of metal on the enemy. You can screw up the tactics, but if you've got the biggest guns and the heaviest shells coming down on the bad guys accurately, you will probably win. There are all sorts of annoying exceptions to this rule, but it still holds most of its water.

The BBs were the rulers of the sea up until the Japanese took their little trip to Hawaii in 1941, then were supplanted by the carriers (out of sheer necessity since the American battleships had been abruptly turned into hazards to navigation). The battleships were relegated to a supporting role and, except for getting dragged out of mothballs for every war we've had since WW II, were pretty much finished.

In the eighties, we recommissioned all four of our *Iowa*-class battleships and deployed them around the world. They carried sixteen-inch guns and fired rounds weighing around 2500 pounds apiece. The effect was like shooting an entire showroomful of Ford Escorts, packed with high explosive, about twenty-five miles. When the rounds hit, they made instant holes in civilization that were the size of tennis courts. I got to see the *New Jersey* fire a broadside at somebody in Beirut once, and I still haven't found the words to describe it.

This was also effective because the people who were fired upon immediately quit annoying their neighbors and repaired to their graves. The surviving terrorists went home for an underwear change and all was quiet for a while.

The battleships have all been mothballed again now and it doesn't seem the same anymore. When one sees a battleship steaming along, one is seeing *Navy* and all that that has meant through the centuries. There is no weapon on earth that will make a little tinpot dictator sit up and take notice like a battleship slowly cruising off his coast well out of *pistola* range with her guns trained on his presidential palace. It sort of gives him a little peek at his relative importance in the grand scheme of things. If that peek stops one firefight, however small, or saves one life, or ensures the fairness of one election, then the battleship has earned her keep.

But, since those things usually happen outside the Capital Beltway, and Dan Rather doesn't mention them, they matter not at all to the geniuses in Washington. Those events have no bearing on the next election, and every congressman knows that money to measure the effect of cow farts on the ozone layer is more far important than wasting it on a battleship. They're quite correct too. It'll help next year, when the bill to teach cows to say "excuse me" comes out of committee.

Beer Day Beverage alcohol has not been permitted aboard commissioned vessels of the United States Navy since a benighted Secretary of the Navy named Josephus Daniels decided that captains might get drunk someday and run their ships aground. The fact that this had never happened was deemed irrelevant. The ship's doctor was permitted to keep a small "medicinal" store of it, but even that went away when we started to become the Corporate Navy in the seventies. The last time I saw *legal* booze on a ship was April 7, 1977, when my carrier, the USS *Independence*, hit a major storm (55- to 65-foot seas and 120-knot winds) and several of us pilots wound up flying in it. When we survived, our flight surgeon gave us each a couple of miniatures to calm us down, which I still think was the right thing to do.

Nowadays, to show the country's appreciation for sacrifice and to boost morale, each member of the crew is authorized two cans of real beer for every forty-five consecutive days at sea (and you didn't believe the Navy was an adventure). There are strict procedures enforced to keep the crew from getting all drunk on their two cans of beer and starting a nuclear war or kidnapping the Pope.

During my last cruise we had two periods exceeding forty-five days, but our beloved captain (a tall, skinny, ex-A-7 pilot and world-class prick) decided that since we were merely the crew and not captains and therefore were not authorized to have morale in the first place, we didn't need any such benefit, so he canceled the beer. He then could proudly point to his record of zero nuclear wars started and zero popes kidnapped by his crew of 5000 scurrilous misfits and thus consider himself a fine and effective officer.

He must have been one. The Navy happily overlooked his pathetic personal morality and his woeful record in leadership and made him an admiral so he could have thousands more men to torment.

There is an odd footnote to this story. There is now an American warship actually named in honor of Josephus Daniels which I believe to be a rather interesting comment on the new philosophies of the Corporate Navy.

433

Gerry Carroll

Command and Control There are few things that piss off commanders more than not having adequate control over their forces. It really torques them to have a bunch of mere subordinates out there fighting and leading and making decisions that the commander cannot directly influence. So, beginning with Alexander the Great, commanders have striven to get more and more control over their troops.

With the invention of radio, commanders had a better shot at it because they could always call up some junior officer who was up to his ears in a hand-to-hand fight with the enemy, just to ask how things were going because *his* boss was on the horn to him with the same question because *his* boss . . . well, you get the idea.

When air mobility came along, things got even better for the commanders since they could requisition a helicopter and orbit over the battlefield, giving orders directly to the units on the ground. This way even the platoon leaders could get the benefit of the commanders' attention as they received their orders to get moving and never mind the twenty-five million entrenched enemy that the platoon had to go through: The platoon was falling behind, and we can't have the generals' timetable disrupted. Many are the small-unit commanders who wished for a heat-seeking surface-to-air missile they could use on their boss.

Today, with satellite communications, we have reached the zenith of command and control. As in the Iran hostage rescue attempt, the President himself now has the capability to get on the blower and screw up the show. This is the ultimate in command and control. The commander in chief doesn't have to wait and worry whether his subordinates will make a mess of the finely tuned plan—he can do it himself.

The good news is that apparently the lessons of the past have been well-learned. In the Persian Gulf war, command and control was carried out pretty well. At least, on the Allied side.

The Iraqis showed the world exactly what command and control can lead to if the commander exercises too much control. And after the commander is proven by events to be a complete idiot, he can always execute the controllees. That'll teach 'em.

Corporate Navy (*See also* Old Navy.) I have used this term several times throughout this novel. If I haven't, then I've displayed what I consider to be a near-saintlike restraint that is totally unlike me. The Corporate Navy came into being when it was discovered that the American people were no longer going to stand for giving their hard-earned tax dollars to a bunch of men who would use them to have as much fun as being in the Navy once was. Taking a leaf from the Air Force, the Navy began to have "assets" instead of men and equipment, and "management" instead of leadership. Everything we did suddenly required a written, approved, and published POA&M (Plan of Action and Milestones) and an MOE (Measure of Effectiveness). Then it became a good idea to create a couple of hundred teams that would go around and visit each command and check up on whether the command was following the newest OPNAV instructions. These were not the dreaded "Inspections" but were "assist visits." If the unit was found not to be doing things right, these "assist teams" would get the C.O. fired and have some new guy in there.

The Navy has come a long way in maximizing their potential for efficacious employment of downsized and semidegraded asset packages. That's Corporate-Navy talk for doing a good job with the diminishing support from Congress. There is an amazing amount of training being done, and it's working. But somehow, to us old farts, things are just not the same.

I saw one of the new training seminars wherein a group of naval aviators sat around and played with balloons in an effort to learn something about military synergy. I saw these guys who were members of what was once a hardworking and hard-playing and wondrously effective brotherhood of arms stretching back over three-quarters of a century all sitting democratically in the room, passing pink ballons around.

At that moment I had no further doubts about having retired.

Dets This is an abbreviation for "detachments." A det is usually a small group sent from a larger parent unit to do some job that is too small and unimportant to be undertaken by the entire unit.

Detachments are usually far from home and can be a great deal of fun when one realizes that many of the restrictive rules and regulations can be dodged in the name of operational necessity when one is on a det. Smart people will volunteer for a det because it is an excellent chance to get away and have some fun in a strange place even though the workload can be heavier than it is back home. The downside of dets is that sometimes the officer in charge (OINC, which may be pronounced "oink," or, it may not) will see the det as a way of demonstrating his leadership abilities to the commanding officer of the parent squadron and then in an effort to get a gold star on his fitness report will work his people half to death. Captain Bligh is a perfect example of this type of OINC. One of the immutable laws of nature is that people determined to demonstrate their leadership abilities usually don't have any in the first place.

Smart OINCs will set the goals for the day and let the troops know that when they are accomplished, the troops may report to him at the beach, where he will have a keg waiting for them. This never fails. It may not get the OINC promoted but it will certainly get the work done.

Flight Deck (a.k.a "The Roof") This is the flat part of a carrier which is probably where they got their cute nickname of "flattops" which no self-respecting carrier sailor or aviator would ever call his ship. ("Bird farm" we can live with.)

The flight deck is about 2½ to 3 acres of steel from which the aircraft are launched by the catapults and then later recovered (landed). Working there is probably the most hazardous job on earth aside from being an S&L manager or a white male in Washington.

An unwary person can get sucked into a jet intake, blown over the side by jet exhaust, beheaded by a helicopter rotor blade, run over by a tow tractor and/or the airplane behind it, de-legged by the arresting cables, or, worst of all, he can screw up and get on the Air Boss's list of enemies.

The deck is loaded with fully fueled aircraft, and after a couple minutes of high-tempo operations it becomes so slick with oil, etc., that it makes taxiing aircraft a real treat—especially in the rain. One of the most frightening moments I have ever experienced was being strapped into an aircraft and suddenly sliding toward the deck edge, completely unable to do anything about it.

The biggest hazard on the flight deck is the mass of joggers that appears within one half of a nanosecond after the last aircraft touches down. They then proceed to run all over the deck in their endless pursuit of ectomorphy. They love to wear dark Speedo clothes and $400 shoes, never carry a light at night, and proudly display their ruined shins to all who come nigh. Tearing off all flesh from the shin by running into one of the thousand or so aircraft tie-down chains around is one of the steps on the road to true awareness, or so they tell me.

I always wanted them to just keep running right off the deck, but for some reason they never did. That's a pity, really, because as they bobbed helpless and terrified in the sea, I'd have loved to have gotten a chance to throw them a cinderblock. I could have been a legend.

Shower Police On ships in the Navy there is no natural fresh water, so the engineering plant must make fresh water from salt-water. First dibs on the fresh goes to the boilers, and the crew gets the leftover. Nuclear-powered ships usually have more than they can use, but on the older "fossil-fueled" ships the supply is very limited, so there is always a strict water-conservation policy in effect. One of the most wasteful things sailors can do is to take a shower, so there have to be men assigned to form the shower police. If a crew member is caught taking too long a shower, he is dragged, still soapy, before whomever the captain has appointed to be this month's water Himmler and is made to undergo a great deal of humiliation for being such a wastrel.

The pressure and temperature vary almost by the second, so the water can go from barely above freezing to just below boiling or the other way in less time than it takes to blink your eyes (which is not an option when there is an instantaneous drop of a hundred degrees in the shower water striking your back or other somewhat more sensitive areas). The system is also prone to get bubbles of air in it, so after a few seconds of rumbling and burping, a slug of water, known as a "water bullet," is expelled at about the speed of a bullet (hence the term). If one is unwary or just a new guy, he can be injured by one of these. One learns quickly to turn one's back on the showerhead when the rumbling starts.

On my old ship there was a problem with the system causing much of the fresh water supply to be mixed with JP-5 jet fuel. It was not unknown for someone to flip a cigarette into a sink in his room and be scorched by a merry little (albeit brief) fire. Fuel was in the showers, drinking water, coffee, and even the onion soup, which really isn't too bad once you get used to it. Periodically, at the captain's strong urging, the ship's Fuels Officer would go on TV and explain to the crew of 5000 that they were suffering from a mass delusion—there really wasn't any fuel in the water, because it was impossible. Being good sailors, we'd accept this as gospel.

The good news is that one medical problem that was completely unknown aboard that ship was constipation.

Gerry Carroll

The Old Navy This is a term used by old farts to tell the young lions how screwed up the modern Navy is. It is one of those generational things that usually fall on deaf ears (i.e. the ears of the young).

About 2500 years ago there was a play by one of The Legendary Dead Greeks Guys From Whom All Ideas Spring by the name of Sophocles. In the play (even the title of which I've deliberately forgotten), Sophocles decried the youth of his day as a bunch of callow, spoiled, pain-in-the-ass youths. Little did he know that those same youths would spend the eons moving over the land and sea like the plague, gleefully screwing things up, until they finally turned their fury full on United States Naval Aviation.

I had to listen to the eulogy for the Old Navy from the veterans when I reported to my first duty station and, along with the rest of my generation, we strove to keep the Old Navy alive. We succeeded too. In fact, I think we did a hell of a job.

Unfortunately, Sophocles' youths came charging over the hill and set up shop right when we were becoming the old farts. They brought in a bunch of management specialists from Harvard or Yale or some other godforsaken place and changed everything. We began having to do endless hours of reports and fiscal justifications and other grim paperwork, which put a heavy blanket over our flying time and our liberty hours. They've even modified the rules so that naval officers can carry *umbrellas,* for Pete's sake. Can you believe that?

They got real serious about safety and forced us to reduce the accident rate by ninety-five percent or so, wiping away aviation Darwinism in a year. Fewer pilots got killed and fewer aircraft got wrecked, so we were stuck with a lesser breed of survivors and had to fly older aircraft, since the replacement pipelines shrank. No more could we fire up the C-1, load it with nurses from the base hospital, and go out for overwater navigation training flights to the Bahamas for the weekend. No longer could we land our helicopters in the field behind McDonald's when the crew began to suffer from starvation. No longer could we just jump in an aircraft, go out, and beat up the sky for an hour and a half. Nope. Now we had to file flight plans and we had to take annual exams and flight checks on the aircraft and the related systems.

Then they began to put computers in the aircraft. We all could hear the bell tolling when the idea sprang up that a computer could do something faster and more accurately than could a good

438

pilot. You could hear the sighs from all over the fleet when the shiny new high-tech replacements for the Phantoms and the A-4s and the H-3s and the A-7s rolled out onto the ramps. We cleaned out our desks and turned in our flight gear. The golden days were but a memory, and the future was featureless and gray.

I hope the young lions realize what they've done and I hope they're happy. But it's a shame that they'll never get to win $250 in a Klondike game, or smell the exhaust from a big ol' radial engine, or bring a single-engine medevac Huey into and out of a tight LZ at night, or pull off a Low Frequency/ADF approach in a thunderstorm, or fly a load of nurses to the Bahamas for the weekend. I suppose the New Navy has its good points, but it could never come close to what we had in the Old Navy. It was fun, then.

Once upon a time.